# Praise for *Until the Rising*

"In our modern age where masculinity is seen as toxic, debut author, Amber Kirkpatrick delivers an astounding story filled with strong male characters whose family ties keep them loving, brave, and courageous. *Until the Rising* is packed with tantalizing secrets, deadly battles and heart-warming moments that show us how romantic love and familial love are both essential in finding where we truly belong." — V. ROMAS BURTON, award-winning author of the *Heartmaker Trilogy* and *The Legacy Chapters*.

"Amber Kirkpatrick has written a masterpiece. With hope and despair, joy and sorrow, strength and weakness, it captures the imagination. In a world so familiar to what we know and yet so different, the Thatcher brothers grab ahold of you and won't let go. You cheer for their successes and cry in their sorrow. It's a book that will linger long after you turn the final page." — ANNA AUGUSTINE, author of *By Blood and Blade* and the *Princes of Allura Novella Collection*.

"*Until the Rising* is an emotional journey through a young man's pursuit of truth, goodness, and the things that are most worth fighting for in this life. With rich world-building, strong themes of brotherly love, and characters that are more like family, Kirkpatrick beautifully ties together raw realities that make this novel not only a story well-told, but a truth worth unpacking and taking to heart." — ANDREA RENAE, author of *Where Darkness Dwells*.

Books by Amber Kirkpatrick

The Aquila Chronicles
*Until the Rising*

The Changed Duology
*Unleashed*
*Released*

# UNTIL THE RISING

# UNTIL THE RISING

## Amber Kirkpatrick

Red
Feather
Press

To my girls,

Ava June, Evangeline, and Clara.

Thank you for the love, the laughter,

and always reminding me to believe in possibilities.

# Contents

# Journal Entry

Excerpt from the personal journal of Daniel Martignoni Lay Brother, Master Historian, and Storyteller Exemplar of Altair Abbey

*The Degenerate Age is the problem of our histories. How can we know so much and yet so little of this era a millennium ago? This power, this magic they wrought—magic they called electricity, which almost destroyed humanity through weaponry, through the destruction of nature, through a reckless sense of their own power. To read their tales of flights to the stars, buildings that touched the sky, roads of packed stone where carriages traveled in minutes that would now take a horse many days—it defies all reason to believe such things. And yet, we know it is true.*

*Why did they choose to remove themselves from the rhythms of creation? How violent were their souls to tear themselves asunder from the love of the Father?*

*My weariness consumes me, but I must finish my thoughts before I sleep, and they are forever lost. Someday the young prince will need to know everything, for the burden facing him is greater than he can imagine.*

*I would that we had burned every article remaining from that era. Too much of their apostasy was saved. Their writings were salvaged for the sake of survival early in our history, but I fear the information we hold here at the abbey could be our downfall. We must ensure the darkness of the past never returns. The weapons that leveled cities...I fear even the evil Sammanon has brought against us in centuries of war is little compared with the evils of the Degenerate Age.*

*The Forbidden Books must remain hidden until Aquila's noble prince wears the crown, as the prophecy—my prophecy—foretold.*

*Only he will know how to wield the secrets they hold.*

*May the Father help him.*

# Prologue

It was the golden hour, and the air was rich with the smells of late summer. The afternoon sun emphasized the derelict condition of the wooden shack as light danced through the cracks in the walls. Inside, a fire crackled in the stone hearth set against the wall, and over it hung an iron pot. For once, the pot was full and bubbling merrily. A woman hovered over it, fearful of ruining the first decent meal in weeks. She tucked aside a lock of black hair laced with silver strands and bent to stir the simmering contents. The woman didn't grasp the spoon with her entire hand. Instead, she held it between two fingers and made graceful swirls in the broth.

Shadows lurked under the woman's bright blue eyes, yet some remnants of a former beauty remained in her fair skin and fine features. Her ankle-length black dress had long ago faded to a dull gray, but it was clean and mended with care. Despite the obvious signs of deprivation and neglect, her quiet dignity had earned her the dubious nickname of "Duchess" from the other village women.

She kept the small shack neat, with none of the careless filth that so often attends poverty. There were other hints of a life less ordinary, including a single shelf containing actual books, although there were few volumes and they all had a battered appearance. Alongside the books, there were several delicate ornaments that seemed to cry out from a glorious, secret past.

Near the hearth, a scrawny boy lay on the dirt floor, mouthing the words to a tattered book and kicking his feet in the air. No one could mistake the boy for anyone but the woman's son. The only noticeable difference between them was the color of their eyes. His were a deeper blue that shifted from sapphire to black depending on the light.

When the woman bent double with a wrenching, phlegmy cough, he looked up with concern. She turned so the boy wouldn't see the blood on the rag she used to cover her mouth.

"Momma?" he whispered.

The mother wiped her lips and glanced over her shoulder at the boy with such loving warmth that a sweet smile broke through his frightened expression. Still struggling to restrain the cough, she took a step nearer to brush her hand through his dark hair. Comforted, he settled back to his book, and she returned to her cooking.

The door flew open, knocking against the wall as a young man charged into the hut. Slamming the bolt, he gulped for air and whispered, "Sammanon soldiers. In the village. *Conscriptors!*"

At these words, a flurry of activity began. They had drilled for this moment many times. She rushed to gather anything worth more than a copper while the man pried loose a stone on the hearth. Together, they flung the items into a deep hole underneath. After replacing the stone, he hauled the stunned boy to his feet, grasping his shoulders. He spoke with fierce desperation.

"Remember! You're Travis Hensley! We've talked about this. Travis Hensley, that's your name. You're seven, not nine. Lie if they ask! They're taking boys your age, but you're small, and I think—I think they'll leave you alone."

A sob broke from the woman. "But if they take you, Michael!"

Muffled screams and the yells of men forced Michael to stifle the panic ready to burst out of him. If he couldn't control himself, all would be lost. He gathered the mother and boy close, forcing his voice to remain calm. "Listen to me. Don't speak! They're going to take me. I won't be able to get away this time. They have archers. I'll be a *willing* recruit." Michael swallowed down these last words with bitterness.

The cries were getting closer.

"You—"

"*Listen.* I'll be an eager, model soldier, and in two months, maybe three, I'll have earned some freedoms. I will escape. You hear me? I'll get away and come back for you, and then we'll leave this hellhole. But you must be strong, Mother."

Michael fell to his knees in front of the boy and caught his breath. "You'll have to work. Tell Duvall what happened. He likes you, and although you won't be able to do much at the livery, he'll be fair. Don't fight these men. When they come here, let them take me, you understand?"

The boy started to argue, but Michael overrode him. "No, don't do it. I know you're brave, little brother. But this isn't the time to prove it. If you fight them, it'll make everything worse for me and infinitely worse for your mother. You must take care of Mother, you hear me?" Michael clutched the boy to his chest, tears filling his eyes.

His brother clung to him, shaking, and Michael whispered in his ear, "I'll see you soon. I promise." Tears falling, he rose and kissed the top of the boy's head.

Bangs and shouts came from a nearby hut.

"And if they want to take you both?" The woman trembled but had otherwise regained control of herself.

Michael had dreaded this question but did not hesitate. "Run. I'll fight them as long as I can, but take him and run, no matter what happens. Don't think of me and don't look back. Just run."

There was a loud knock at their own shack, and all three jumped. Michael strode to the door while brushing away his tears. He cast a troubled glance at his brother, not confident his orders would be obeyed. With a silent prayer, he slid the bolt. Three burly men stamped into the hut, their presence overwhelming the small space. The largest of the men studied the two boys before speaking.

"Two males here? That's what we were told."

The mother raised her chin like a queen. "I have two sons, as you can see. I believe Michael is excited about this...opportunity, but I fear my youngest is not yet old enough."

Michael stifled a sudden desire to laugh, for her performance was so perfectly careless. But one glimpse at his brother's distraught face and the laughter died in him. A bearded soldier grabbed Michael by the arm and circled around him.

"Not tall, but strong," he declared. "How old are you?"

"I'm twenty-one, sir. I'm afraid this is all you get," Michael said with a relaxed smile.

"What's your name?"

"Hensley. Michael Hensley."

The first soldier narrowed his eyes. "You aren't scared of us."

"Why should I be? I was born to be a soldier, and I'm eager to join."

"Humph. What about this one?"

Michael eased his way in front of the boy. "He's seven, but..." he leaned in confidentially and tapped his head, "to be honest, he's not quite right." Michael could almost feel the waves of indignation rolling off his brother. Yet the boy kept his eyes lowered and remained silent.

"That so? Can he work?"

Michael's heart raced faster. The soldiers would as soon put a spear through his brother if Michael portrayed him as too much of an idiot. They wouldn't tolerate one more potential beggar in the village. On the other hand, he must *not* be conscripted. Michael would sooner die than allow that to happen. With a wave of his hand, he forced a laugh. "Oh, he works with horses a bit. One dumb beast recognizes another."

"Right." The bearded soldier shoved Michael, separating him from his family.

The woman forgot herself and gasped. Tears were sliding down his brother's cheeks as his thin body shook with silent sobs. Michael ignored them until almost passing through the door. He twisted around to face the largest of the soldiers and muttered, "May I tell them goodbye?"

"Meh. Be quick about it."

Aware that every movement was being watched, Michael pulled his mother and brother into an embrace, whispering, "I love you both very much. Never forget that." He kissed his mother's cheek.

Before he could stop himself, Michael crouched and grabbed his brother, holding him close. There were many things he wanted to say, but he knew if he tried to speak, he would begin weeping and never stop. After one last squeeze, Michael rejoined the soldiers at the door. There he paused and flashed that kind, cheerful smile they knew so well. Then he was gone.

Mother and son remained still in the silence that followed. The pot over the fire bubbled merrily.

They never saw Michael in the hut again.

# PART I

# Chapter 1

# The Vagabond

Lord General Andrew Kavanaugh was having an inauspicious start to his day. At dawn came the stableboy, proclaiming Andrew's new prize mare had broken free from her stall. Having been warned the horse was an escape artist, Andrew had ordered his men to take extra precautions. Either they had not done their job, or the mare was indeed an expert in seeking the wide-open country. After this discovery, he had the misfortune of opening the letter from Lord General Stuart MacClaren over breakfast.

His stomach curdled, ruining his appetite. MacClaren! Just the name made Andrew grind his teeth. Lecherous, ill-tempered, scheming—MacClaren and Andrew were diametrically opposed in all things, and the two had long held a grudge against each other. Why Queen Charlotte had allowed the man to reach so high in the military ranks was beyond Andrew's understanding. But even if her decisions were sometimes enigmatic, they were always practical. MacClaren must be serving some purpose Andrew couldn't perceive.

Andrew stepped outside his study, a small, low stone building, separate from the main house. Short of hiding in the stables, the study was the one place he could go to find any peace on an estate full of flitting, chattering females. He peeked toward the manor, fearful his wife might be watching through the windows. Judging himself safe, he lit a hand-rolled cigarette. The cost of tobacco had risen to outrageous amounts since the crops in the southeast had failed for the past two years. Andrew did not smoke often, but today he believed the indulgence to be richly deserved.

He paced the length of the building before sitting on a stone bench near the door. The spring morning was mild, birds twittered, and Andrew relaxed as he inhaled. Hang it all! Tobacco might be expensive, but nothing soothed him better than a smoke. Andrew rested with his back against the wall and closed his eyes, reveling in the warmth of the spring sunshine.

He loved this time of year when they weren't at war. He could rest easy at his estate, surrounded by a riot of beauty, with his wife's many flowers paying allegiance to their mistress. Mariah fussed over her blooms far more than she ever had over their children, but that seemed to have worked out well. Andrew assumed children raised themselves for the most part, a philosophy Mariah would have objected to rather strongly had she known he thought it. He smiled, for Andrew loved his wife. A deliciously plump woman with fiery red hair and sharp blue eyes, she provided an amusing contrast to his lanky height and black skin.

In wartime, spring was a nasty, messy affair. Andrew's smile faded, thinking of the last one. Between the melting snow and the seasonal rains, the camps were a sopping mud bath. Chaos ruled over the men. They itched to fight each other when not engaged in battle, and yet when required to bear arms, all the discipline of the winter months fell apart.

If they had wintered far from any villages, the camp whores descended upon them after the snow melted. Andrew shuddered, thankful there was no war with Sammanon now. There hadn't been one for several years, and the next war wouldn't be happening anytime soon. Taking in the fragrance of the flowers and the pleasant morning, he yawned. *And look*, he thought, *there's a horse coming up the path.*

Andrew shook his head to clear it and sat straight. There *was* a horse coming along the path, and not any random horse, but his own errant mare. As they came closer, Andrew caught sight of a boy leading her, murmuring horsespeak all the while. She must have liked it because the irascible beast was twitching her ears, as calm as any old broodmare. Andrew approached the horse, but she tossed her head and swept back her ears. The boy glanced over at Andrew.

"I wouldn't, sir. She's awfully mean-tempered. Is she yours?"

"Indeed she is." Andrew grunted. "But I believe she may prefer you."

The boy offered a tight smile. "I've been told I have a way with horses. They seem to like me."

Andrew studied the lad. He looked young, but the rich timbre of the voice did not belong to a child. He was a small vagabond, no doubt homeless and hungry, with a bulging sack thrown over one shoulder. No shoes, ragged clothing, and yet...Andrew took a safe step away from the horse before calling out, "Joe! C'mon, lad, come here."

A nervous stableboy poked his head around the corner and groaned when he saw the mare. He trotted up like a skittish colt himself and reached for the lead rope, but she turned on him quicker than a snake, her teeth bared. Joe fell back, cowering.

The small stranger let forth a sound of exasperation, reflecting Andrew's own feelings about the matter. "Perhaps it would be better to lead me where you want her," the boy suggested. Joe was more than happy to relinquish the task.

"Come to my study when you are done," Andrew said, walking to the door of the small outbuilding. The boy waved a hand to indicate he heard, never taking his eyes off the mare as he followed Joe to the stable. Andrew reached for the bell hanging outside the door and rang it. A few minutes later, an aged servant hobbled inside.

"Ah, Merrick. A boy located the mare and is putting her in the stable. He appears as if he's been living rough. Could you bring a tray of food for him?" The old man bobbed his head and made to leave, but Andrew narrowed his eyes. He knew Merrick would be loath to feed even a derelict child if left to his own devices, the snob. He put a hand out to stop the servant, adding, "And please make the portions generous, Merrick." Sure enough, Merrick grimaced, but nodded his assent and shuffled off. After some time, a light knock tapped at the door. Andrew beckoned the boy inside, inviting him to sit in a chair near the fire.

"Tell me, where did you find the horse?" Andrew asked in a pleasant manner.

"When I first saw her, she was enjoying a gallop in a pasture about two miles south of here. She led me on quite a chase before I caught her. I had heard m'lord had lost a horse, a fine mare I was told, and I wondered if she might be yours."

"I regret to say the devilish beast is mine. May I have the name of her rescuer?"

The boy hesitated before answering. "Hensley, m'lord. Travis Hensley."

The name Hensley sounded familiar, but Andrew couldn't recall any specifics. "You say you heard about the mare. I thought I knew all the village children, however, I don't remember seeing you before."

"No, sir. I was passing through and stayed a few days to earn a coin or two." Travis heaved a breath. "Actually, I came this way to meet you, sir."

Before Andrew had time to react to this astonishing statement, Merrick returned with a tray. Thankful for the distraction, Andrew raked his eyes over the food and nodded, pleased to see Merrick had obeyed his order, bringing an assortment of bread, cheese, butter, and dried meat. Andrew brought a small table closer to the boy's chair and took the tray. Dismissing Merrick, he placed the tray on the table. "Please eat."

Travis's stomach rumbled at the sight of the food, but rather than digging in, he paused and bowed his head before crossing himself. *One of the Faithful*, Andrew thought. As if this weren't startling enough, Travis picked up the knife and fork with care. Observing his correct use of the utensils, Andrew began to consider that this boy was no ordinary stray.

Travis seemed aware of his curiosity but not concerned enough to stop eating. A handsome lad, he had high cheekbones and pale skin. His coloring was offset by black eyes and a thick mop of black hair with loose curls that fell over his forehead. Andrew would have guessed his age to be about ten if it weren't for his voice, which told him the boy must be several years older.

Andrew almost snapped his fingers when he discovered what had intrigued him about Travis from the first—he was remarkably clean. His clothes had been mended by a clumsy hand, and his shaggy hair showed signs of brushing. Though dusty, the boy's bare feet didn't show the grunge of walking endless miles. He spoke well, even if he did have the distinct accent of the mountains. The table manners, the cleanliness...and there was something indefinable about him; he carried himself like a young prince. A long-lost changeling child? Andrew hid a smile at his own foolishness.

When Travis finished his food, Andrew poured a small mug of ale and set it before him. The boy's eyes brightened when he tasted it, and Andrew caught himself grinning.

"I'm glad you didn't eat too fast, lad. It wouldn't do to have it all come back up again."

Travis blinked, startled, before a lopsided grin broke through. "No, m'lord, it would not."

They sat in companionable silence until Andrew cleared his throat. Travis took the hint, moved the tray aside, and straightened.

"Now, young Master Hensley, would you mind declaring your business? For you have me surpassingly curious. But first, may I ask, how old are you?"

"Thirteen, sir. Well, almost. In June."

"I'm surprised, I would have thought younger. You are rather..."

"Though he be but little, he is fierce," the boy murmured, with a smile tugging at one corner of his mouth.

Andrew stared at Travis. "Where did you hear that?"

"Shakespeare."

Nonplussed, Andrew demanded, "Surely you can't read!"

"Surely I can," Travis insisted. His tone implied this was a normal state of affairs for an orphan of twelve. At Andrew's look of skepticism, the boy snorted and reached for the sack at his feet. He dug into it, muttering to himself, even poking his entire head into the bag to search. Hauling out two thick leather-bound books, he paused, fear clouding his eyes. "I didn't steal these, m'lord."

"Of course not," murmured Andrew, regretting his sharp tone. It never would have occurred to him to suspect the lad of thievery, though many might have done so. But everything about Travis indicated he had been well-educated, perhaps even loved.

Andrew reached for the books, but the boy hesitated before passing them over. He watched as Andrew studied both books, a Bible and a volume of Shakespeare. The Shakespeare was falling apart at the binding, and the Bible fared worse. Andrew stifled his disappointment when he saw the page that should have held the family history was missing—long ago fallen aside or torn out. Both were ancient tomes, perhaps created at the beginning of the second age of the press.

"These are treasures." He smiled at the boy, returning the volumes. Travis placed them in his bag with great care. "Have you read them both?"

Travis cocked his head, thinking. "Most of the Shakespeare. I was taught to read from the Holy Book, and my mother told me I must always read a little every day. I'm not done with it yet."

"And where is your mother?" The boy averted his eyes to the fire and said nothing, but Andrew saw him blink back tears. His heart squeezed for the lad. "How long have you been on your own, son?"

Travis counted on his fingers, made an exasperated noise, and started over. "About a year, I think? Maybe more? I've lost track."

Andrew nodded. "Well, you have been quite tolerant of my questions. What can I do for you?"

Travis leveled his gaze straight at him, and Andrew realized for the first time his eyes were not black after all but an intense dark blue. Those eyes stirred a memory.

"I need you to find my brother."

# Chapter 2

# Shadows from the Past

Andrew leaned back in his chair and studied the boy. Travis returned his look calmly, but fear and uncertainty showed in the way his shoulders bunched stiffly. A moment passed before Andrew asked, "Why do you think I can do this?"

"My mother told me you could. She said you were the person I should go to when she—that you might know how to find him."

"What is your brother's name?"

"Michael."

"I know many Michaels, but no Michael Hensley. How old would he be?"

"Twenty-five. He was twenty-one when they took him."

"Took him?"

A shadow passed over the boy's face.

"What happened, son?"

"A few years ago, we were living in Curie and—"

"You were in the Shadowlands?" Andrew asked, astonished. It was inconceivable to imagine a well-educated child coming from the mountains.

"Yes, sir. Sammanon conscriptors came and took my brother. He didn't fight them. He said if he resisted, they would harm my mother or me. Mother was already unwell and weak. We let him go. I should have fought!" The boy's voice grated with emotion.

"No, lad. He was correct. You did the right thing," asserted Andrew. He shuddered at the thought of what could have happened to Travis had he fought back. Andrew saw no need to point out the boy's brother might not have survived his capture.

"Without his wages, we couldn't pay rent. I tried!" Travis exclaimed. "I worked at a livery, but I was small and couldn't do much. We wanted to move on, to head northeast. Our family came from Aquila, and Michael wanted us to go home. He and I could have traveled, but Mother was always ill. It was difficult to get very far, even when Michael lived with us. After he was gone, it became impossible."

"If you were from Aquila, how the devil did you end up in Curie?"

"I'm not sure." Travis raked a hand through his hair. "I was young, not quite four. Once or twice I asked, but it set Mother to weeping, and I couldn't bear that. I know we were traveling on the southwest road. When we approached the southern border, the village where we were staying was attacked. Somehow we were all separated. Mother said that my father was killed. We were herded farther west into the Shadowlands."

"Rounders," muttered Andrew.

Travis sat straighter. "I've heard that word before. Who are they?"

"Your brother was taken by conscriptors. From whom do they conscript? Villages run out of men. Rounders are gangs paid to ambush travelers or small hamlets, driving the people deeper into the Shadowlands.

Sometimes they'll cross the border into the southern kingdoms or even the far reaches of Aquila. They're few in number but well organized and very fast. It's difficult to stop them or escape when they're hunting you down." Andrew sighed. Travis remained silent, deep in thought. "What happened next?"

Travis broke from his reverie. "We wandered, and I tried to find work whenever I could. Mother would do laundry. It was awful for her. We sold everything we had of value."

"Except for these books?"

"There were others. Not many, but a few. We sold the rest."

"Books are expensive."

"I know. Before they took Michael, we did well enough, though we never had much. He and my mother set a great store by books and would save coppers to buy the most worn copies. But Mother and I couldn't part with the last two. In the end, I would have sold even those to feed her if I could, but she hid them from me until after..." Here the boy stood. He walked to the open window and leaned against the frame, silent for a long time. Andrew remained quiet, allowing Travis to wrestle with his thoughts.

Continuing to gaze outside, Travis spoke in a low voice. "Before she died, she told me how to find you. She gave me very specific instructions."

"And then you were on your own," Andrew stated. He picked up the fire iron and poked at the glowing embers, already dreading his next question. "Why do you assume your brother is even alive?"

"He's got to be," Travis muttered, clenching his fists. "I would know if he was dead. He's alive somewhere."

At a loss for words, Andrew stared at the fire, thinking. The story wasn't unusual. Variations of the same sad tale had been passed around for years, but the boy's account touched a deep chord in Andrew. Traveling alone as he had, all the way from the Shadowlands.

"Travis, I would do anything to assist you. I promise. But I can't place the name Hensley, or why your mother sent you to me, a stranger. Did she provide any explanation, or a letter?"

Travis remained so still, Andrew wasn't sure his question had registered, but the boy turned from the window with a peculiar expression on his face. He retrieved his sack and bent over it again, withdrawing a small, dusty bundle of velvet. Sitting across from Andrew, Travis stroked the object in his hand with a gentle finger before handing it over.

Andrew unwrapped the worn layers of fabric to reveal a magnificent garnet hanging on a long, golden chain. Stunned, Andrew stared at it. He held the gem to the light of the fire. A hundred memories flooded his heart as the flames danced off the facets. Minutes passed, and he brushed at the moisture that had formed in his eyes.

"What was your mother's name, lad? You never told me." Andrew struggled past the thickness in his throat.

"Anna, sir."

"And she gave this to you?"

Travis nodded. "She said I must never show it to anyone, but to you alone. That you would know where to find any family that might still be alive. And if there was no one left, you would take care of me. Do you know why?"

"Yes, I know why," he whispered. He placed the jewel back in its velvet shroud and returned it to the boy.

Andrew tugged Travis to his feet and steered him to the window to study him once more in the light. There were the eyes, those deep sapphire eyes that had teased Andrew's memory. The hair was not a true black as he had first thought, for subtle glints of red caught the sunlight, turning it into a dark mahogany. *A few fragments of his father*, Andrew thought. The rest of him—the shape of his face, the fine bones, the way he carried himself. How had he not seen it before?

"I have a friend," Andrew spoke as though his mind were miles and years away, "a very dear friend who had a wife and four sons. His wife was in poor health, and he believed taking her south might aid her condition. That particular year the Rounders were worse, bolder than ever, and the family was torn asunder. He escaped with two boys while his wife and the other two sons—the eldest and youngest—disappeared."

"The father escaped!"

At these words, the boy's natural pallor intensified, and Andrew feared he might faint. "Your name isn't Travis Hensley, is it?"

Travis closed his eyes and shuddered. When he could speak again, his voice was hoarse. "Can you help me?"

"I may be able to help you, son. However, you must be patient. It takes time for letters to find their way to the right people, do you understand?"

Travis slumped against the window, relief plain on his face. "Yes, sir."

Andrew gave his thin shoulder a squeeze and told him to gather his things. Together they walked to the main house. The moment they crossed the threshold, the peaceful quiet of the morning was shattered as what seemed to be dozens of chattering voices crashed over them. Flurries of skirts flew about, and Travis halted, stunned by the instantaneous mass of feminine energy. Andrew chuckled at the boy's reaction but sailed through undisturbed while calling for his wife. Mariah Kavanaugh appeared, a harassed but good-humored woman. If she was shocked at her husband leading a random stray human into her home, she showed no sign of it.

"Mariah, dear, this is Travis Hensley, and he will be staying with us for a while. I want him to have a proper room and be treated as a most important guest." He dropped his voice and whispered in her ear, "I'll explain later."

Mariah studied the boy and gave a curt nod. "A bath, haircut, new clothes, and as much food as he can eat. That should do the trick!"

Travis gulped over her assessment, but the promise of food encouraged the lad. Nevertheless, Andrew knew his wife's enthusiastic nature could be overwhelming. A thought clicked in his head. "Wait a moment. Travis, come with me." He led the boy down a corridor and into a room full of books. His library was modest compared to the castle or abbey in Altair, but he was proud of his collection.

"You are welcome to read any of the books in my library. All I ask is that your hands are clean and the books stay in the house." He grinned at the awe on the boy's face.

Andrew returned to his office in a distracted state. Light footsteps chased after him, and he smiled. He had known Mariah would be wild with curiosity. Andrew remained at the door, holding it open for her as she swooshed in. He then sat at his desk and gazed at her with pretend innocence. His playful anticipation was deflated by her first words.

"Is that child Anna Lockhart's youngest son?"

Andrew's jaw dropped. "However did you guess?"

"Because he could be her twin, that's why. Look at him! And with his father's very eyes peering out at me. I would recognize those eyes anywhere."

"You never cease to amaze me, my dear." Andrew marveled at his wife. She had seen in moments what had taken him an hour to work out. "Remember, the boy wishes to be referred to as Travis Hensley. I have no idea why, but let's abide by it. No mention of the other. Now, I must write to Thomas. And by the way, Anna Lockhart hasn't been a Lockhart for well over twenty years."

"Once a Lockhart, *always* a Lockhart. But where is she?"

Andrew was silent, and Mariah understood. "Oh, dear Anna..." she whispered as she sank into a chair and dashed tears from her eyes. There she remained, lost in memories as Andrew made ready to write. He uncorked his ink bottle, but she placed her hand over his.

"Don't write to Thomas. He's become utterly despondent over this whole thing. And what if we're wrong? I don't think we are, but consider what it would do to him!"

Andrew pondered the problem, considering his wife's words. Mariah had made herself invaluable to him over the years with her instincts about such matters, and he took her advice seriously. He drummed his fingers on the desk a few times before nodding. "Perhaps you are right. I'll send this to his eldest, and he can decide whether to tell Thomas or no. Meanwhile, go fuss over the lad and see about fattening him up. I know that will bring you unceasing joy."

Mariah gave him a dirty look before flouncing off. As she passed through the doorway, she called over her shoulder, "Hensley was the family name of Thomas's mother." At Andrew's jubilant exclamation, she departed with a pleased expression on her face.

Andrew laughed, his heart lighter than it had been all morning, and dipped his quill into the ink bottle. Perhaps his previous notion of a changeling prince wasn't so far from the truth after all.

## Chapter 3

# The Red Feather

In the far western wilds of Aquila, that spring had been exceptionally wet. The snow was late leaving and the rains early arriving. Michael Thatcher hated the wet. He liked a clean, neat camp, and these were impossible standards to meet in the constant slop. Horse manure mingled with mud, it was difficult to keep food dry, and Michael felt as though he had been living in soggy clothes for weeks. His good wool cloak smelled of damp sheep. He didn't know why they were already in the mountains instead of finishing out the winter at Castle Altair. And yet, here he was, swimming in muck, when back east it had been a beautiful spring for a month at least. He shook his head. Someday he would get married and stop wandering the country. Although cheerful and lighthearted as a rule, the wet did try Michael's patience and recall dark memories. He had several to choose from.

He searched in vain for a dry spot to sit and settled for a musty stump, peering through the trees to see if the sun would break through the clouds. A voice calling his name broke into his thoughts, and he jumped. Chiding himself for daydreaming, he smiled at the rangy redhead sauntering toward him, bare to the waist, with faded trousers rolled up and a fishing pole over his shoulder.

"Woolgathering?"

"Maybe."

"Dinner," the redhead said with a grin, displaying a string of fish.

"Fantastic! Guess that means I'm cooking?"

"I caught 'em, you cook 'em. Besides, you're a much better cook."

Michael laughed, for he couldn't deny the truth of this. Mealtimes were an adventure whenever his brother James took the helm. Michael knew he was a boring cook, but at least his food promised to be edible.

"Do you know when Dad will be back?" asked the youth, handing the fish to Michael.

"No idea, but it could be another few days."

"What say you and I haul up the camp and head east? Find a nice sunny spot and a few girls?"

"That would be no." Michael chuckled even as he gave James a mock-stern look. "Absolutely not. Instead, how about you scout for a new place to tie the horses? I'm worried about them standing in the wet."

James spun about to begin searching for a drier section of the forest, calling over his shoulder, "Coffee?"

Michael grunted a vague reply. Their father wouldn't like how much coffee the two of them had been drinking during his absence. Sailed across the sea from tropical islands over a thousand miles southward, they considered coffee to be a precious commodity. But for Michael, nothing fought off the wet chill better than coffee or whiskey, and the whiskey they had was strictly medicinal. Moving to a crude, precarious table that was simply a board placed between two uneven boulders, Michael glanced at the fish and sighed. More wet things—wet fish, wet guts, and wet hands that would smell for days. He set the coffeepot to boil first, and yanking out his knife, he began to gut the trout.

In spite of the unpleasant job, soon his rare, dark mood lifted. It was pleasant to hear James talking to the horses and mules, with the burble of the creek nearby. The thought of fish, fresh from that same creek and fried on a hot skillet, went far in cheering him.

A crackle in the woods interrupted his thoughts.

"James?" Michael called, although the noise didn't come from where James had led the animals.

His brother came out from the trees behind Michael and replied in a low voice. "I heard it too."

Michael remained calm as he continued cleaning the fish, but his gaze darted to his hunting bow and longsword, both leaning against a stack of wooden crates. He gripped the knife in his hand. To be sure, the smell of fish guts alone might be enough to frighten anyone off. Michael almost laughed at the thought.

"Whoever it is, they are making a terrible racket," James murmured as he came near Michael, tugging on his homespun linen tunic, sword already strapped to his side. "Can't be an animal. Not this close to camp."

A horse nickered and then silence fell. Michael and James looked at each other, and Michael jerked his head, indicating to James to start a perimeter sweep to their left. Michael adjusted the grip on his knife and took a step toward his sword. He and James froze when a quavering voice called out, "Thatcher?"

"Ollie?" Exasperated, Michael relaxed. "You scared us half to death! What are you doing, lurking around?"

Ollie fumbled out of the forest, leading his horse. "I scared you? I never know where to find you folks, and who knows what might be in these woods, yet *I scare you*!"

James rolled his eyes. "You need a different job if you can't handle poking around a few trees."

"It's not the trees that worry me," Ollie muttered. "I've seen bear scat out already. You know how they are this time of year. Wolves are hungry too. Anyway, here's the mail. Do I smell coffee?"

Michael caught the leather satchel Ollie tossed to him while James grabbed a few clay mugs and poured coffee for everyone. He handed a mug to Ollie, who was about his own age, and they settled before the fire to talk over any news Ollie brought while Michael finished prepping the fish.

"You staying the night, Ollie?" Michael interrupted.

"Might depend on what's for dinner. Is that trout?" he asked as Michael gestured to the fillets stacked up. "I'm staying!"

It wasn't long before the sizzling sounds and smell of cooking fish hung over the camp. Ollie contributed a flagon of ale, and the brothers hailed him a hero.

"Where's your father?" Ollie asked.

"Off somewhere west, deep on the mountain border. He's training some new men."

Ollie lay against his saddle, which served as a makeshift pillow, and eyed the young men working together to prepare the food. "You know, I never could figure how the two of you are related, much less brothers. I've never seen two men less alike."

Michael and James grinned at each other, for this was an old joke between them. It was true they were nothing alike, although both drew the appreciative eyes of the young ladies in the local villages. Even at seventeen, James was tall and broad-shouldered, showing promise of more to come, with a ruddy face that already needed a daily shave, and bright auburn hair that curled if left to grow too long. Michael had topped out years ago several inches shorter. His pale skin and smooth complexion were a sharp contrast to his straight, jet-black hair and brows. Their one shared characteristic were eyes as blue as the summer sky.

"You're exposing a family scandal, Ollie," James said, arching an eyebrow at the courier. Ollie appeared chagrined until James hooted with amusement.

"Ignore him." Michael laughed as well, poking at James. "The fact is we're cousins by blood. My parents died in that awful plague years ago when I was a wee tot. Don't even remember them. The Thatchers raised me as their own son, so James and I are brothers as far as we are concerned."

"Don't you also have brothers who live back east?"

"Just the one. Ethan," Michael replied, all signs of amusement gone from his face. Ollie took the hint and said nothing more on the topic. Tossing the last of the fish into the pan, Michael caught James glancing in his direction with a rare shadow of sadness in his eyes.

Michael threw a fresh log onto the fire with unnecessary violence. Dear, sweet Anna, twin sister to his natural father, Gareth. She had been beautiful and kind, a wonderful foster mother to him, taking him in even before she had married Thomas Thatcher. It had been years since he had seen her, or...*Don't go there*, he told himself when his heart thudded with an old ache.

After Michael finished cooking the fish and they were all enjoying both food and drink, Ollie jerked his chin toward the satchel Michael had set aside. "You might want to go through the mail, that way if anything needs an immediate reply you can write it before I leave in the morning."

Michael grunted his assent. He reached into the bag and fished out a few letters. "I'm surprised they bothered sending you. There's not much here."

"Aye, that's what I thought, but there's an urgent letter in there, you'll see it."

With his father gone, Michael was in charge and free to open anything as he saw fit, the one exception being letters from the queen herself. He wondered if that might be the pressing missive, but there was nothing from Castle Altair. Finding the letter stamped with the red feather, Michael's forehead scrunched in puzzlement. The letter in question was addressed to him from Lord General Andrew Kavanaugh. He tapped the parchment against his leg, considering. A close family friend, Andrew exchanged letters with both him and his father, but to send an urgent message to Michael was unusual.

Michael watched the two young men talking by the fire, wondering if he should read the letter at once or wait for more privacy. Apprehensive, he took another swig of ale and broke the seal. He relaxed as he read the first few lines. It seemed a perfectly normal letter. In fact, one passage had him laughing, catching James's attention.

"What is it, Michael?"

Michael gasped for air and waved the letter. "Andrew."

"How's my Cat?" James asked with a wicked grin as he shifted closer to Michael.

Seeing the confusion on Ollie's face, Michael explained, "Lord General Kavanaugh has a bevy of daughters and an untold number of house cats roaming about the estate. One time James compared the girls to a pack of feral felines, and the oldest daughter took particular offense to his comments. Her name is Catrina, but she's always gone by Cate. James started calling her his Cat years ago to rouse her temper. They've developed quite the combative relationship."

"What did Andrew say?" asked James as he leaned over Michael's shoulder.

Choking down his laughter, Michael read aloud. "'Tell James his most recent letter referring to recommendations on how to declaw his favorite Cat did not go over well. She wishes him to know her claws remain intact, sharpened daily, and she will take delight in scratching out his eyes at their next meeting.' You're in for it now, James."

"Let me see that!" James tried to snatch the latter but Michael jerked it away.

"No, wait until after I've finished. Go eat your fish."

Michael continued reading to himself, unable to stop chuckling.

*I have a situation here at Lawnwood Manor, and I'm hoping you can help me puzzle it out. My new mare escaped, and an urchin brought the beast home. I fed him well, and afterward we proceeded to have the most extraordinary conversation. He came to me expecting assistance in finding his brother, which baffled me at first. He claims his name is Travis Hensley—*

Michael went rigid. Ollie was cackling over a story James had told him concerning Cate. Neither of them noticed when Michael stood and walked some distance from the fire before continuing.

*He claims his name is Travis Hensley, his mother was Anna, and he's seeking his brother Michael. He says he's almost thirteen but is small for his age and certainly has the Lockhart look to him. I didn't recall hearing the name Hensley before, however my wife suggested it might mean something to you or Thomas.*

"Michael?" James's voice came from far away.

*I almost keeled over when he brought forth the garnet pendant—Michael, that garnet is a Kavanaugh family heirloom. I gave that necklace to your Aunt Anna years ago, hoping she would marry me. We know how that turned out, but I insisted she keep it (much to my father's annoyance).*

*Mariah suggested I write these things to you and not Thomas, knowing his feelings on the matter after so many false hopes. I'm positive this boy is Tristan. He hails from the Curie region, and a change of name may have been deemed safer. He is—*

Michael staggered against a tree, his breath coming in short gasps. James jumped up and ran over to him, catching him by the arm.

"Michael! What's wrong?"

Speechless, Michael passed the letter to James. It took him a moment to find the passage that had affected his older brother. James's eyes widened, and he gaped at Michael.

"I need to go." Michael gulped for air. "Right now. You'll be good here until Dad gets back?"

"Don't be daft!"

"He won't like it, me leaving you." Michael frowned, thinking hard.

"Go, Michael! The date—it's been weeks already. Do you think..." James hesitated. "Do you think Mother..."

Anguished, Michael shook his head. "I don't know. Andrew says nothing about her."

Michael stood there, lost in his own thoughts. James hovered beside him, bursting with impatience, but knowing to leave him alone. Michael never acted rashly. He thought through every situation, considered every point. At last he looked at James, his eyes gleaming.

"Right. I'll leave at first light. If the Father wills it, I'm bringing our brother home."

# Chapter 4

# Lawnwood

Lawnwood Manor was an old, mellow house. Although only two stories, it sprawled over the landscape with multiple wings. Ivy climbed the walls, threatening the rare mullioned glass windows of the formal lower rooms. In the spring and summer, Mariah's work in the flower gardens made the manor a showcase to rival any grand estate in Aquila. The house had a tranquil appearance that belied its exuberant interior life.

It was clear to all who knew the Kavanaughs that Andrew and Mariah had one of the happiest marriages in the kingdom, as evidenced by their many daughters. The eight women of the house ran the estate without the slightest interference from Andrew, allowing him to attend to his horses and military matters. Known as a generous yet firm mother, Mariah Kavanaugh indulged in the high spirits of her girls while keeping them thoroughly in hand. One more addition to the brood in the form of Travis presented no hardship, even if he was "just a boy," as the eldest daughter Cate had sniffed the day he arrived.

The last few weeks had been wonderful for Travis. Mariah took over his care with a zeal that would have terrified Andrew. Within hours after his arrival, Travis was bathed and dressed in a proper linen shirt with trousers and new boots. He protested weakly when Mariah brought forth the shears to address his hair, but she remained undeterred. Even so, she did not crop it as closely as she might have, given the lack of vermin. He cut such a handsome figure that evening at the dinner table that the youngest daughters tittered, causing the poor boy to blush. Andrew wondered how Mariah managed to find the lad clothes and boots that fit him in a single afternoon but shrugged it off as one of his wife's many mysterious attributes.

Not wishing to be idle, Travis worked alongside the stablehands every day, determined to earn his keep. Andrew left him alone until a disgruntled report from his head groom declared that although young Travis handled horses well, he sat on them like a sack of potatoes, and could *something* be done before he shamed the very name of Lawnwood? With that, Andrew himself instructed the boy in the finer points of riding.

Travis had a kind nature, if somewhat quiet, and it wasn't long before he won the hearts of everyone on the estate, including Cate. He had an obvious affection for Mariah, making himself available to assist her with minor jobs when the stables could spare him. However, Travis spent most of his free time in the library. After the stables, he was happiest there. It was a snug chamber with just enough chairs—but not so many that the room invited those who didn't come to read. Even though the days had grown warm, at dusk Andrew often lit a small fire in the flagstone hearth for the cozy atmosphere it provided.

The first time Travis tip-toed into the room, Andrew was already sitting with a mug of ale, lost in a book. Out of the corner of his eye, he watched the boy take in the shelves, the candles, the many books. He seemed especially fascinated by the windows.

"Is this actual glass?" he whispered to himself, touching a pane with a careful finger. He spun and stared at Andrew. "I've never seen glass windows before."

Andrew chuckled. "They are rather ostentatious for a family room, I'll admit. But I believe a library should have good light, and using shutters wouldn't protect the books from the wet."

Travis nodded before murmuring, "Momma told me stories about the great houses with libraries. I was never sure if I believed her."

Andrew bit his lip, recalling Anna Lockhart's love of books. It warmed his heart to see the boy had inherited the same eagerness to read.

They passed many long hours together in the library, each in a chair reading his own book of choice. Sometimes Andrew would pick out a passage and read aloud in an attempt to draw out the boy's thoughts. At first reserved, Travis soon grew comfortable enough to voice his opinions, delighting Andrew with his fresh perspective, untainted by the cynics. One evening, in a fit of inspiration, Andrew also started teaching him chess, to the great enjoyment of them both.

Good food, solid work, and a soft bed gave the boy a healthy vigor. Despite this, a haunting sadness lingered in his eyes. Andrew fervently wished he could find a way to bring some joy to the boy's expression.

Almost two months had passed since Travis had arrived at Lawnwood, and Andrew expressed concern to Mariah that his letter to Michael might have been lost. He was sitting in the library, watching his wife fuss over the dust on the mantel.

"I shouldn't wonder, since we've not heard from any of them." Mariah sniffed, battling a sneeze. "Travis can stay with us until Thomas returns to winter in Altair. He always passes a few days here. No one will mind. Although I'm sure you'll miss the boy when the time comes for him to go."

Andrew grunted in a noncommittal fashion, causing Mariah to peer at her husband for a long moment. She moved to lean over his chair and raised a hand to his cheek, bringing his eyes to her own.

"I know you wished for a son, Andrew." Surprised, Andrew started to speak, but Mariah silenced him with a shake of her head. "I see how you are with him, and while you have been an excellent father to our daughters, I also see glimpses of things you have missed by not having a son of your own. I'm sorry you never had the opportunity."

Andrew reached for his wife and drew her down onto his lap. "My dear woman, I would not trade my girls for all the boys in the land, don't you know that? Perhaps I'm waiting for grandsons!"

Rolling her eyes, Mariah was dropping a kiss on his head when the door opened and the very subject of their recent conversation stepped into the room. Beholding his patrons in such an intimate display of tenderness, Travis drew back in abject horror. Andrew called out to him, and Mariah stood, laughing as she straightened her skirts.

"I'm sorry you had to witness that, lad," Andrew said with a sheepish smile. "Do you need anything?"

Two spots of color appeared on Travis's cheeks, but he grinned at Andrew. "Merrick wanted me to warn you that a solitary rider is coming in fast. The horse looks to be under the whip."

"Thank you, Travis. Why don't you come with me? You can take care of his horse. Sounds like it'll need some attention."

Travis slipped out a side door to grab a lead rope from the stable as Andrew went through the main doors of the front hall to greet his guest. The rider was indeed coming fast, and lather flecked the horse's neck. Not until they pulled up in a swirl of dust did Andrew recognize Michael Thatcher, possible brother to one local waif named Travis. It had been about eight months since Andrew last saw Michael, and now as he stood there in the flesh, any lingering doubts Andrew might have had about his relationship to Travis were erased.

"Andrew!" Michael grasped the hand of the older man. A thin stubble glazed his cheeks, there were shadows under his eyes, and he was breathless. Andrew couldn't tell if it was from the hard ride or some inner agitation.

"Michael, m'boy! How are you? Where are the others?"

"I left them as soon as I received your letter. Dad was deep in the mountains, and I couldn't wait. Is he here?" Michael cast his gaze about the estate, suppressed excitement thrumming through him.

"Yes, yes, he should be here any mo—" Andrew broke off when Michael's entire demeanor shifted. He pivoted to see Travis coming around the corner of the house, swinging a lead rope while humming an off-key tune to himself. At that moment, Travis saw the man standing beside Andrew and stopped in his tracks.

They both stood there, staring at each other. The boy broke the silence first, taking a single step forward, his eyes questioning. "Michael?"

"Tristan!"

In a flash, Michael bounded to him and fell to his knees even as he jerked the boy into a rough, strong embrace. His heart pounded, and he wept without shame. After all these years, when hope was nearly extinguished, he was holding his precious baby brother again, the person he loved more than any other on earth. The one he had tried to protect but had lost. Michael almost smothered the boy. Pulling himself together, he cupped the boy's face with trembling hands. "Look at you!" His voice rasped with emotion. "You've grown so much!"

Tristan had tears in his eyes, and he gave a shaky laugh. "Still not very tall."

Michael laughed as well, even as he swallowed his own tears. His eyes were all over Tristan, taking the boy in. It was true; he was small for his age, but he had grown a great deal since Michael's farewell glance. Michael looked over Tristan's shoulder at Andrew. "I can't believe this. I can never thank you enough."

"What this will mean to your father," Andrew murmured in disbelief.

Michael turned back to his brother, his face sober. "Tristan, what about Mother?"

Tears falling at last, Tristan shook his head. "I tried to take care of her, Michael," he choked. "She kept getting weaker and weaker and I—" He couldn't get any more words out and his voice broke.

A sob tore from Michael's throat as he drew the boy close once. "Shhh, Tristan, never mind. I've got you now. And I'm not going to lose you again, I swear it. Never again."

# Chapter 5

# In the Library

"Why the devil didn't the boy tell me his real name?"

After a long dinner, Andrew and Michael escaped to the library. Andrew dusted the bottle of brandy he brought out when particular friends visited, pouring a generous tot into rare cut crystal glasses for Michael and himself.

Michael had gathered the most pertinent information on Tristan's life after his forced removal, but even he couldn't extract anything from the boy regarding his mother's death. On that topic, Tristan shut down and could not be budged.

Accepting the brandy with a silent prayer of gratitude, Michael mulled aloud. "Simple fear. After the Rounders separated us from the others, we were pushed farther into the Shadowlands, almost to the border of Sammanon itself. We had to change our names. Even that far west, Thatcher was problematic. For years it's been known that one of the queen's closest confidants went by that name. And my true family name was impossible. Lockhart is one of the most powerful houses in

Aquila! No, we had to come up with something else. Hensley seemed harmless enough, yet it was a name Dad would recognize."

"Why change his first name?"

"Tristan? No child of the Shadowlands would have borne the name of Aquila's greatest king, it would have meant death. We had to change it."

"But he knew his real identity all along, didn't he?"

"Of course he did. But with no memory of you, and after what he has been through, I'm not surprised. We had hammered into Tristan's head that he must never reveal his true name. I thought Dad told you the whole story after I returned to Aquila."

Andrew gave Michael a searching look before saying, "What your father *didn't* tell me was that you'd been conscripted by Sammanon soldiers. Horrid business. I should have known you would have never allowed yourself to be separated from Anna and Tristan on your own."

"No," replied Michael with bitterness. "I asked him to keep that between ourselves."

"Well, Thomas may have told me about Hensley at one time. Mariah figured it out at once. That woman remembers everything. Why did Anna send the boy to me? She could have sent him to Altair. His most powerful relations are there and would have helped him."

"Because you were someone Mother trusted without question. Remember, she believed her husband to be dead, her whole family gone. She had no idea whether I was dead or alive. And Dad always had enemies among the nobility. Send Tristan alone to Altair? I'm sure Mother feared his life could have been in danger. All great families have enemies, and the Thatcher boys have ties to several powerful houses."

Andrew stood to stir the small fire in the grate and topped off their glasses. Michael's mind drifted. The days of urgent riding were catching up to him, not to mention the emotions of reuniting with his youngest brother. A shudder of a yawn ran through him. Andrew sat again and tapped his fingers on his glass, thinking.

"Michael, there is one thing you should know. I'm not sure if Tristan remembers James and Ethan, much less his own father. When I revealed that they had escaped from the Rounders, he seemed stunned, but he's not mentioned them again. He's only asked about you."

"He was so young when the family was separated, not even four. We thought they were all dead, and what was the point of reminding him of brothers he couldn't remember?" Michael sighed. "When he was older, I tried to talk about them, but Mother would become emotional, and Tristan couldn't bear to see her cry. We never discussed the past. He knew we were in fact cousins by blood, although we were all raised as true brothers. But he has no clear idea about the Lockharts, the Reynards, or any of his extended family or history."

Andrew lifted his mug toward Michael. "Well, here's to many joyful reunions!"

Michael smiled as they both drank but remained thoughtful. "Andrew, you've had Tristan here for some weeks. What's he like? I know what I remember, but I want to hear what you think."

Andrew considered his response for a moment. "Smart. Quite intelligent. He reads at the level of the most well-educated adults I've met. All you boys read well, but Travis—forgive me, Tristan—he soaks books in like a sponge. Granted, he has no training, no skills. Well, no, that's not true. He's excellent with horses. Of course, Tristan's behind where the rest of you were at his age. I doubt he's ever touched a sword or a bow."

The fact that Tristan was intelligent came as no surprise to Michael. He himself had taught the boy how to read when Tristan wasn't much more than a toddler. But Andrew continued speaking.

"He's special, Michael, very special," Andrew said, his face softening. "Honorable. He's kind and gentle, brave and strong. I suspect he's dealt with some atrocious things. Tristan hasn't told me much, to be honest, and yet he's survived them with his integrity intact. Not everyone his age could manage that. There aren't many adults who could either, for that matter! And to be reunited with those who will love him, and nurture his gifts? Michael, m'boy, he will grow to be a prince among men, believe me."

Michael could only nod. His throat was tight and tears stung his eyes, but his heart was full of joy and a fierce pride.

A light knock interrupted his thoughts, followed by Mariah and Tristan entering the room. Mariah set down a tray with a crock of ale and several mugs. She took a seat close to Andrew while Tristan curled up in a chair near Michael with one of the many house cats snuggled into a ball on his lap. A sense of expectation filled the air, and all eyes were on Michael.

"Right," he said. "Tristan wants to know what happened after I was taken."

Michael huffed a deep breath and drained his brandy. He shook his head when Andrew offered him the bottle. Instead, he poured himself a mug of ale and sat. Michael leaned forward, his elbows resting on his knees, staring at his mug and marshaling his thoughts.

"When they took me, I told you I would try to escape in—what did I say? Two or three months?"

Tristan nodded, his body rigid with anticipation.

"I made that claim based on stories I had heard from conscripted soldiers who had escaped. I always paid attention to those stories. Nevertheless, I did make a few mistakes. I didn't count on my accent for one. You would have been better off on that point, Tristan. You grew up in the mountains and foothills of the Shadowlands, and your speech shows it. But your mother and me? No one would mistake either of us as being from anywhere but far eastern Aquila, even Altair. Such nonsense too. I could have corrected my accent, but I didn't think to alter it until it was too late.

"And I had another problem. I was too good with a sword, at least for a youth they viewed as a mere peasant. I hadn't sparred for years and was out of practice, but I had started training at seven years old. At first, I tried to appear inept on purpose. I'm ashamed to say my pride got in the way. I was good, I knew it, and I wanted to show off."

"You were excellent," Andrew offered. "Thomas wrote with such pride of your swordsmanship. Didn't you fight in the last war?"

"Yes, a little. Toward the end."

"I'm sure it felt good to hold a sword in your hand once more."

"It did, I won't deny it. But at the expense of being away from Tristan and Mother? No. I should have controlled my pride for their sake." Michael stood and paced the room, troubled.

"The fact is, even though a part of me wanted to get back to you, I enjoyed being among men again. I was young and selfish, and tired of living a neutered life. The months before I was taken had become so frustrating. I was desperate to bring you and Mother home to Aquila, to salvage whatever we could of our previous life. You were old enough for us to traverse even dangerous lands. Mother though...she was sick and fearful of everything. I couldn't budge her. It would make me so angry, I would—" Michael stopped and braced his hands against the mantel.

"You were very young," soothed Mariah.

"I was still a man and should have behaved like one." Michael returned to his chair and raked a hand through his hair.

"Anyway, I was far too good for a country rustic. Between that and my accent, I had a problem. They grew suspicious of me, and their suspicions increased when those in charge were told I came along without a fight. They were convinced I was some sort of spy. It took longer to earn their trust than I thought. I became more prisoner than recruit, and they even flogged me. I suppose they hoped to beat the truth out of me."

Tristan winced and his stomach churned. He had seen public floggings before and tried to banish the image that flashed into his mind—Michael, stripped to the waist, blood pouring down his torso, his flesh shredded.

Michael knelt in front of the boy. "It wasn't bad, Tris," he whispered. "It hurt, yes, but not like those floggings we would see in the villages. I was valuable to them as a soldier. They wanted to be sure of me, not ruin me."

Michael wished Tristan were younger so he could hold the boy on his lap like he did years ago. Instead, he tousled Tristan's hair and sat once more before taking a gulp of ale.

"The irony is their fears were justified in the end. I handed over a great deal of information later. From that point forward, everything went as I had expected, including escape, but it was months later than I anticipated. By the time I got away and journeyed back to the Curie region, you were both long gone. I visited Duvall in the dead of night and almost sent him to an early grave, he didn't recognize me at first. He said you and Mother had been kicked out of the last place. He claims he tried to help, but it wasn't enough."

"Duvall was good to us, he really was!" Tristan exclaimed before his voice dropped off. "But no, it wasn't enough."

"He said you took to begging before you left the village."

Surprised, Andrew stared at Tristan, who had never mentioned this before.

"I did," Tristan said with defiance. "And I should have done it sooner."

Michael wanted to ask more but decided to forgo the topic until another time. He was also anxious to finish his story, for he took no joy in reciting it.

"After I left Duvall, I spent several months trying to find you and Mother. I could track you easily enough in the beginning, then the trail ran cold. Dead cold. As near as I could tell, you fell off the face of the earth. I was forced to make some decisions. I had military information on Sammanon I needed to pass on as soon as possible, and I wondered if it would be easier finding you if I had help. Andrew, you and Mariah know the rest. I made my way to Castle Altair and reunited with Her Grace—"

"Wait! Her Grace? You can't mean the queen?" Tristan exclaimed.

"Yes. And—"

"How? Surely not anyone can walk into the castle and ask to see her?"

Mariah laughed. "Why wouldn't he see Her Grace? Don't you know that Michael—" She stopped when her husband put his hand over hers.

Confused, Tristan looked at Michael, who shrugged and rose from his chair, pacing again. "Let's just say I have some connections with the queen and her family."

"That's one way to put it," murmured Mariah before sipping her ale. Andrew squeezed her hand in warning.

"Queen Charlotte put me in touch with family. Others who had been searching for us since our disappearance years ago. They were doing work in the Shadowlands, watching the borders, hoping to run across us someday. Together, we returned to where the trail grew cold. Nothing. Not even a clue to indicate whether you were alive or dead. So, we continued watching the border. It's valuable work, to be sure, but the truth is I stayed with it, clinging to the hope we would find you. Instead, you found me." Michael offered his brother a warm smile.

At this, everyone fell quiet, each mulling over their own thoughts. Tristan yawned, and the silence was broken with laughter. Mariah stood and patted Tristan's head.

"Well," she said, "I'm sure Tristan will be leaving with you and keeping a man's hours soon enough, but in this house it's long past time for bed."

"Yes, ma'am," said Michael with a wink.

"Tristan, I've put Michael in the room next to yours. Come along." Mariah moved to sweep the boy away, but Tristan stopped to hug Michael hard before leaving. Michael chided himself for going soft as his eyes filled with tears.

"I'll see you in a bit. Get along with you."

Chapter 6

# Dark Memories

The weary days of hard riding were making Michael's muscles scream as he dragged himself up the stairs, but he grinned when a loud snore erupted from a nearby bedroom. Tristan had snored since he was a small tyke. It used to drive Michael mad when his brother would fall asleep first and the noise kept him awake. Yet throughout all those nights in the Sammanon camp, and the painful years that followed, how Michael had longed to hear the familiar sound once more.

Michael tiptoed into Tristan's room and sat on the edge of the bed, thinking about what he had said downstairs. He had skimmed the edges of his story, giving the barest outline.

There was the flogging to start. He supposed one day soon Tristan would see the scars on his back, but there was no need to burden him with that. Best let the boy believe it had not been too awful, for knowing otherwise would serve no purpose. Michael had always been strong in both mind and body. When they had brought out the whip, he clamped his teeth on the leather strap they forced into his mouth and submitted to every stroke. To give in would have meant certain death, and the last assurance of being reunited with his family would have been lost. The whipping also cleared his mind of his recent fall into pride and self. It refocused his priorities to escape and return to those who needed him.

After the flogging, life in Sammanon's army had not been too bad, if you discounted the homesickness, the yearning for his sick mother and young brother, and the desperate fear for their safety. If you could forget you were a slave, forced to fight on behalf of your beloved country's darkest enemy, it was endurable.

He had spoken the truth about gaining intelligence on Sammanon. Michael recalled all he had passed on to Queen Charlotte. He might have staved off another war for a few years with the information he had gathered concerning their armies. Few would ever appreciate what he had done. Not even a handful of people knew he had provided information, and he had sworn them all to secrecy.

Once the Sammanon officers' suspicions were eased, escape required nothing more than careful planning and a delay of a few more weeks. Looking back, Michael wondered why more conscripted soldiers never bothered trying to get away. He supposed the promise of regular meals was enough to sway the half-starved men.

The journey to their village had required days of travel with no food and few streams along the way. Michael remembered the joy in approaching the village, only to be undone by the abandoned shack. He had fallen to his knees at the cold stone hearth, the shock of finding the place long deserted too great to bear. It had been nine months since he had been taken. How could he have believed he'd be returning to the same bubbling stewpot? Had his mother and brother left, or were they both dead, thrown into a pauper's field? He stifled his tears and staggered to his feet, finding his way to the one friend he had in the village and terrifying poor Duvall by his unexpected appearance.

The friendship of that man! Michael would never forget it. Furious when he discovered Duvall had dismissed Tristan, he had lashed out before collapsing in exhaustion and hunger. He awoke in Duvall's own bed, feverish and despondent, with Duvall hovering over him. At last Michael gave his old friend a chance to explain. Yes, Duvall had dismissed Tristan, but his reasons were sound. He knew Sammanon men had been watching Tristan. Whispers in the village hinted that a boy who could earn a bit of coin working in a stable was old enough to be conscripted. He had to let Tristan go for his own safety, but Duvall found a way to work around Anna's pride and continued to provide for them as much as he could. When the two were evicted from their shack, he had searched for days, hoping to shelter them in his own home. But he never discovered a trace of them. After Michael recovered, Duvall even loaned him a horse so he could continue the search.

Spring slipped into summer, summer to autumn gold, and still Michael sought them out. Searched relentlessly all those months. It was a struggle for him to survive. He had grown up in the capital city of Altair, and though the recent years had been difficult, he had never needed to live off the wild before. The muscle and health he had gained from the good food in the Sammanon camp began to disintegrate into a waste of flesh and bone. When the first snow fell, he turned northeast, heartsick with grief. The trail had long since grown cold, and with winter approaching, he had no hope of discovering anything new. Perhaps he could find help and try again next spring.

His sudden arrival after being missing for years caused quite a stir at Castle Altair. He had been a green, sixteen-year-old youth when his family had left Altair six years before, but he returned a gaunt, broken young man. Queen Charlotte had wept over him. He had been dazed in his grief, with a dead heart, until the queen said those fateful words as she embraced him. "Your father will be overjoyed to see you."

"My father? He's dead, Your Grace," Michael said tonelessly.

"Not Gareth, dear Michael. Thomas, your foster father." The queen's voice was insistent as she tried to draw him out of his stupor.

Michael's heart stirred to life as he stared at her in stunned surprise. "Thomas...Dad...he isn't dead?"

"No, my dear, he's here. He has been seeking you and..." She hesitated, fearing to mention the still-missing mother and son. "He has sought you all these years."

"The boys? James and Ethan?"

"They are well, Michael. Very well."

Michael gaped as Thomas came rushing into the Great Hall, followed by two boys. His heart bled at the sight of the brothers, whom he had remembered as young children from years ago. And Ethan—Michael couldn't bear to see Ethan, one year older than Tristan, with features so much like him.

Thomas stopped a few feet before Michael, his mouth opening and closing again, speechless. He placed his hands on Michael's shoulders.

"Michael. My dear son. Is it really you?" Thomas asked, his voice breaking.

"You're alive?" Michael choked out.

Thomas nodded, overcome with emotion. James stepped forward, his bright blue eyes looking around. "Tristan? Mother? Where are they?"

Michael shook his head as tears filled his eyes, and the boy wheeled away to hide his intense disappointment. Shame consumed Michael, and he started sobbing, unraveling after all the months, all the years, of holding himself together.

"I lost them! Dad, I had them, I was with them, and I lost them both." Michael fell into his father's arms, brokenheartedly repeating over and over again, "I'm so sorry! I lost them..."

"Michael?"

Michael jumped, for he had been lost in his memories. Tristan was sitting up, rubbing his eyes, looking more like the small boy Michael had left behind all those years ago. He smiled at the sight. "I'm sorry. Did I wake you?"

"No." Tristan yawned. "Michael, when I first came here, Andrew said things about our family. I didn't know if I believed him at the time, but...is our father alive?"

Michael eased the boy down onto the bed. "Yes, and he'll be overjoyed to see you. Our brothers as well."

"Andrew mentioned I had two more brothers. I don't remember them."

Tristan sounded confused and upset. Michael tucked him under the covers. "I know, and I'm sorry about that. They're wonderful boys. You'll love them."

"Where was he all those years when we were on our own? Did he not care about us?"

"Oh, Tristan, he cared very much. We'll talk more about it tomorrow."

Almost asleep, Tristan winked one eye open and whispered, "You promise you'll be here in the morning?"

The boy's fear of being abandoned was palpable. Michael flinched at his need for reassurance.

"I'll be here, I promise."

He sat on the bed until the snore burst forth once more. Michael sighed, breaking free of the dark memories for the last time. He could do nothing for his sweet mother Anna, but Tristan was here now, and Michael would not be parted from him again. With his heart full of thankfulness, he brushed back his brother's hair and kissed his forehead before leaving.

# Chapter 7

# Dun

Breakfast at Lawnwood was always a noisy affair. Michael admired Andrew for his ability to start each day with so much feminine chatter at the table. He met Tristan's eyes and almost laughed at the boy's exasperation with the younger girls surrounding him.

Mariah often referred to Michael as "catnip for the ladies," and he was lavished with attention by several of the oldest daughters whenever he visited Lawnwood. He enjoyed their flirtations and did his share of teasing back, especially with Cate. Michael sucked in his breath when she flounced into the room and sat opposite him. She was quite fetching that morning, with her long, black hair made up in a complicated braided twist. Michael's fork skittered across his plate. Mariah, not one to miss a thing, raised an eyebrow in his direction with a knowing smile.

Michael cursed his weakness. Cate was a beautiful girl, and she knew it. Statuesque, she was not as dark of skin as her father. Nevertheless, the inheritance of her mother's blue eyes created a sharp contrast with the rest of her coloring. They reflected almost violet in her gaze. The effect was startling, and Michael never ceased to melt at the sight of her.

Although he had harbored some secret hopes concerning Cate for well over a year, he kept biding his time for reasons he couldn't explain. Not that she wasn't old enough. Most men his age would have pursued her without reservation, but he couldn't shake the urge to wait. However, Michael knew that if he didn't make a decision soon, another swain would come calling.

"How is James?" Cate asked as she held up her knife for inspection, her eyes narrowed.

Michael had just taken a bite, and her question caused him to swallow wrong. He strangled on a fit of coughing. A bit red-faced upon recovering, he choked out, "He's strapping, Cate. I'll tell him you asked."

"I wonder why he didn't come with you," she mused.

Michael grinned. "I'm sure he was fearful of your claws."

"I doubt that." Cate stabbed at a piece of meat, and Michael thought she seemed disappointed not to have a round or two of verbal sparring with James. Michael had never before considered he might have competition with his own brother for Cate, but now he wondered.

Mariah broke into the conversation. "Tristan, dear, why don't you take Michael to the stables? It's a delightful morning, and I'm sure he would appreciate seeing how well you ride."

"I'm not that good," Tristan mumbled, flushing.

"Nonsense." Andrew glanced up from the letter he was reading. "You are much improved, and Michael will be pleased to see you in the saddle."

"I'll need a mount," Michael inserted. "My poor horse deserves a rest after the way I rode him here."

"Not a problem. Tristan, pick one out for him. You'll know who needs the exercise."

"Well, shoo, the both of you. The day isn't getting any younger, and I want all you men out of here!" Mariah commanded.

"Yes, ma'am." Michael saluted, and she gave him a playful swat. He was still chuckling when they left for the stables. "Mariah could have been a general herself."

"Andrew once told me he knew he wanted to marry her when he saw how she handled a sword," Tristan offered, grinning.

"That I didn't know," Michael murmured. He wondered if Mariah had passed those skills on to Cate but tucked that enticing thought away to consider later.

The farther they walked from the house, the quieter Tristan became. As a child, he had exhausted Michael with his ceaseless chatter and curiosity. Michael hoped the silence was due to the years apart and would dissolve over time.

Reaching the stables, Tristan pointed to a stall and asked, "You want to see my favorite?"

Michael nodded, curious what kind of horse had Tristan's eye. The boy made a clicking sound with his tongue, and heads appeared over various stall gates. One horse nickered back and tossed its head in greeting. Tristan laughed and approached the horse with a treat he had hidden in his pocket. Michael watched the two interact, remembering how even as a child Tristan had shown a special connection with horses. It had not diminished over time.

Tristan led a yellowish-brown gelding out of the stall, and Michael leaned against the door, studying the horse. He wasn't a large animal and would never be considered a beauty, but he was compact and well built. Noting the calm eyes, Michael came forward and let the animal have a sniff before rubbing its muzzle. The horse gave a whuff of approval, and Michael chuckled. Many boys would have chosen some flashy wild stallion as a favorite mount, and Michael thought Tristan's choice showed his good sense.

"Do you like him?" Tristan asked. "I know he's not—"

"I like him very much. How does he ride?"

The boy's face flushed with happiness. "Faster than he looks. Sturdy too. His name is Dun, and he's a good all-around horse, aren't you, boy? You want to go for a ride?" Dun nickered and pricked his ears.

After some consideration, Tristan led out a young, dark bay mare for Michael, and soon both animals were ready. Michael observed Tristan, pleased to see his riding was more than sufficient. He had some work to do, but with a steady mount he rode well enough for the mountain trails.

After years of longing for this moment, Michael found the silence awkward, and he wasn't sure how to break it. Tristan had resisted speaking of his mother the previous evening, and Michael didn't want to force the topic. On the other hand, the boy had asked about his father and brothers the night before. Maybe that would be the best place to start. Michael eased into the conversation, treading with care.

"You used to talk my ear off, Tristan. What happened?"

The boy shrugged. "Out of the habit, I suppose. It's hard to get a word in with all the girls."

"I can imagine! But how about we stop and talk awhile? I feel like there's much I need to tell you."

Tristan agreed, and they dismounted at the edge of a pasture, under the shade of a large oak. Mariah had given Michael a satchel before they left, so he dug in and found fresh bread and a hunk of cheese. They both sat on the grass warmed by the sun and ate. Frustrated that his brother wasn't helping with the conversation, Michael broke the silence again.

"I know Andrew told you about the Rounders. Do you remember that night? Or before?"

Tristan closed his eyes and put a hand before his face, as though reaching for something in the darkness. "It's strange. There's this black curtain covering my memories when I go back too far." His eyes blinked open. "I don't remember much of anything. You and Momma, that's the life I recall."

"I'm not surprised, but I'm sorry. Those can't have been happy memories. I wish you could remember the days before we left Altair."

"They were happy for me. At least, I thought we were happy together." Tristan fisted his palm, his jaw clenched. Michael didn't blame him. Their little family had fought every day for the happiness Tristan remembered.

Tristan stood and paced back and forth a few times. Michael tore off a piece of bread and ate, allowing the boy to work out whatever was bothering him. Tristan made a sound of frustration and spun around toward Michael. "Why didn't he come for us? Our father? It was one thing when we thought he was dead, but he wasn't! Why did he abandon us, leaving us to starve, leaving Momma to—" He stopped himself, his face white with anger.

Michael groaned and shook his head. "It wasn't like that. He searched for us for months, years! Remember, overnight he was left alone with two children, with no mother, no wife. He had to get the boys to safety, but he came back to look for us. Dad uprooted everything. Even when I returned, he was still searching the mountains and foothills of the Shadowlands. I don't think he gave up until this past year. To believe he had lost you and Mother forever was the worst thing to happen to him. You have no idea what it will mean to Dad to see you again."

"You didn't give up!"

"No," Michael said, cautious with his words. "Not exactly. But Tristan, think! It's been nine years since the family was separated. Not many men could have held on to hope that long."

Tristan sat again and spoke in a strained voice, "Why don't I remember them? My father. My brothers? I'm trying, but I can't."

"You were three the last time you saw them, and it was very traumatic. Even I was terrified. It would have been better if we had talked about them more. There were many things we should have talked about, but it upset Mother, and you wouldn't allow it."

"No," whispered Tristan. "I couldn't bear to see her weep."

Michael fought to control his emotions, remembering their sweet, sensitive mother. Tristan had always been like her, wanting everyone around him to be happy and content. His desire to protect their mother at all costs had pitted Michael against his brother more than once, especially in the months before he was taken.

"Tris, what happened?"

Tristan blinked back tears. "I can't."

Michael huffed, fighting the urge to shake the truth out of his brother. What had been so horrible that Tristan couldn't even speak of it? But then Michael's frustrations melted. There was no telling the terrors the boy had faced in the last few years. Michael cleared his tight throat. "You know I'll be needing to leave in a day or two. I assumed I would take you with me, but I never thought to ask how you might feel. Do you want to stay with Andrew and Mariah?"

"Don't *you* want me?" Tristan asked, his face pinched and anxious.

"Don't be daft. Yes, I want you with me—with all of us. But I also want you to have a choice. Our life—the life I would be taking you to, it's not an easy one."

"It can't be any harder than what it's been," Tristan muttered. In a louder voice he added, "Besides, I would be with you and...the others. Tell me about my brothers."

Michael grinned, ignoring his disappointment that Tristan didn't ask any more about his father. "Your brothers. James is seventeen, a tall, brawny redhead. He looks just like Dad. He has always wanted to be a soldier—well, he would say a general. James likes to think he's funny, but he's a terrible tease and can be a bit thoughtless at times. He has a good heart, though. Dad told me for months after the separation, James asked about you constantly."

Tristan's eyes brightened. "And Ethan?"

"Ethan is a year older than you. He's a quiet sort, and I'm convinced you won't find a kinder person in all of Aquila. I'm not around him quite as much. He lives in Altair all year, unlike the rest of us. He wants to be a healer and studies at the abbey."

"Where do you live?"

"Spring, summer, and fall, we're out in the wilds, in and out of the Shadowlands. We're border watchers, spies, even militia-on-call should the border towns need us. Mostly, we observe and report anything amiss. Since the winters are too harsh to be out in the mountains, we go east and overwinter in Altair."

"I can't imagine living in the capital city."

"This may surprise you, but everyone in our family was born in Altair, or close enough. Except Dad."

He thought this might tease Tristan's curiosity concerning his father. The boy remained silent, not taking the bait. Michael sighed to himself and decided to let it go for the moment, not sure how to break past the anger.

"What will you do, Tristan? Come with us and find out who you are, where you come from? Be a part of our ragtag family? There's much more I haven't told you, but if you want to stay here, I'll understand. You'd be happy here, and safe."

His words were true, even if Michael knew it would tear him apart to leave his brother after finding him. He didn't dare to think what his father and James would say if he returned without Tristan, but he would deal with that as it came.

Tristan surveyed the fields surrounding them. It was quiet here at the estate, feminine chatter notwithstanding. Tristan had a warm heart and already loved the Kavanaughs. *Even the girls*, he thought with some humor. He hated the idea of going back into the world, which he considered to be a cold, unforgiving place. However, to be apart from Michael...He didn't feel much beyond curiosity for the brothers and father he couldn't remember, but he refused to be separated from Michael again.

When at last he spoke, a dreamy expression lit up his face. "I remember feeling sad one time, when we were forced to another village. I don't remember *why*. There couldn't have been anything special about it, but I must have liked the place we were living in." Tristan offered a sheepish smile. "You told me as long as we were together, we were home. Being together is what mattered, no matter where that was."

Michael watched his brother, holding his breath. Tristan hauled himself to his feet and moved to untie Dun. Before mounting, he turned to Michael. His eyes were bright.

"Home is the only thing I've ever wanted. Let's go find it, Michael."

Michael let his breath out, relief flooding through him. "All right. Let's go."

# Chapter 8

# A Tankard of Ale

Michael and Tristan made their departure two days later. The parting between the Thatchers and the Kavanaughs was affectionate and filled with promises for a return visit in the fall, topped off by a friendly argument between the men concerning who had arrived at the decision to gift Dun to Tristan. Mariah ended the debate by stating it was, in fact, *her* idea, and neither man dared contradict that formidable woman. Tristan was delighted that he and his favorite horse would be traveling together.

The first few days passed slower than Michael would have ridden had he been alone. He grew anxious with the delays, thinking how long it had been since he had left the camp. There was no telling where Thomas and the others were now. It had taken many days of hard riding to get to Lawnwood, and then time to rest. He knew Tristan couldn't handle the same pace, and once in the mountains they would need to find the others. Still, they made good time, and Tristan hardened to life in the saddle all day.

The two grew more comfortable with each other, recapturing the way they used to be together. Tristan chattered, asking Michael many questions as they rode. Michael told stories of his travels with their father and brothers, hoping to build some anticipation for the reunion. As for Tristan, he could sometimes be prevailed upon to tell a story of his own, however he never mentioned his mother. Michael decided to leave the topic alone but wondered at his reticence.

After two weeks of travel, Tristan was surprised when they rode into a small town in the foothills. Most days Michael preferred to stay on the fringes or avoid towns altogether, but when they came to Haddox, he rode straight down the main street. They arrived at a tavern and left the horses at the livery.

"This place can be rough," warned Michael as he handed the reins of his horse off to the stableboy while slipping him a coin. "They're not a bad sort, but if they've had too much to drink you'll need to be careful. Stay close to me until I say it's good."

"What are we doing here?"

"First, staying the night. I want one more sleep in a decent bed before heading back into the mountains. Although *decent* might be overstating what we'll have here. Better than camp anyway. Second, getting any news that may be useful."

"What kind of news?"

"Useful news," Michael said shortly. "Watch yourself here and don't talk more than necessary."

When they walked in, several men hailed Michael, and a bushy-haired tavern keeper poured out a fresh brew for him.

"Ah, young Michael! It's been an age! Here ya are, lad. I know what ya like. I never knew ya had a son! Laws, he looks like ya."

Michael grinned. "Not my son. Truly, Jack, do you think I'm old enough to have sired a boy his age? Nah, he's my younger brother, is all."

Tristan's eyebrows rose when Michael spoke with the local dialect, but he said nothing. It had been months since he had last entered a tavern, and he took a good look around. The place wasn't much more than a large, thatched house, with log stairs leading to another level. Though dark inside, it was warm and homey, with a bright fire blazing in the center of the room and plenty of thick candles. Long tables were lined up, and most of them were full of men talking. Tristan did spy a single old woman with a pipe dozing in the corner. Off to one wall were several barrels of what Tristan assumed to be ale and other brews.

"A brother of Michael is a friend of mine! Have a drink, lad!" Without waiting for a reply, Jack poured an immense jug of ale and slid it before Tristan. He gazed in wonder at the foam-topped vessel. Like most children, Tristan had grown up on ale, but in small doses. To have a week's worth of ale slopped over to him in one go was a pleasant surprise. He took a cautious sip. It was by far the best ale he had ever tasted.

Jack and Michael whispered a few words to each other as they both regarded Tristan. Jack guffawed and clapped Michael on the back, almost knocking the younger man over. Michael made his way around the tavern, gesturing to Tristan to stay where he was. Tristan hunkered at the end of a table, watching Michael and sipping his ale. Michael wandered over to a gathering of men who greeted him with amiable nods. After chatting with them, he angled his position to whisper in the ear of one of the men, who nodded and rose. Together they went to another table, with the man introducing Michael to the new group. Michael sat in a relaxed manner and began talking among the men.

Tristan yawned. The long days in the saddle had been harder than he cared to admit to Michael, and the ale was wonderfully soothing. A gentle belch burst forth, and Jack, who was wiping some mugs nearby, roared with laughter.

"Aye, fresh ale is good for a boy, don'cha know? Drink it down, lad, and ya'll sleep like a log tonight."

Tristan gave him a weary nod of thanks, but after another long drink, he pushed the ale away. Jack grunted with understanding and departed around a corner. He returned with a tray of bread, cheese, and some sort of paste and set it before Tristan.

"Here ya are, lad, put a base under that ale."

Michael continued to wander around the tavern, doing the job he did best, gathering information from the locals. Most would be useless—village gossip, scandals, and tattle. But here or there might be dark whispers of strangers armed and on the prowl, or the murmur of Rounders a hundred miles south.

An hour passed before Michael came back to where he had left Tristan. The boy had curled into a ball to sleep on the wooden bench.

"Poor, wee lad," Jack declared. "It's that sad when a healthy boy can't handle good brew. He only drank half his ale." The barkeep heaved a mournful sigh. "Ya'll have to build him up, young Michael. At least he ate a good amount."

Michael's heart warmed at the sight of Tristan, flushed and sleeping, and he half-carried the boy upstairs to their room. Tristan crashed into bed, snoring. Michael chuckled as he dragged the chamber pot closer in case his brother needed it during the night.

Tristan woke groggy and flinched at Jack's enthusiastic greeting when he came downstairs in the morning, but otherwise he was no worse for wear. He spied Michael at a table, again head-to-head with some local men. Another tankard of ale appeared at his elbow seemingly by magic, and Jack winked at him. Tristan took a small sip, his awe of the brew dissipating. A short time later, Michael approached and stole Tristan's drink, pouring half of it into a mug for himself.

"Drink half of what's left and you'll do well," he said with a smile. "Jack will kill you with kindness if he's not careful."

"What happened last night?"

"You drank ale, ate food, and fell asleep. I'm sorry for deserting you. I knew Jack would keep an eye on you, but I should've let you go to bed."

"Did you get the news you wanted?"

"Hmm, more or less. I think I know where Dad and the others are."

"What! You didn't know where they were?"

"I knew the general area, but no, not specifically. They're about three days southwest of here, not too bad."

Jack interrupted them with a tray of the same foodstuffs as the night before. Michael scowled at the platter. "The food is consistent at least. C'mon, eat up and we'll get out of here."

Once they were well out of the village and picking their way across an unused trail into the forest, Michael explained his behavior the previous night.

"We all have different jobs as border watchers, depending on our skills and personality. James and Dad are soldier types, and good ones. They can organize, muster, do anything military related. But with their red hair and size, they can't blend into a crowd. I like people and can talk to them, earning their trust. No easy task here with the mountain folk.

Plus, I don't have a threatening appearance. People are always at their ease around me."

"They've never seen you handle a sword." Tristan had caught Michael sparring for fun with one of Andrew's captains when they were at Lawnwood, and even with his inexperienced eyes he could see Michael was a formidable fighter.

"There's nothing wrong with being underestimated, don't forget that. I'm guessing you'll not be physically imposing. Your build is too much like mine, which means you'll have to work twice as hard as the rest of them. But if you can learn a weapon and master it, you might find yourself with an advantage over anyone who thinks you can't fight."

At these words, Tristan remained silent for some time. Having grown up in poverty, the height of his ambition was to own his own small parcel of land and work with horses. He didn't care whether he learned how to use a sword or not. It seemed important to his brother, however, so he didn't comment on what Michael said. Instead, he asked, "When you were gathering information at the tavern, was there anything significant?"

"No, most of it amounted to nothing. There were a few items of interest I'll pass on to Dad when we find him."

That night before the fire, Tristan watched Michael polishing his sword. Michael smiled, gesturing to the weapon. "Been in the family for generations. I can trace it back to King Emery. After that it gets murky. The stories are rather far-fetched, to be honest."

"What do you mean?"

"You know the type. Forged sword of destiny, all the usual nonsense. Then again…" A dreamy gaze came into his eyes. Shaking himself, he shot a peculiar look at Tristan. "Well, maybe. Here, take it and see."

"See what?"

"Take the sword."

Aware that Michael was watching intently, Tristan reached for the sword. The instant his hand touched the hilt, a tingle started in his fingers and crawled along his arm. Tristan jumped and thrust the sword back at Michael, eyes wide and startled.

"Did you feel it?"

"What was that?"

"It's a mystery to me! Most don't, whatever it is. Dad doesn't. Neither does James or Ethan. I like to think the sword recognizes a kinship with some people, but Dad says that's bunk. He's probably right. I do tend to let my fancy run away with me. That said, if you felt it…Want to try again?"

Tristan shook his head. He remained quiet until Michael finished the polishing and thrust the sword into the scabbard. When Michael stirred the fire, Tristan spoke again. "I don't know if I understand what you do as border watchers. I mean, you just wander up and down the mountains?"

Michael chuckled. "Well, you might be oversimplifying it, but I suppose it isn't too far off." He grabbed a stick and drew in the soft dirt near the fire. He marked the continent's wide eastern coastlands all the way west to the foothills and mountains. The mountains ranged from north to south, roughly parallel to the sea.

"Here is the great Lantic Sea, with Aquila spreading out from the coastline. Up here to the north and northeast is the kingdom of

Woodraven. You have some family there on Dad's side. Beneath us are the southern kingdoms—Austella is the largest. You following this?"

Tristan nodded. "And we're heading west, into the mountains?"

"Yes, we are about here, in northwest Aquila." Michael waved the stick over the western edge of his makeshift map. "You'll remember, of course, up there in the mountains the locals use the ancient name of Appalachia. Those in Aquila have always called it the Shadowlands because the people there don't belong to any country. The mountain folk claim no king or queen, no leader, and are on the fringe of society. They hate Sammanon, but neither are they willing to subject themselves to Aquila's rule. Heaven knows why, they suffer much from Sammanon. They trust no one and simply want to be left alone. They are a people apart."

"Where's Curie on this map?"

"Here, in the southern reaches of the mountains."

"Is that town where we stayed a part of the Shadowlands?"

"Haddox? No, we're still within Aquila's borders, but you'll find a great many of the mountain folk coming down to the foothills to trade in towns like Haddox."

Michael sat back on his heels, surveying his rough map. "The mountains are where we work. Sometimes we might range farther down, for Sammanon isn't above tackling the smaller, poorer southern kingdoms when they don't have the numbers to attack Aquila or Woodraven, so we offer support there too."

Tristan pointed at the outline. "And what's to the west of the mountains?"

"Sammanon. Beyond that, no one knows. There are stories of a mighty river cutting through the known continent."

"You've never been that far west?"

"No one from Aquila has, at least as far as I'm aware. I've never traveled beyond our side of the mountains."

"Is there anyone else doing this stuff?"

"Oh, yes. Dad started the whole idea, but there are several groups of us. He's training some new men this year. We all cover sections, and there's often some overlapping. In fact, I'm hoping we won't have to continue doing this much longer."

"Are you all soldiers?"

"More or less. James wants to be one as soon as he gets a chance to fight. I've fought, but it's not something that brings me any pleasure. But Dad is the consummate soldier and leader. He should be a general—"

"Was he like James, wanting to be a soldier?"

"No, he wanted to be a healer. And he might have been a good one. He did have some formal training. Unfortunately, there were objections from his family, who expected him to go into the military. As it is, he received enough education in the healing arts that it comes in handy with injuries. Between you and me, I think it was for the best he went into the army. Dad has a wicked sword arm and understands battle tactics far better than he'll admit. He might disagree though, I'm not sure."

Tristan lay down, staring at the stars overhead. He was torn between curiosity, anger, and sadness toward this unknown person, this father whom he didn't remember. Every night he tried to pull up a memory, any memory at all. And night after night, nothing came to him. As far as he could remember, Michael had always been both father and brother, and he was the only father Tristan thought he wanted.

# Chapter 9

# The Voice

The two brothers were deep within the thick mountain forest when Michael reined in his horse late one afternoon, waving a hand for Tristan to stop as well. They sat in silence as Michael waited. He grinned when the whistle of a bird broke through the trees, and he whistled back, causing Tristan to jump. Tristan was further startled when a figure dropped from the branch of a nearby oak.

"James!" Michael leaped from his horse with unwearied enthusiasm. Tristan dismounted with a groan. The two brothers hugged, but James couldn't take his eyes off the boy.

"Tristan, this gangling idiot is your brother, James."

"Tristan!" Ignoring Michael's restraining hand, James rushed at his younger brother, engulfing him in a crushing hug while laughing with unfettered joy. Tristan squirmed in his strong grasp, and James let him wriggle free. "He looks *exactly* like you, Michael. It's downright uncanny!"

"Everyone tells me that," Tristan blurted out. James chortled, and even Tristan choked out a laugh.

Michael kept his eyes on Tristan. He had been holding no small amount of anxiety about this reunion. It was hard to resist James's enthusiastic nature, but Michael could sense the tension simmering.

"James, come here. I need to talk to you. *Now*." Michael yanked him off to one side, and the two had a hurried, whispered conference. James nodded, and with a questioning glance at Tristan, disappeared into the forest. Michael heaved a breath.

"C'mon, we're heading this way."

"What was that all about?"

"I was explaining to James that you don't remember him, and he might need to go easy on you at first."

James rejoined them, his manner more subdued, much to Tristan's relief. As they walked farther into the woods, Tristan couldn't help but stare at this new *brother*. James was a tall, muscled boy—a young man, really—with sky-blue eyes and a roguish, kind smile. Nevertheless, he was a stranger to Tristan. James and Michael chatted, with James asking many questions regarding their time with the Kavanaughs. When Michael asked about their father, James muttered, "He's been worried, figuring you should've been back long before. He wasn't happy when you left."

Tristan edged closer to Dun.

A stream burbled from a distance, but Tristan could see no sign of water through the thick trees. Without warning, they broke out of the dark forest and into an open, sunny glen. Several canvas tents were scattered in a semicircle with a low fire in the center. Dun nickered at the nearby horses and mules, and Tristan shushed him with a quiet word.

A giant man shoved his way out of a tent. Though his hair was a darker auburn, no one could mistake his relation to James, with the same ruggedly handsome face, if more careworn. A threadbare, rust-colored duster whipped out behind him. Like Michael and James, he wore a simple, rough linen tunic and trousers beneath the long coat, the bottom half of his legs obscured by boots of ancient leather.

The man bounded across the ground. "What were you thinking, leaving James alone while you go gallivanting over the countryside? The Sammanon army is at our doorstep, and you run off without even by-your-leave!"

Tristan staggered back a few steps, but Michael stood his ground and chuckled as the big man barreled toward him. He cuffed Michael on the head, then embraced him in a bearlike hug, lifting the much shorter Michael off his feet. James joined in, and the three of them laughed and talked in low voices. The man shifted his attention to Tristan. An extraordinary expression came over his face, and his entire demeanor softened.

"It *is* him," he murmured in wonderment.

Thomas Thatcher took a few steps in Tristan's direction, his eyes searching the boy's features. He raised his hand as though to reach for his son, but Tristan stiffened, and the man stopped short of touching him.

"Tristan, son. Do you remember me?" His voice was a low rumble and surprisingly gentle.

A long-forgotten memory buried deep within Tristan melted when Thomas said his name, but he shook his head. "I don't. I'm sorry, sir."

"You're...so like your dear mother," Thomas rasped. No one could doubt the tenderness in his eyes as they took Tristan in.

These words startled Tristan. Everyone always commented on how similar he was to Michael. To hear this man compare him to his mother touched his heart, although Tristan couldn't say why. Distracted by this thought, Tristan jumped when he realized Thomas had asked him a question. "My mother? She's dead, sir."

Thomas closed his eyes and shuddered. James placed his hand on his father's arm in a gesture of comfort. Ugly feelings roared up in Tristan.

"Why didn't you search for us?" he demanded, his hands balling into fists as he stepped forward. Dun tossed his head and whinnied.

Thomas flinched at the sudden change in Tristan's demeanor, and a groan escaped him. Michael tensed. "Tristan, we talked about this—"

"No, I understand why he couldn't find us later. Years later. But when the Rounders showed up, why didn't you come after us?" Tristan's voice began to rise. "Michael did, he found us. If he hadn't, we would have died. You abandoned us!"

"He didn't!" James choked out, but Thomas held up his hand.

"Tristan, how much do you remember about that night?" asked Thomas. In contrast to Tristan, his voice remained calm, his countenance guarded against any further treasonous emotions.

Tristan heaved a breath, trying to recall those memories. They used to frighten him, and he had been prone to nightmares as a child. At some point he had begun to mix his dreams with reality. Years ago, he had started blocking off these memories altogether, but now they rose, sharp and vivid. He squeezed his eyes shut.

"I remember fire. And smoke. Screams. Mother crying. She had somehow become lost or bewildered. I remember a man being shot down by an arrow, right in front of us. She thought it was you. I don't know, it was confusing." Tristan's body went rigid as he snapped, "It doesn't matter! Michael came out of the smoke and found us. *He* took care of us."

"Yes, I was trying to handle your brothers," Thomas said, his face pale and strained. "Ethan was four and James…" here he glanced at James, who in turn stared at Tristan, biting his lip, "but you were small, and I thought your mother having you alone would make it easier for her to keep up. The Rounders set fire to the entire village. It was chaos."

Tristan leaned against Dun, fighting off the tears lurking beneath the surface. Thomas winced at his son's pain and ached to hold him, his beloved son missing for so many years. He eased a few steps closer.

"Don't!" Tristan growled. Thomas stepped back, hurt and shock showing on his face. Thrown into confusion by his father's response, Tristan spun around to Michael, whose obvious disappointment shattered him. To Tristan's dismay, tears stung his eyes.

"It's all right, son. I won't force you," Thomas whispered. After a final lingering look, Thomas turned to Michael. "Take the boy to your tent. He needs warm food and rest more than anything else right now."

"I need to take care of Dun," mumbled Tristan.

"I'll do it. You come with me," Michael said as he grabbed Tristan by the arm and dragged him to a tent. Thomas watched them disappear before tugging James to follow him, and they talked between themselves.

"Please, don't be angry with me," Tristan pleaded. The tears that had been gathering in his eyes were close to falling.

Michael glared at him, but then his gaze gentled. The boy was pale, hungry, and frightened. Michael dragged a weary hand through his hair. What did he expect with everything Tristan had been through?

"Give him a chance, Tris, that's all I ask. But he's right, you are done in. Get some rest and maybe, later today, we can try again."

Tristan *was* tired, and he slept through most of the evening, waking long enough to eat a few bites of food before falling asleep once more. Michael chided himself for pushing the boy too hard on the trail. He might be almost thirteen, but he was a little mite and not hardened to their life.

And, as Michael recalled, Tristan had not once complained, even during their many long days in the saddle when he must have been sore.

Michael allowed Tristan to sleep later than usual and, upon the boy's waking, urged him to the fire. As they sat warming their hands in the chilly morning air, Thomas approached and asked Michael to saddle Dun before turning to Tristan. "Come on a ride with me. I want to make sure you know the lay of the land around here. This forest is thick, and it's easy to get lost."

Tristan's mouth went dry, wondering if perhaps Thomas might beat him for the way he had spoken the day before. Most men would not have tolerated such disrespectful words from their sons. He stared hard at the man, but Thomas's face was a stoic mask. Tristan shivered. He couldn't count how many times the strap or rod had been laid upon his backside while working his odd jobs over the years for moving too slow, being too small, or questioning an order. There was no telling what this man might do to him.

"It'll be all right, Tris," Michael murmured as he cinched Dun's saddle, not understanding the boy's fears. Tristan didn't say a word. Michael turned to Thomas. "Perhaps I could come as well?"

"No need," Thomas said, and he gestured for Tristan to mount and follow.

Tristan shot a desperate look at Michael before hanging his head and clicking to Dun to catch up.

Over the next hour, Thomas pointed out certain landmarks in the region and asked Tristan questions about life alone on the road, his work with horses, and his weeks with the Kavanaughs. Tristan did his best to answer, but fear choked his words into vague mutterings.

After some time, the tension inside Tristan reached a breaking point. His heart thumped erratically. He knew from experience the anticipation of a beating could almost be worse than the strap itself. He screwed up his courage and reined Dun to a stop. "Sir, if you don't mind, I would rather get it over with."

Thomas halted his giant chestnut, arching an eyebrow at Tristan.

"Whatever you plan to do. I would rather just have it done." The boy huffed a painful breath.

"What the devil are you saying?"

"For the way I spoke to you yesterday. I know I deserve the belt for that." His expression clouded. "It wouldn't be the first time a man used the strap on me."

Not quite meeting his eyes, Tristan couldn't make out Thomas's face, but he heard incomprehensible mumblings. Thomas cleared his throat. "Right. Get off your horse, son."

Tristan gulped and dismounted. He stared at the ground as Thomas approached him. The man placed his large hands on the boy's shoulders. Tristan flinched at his touch, and Thomas sighed.

"Look at me, Tristan," he commanded. When Tristan dragged his eyes upward, he was startled to see the deep love in his father's eyes. "I cannot answer for all the things you have faced in the past. I'm sorry I was not there to protect you, as you deserved to be protected. And I accept you don't believe this, but you are my son. You—and your brothers—are everything to me. *Everything*. You may always speak your mind. Even if the words are harsh, I would rather have them out than festering inside. Do you understand?"

No. He didn't understand. The expected blow had been a soft word and gentle touch. Tristan smothered his confusion with a whispered, "Yes, sir. I think I understand."

Thomas wanted nothing more than to take his son into his arms but settled for squeezing Tristan's shoulders. He nodded to the horses. "Let's move on, the day is passing."

On the trail, both of them were quiet, weighed down with their own thoughts. Tristan cast a furtive peek at the man riding beside him. Without memories of a father, he didn't comprehend a father's love. But he decided he was at least safe with Thomas. If Michael trusted him, surely he could do that. Forcing his trepidation aside, Tristan asked, "Michael said you aren't from Aquila?"

"No. I was born in Woodraven. Have you heard of it?"

"Yes, sir, but I don't know anything about it."

"You aren't missing much."

Thomas's wry tone made Tristan pause. Trying a different tactic, he braved another question. "How old were you when you left?"

"About the age of James, give or take a year."

"Why did you leave?"

Thomas didn't speak for so long, Tristan thought he wasn't going to answer. Then he said, "That's a story for another day. I'll say this. I wanted a better place to raise my own family later."

"You were awfully young to be thinking of such things, sir."

"It may surprise you how soon a man starts to think on these matters."

"I guess."

Tristan urged Dun to move ahead. Everything about Thomas defied the ideas he had formed of the man since discovering he was still alive. A riot of emotions fought within his heart. Tristan reined in without warning, and Dun gave a snort of indignation.

"Why did you take us south? Take us into—" He choked on the anger that had begun to rise once more.

Thomas again hesitated before replying. "Well, there were several reasons, including your mother. She was never strong, but over the years she had grown weaker. More after you boys were born. I hoped maybe a different climate would help."

"That's ironic," Tristan muttered. "Take us out of the city for our own good only to be met with disaster."

"Well, I'm no fortune teller," Thomas said.

Tristan relaxed as they rode on, but he had a difficult time believing this big man was his father. Thomas was muscled and solid, several inches over six feet. When they dismounted to water the horses at a burbling creek, he towered over Tristan.

"Sir?"

"Yes, Tristan?" Thomas answered, very much wishing the boy would acknowledge him as his father.

"What happened after...I mean, what did you do? You had my brothers with you."

"Ah, well, that's a story I can tell. Let's sit." Thomas smiled with such warmth, Tristan's heart leaped. Even Michael had never looked at him quite the same way. After tying the horses, they sat together on a moss-covered log. Thomas handed a waterskin to Tristan.

"Michael warned me you were a chatterbox once you open up," Thomas teased. Tristan flushed, but Thomas chuckled and gave him a nudge. "I don't mind. Right, you asked about your brothers. Ethan was quite young, let me think. He would turn five a few months later. His age was a problem, more so than James. Although James was terrified, he was also older and more independent. He could ride a pony and even had his first sword. But Ethan...I was alone and couldn't care for them while searching for you all. It became clear I needed to be free of the boys. I took them to Altair where they would be better cared for.

"With that, a routine began with me searching for you in the good weather and returning to Altair in the winter to be with the boys. It wasn't ideal. I missed so much time with them, but I couldn't stop. And throughout my wanderings, I gathered important information on Sammanon, and that grew into what we do now. A few years later, James was old enough to ride with me, and about then Michael returned as well. Ethan chose to remain in the city to study. Michael explained our job to you, yes?"

Tristan couldn't speak. He was beginning to see the full range of heartbreak when the family had been torn apart. Mother, father, brothers...no one had been left untouched. All his thoughts wearied him, and he slumped. Thomas eyed him with concern.

"I think perhaps Michael may have pushed you beyond your strength on the journey here. How about we say this is enough for today. Mount up, son."

When they arrived at camp, Tristan offered to rub down both horses. Thomas agreed, touching the boy's shoulder in affirmation, thankful that Tristan didn't shrug him away.

Seeing Tristan wrestling with his father's saddle, James strolled over and took the horse in hand. "Let me help you. Marley is a big boy, might be hard for you to reach the top," he said, winking. Tristan couldn't stop himself from grinning. He was liking this tall, redheaded brother more and more.

For a time, they brushed and curried in a companionable silence until James sighed. "It was all my fault."

Tristan stopped brushing Dun. "What?"

"It was my fault, that night. Why you and Mother were separated from the rest of us."

"What—what do you mean?"

"Dad had you and Ethan. His babies, that's what he called the two of you, even as old as you were already. He loved you both so much—anyway. He had given me to Mother thinking I could keep up with the running. You and Ethan were more or less paralyzed with the terror of it all, but too small to run, so he was carrying both of you. But I became uncontrollable."

James paused for a moment. Tristan's heart thudded as images of that horrible night flashed in his head, all the more vivid with his brother's story. James took a deep breath and continued. "I guess that was the last time she held me. Dad switched us up, taking me by the hand while holding Ethan, and giving you to Mother. I was screaming, and it was all he could do to keep me moving. If Michael hadn't been watching, you and Mother would have been on your own. I'm sorry, Tristan."

"How old were you?" Tristan whispered.

"Eight."

Tristan bowed his head against Dun and rubbed his face into the warm hide of the horse. He flushed with shame, thinking once more of the words he had hurled at Thomas the day before. In hindsight, they seemed beyond cruel. His throat hurting, he said in a strangled voice, "You were a child yourself. It wasn't your fault. It wasn't anyone's fault."

James came around both horses to face Tristan. "Do you mean that?" he asked. At Tristan's nod, he continued, "Please, go easy with Dad. You didn't see him after he lost all of you. I know what it was like. He was almost mad for months, and even after...It's been like a slow death to him."

Tristan gulped. "I'm trying, James."

"Fair enough." James walked a few paces before stopping. "Tristan? I'm glad you're back. I know you don't remember me, but I missed you. More than you'll ever know."

James left Tristan alone with the horses. It was a long time before Tristan could finish rubbing Dun down.

Thomas swiped a hand over his eyes, suppressing a yawn. He had not slept well the night before, his mind racing with the events of the day and the torment of memories. He hoped he had made some headway with his youngest son, but he was unsure if Tristan accepted him yet. And now Michael was yammering on about his news from Haddox.

"Get to the point," he snapped, sharper than he intended. At Michael's raised eyebrow, he gave a rueful chuckle. "Sorry. Your descriptions are always more...*colorful* than necessary. Just give me the important bits."

Michael pointed to a map. "Rumors of Rounders were cited here..."

He kept talking, but Thomas wasn't listening. His attention was arrested by the sight of Tristan wandering the camp. The boy spotted the pair of them and made his way in their direction. *He's wanting Michael*, Thomas thought, struggling with the fact his own son viewed him as nothing more than a stranger. He covered his feelings with a huff. "Wait, Michael. You keep saying near Quiller, but that's not where you're pointing. Get it right."

"I *am* pointing at Quiller."

"Don't be daft, you are waving your hands all over the region, how am I supposed to know where you're pointing?"

Tristan came closer, and Thomas was startled to see the boy watching *him*, not Michael. He stood nearby and fidgeted, trying not to interrupt. Thomas held up an exasperated hand at Michael, far more interested in hearing what Tristan had to say. "Hold up here a moment. What is it, Tristan?"

"I remember your voice," mumbled Tristan, not quite meeting his eyes.

Thomas's breath caught. "What was that?"

Shaking his head, Tristan struggled to get the words out. "When we were riding here, I was trying to see if I could remember you or my brothers, and I couldn't. I couldn't see your faces, I couldn't recall anything about you. But the first time you spoke to me, I recognized your voice. How did I remember your voice...Dad?"

Thomas stared at Tristan, remembering the nights he stayed awake cuddling his youngest child, singing and whispering the small lad to sleep. Tristan had been the sweetest tyke, constantly begging his father to be picked up and held. Thomas's heart thudded with hope, but he kept his tone even. "I don't know, son."

Tristan gazed with wonder into his father's eyes. "I would have known your voice in an army of men."

With a rush of emotion, Thomas gave in to the longing to hold his son, bringing Tristan close. Though the boy didn't relax into his embrace, neither did he reject his father's touch. Thomas fought the tightness in his throat. He caught Michael watching them and smiling. Thomas coughed and eased Tristan away, roughing his hair, then turned back to the map. With a gruff voice he barked at Michael, "Right. Now, Michael. Point directly at Quiller and where the Rounders were last seen."

# Chapter 10

# Broken Walls

By the time Tristan and Michael had tracked their way to the campsite, the spring rains had dried up, and it was turning into a beautiful summer. These were good days for Tristan, who found himself to be safe and loved when his thirteenth birthday rolled past.

To be living amongst men was an unfamiliar experience for the boy. For as long as Tristan could remember, his world had been governed by women. Even before Michael was taken, both he and Tristan had always deferred to the wishes of their mother. They had been led by her in all things, which Michael regretted later. The weeks spent at the Kavanaugh estate were also heavily influenced by the women of the house, and it had been all Tristan could do to find respite in the library or stables. He was now supported by three men devoted to his well-being. Food and solid work were their prescription for raising a boy in the wilds. Under their watch, Tristan couldn't help but thrive in his new environment.

Aside from the Thatchers, there were three other men in the camp learning under Thomas. One of them was highly regarded as a horseman, and David took Tristan under his wing to further his riding education.

Tristan's natural affinity with the animals served him well, and by the end of summer he was as good a rider as any in the group. Since everyone agreed Tristan was too young to participate in their regular work as scouts, he was declared Head of Horse with great pomp and ceremony; both he and the horses benefited from this arrangement. The mules especially liked his gentle hand and brayed when they saw him coming.

Tristan didn't have much to do with the other two men, Jeffords and Smythe. They were kind men, but older and serious about their work. For it was serious work, and dangerous at times. They were always moving, never staying more than a week or two at each location as they made their way south. After getting the camp settled, two or three men would ride deeper into the mountains to scout and might not return for several days. Once, a group rode back with Smythe injured, an arrow piercing through his upper thigh. Although Thomas doctored it, it became infected, and Smythe was fortunate to recover with his life and limb intact.

The first few weeks after Tristan arrived, Michael stayed close by, but eventually he had to resume his own duties. During these absences, Tristan had to fight the fear that Michael might never return. He grew used to the routine, but a rush of relief would hit him when Michael rode back into camp, safe and sound.

As for Tristan's further training, this topic provoked some disagreement between father and sons. Michael desired to start the boy in archery, while James wanted to involve Tristan in learning swordplay with real steel, but they had no swords small enough to suit the boy's size, nor any bows he could handle. After much debate, Thomas left to rummage about in his tent, returning with a sheathed dagger.

"Tristan, take this. It's no sword, but you need to arm yourself with something, and it's the best I can do out here. My foster father gave this to me when I was about your age, passed down through his family. There are few things of Woodraven I may boast about, but their metalsmithing is superior to anything in Aquila. I would be pleased if you would have it."

Tristan fingered the knife gingerly. It was a beautiful weapon, with many strange carvings cast in the metal. Even Tristan could see it was the work of a master.

"Thank you, sir. Dad." Tristan still struggled over the word. "I don't know though, shouldn't this belong to Michael, or James? What if I lose it?"

"If it saves your life someday, it will be worth it. Nothing is more valuable to me than that. And as for your other question, I've been keeping it for you all these years, if you were ever found."

With a careful hand, Thomas tousled the boy's messy hair. A tiny quirk of a smile flitted across Tristan's face. Overjoyed he had coaxed that much from his son, Thomas turned back to the rest, covering any emotions lurking beneath the surface. "Michael, show him how to use it. James, if you want to teach Tristan the sword, find some solid sticks and begin with those, the same way you started. You absolutely will not use steel on your untrained brother, are you daft?"

Tristan and James formed a strong attachment right from the start. Being older when the family broke apart, James remembered Tristan well as a toddler and teased that he had been an annoying little shadow. Yet anyone could see James held a deep affection for his youngest brother. But Tristan also discovered another side of him when they sparred with sticks. James was serious about becoming a swordsman and soldier, which showed even when fighting Tristan. If James had any regrets in trouncing his brother black and blue, Tristan wasn't aware of it. Consequently, although Tristan had no great desire to learn swordplay, James forced him to master a few moves in self-defense.

Thomas would often take Tristan into the forest to teach him the basic elements of woodcraft. His father was patient, praising Tristan for what he learned and never shaming him for the many things he didn't know. Thomas could be stern on occasion, but he was mild compared to what Tristan had experienced in the world, and Tristan grew to respect him.

Learning to love his father was another matter.

Ever since being told Thomas had not perished on the night the family was torn apart, Tristan had built a strong, cold wall around his heart concerning his perceived abandonment. Even though he understood what happened wasn't his father's fault, that wall would not come down easily. And every time a few bricks loosened in the face of Thomas's kindness, Tristan would think about his mother, fortifying his previous resistance.

Tristan sometimes caught Thomas looking at him with a yearning expression, but it disappeared when he saw his son watching. There were times Tristan wanted to spill his heart out to Thomas, and then the old anger would take hold. Nevertheless, met with his father's persistent, unwavering love, over the weeks that wall began to crumble.

High summer was upon them when Thomas and Michael set out one day to hunt. Come midmorning, Thomas's chestnut galloped into camp riderless, covered in sweat and wild-eyed, shocking them all. It took

David, James, and Tristan an hour to catch Marley, and the horse would allow no one except Tristan to handle him.

Consternation ran through the camp. James and Tristan wanted to search the surroundings at once, but the older men dismissed the idea. Perhaps the chestnut had bolted, they argued. There was no need to assume anything terrible had happened. Even the best rider could be unseated. Tristan knew the horse's disposition well and grudgingly admitted they could be right. The afternoon sun was hanging above the trees when James yelled, and everyone rushed from their various jobs to see Michael walking into camp. He held his own horse by the lead with Thomas riding. He was slumped over the mane, his face ashen.

"Bear," muttered Michael as he helped Thomas off the horse. His tunic was ripped to shreds, and blood flowed in rivulets along his side. Jeffords and Michael maneuvered Thomas to his tent while James gathered medical supplies.

Tristan knew he should take care of Michael's horse, but one glimpse at his father's face made him loop the reins around a tree and scurry after the men helping Thomas. Due to his smaller size, even in the crowded tent he could hide in the corner as they laid Thomas on his bedroll. Tristan stayed where he was until Michael ripped his father's clothes aside, revealing five gaping furrows running across Thomas's waist. A paralyzing fear gripped Tristan. He knew little about wounds, and the volume of blood dripping onto the ground appalled him. His breath hitched, and a cold sweat broke out while bile rose in his throat. He left the tent in a hurry, with James following.

"Tris?"

Tristan tried to speak. Instead, he retched on the yellowing summer grass. James patted his back in a gentle, albeit clumsy, manner.

"Don't worry about him. I know it looks bad, and Michael said he lost a lot of blood, but trust me, he's had far worse." He paused before adding, "I'll take care of Michael's horse."

Tristan started to object, but James ignored him. So he waited outside the tent until Michael came out, wiping his hands on a bloody rag. Tristan's stomach roiled again at the sight of the blood-soaked fabric. Michael looked tired but otherwise untroubled.

"There you are, Tristan. Did you see to my horse?"

Tristan shook his head, trying to peer past Michael into the tent.

"Has he been waiting out there all this time? You should have—" He stopped upon seeing Tristan's pale face. "Tris? Hey, come here." He hugged Tristan, whispering, "He's not going to die."

When Tristan didn't speak, Michael nudged the boy far enough away to study him. "Do you want to sit with him? He's resting, but you can go in. I doubt he'll even wake up." Michael gave him an encouraging nod and Tristan slipped into the tent. Michael waited a moment before leaving with a thoughtful expression.

Shy and hesitant, the boy moved to where Thomas lay with his chest bare and waist bandaged. His eyes were closed, and he appeared to be asleep. Tristan thought his color had improved, though lacking its usual ruddy vigor. He knelt next to him and took his father's large hand in his own, relieved to feel its warmth. The memory of his mother's icy hands as she lay gray-faced and dying overwhelmed Tristan.

"I'm sorry, Dad. For everything I've said," he whispered, fighting an onslaught of tears without success. "Please, don't leave me. Not like Momma."

With a moan, he bent over Thomas, putting his arms carefully around his father's chest, snuggling as close as he dared. His pleadings became prayers. "I *just* found him. I'll try to do better, promise I will. Please, don't take him too."

Later, soothed by the sound of his father's steady breathing, Tristan wiped his eyes and left the tent.

By evening, Thomas insisted he had regained enough strength to gather with everyone at the fire. When Tristan joined the circle, he did not sit near Michael as usual. Instead, he settled next to Thomas. Tristan sat quietly while Michael told them about the bear attack. It was a fun story now that the danger had passed, and he regaled it with great gusto. During a lull in the conversation, Tristan said, "I want to tell you about Mother."

A dead silence fell over the circle. Smythe and Jeffords looked at each other and got up to leave. David, who was younger and more curious, tried to stay, but Jeffords dragged him off. Tristan began speaking in a stilted, halting manner, as though it were difficult for him to find the words.

"Michael asked me a few times about Mother, and I couldn't talk about it. The simple truth is she wasted away. You said she had been sick before? Maybe this was the same thing. I don't know. Always a little sicker, a little weaker. When Michael was with us, it felt like we kept it at bay. Between the two of us we could earn money for food, blankets for warmth, and a book every now and then to feed our souls. But even with Michael there, she faded. Didn't she?"

At this, Tristan looked across the fire at his brother. Michael nodded mechanically, lost in the same memories.

"After they took Michael, I kept on, doing the best I could. I worked, I begged, once I even stole. Mother wasn't so sick as to let me think *that* was acceptable." Tristan allowed himself a faint smile at the memory. "I was desperate to feed us both. I sold books, the few fancy things she had clung to, her very past. Sometimes I sold them as she wept at their leaving. It made me feel awful. Then to be removed from the shack that we called home, it devastated us. She was coughing up blood by that point, but it didn't matter. We had to move on."

Michael shuddered and half-rose to his feet to reach for Tristan. Instead, Thomas put his arm around his son's shoulders. Michael settled back once again.

"At our last place, she couldn't leave the bed. She was that weak. She would...soil it. Soil herself. I was already working hard to take care of us both while trying to earn a coin or two, and that...too much, it was all too much. I was tired and constantly hungry. It made me angry she couldn't even get up to do that, and I had to clean her. And I was ashamed. We both were. To see my mother that way, to clean her mess. I realized she was dying. I suppose it was stupid I didn't see it before. But I kept thinking..."

Tristan's voice caught, and he stopped talking. Unmoving, James stared into the fire. Michael didn't bother to wipe the tears falling from his eyes. Easing Tristan closer, Thomas brought his cloak around the boy. A sob escaped Tristan as he leaned into the warm bulk of his father, the love drawing him in. He worked a small drawstring bag out of his pocket and handed it over to Thomas with a shaking hand.

"She hid these to keep me from selling them. Her wedding ring and some other jewels. I had no idea she had them until right before she was gone. She begged me to get them to Queen Charlotte of Aquila if I could find no other family. I thought she was mad. Why would the queen care? Mother would tell me all sorts of things I didn't understand. Even now I don't know if they were true or the lunacy of sickness. She would alternate between delirious and lucid, then there were times...it was hard to know. Toward the end she told me about Andrew Kavanaugh, where to find him, and what to tell him. She seemed herself. Still, I wasn't sure I believed her.

"When Momma died..." Tristan drew a ragged breath and struggled to keep speaking, gasping out the words in short spurts. "When Mother died, there was no one else to take care of her body—but I can't speak of that. I buried her myself. We had no priest and no money. I knew she'd be thrown into a pauper's grave, and I couldn't let that happen. I had a friend, a baker, he was a good man—but that's another story—he helped me take her to a place outside of town, under a beautiful old oak. We dug the grave. I'm sure we made a shoddy job of it. It was far too shallow, but I buried her. Read the Bible over her. I—Momma—"

Here he stopped, unable to speak. Michael covered his face and let out a sob before commanding control over himself. Without a word, James stood and walked into the forest. They didn't see him again until the morning.

"Tristan," said Thomas, and his voice sounded strange to the boy. Tristan looked up and was stunned at the tears on his father's face.

"Thank you, son. Thank you for telling me." He put his hand over his eyes. "My sweet girl, my lovely Anna..."

At the sight of those tears, the wall in Tristan's heart crumbled, and he sank into his father's warm embrace. Thomas wrapped his arms around his son, holding him fast as they wept together, and an ocean of deep love for his father swept over Tristan at last.

# Chapter 11

# Journey to Altair

Tristan woke one morning to a light frost on the ground. The summer had been long and glorious, so the sharp chill took him by surprise. He was thankful for the thick woolen cloak his father had purchased at the last village they had passed through. Tristan wrapped himself in the warm folds and pulled the hood up, delighting in the beauty of the frost.

Michael grumbled, for he was not fond of the cold, but kept it between himself and Tristan. The other men had left a month before to prepare for winter. Next spring, they would go out on their own. The Thatchers continued to travel southward along the mountain range. Michael hinted a few times about beginning the journey east, but Thomas paid no attention.

When the first snow arrived, however, Michael could be silent no longer.

"Every year it's the same thing!" He exploded in an outburst of temper. "Just because you like riding through drifts as deep as your knees doesn't mean I do!"

Tristan looked around, bemused. There was a scant inch of snow on the ground. But Michael wasn't done. "And what about Tristan? He's barely thirteen and you're keeping him out in the cold!"

Tristan tried to intercede. "I'm fine, Michael, I don't mind."

"Be quiet, Tristan. I'm discussing this with Dad, not you."

Tristan's own temper rose at the condescension in his brother's voice and stood straight. "See here—"

James dragged him away, laughing all the while. Even far into the forest, they could hear Thomas and Michael bellowing at each other.

"You don't want to get in the middle of *that*! Michael hates the cold and snow, and Dad can't move out of the mountains fast enough for him. Don't bother them. They fight about this every year and, to be honest, I think they enjoy it. I bet Michael's thrilled to have you as an excuse to leave."

"Except I don't mind the snow."

"You don't now, but you will. Michael is right. We've been caught in the mountains during these early blizzards, and it's not fun. C'mon, it's getting colder. Let's go find some firewood."

When the boys returned to camp, the tension had not abated much. Thomas was poring over maps by the fire, and Michael hid away in his tent, muttering to himself as he cleaned his sword. Tristan looked from one to the other, at a loss not knowing what to do. He had come to love his father deeply over the summer months. Still, his heart ties to Michael were no less and Tristan hated seeing them at odds.

He meandered over to Thomas and sat, poking at the fire. Thomas didn't look up from his map but roughed Tristan's hair. Reassured by the smile teasing at the corner of his father's mouth, Tristan cleared his throat.

"Ethan is in Altair, isn't he?"

Thomas grunted. Tristan waited a moment and tried again.

"He's a year older than I am, right?"

Thomas kept his eyes on his map but nodded. "Yes. Well, less. You're less than a year apart. You and Ethan were already close together, and then you decided to come a bit earlier than we expected." Far too early. Thomas remembered the fear that had gripped his heart when they thought the wee Tristan might not survive past his first few days of life.

"Does that mean we're twins for a few weeks?"

Amused by his reasoning, Thomas responded with a gruff rumble.

"Are we a great deal alike?"

Thomas scratched his chin, considering. "James and Ethan have very different personalities, opposites in many ways. I would say you fall somewhere between them. He's quieter than you, thank heavens."

"What does he look like?" Tristan continued, ignoring the gibe.

Thomas pushed aside the map, smiling at Tristan's sincere curiosity. "I forget you don't remember him. He's a taller version of you in some ways."

"Everyone is taller than me, Dad. *Everyone*," Tristan declared mournfully.

Thomas laughed, his grumpiness dissipating. "I meant his build is similar. He's not the bigger, muscular type like James or myself. He's tall with long, lean muscles. His hair is more blond-red and, like you, he has your mother's face." He gazed at Tristan, pausing as he took in his beloved wife's features in his youngest son. "He has those bright blue Lockhart eyes, like James and Michael."

"Your eyes are blue."

"Ah, but they are significantly darker, like yours." Here he winked at Tristan before shuffling through a few different maps, searching a particular one out.

"Maybe if Ethan and I are similar, that means I'll grow taller soon," mused Tristan. Thomas suppressed a chuckle. He suspected Tristan had far too much of the Lockhart side in his blood, but he didn't care to dash his son's hopes.

"Does he know about me?"

"Indeed he does. I've written a great deal about you in my letters. He is excited to see you again."

"And he stays in Altair to study medicine? He's awfully young for that."

"You have to start young, there is much to learn. Bones, muscles, organs. Plants take years to learn medicine making. And Ethan is interested in plagues, of all things. He'll be studying for a long time."

"Michael told me you wanted to be a healer?"

Thomas grunted again and refocused his attention on the map before him.

"Hmm." Tristan went for the final thrust. "I can't wait to meet him. Ethan, I mean. My *brother*. It's been such a long time."

Thomas froze, his eyes flashing toward his son. He folded the maps with calculated slowness before bellowing, "Right! We leave tomorrow! Pack up." He regarded Tristan with amused resignation. "You're better at this than Michael. He could learn from you."

Tristan chortled all the way to his tent, where Michael sat in disbelief.

That evening, while Michael and Thomas were deep in conversation, Tristan's stomach was beginning to rumble, and he took it upon himself to cook dinner. But despite Michael's tutelage over the summer months, the stew began to misbehave. James's attempt at helping his younger brother only enhanced the noxious fumes wafting over the camp, causing Michael to rush over. While they tried to salvage the meal, Tristan noticed Michael casting furtive glances at him.

"What?" he demanded.

"Ah, I need to talk to you about something," said Michael. He waved over Thomas before turning back to Tristan. "Here, put some more of this into the pot and sit. I'll take over. Actually, let's *all* sit a moment."

It was unusual for Michael to appear so uneasy. Tristan looked with some concern at his father, but Thomas was smirking. Michael coughed. "We think it's time to tell you more about our extended family, since you'll be seeing them at Altair. Besides Ethan, I mean."

"Our family?" Tristan directed his question at Thomas, who shook his head.

"Not my side," he said.

"Yes, Dad's side is a whole other problem. For today, let's stick with the Lockharts. My father, I should say, my father by blood, Gareth was his name. He and your mother Anna were the sole surviving children of Lord Edward Lockhart. The Lockhart name is an old and noble one. I won't go into all the stories and complications, it would take far too long, but the essential point is we are related to the royal family."

Thomas snorted. Michael glared at him and shot out, "You want to talk about *your* family next?"

"How are we related?" interjected Tristan, not wanting to see tempers flare between them again.

"Well..." Michael hesitated. "You might have heard me refer to Cousin Charlotte on occasion?"

"Yes, I always thought it was funny you had a cousin with the same name as the queen."

"Funny. Right. The fact is, Cousin Charlotte *is* the same as the queen. Queen Charlotte. And she's your cousin, too, on the Lockhart side. A far distant cousin, mind."

With a slight edge to his voice, Tristan asked, "How distant?"

"Oh, who knows. It's not important," insisted Michael, with a vague wave of his hand.

Again, Thomas snorted. "Don't act like you don't know to the precise generation."

Michael pressed his lips together in exasperation. "She's your third cousin once removed."

"Third cousin!" cried Tristan, jumping to his feet.

"Once removed."

"I thought she was our fourth cousin?" James inserted.

"No, Justin and Christiana are our fourth cousins."

"Why aren't they our third cousins twice removed?"

"Because..." Michael stared hard at James, working it out in his head. James snickered.

"Stop it," Michael said. "Anyway, our common ancestor goes back over a hundred years."

Tristan exploded into the conversation. "I don't care what kind of cousin she is! How could I not know this? What the hell, Michael!"

"Don't you be using that kind of language." Michael stood as well, his jaw jutting forward.

"You say it all the time!"

"That's different, and I'm older. When you're my age, you can say whatever the hell you want!"

They stood glaring at each other, Tristan a miniature version down to the very look he gave Michael. James cackled at them both.

"They say both the Thatchers and Lockharts are known for their hot tempers," murmured Thomas. "I'm afraid you might have received a double dose there, Tristan."

Tristan snorted like his father and thumped onto his seat. "Right. What does this mean anyway?"

"Nothing much. I wanted you to know, that's all. You'll be meeting them."

"Who 'them'?" Tristan growled.

"The family. Our royal cousins, the Reynards—Queen Charlotte and her children, Justin and Christiana. Oh, and we stay at the castle over winter."

"Castle Altair?"

"It's the only one I know of in Altair."

Tristan mulled this over and nodded curtly. "Anything else?"

"Not that I recall." Nettled, Michael turned back to the stew and gave it a vicious stir.

Tristan glowered at him before turning to Thomas with a stubborn set to his jaw. "What's he not telling me?"

Thomas stifled a chuckle and shot an amused glance at Michael, who fidgeted. "You may hear me referred to by my formal title."

"Formal title?"

"Lockhart, of course," said Michael.

"As in His Grace, the right and noble *Lord* Lockhart." James bowed with a flourish before Michael, who threw a filthy cooking rag at him. Fed up with the conversation, Tristan turned back to the smoking pot.

Together, they gathered around the warm fire for bland, overcooked stew. Michael and James exchanged stories of Altair, hoping to get Tristan excited about traveling there. However, it had been a long day, and Tristan contented himself with leaning against his father, yawning. Thomas put an arm around his son, almost cuddling him. He had a passing thought Tristan might be too old to be held, but he didn't mind. Not truly. He had missed most of Tristan's childhood, and the boy still seemed quite young in some ways.

As stars emerged overhead, Tristan snuggled closer and relaxed against his father. Moments later, a light snore wafted up. Michael and James chuckled at the sound. *Hang it all*, Thomas said to himself as he hugged the sleeping boy close and kissed the top of his shaggy head. Tristan sighed in his sleep and burrowed deeper into his father's arms. Thomas thought his heart would burst with joy.

James had been right. Before they left the foothills, a proper snowstorm hit them. It wasn't especially dangerous since the winds were low, but Tristan started to understand why Michael had wanted to leave when they did.

They stopped at Lawnwood for a few days on the way to Altair, and Tristan was thrilled to see the Kavanaughs again. He considered it odd that Cate enjoyed the sharp banter with James more than the sweeter attentions from Michael. But then, Tristan thought most girls *were* peculiar. Michael didn't act as though he minded, but occasionally Tristan caught a wistful expression on his face at the sight of James and Cate together.

Mariah gushed over "her boys" and fed them to bursting. Andrew couldn't stop admiring how fit and happy Tristan looked. Before, Tristan had been a subdued boy with sad eyes; now he chattered nonstop, and his eyes sparkled with merriment.

From Lawnwood, they continued to the capital city. Tristan had no memory of living anywhere but the small villages of his childhood, and the towns they encountered grew larger than he thought possible. He said as much to Michael, who laughed and said, "Just wait."

The air changed as well, kindling a deep memory in Tristan's heart, awakening strange dreams. He wrestled with it for several days before mentioning it to his father.

"It's the sea, Tristan. The salt in the air. Anyone born in Altair has it in their blood. Babies are christened with seawater, bridal beds are sprinkled with it, and it is poured out in offering over the graves of the dead."

Aquila was a happy kingdom when at peace, with the capital city of Altair its shining beacon, the epicenter of all that was good in the country. Situated on a rolling plain that extended all the way to the great Lantic Sea, a river inlet outlined the northern section of the city. High, rocky cliffs spread north and south along the coastline of both the river mouth and the sea. These cliffs offered ample protection from invasion by water, although such events were the stuff of myth and legend. A few miles south of Altair, the cliffs descended, affording easy access to the water through the coastal village of Newmoth. The sea wasn't visible from within the city, but there were rumors it could be seen from the highest point of Castle Altair.

Altair formed a roughly triangular shape, with the castle at the easternmost tip and the city fanning out westward. The city had no walls, and some military leaders bemoaned this fact while others pointed out Sammanon forces had never broken past the western edge of the coastal plain. Hence, the issue remained dormant. There was no doubt it made for a welcoming view when approached from the west.

However, a wall did separate the castle from the city. To enter the castle grounds, one had to pass through a heavy portcullis guarded by soldiers at all hours. Once through this gate, a paved lane led to the left around the castle until it widened into an expansive stableyard with multiple stables, granaries, many chickens, and even a pigsty. At this point the wall gave way to the swelling pasture lands beyond the stables.

There was a grander entrance to the castle on the southern end, away from the city. Its prospect was pleasing to the eye, and guests crossed a large vista of lawn before reaching the castle's tall imposing doors.

The castle itself was a sprawling building built in stages over several centuries, giving it an inconsistent design. It was not uncommon to find odd stairways—up ten, down seven, up fifteen, and so forth. It did not possess secret passageways as much as long-forgotten ones, and few people knew them all anymore.

It was by the city road the Thatchers approached the castle in the bustle of midday, and Tristan was amazed at every turn. He had never seen so many people or buildings in one place. It invigorated and overwhelmed him all at once. He kept tugging on Dun's reins to see everything until an exasperated Thomas had to urge him to keep riding.

"Don't worry, Tris, you'll have all winter to get to know the city," James called with enthusiasm. "You don't know what you've been missing!"

Thomas groaned and urged his horse forward. James laughed. "You never worry about Ethan being alone in Altair."

"I can trust Ethan to be responsible," Thomas said. "There's no telling what you get up to here. I'm not letting Tristan loose in the city with you at his age."

James winked at Tristan, and they both cackled.

At the castle gates, soldiers stood at attention and saluted, causing Tristan to gaze with wonder at Michael. "Were they saluting you?"

"Hmm, I'm not sure. Dad or myself, we're both well known here."

When they arrived at the stableyard, several men came out to help them with the horses. Tristan cast a suspicious eye upon the old groom who approached to take Dun, but his kind smile convinced Tristan to hand over the reins.

"No need to worry, son," Thomas reassured him. "He'll be treated well, I promise. No one cares for horses better than George here. You can check on him later, but for now, we need to go in."

"Do I grab my things?"

"No, leave them. They'll be brought to our rooms."

The stableyard contained an odd mix of smells that tickled Tristan's nose—manure and fresh bread, hay and roasting meat. He understood the reason when they entered the castle through a small door off the stableyard. The kitchens were immediately to their left. Tristan's stomach growled with the rich scent of food wafting so near. But his father steered him right. They passed a bathhouse and went up some stairs into a wide, airy corridor. To the right were open, arched windows that overlooked the stableyard and a few paddocks. The windows had no glass and were quite large, allowing light and air to flow through, but with shutters on either side to shut in bad weather. On the other side of the corridor was a series of doorways.

From there they jogged up and down more stairs, passing through various rooms and chambers until Tristan became hopelessly lost. At last they came to a central entry hall—it was all stone, with thick wooden support beams. On one side were mullioned glass windows. Tristan would have been in awe of the castle for the windows alone. Breaking the visual flow of all that glass stood a pair of wooden doors. Later Tristan would learn the doors led to an enclosed courtyard.

Standing there in the entry hall, across from where they had arrived, was a sweeping staircase. Curious, Tristan took a step toward the stairs, gazing upward, but he stopped at the sight of a soldier approaching Thomas. The man was armed with a sheathed sword and multiple daggers, and Tristan squirmed with no small amount of anxiety. But the two men greeted each other as friends and then spoke too low for Tristan to hear. Thomas muttered some response in the affirmative, nodding toward immense oak doors to their right. He strode over and threw them open.

"The Great Hall. Also doubles as the throne room," Michael whispered to Tristan as the boy hung back, stalling his entrance. "Don't worry, Tris. She's just the queen."

He grinned as Tristan glared at him.

Chapter 12

# The Queen

The Great Hall was the largest room Tristan had ever seen. Rectangular in shape, there were many heavy oak tables and benches arranged in rows along the length of the space. The exterior wall, opposite the side they entered, was lined with more mullioned glass windows. They loomed high, starting near the floor and reaching up twice as high as a man. Like the entry hall, heavy wooden beams and pillars supported the high, arched ceiling.

An enormous flagstone fireplace dominated the same wall as the entry doors. Tristan guessed a whole bull could be roasted in it if desired. But here in the east, the weather remained mild, and the fire was kept low. Tristan's eyes roamed, and he saw a large, spiked iron wheel set to the side of the hearth with a heavy chain coiled around it. Curious, he wandered over and fingered the chain.

"Careful," James murmured as he grabbed Tristan's hand, lifting his eyes upward. Tristan followed his gaze and gulped. The chain ran up to the ceiling, and from that hung an enormous black iron candelabra. It held dozens of thick beeswax candles. "They use the chain to bring the candles lower to light. We wouldn't want that crashing down on us, would we?"

Thomas led them to the far end of the room, where a dais was raised. Nothing ornate lined the walls. Even the dais was relatively unimpressive, with a simple wooden throne, modest in its carvings. Dark red velvet curtains ran along behind it, and Tristan wondered if there was a private entrance for the queen hidden there. Thomas stopped and knelt before the dais. James and Michael did likewise. A little confused, for he saw no one else about, Tristan followed suit with what he hoped would be considered an elegant pose. A faint giggle reached Tristan's ears, and he stiffened.

"Are we this formal, Your Grace, that we meet at the throne?" Thomas asked with a hint of a chuckle.

A woman came out of the shadows. "Be quiet, Thomas, and kiss the royal hand." The woman and Thomas laughed, and he stood to allow her to kiss his cheek. She directed her attention toward Michael and greeted him.

Tristan took his first look at Queen Charlotte, House of Reynard. He had expected a tall beauty, so her petite size was a surprise. Nut-brown hair with a streak of pure silver weaving through it tumbled down her back, leather cords restraining her long, soft curls. Her simple dress of muted green fell to her ankles and reminded Tristan of his mother, except a dagger hung from the belt cinched around the queen's waist. She wore no jewelry other than a band of twisted gold on her right hand and a gold coronet.

Tristan caught himself staring and lowered his eyes, flushing. All the while, he had the disconcerting sensation someone was watching him. He took another glimpse and saw a girl behind the queen. She was small and had the wildest head of hair he had ever seen—long tresses of copper-gold curls contained with a burnished silver clasp. He couldn't see her face, for she held one hand over her mouth in an attempt to suppress her giggles as she stared right at him.

He rolled his eyes in annoyance. Tristan had quite had his fill of girls while staying with the Kavanaughs. Having lived in a man's world for months, he groaned at the idea of meeting any more girls, especially one who *giggled*. Nettled, he peeked again. Her countenance had turned serious, but her bright green eyes were sparkling with amusement. She gave Tristan an impish smirk, and to his dismay he chuckled out loud before he could stop himself. He tried to cover the sound with a cough, which set her giggling again.

Michael and Thomas had been talking to Queen Charlotte all this time and, after a quiet greeting to James, she approached Tristan. Holding out her hand, she said, "Stand up, my dear boy. Let me see you."

Tristan stumbled to his feet, and another titter escaped the girl. He avoided looking in her direction, but he wasn't quite sure where his gaze should land. When the queen's hand lifted his chin, he studied the floor until she said, "Come now, Tristan. I promise I won't bite."

He dared to meet her scrutiny and was startled to see her brown eyes glazed with tears.

"By heavens. He's so much like her," she whispered. She nodded to Michael. "And yes, like you. He is a Lockhart."

"I'm a *Thatcher*." Tristan's voice rang out, clear and firm. He caught a glance from Thomas, and the pride in his father's expression filled his heart.

The queen blinked and then released his chin with a wry smile. "You are indeed your father's son, Tristan *Thatcher*. Forgive my presumption, I should have seen him in your eyes. But your sainted mother was my dearest friend, and I loved her. Like your father here, I have grieved many days and nights for the loss of her. To have you back is a gift, my dear boy. I hope you will be happy here."

"Thank you, ma'am. I mean, Your Grace."

Charlotte's laughter rang out. "When it is family, Charlotte is appropriate. Alas, if others are present, we must observe the formalities." Despite the words, mischief glinted in her eyes.

With an indulgent wave of her hand, the queen brought the young girl forward. "And here is my daughter, Christiana, whom you might not remember, although you were playmates as tots. You were born mere months apart, and she will be happy to be friends, if you can tolerate her animal impulses."

"Hello, Tristan," said the girl, holding out her hand, all traces of amusement gone and replaced by a sweet smile. Tristan couldn't believe this small, giggling creature was the same age as himself. Not knowing what else to do, he took her hand and jumped when she leaned forward to kiss his cheek. Before he recovered, she had launched herself at Michael.

"Michael!" she cried as he caught her up in his arms to swing her around.

"How's my girl?" he asked, setting her on the ground and tweaking her nose.

"I am most excellent, thank you, kind sir," Christiana said, making a funny little curtsy. Michael laughed and bowed to her. James lurched over to grab her by the shoulders from behind, and she spun around to hug him. Tristan decided he had been let off easy with a peck on the cheek. After their chaotic greetings were done, she whispered into Michael's ear, peeking at Tristan all the while.

"No, he's not shy," he mock whispered back to her. "But how anyone can get a word in edgewise with you, I don't know."

"Where's Justin?" James asked.

"Coming, coming…" A youth close to James's age entered the room in a rush. He could have been Christiana's twin if not for being several years older. All the Thatchers inclined their heads at his approach, Tristan after a nudge from Michael. Tristan studied the queen and decided her children must take after their father. Prince Justin strode over to Thomas and shook his hand. "My apologies for not being here upon your arrival, sir."

Thomas led Justin to his youngest son. "Your Highness, you may remember Tristan, although he was quite small the last time you saw him."

"Tristan! Mother wrote you had reappeared from the Shadowlands. How old are you?"

"Thirteen."

"Wonderful! Old enough to spar a bit, we must have a round later."

Tristan stepped back in alarm, and James came to his rescue. "Tristan hasn't handled a sword yet. We need to have one made for him here at Altair."

"Justin returned from a diplomatic visit to Woodraven," Charlotte stated with a pointed look at Thomas.

"At his age?" Thomas frowned. "You risk much in sending the heir to Woodraven."

"I would have preferred sending you, but as always your arrival was delayed," Charlotte responded primly.

"Not my doing!" Michael insisted, holding his hands in a gesture of surrender, and everyone laughed.

Thomas wasn't done with the topic of Woodraven. "Did you see King Holden?"

"I did, sir, but it was brief. Most of my conversations were with Counselor Kingsley."

"Kingsley is a good man, at least as good as you can find in that court," said Thomas.

"Yes, sir, I thought the same. I would appreciate the opportunity to sit and talk to you about the visit later."

"I am happy to discuss anything with you, Your Highness." Thomas directed the conversation back to the queen. "Why did you receive us here? I jested earlier, but it is rather formal."

"Tush, I had to meet with someone disagreeable today. Lord General MacClaren, of all people, and I wanted to show my full hand. Let us go to the common room, it will be far more pleasant."

"I think," Michael said, giving Tristan a gentle shove, "it might be better if Tristan and I go to our rooms to get our things in order. This is a new place for him after all. And where is Ethan?"

"He had examinations today. No doubt they held him up. But yes, that's an excellent notion. Please get settled and comfortable. We can gather together later in the day to tell our stories of the summer. Tristan, my dear boy, please consider this your home." She sailed from the room with everyone but Michael and Tristan following her.

It was quiet after their departure. Tristan blew out a big breath. Michael winked at him and said, "C'mon, we're going back the way we came."

Tristan tried unsuccessfully to follow the maze of hallways. Somehow, they ended up in the large, airy corridor they had passed through before. A groomsman had set all their bags and bundles in the corridor in a neat pile. Michael pushed open the second door on the right and said, "Here you go, Tristan."

Tristan stepped over the threshold, and a pleasant shiver passed over him. It was a nice, wide room. The wall to his left held a smallish hearth laid with the same flagstones as the Great Hall's fireplace. Two squishy, worn-looking chairs were placed before it. Taking up the rest of the wall and surrounding the fireplace were bookshelves, nooks, and cabinets. On the opposite side of the room, a large, plump bed caught his eye.

The far wall was bare other than two long, vertical windows. No glass, of course, but securely shuttered. The dust set Michael sneezing, and he strode across the room to throw open the shutters. Fresh air and the late afternoon light flooded in. Tristan stood on tiptoes to peer out. The window looked upon a courtyard below, enclosed on all sides by the castle. He wondered if it was the same courtyard he had seen from the entry hall, or if there were others. Tristan spun around. Previously hidden by the open door, that side of the room held a tall wardrobe and a writing desk. There was another door in the far corner near the bed, but when Tristan tried the handle, it was locked.

"Home at last, at least for the winter." Michael smiled. "Charlotte keeps the rooms in this corridor for us, so you can take it over as much as you like. This one is all yours."

"Mine? Where are you?"

"I'm next door." He took an iron key from his pocket and unlocked the door in the corner. It opened to another room as deep as Tristan's chamber but narrower. "I've always liked to bunk here, I don't know why. It's my favorite, perhaps because it's small and cozy. We can leave the door unlocked, though, since you're in this one now. And it has a door going out that way, so I don't have to pass through your room." Michael pointed to another door that led to the corridor.

"Are you sure you don't want the other room? It's bigger."

"I'm certain. I've stayed here as long as I can remember. Look around, you can see all my things," he said as he started to unpack. Michael's room was cluttered with an array of personal items. Books had long since overwhelmed the shelves and were stacked along the wall. His desk spilled over with parchments and tattered quills. It was oddly messy for Michael, who made sure their camp was kept neat and in order. Tristan peered closer at the papers, some of which had the Lockhart crest of a rearing unicorn emblazoned upon them.

"Michael, if you are the Lord Lockhart, why don't you live at your manor?"

Michael mulled over the question before answering. "It's never really been home for me. A steward manages the estate, and I visit once or twice a year to check on things. I didn't grow up there. Altair has been home for as long as I can remember, aside from our time living in the Shadowlands. What do you think of Christiana?"

This random change in topic caught Tristan off guard. "Wha—oh, that girl. She's, ah…" And to his surprise, he found himself grinning. "She's something."

Michael burst out laughing. "She chatters nonstop, you'll see. Almost as bad as you. I adore her though. She's the brightest little thing, pure sunshine."

"She might be all right," Tristan admitted. "Pity she's a girl."

"You've been ruined by that henhouse of Andrew's. Christiana is nothing like them except…well, maybe Cate." Michael appeared to busy himself unpacking. Tristan shoved down the odd prick of jealousy.

"Do you like her?" he blurted out.

"Like who?" muttered Michael, his face showing some color. "Cate?"

"Who else?"

Michael shrugged off the question, but abruptly his entire demeanor changed. He locked eyes with Tristan, his gaze wary. "What do you know about such things anyway?"

"What things?"

Michael hesitated and turned away. "Never mind."

"C'mon Michael, I know all about that stuff. And James has told me everything he knows." At Michael's alarmed expression, Tristan tried to restrain himself from smirking, but it was a complete failure.

"Oh, get out of here, you young pup," Michael barked. Cackling, Tristan passed through the doorway to his new room and out to the corridor to retrieve his things. He tried to make sense of the odd assortment of belongings but soon gave it up as a bad job and he decided to check on Dun.

Finding his way outside was far simpler than navigating the interior of the castle. There were several fine stables, but he found the correct building easily enough. Inside a tall boy was stroking Dun's head. He was a handsome lad, with tousled strawberry-blond hair.

"Is he yours?" the boy asked as Tristan approached. When Tristan nodded, the boy beamed. "He's a grand horse! Look at his eyes, so intelligent. He nickered at me as I walked by, and I couldn't help introducing myself. I hope you don't mind?"

"I don't mind at all, and yes, he is quite smart," Tristan responded with enthusiasm. If Tristan had one bone of contention with James, it was the way his brother poked fun at his *pony*. He used this moniker most often during sparring practice to rile Tristan into fighting back, and the word pony had caused many dark bruises and painful nights. Tristan knew Dun might be smaller than the average horse, but he was no pony! To hear a stranger speak such praise about his horse was inordinately pleasing.

Tristan slipped into the stall. Dun was indeed well tended, with a warm bed of deep hay. He had been groomed, and Tristan could find no fault with his care. The other boy continued murmuring to Dun, the horse's ears showing how much he liked it. When Tristan left the stall with one final pet for Dun, the boy followed him, carrying a bulging leather satchel. Although quiet, he had a relaxed, pleasant air. Tristan noticed he was well groomed and wondered if this was typical for those living in the city. Years of poverty and wandering the mountains all summer had left Tristan rather grubby by comparison.

"Are you staying at the castle?" the youth asked when they both approached the entrance, and Tristan affirmed with a grunt, distracted while trying to kick some horse muck from his boots before stepping inside. The boy watched him and gravely checked his own boots. "I've never seen anyone be concerned about tramping mess indoors before," he teased.

Tristan chuckled and passed through the castle door. "My mother insisted on clean habits, and it's unfortunately stayed with me."

"Is she here as well?"

"No, she's—" Tristan huffed a breath, and the boy gave him a knowing smile.

"Mine too. Long time ago. It's nice that you have memories of her. I don't have many of my own mother. I wasn't much more than a tot the last time I saw her."

Tristan had to think about this for a moment, recognizing the truth of the words. Many children grew up without their mothers, but at least his hadn't died at birth or in his infancy. Gratitude for the memories flooded through him, even if some of them darkened his dreams at times.

"Yes, it's good I can remember her. I'm Tristan, by the way."

The boy skidded to a halt, his jaw dropping. "Tristan?"

His words sounded strangled, and Tristan stopped to study the boy. It was as though he were looking into a warped mirror, where the reflection wasn't *quite* right. The boy's face had the same high cheekbones and well-defined nose as his mother and himself. Something in Tristan shook loose like the first time he heard his father's voice. A sudden memory rushed at him. The seashore. The cry of gulls. Gravelly sand beneath his feet, his hand held by another, and a small child's piping voice—*Come with me, Twistan. Let's find a pwetty shell for Momma.*

"Ethan?" Tristan choked. With an exuberant laugh, Ethan dropped his satchel and leaped to embrace his brother. In that moment, the last missing piece of Tristan's life fell into place.

It felt almost like home.

# Chapter 13

# Life at the Castle

The next morning, Tristan slept later than he had in a long time, and he reveled in waking to a warm fire. The evening before had gone late, for with all the Thatchers together once more, there had been much to hear and tell. Ethan had many questions for Tristan concerning their mother. Of the brothers, he had the fewest memories of her, and Ethan treasured every story. He never asked about sad or painful moments, but rather sought to know all the sweet, insignificant details too often forgotten. It was a joyful occasion for them all, and Tristan was excited to begin life at Altair. When he left his chamber to find the corridor empty, he huffed, knowing it was up to him to navigate his way around the place. After a few wrong turns, Tristan stumbled into the common room, where Michael was writing letters.

"Where is everyone?" he demanded.

Michael set his quill aside and looked Tristan over, his brows knit together with a stern expression that was belied by a twinkle in his eyes. "Good morning, or should I say good afternoon?" He glanced outside and shook his head. "No, still morning."

"C'mon, Michael."

Michael chortled and shuffled his papers. "Dad is conferring with Justin, talking over his recent visit to Woodraven. James is in town, and heaven knows what mischief he's up to already. Ethan has studies in the mornings, remember?"

"Right. Why are you dressed like that?" After months in the mountains, Tristan was surprised at the change in Michael's appearance. He had bathed, trimmed his hair, and donned much finer clothing than Tristan had ever seen him wear. His shirt was of a smooth, tightly woven linen, his boots were polished, and he wore a knee-length jacket like their father's duster but it had a far more elegant cut and was embroidered at the edges. Instead of his sword, Michael had his dagger belted around his waist.

"We are in Altair, Tristan. Civilization. Which reminds me, I need to talk to Dad about getting you some new clothes. You could do with some...sprucing up." He eyed Tristan's shaggy dark curls, which had grown too long over the summer. "Anyway, I must get these letters written today. Estate business. Why don't you have Christiana show you around the castle? She's been waiting all morning for you to decide to wake up."

Tristan was about to object that he didn't wish to spend his day with a strange girl, when a voice piped behind him, causing him to jump. "Oh! I would so enjoy that! Please, Tristan, let me!"

He whirled and there she was, the precocious wee thing, curled up in a chair by the fire with a book. Tristan hadn't seen her upon entering the room. He was on the verge of declining, but her smile charmed him so completely he could deny her nothing. She hopped to her feet and grabbed his hand, hauling him away. Alarmed, Tristan shot Michael a glare over his shoulder, but his brother was shaking with silent laughter.

Tristan soon realized Michael was right. Christiana wasn't like the Kavanaugh girls. Yes, she was talkative, but there was nothing silly or heedless in her manner. Her chatter was a steady stream of bright conversation.

As it turned out, Christiana was the perfect guide to the castle, for she had been roaming it since she could walk. No one knew the passages better, and she took Tristan everywhere, giving him hints on how to navigate his way around. She was forever providing information about life in the castle, important tidbits such as, "When I introduce you to Cook, do be charming and flirt a little. If you can pull it off, you'll be able to go into the kitchen at any hour, day or night, and she'll feed you."

His presentation to Cook went off without a hitch, and they ran from the kitchens to the stables, laughing like young children. When he introduced her to Dun, she sang praises for his horse. Since Christiana had brought a carrot with her, Dun took to her as well. He whinnied his approval, bobbing his head up and down.

Tristan's face lit up with merriment. "He says, 'Thank you, Chris!'"

"Whatever did you call me? Did you say Chris?"

"I never!" Tristan exclaimed, attempting to stifle the laughter bubbling up without much success. "*Dun* called you Chris, not me. See here, Dun, I know Christiana is a mouthful, but Chris is a ridiculous name for a girl."

"I love it! Momma sometimes calls me Christy, but I don't care for that at all."

Tristan studied her, rubbing his chin. "No, you are most definitely *not* a Christy."

"Thank you, Dun. And *you* may also call me Chris, if you wish," she said to Tristan, standing on her tiptoes and kissing him on the cheek before leaping away like a deer. Tristan's face and neck heated. Christiana's high spirits were infectious, but then she did mad things such as kissing him. One never knew what she might do next. Yet despite his embarrassment, when she called for him, he bounded after her.

As they raced along the halls, she skidded to a stop and paused before a pair of ancient-looking doors. Christiana considered them with a serious expression that surprised Tristan.

"I don't know," she whispered to herself, taking a peek at Tristan. "Would you like to see the chapel?"

"The castle has its own chapel?"

"Of course," said Christiana, and with a considerable effort for some-one so small, she forced the heavy wooden doors open. They stepped in, and Tristan let out his breath. It was a silent, dark space, and he could almost hear the whispered years of prayers.

"This is one of the oldest parts of the castle," she murmured.

Tristan blinked back unexpected tears. He couldn't remember when he had last been in a church of any kind. It was a loss his mother had mourned, for churches were not common in the Shadowlands. He knelt and crossed himself before sliding onto a bench. Christiana sat next to him, eyeing him curiously.

"Are you one of the Faithful, Tristan?"

He nodded but didn't speak for a moment. Without taking his eyes from the altar, he reached for her hand and grasped it. "Thank you for showing me this. May I visit at any time?"

"The doors are never locked. I come here often myself."

"Do you?" He leveled his gaze upon her with a soft smile.

"Yes, I love it here. I believe as well."

Tristan squeezed her hand and looked back at the altar. He was so still that after several minutes, she said, "I should go. Can you find your way?"

His lips moved, but no sound came forth. Christiana slipped out of the chapel, leaving Tristan alone with his thoughts.

The sun had already made its early descent when the household of the castle gathered within the warm common room. The large chamber was cozy with a bright fire, and during the winter months when few visited, it served much better than the drafty Great Hall as a place to spend the evenings. Here they would read, write letters, talk over the day, roast nuts, and enjoy each other's company. Despite declaring she had no time for such foolishness, Queen Charlotte frequently joined them.

"I never thought I would live to see this day, all my sons together again," Thomas said to Charlotte with deep feeling, watching his boys. Ethan and Michael were immersed in a game of chess. James was holding Tristan down, allowing Christiana to tickle him with enthusiasm. Thomas grinned at the sound of Tristan's cackles. "Your daughter is very good for Tristan. I've never heard him laugh so much."

"Christiana is such a child. She knows how to play, which I suspect Tristan did not experience growing up in the Shadowlands," said Charlotte. "I should tame her, but I confess I love her high spirits."

"Don't tame her, time enough for that later. She reminds me of you sometimes. Well, I suppose you were older when we met."

"Perhaps, though I was never allowed to be so young, even when I was her age. I have guarded her childhood jealously. Although the day is coming..." Charlotte glanced at Thomas and pursed her lips before speaking again. "You know the plans Anna and I made."

Thomas kept his eyes on Tristan and Christiana, who were wrestling on the floor. Justin had entered the room, and James redirected his attention to discuss battle tactics with the prince. Without his older brother restraining him, Tristan had the upper hand, and the girl was giggling madly. Thomas shook his head, not liking where the conversation was going. "The plans *you* made and led my Anna into."

"She had more of a say in it than you may believe."

He sighed, for he did believe it. "Promise me you won't force it. Let it happen on its own, or not at all."

"Thomas, think. You are my oldest friend and my greatest confidant. Knowing what you do of my life, would you suppose I would ever force anything between them?"

After a long silence, all he would say was, "I hope not." But she seemed satisfied with this answer.

Two weeks after their arrival, Christiana took Tristan to see the castle graveyard. After an hour of rambling about, a particular headstone captured his attention.

"Is this your father?" he asked, pointing to it.

She stopped short, staring at the stone. In a choked voice she whispered, "Yes." But there was some other emotion there Tristan couldn't identify. It occurred to him that he knew nothing concerning Queen Charlotte's deceased husband. Neither Christiana nor Justin ever spoke of their father. Christiana spun away and hurried off. Bewildered, Tristan looked once more at the stone. It was a simple epitaph with the name *Lawrence Marchant*, followed by the dates of his birth and death. There was no additional script or ornamentation at all.

He turned to follow her. As soon as he caught up, he grabbed her hand. "Chris?"

The girl shook her head, but she slowed to a stop and leaned against him. Tristan gave her an awkward pat before they continued to the castle in silence. When they came to the entry hall, she mumbled a few words about not feeling well and raced up the stairs.

Thus abandoned, Tristan wandered the castle toward his bedchamber. The door to his father's room was open, and he peeked inside. There stood Thomas, sorting through a vast array of weaponry laid out on the bed and floor.

"Off to fight giants, Dad?" Tristan asked with a grin at the sight of so many daggers and swords on display. He walked around, admiring the collection, and almost tripped over some unstrung bows resting against the wall.

"Taking inventory and inspecting to see if any repairs are needed. Have you and Christiana enjoyed your morning?"

"I suppose. We went to the castle graveyard."

"Hmm," was all Thomas said, distracted as he examined the edge of a sword.

Tristan picked up a dagger and twiddled with it. Thomas coughed pointedly, and Tristan put it back in its place.

"Sorry," he muttered. Thomas snorted and continued to study the sword in his hands. Tristan took a deep breath and burst forth with a thought that had been weighing on him. "Dad, do you ever wish Mother was buried where we could visit her?"

The question startled Thomas. "Sometimes, yes." He put the sword down and gave Tristan his full attention. "But the truth is, when someone passes, the body is nothing more than a shell left behind. I can—and do—talk to your mother whenever I wish. I don't need a gravestone to do that."

A sudden longing for his mother washed over Tristan, and a lump formed in his throat.

"I miss her," he whispered. "Momma. Not always, but…"

"I know, son, I know. Me too." Thomas squeezed the boy's shoulder. They both stood in silence before Thomas cleared his own throat. "What brought this on? Something from services?"

Tristan looked askance at his father. He himself never missed a service at the cathedral that graced the center of the city; Michael and Ethan came with him as well. His father, however, rarely attended, and James never. This bothered Tristan a great deal, although he wasn't quite sure how to address it.

"No, sir. I guess being at the graveyard. And Chris suddenly started acting odd. I found her father's stone and asked about it. I wasn't trying to be rude, but she upped and left."

"Oh. Him." Troubled, Thomas opened his mouth but stopped and thought a moment longer before speaking. "Her memories of Lawrence may not be entirely pleasant."

"Was he cruel to her or—"

"Not at all. I believe he was a kind father." Thomas hesitated. "It might be best not to bring him up again."

Tristan had too many questions in his eyes, and Thomas decided to change the subject. "You know, if you would like, we could commission a memorial stone for your mother in the castle graveyard. Would that make you feel better?"

Tristan mulled the idea over before shrugging. "I don't know, it wouldn't be her."

"Even where you buried her, son, it's not her. Not truly. Think about it. I would be happy to do that for you, if you wish."

Tristan thew his arms around his father. Surprised, Thomas hugged the boy back, then thrust him aside, rumbling, "Get out of here. I have things to do, and your chatter is distracting me."

With a grin, Tristan left.

# Chapter 14

# Swordplay

No doubt those who lived year round at Altair thought the winter months quiet and uneventful, but for Tristan, it was far more social than anything he had been used to. At Christmas there was a dance, with the castle full of people willing to leave their homes, even with the ever-present threat of sudden snowstorms. Tristan laughed hard as Christiana tried to teach him some simple reels without much success. Although he was fond of the larger gatherings, he came to love the stormy winter days best. These were the times that nourished his soul, when he could read the many books in the castle library, play chess, and enjoy his family.

When the weather was fair, there were riding parties, and Tristan often rode to the cliffs to see the ocean. He would inhale the salty air into his lungs with deep breaths while the Lantic spread out before him, terrifying and glorious. Tristan yearned to sail the waters and said as much to Michael, who smiled in sympathy.

"So you're a son of Altair after all. There's not one of us who hasn't dreamt of doing the same. We long for the sea."

"Speak for yourself." Thomas laughed, but it had a hollow sound. "I sailed once and got seasick. Even seeing it makes me ill."

Thomas wheeled his horse around and rode away from the cliffs. Tristan wanted to follow out of concern, but Michael stopped him with a sad shake of his head.

"Seeing the water doesn't make him sick. Mother loved the sea. He took her sailing on their wedding night. It reminds him of her, and he can hardly bear the ache, even after all these years. Give him a moment."

Chess provided much-needed entertainment during the evenings or bad weather. Tristan had enjoyed learning how to play when living with the Kavanaughs, but the long summer months with no practice had weakened his game. Now at Altair, he played daily, but he could never win against Michael or Thomas. At best, Tristan won sporadically when playing Ethan. Christiana also proved to be a formidable opponent. After seeing her beat Michael on several occasions, it baffled Tristan after he won a few times while playing against her.

Michael chuckled to himself, knowing full well she had lost those games on purpose. He suspected the girl was sweet on Tristan, and he wondered if that might be why she allowed him to win, for she had always been a very competitive player. However, Christiana wasn't above showing Tristan up in other matters.

On fine days the boys would practice archery and sword work. Armed with a bow and arrow, most of the older youths were good enough for hunting large game, but Michael alone had any exceptional shooting talent, for it was a Lockhart tradition that the men were renowned archers.

It soon became apparent to everyone that Tristan had no talent for archery. Much to the amusement of the others, Michael could be seen bouncing about, alternating between encouragement and exasperation, as he endeavored to teach Tristan the basics. Try as he might, Tristan could not land an arrow remotely near the target, and the other boys learned to race far off the range whenever he attempted a shot. At last even Michael was forced to admit Tristan was downright awful.

Christiana loved coming out to watch them shoot, bundled in woolens and nestled in a bed of straw. One day she giggled at Tristan as an arrow skittered off a stone wall more than five feet from the intended target. Hurt and infuriated by her laughter, he whirled to face Christiana and said with a touch of scorn in his voice, "I'd like to see you do better, *Princess!*"

Justin, who stood nearby, groaned. "You've let yourself in for it now, lad."

Christiana narrowed her eyes before fighting her way out of the straw. Throwing off her cloak, she snatched Tristan's bow, stole an arrow from his quiver, and shoved him aside. In one fluid motion, she nocked and drew the arrow back before letting it fly straight into the target's center. Tristan's jaw dropped while the other boys murmured their admiration. Michael chuckled to himself. He had not seen her shoot since the previous winter and had forgotten how good the girl was. Christiana returned the bow with a sharp nod before departing for the castle, satisfied and a bit smug. As for Tristan, his eyes followed her with undisguised awe.

The inner courtyard was protected from the worst of the snow, and there the restless men of the castle would sometimes temper their hot blood with sparring matches. They worked with a sword master in the mornings, but Michael would often tutor some of the younger men during the afternoon sessions. He was an excellent swordsman, and Tristan admired his technique. If James fought like a bruiser, using his height and strength to every advantage, Michael combined power and grace when he wielded steel. Tristan thought there was a certain beauty in his movements, deadly though they were.

Tristan expected James and Prince Justin to spar, and everyone enjoyed watching them go at it. However, he did not expect to see Ethan join in some sparring sessions and perform quite well. Tristan had assumed his brother's desire to be a healer meant he wasn't much of a fighter. He didn't know that all men of Altair were taught to fight, and Ethan had been training since he held his first sword at age seven. He didn't practice more than necessary, but a natural aptitude showed.

Seeing Ethan's casual display of skill frustrated Tristan. Michael had worked with him throughout summer on throwing the dagger, and he wasn't so bad at that, but he remained far behind other boys his age with the sword. Tristan conveniently forgot he had never so much as touched a sword until the past summer and grew discouraged. One afternoon, after a more pathetic performance than usual, James taunted him that after months of practice he continued using wood to spar. Tristan knew his brother didn't mean any harm, but he had to fight off hot tears of shame. He could see Christiana watching. In a fit of self-disgust, he threw the sparring stick to the ground with a few choice swear words that caused Michael to give him a clout on the head.

James snickered and called over his shoulder as he walked away, "Nice try, *little* brother."

With those words, Tristan lost his temper entirely. He rushed at James, but Michael grabbed hold of him before he pummeled his brother.

Lifting the boy off his feet, he tossed him into a snowbank on the edge of the courtyard. Tristan jumped up, sputtering wet slush. By then his anger had passed, and he slumped, defeated. Michael threw an arm around Tristan's shoulders, murmuring a few words of encouragement, but Tristan caught the smile his brother was hiding and shook Michael off in frustration.

At that moment, Thomas came into the courtyard with his great war sword. None of them had ever seen their father spar, for he always practiced alone or with far more experienced fighters. He beckoned to James. His son jumped forward as catcalls arose from the other men in the courtyard. Michael tapped Tristan on the arm and murmured, "Watch this."

His blue eyes gleaming with excitement, James brandished his weapon with a few measured swings while his father stood by. James clenched his jaw in concentration and took his stance. Thomas looked bored, even squinting up at the sun as though checking the time. Seeing James ready, he shrugged and raised his sword. "Come along."

After a few lazy strokes, Thomas had James on his rump, gasping for air, with the blade's point hovering over his head. Smirking, Thomas leaned over and whispered into his son's ear. James nodded, his eyes flitting to Tristan and back to his father, and he gulped. With a grin and a wink, Thomas held out his hand and hauled James to his feet before roughing his hair. Lesson learned, James backed off from teasing Tristan so much.

About a week later, Tristan was slumped on the ground, back against the courtyard wall, watching James and Ethan fight. Listless, he poked at his stick sword. Michael suppressed his amusement at the pitiful behavior and instead slid down beside him. Without saying a word, he passed a sheathed sword to the boy. At Michael's nod, Tristan withdrew the sword and studied it. Although smaller than the weapons his brothers used, he could see the sword was of the highest quality.

"Check the balance and tell me if you think this will suit." Michael grinned at the look of speechless wonder on Tristan's face. "For someone who's said for months he didn't care if he learned to use a sword, you seem rather pleased."

Tristan jumped to his feet. He held the blade up, parrying an invisible opponent. Michael stood, drawing his own sword, and they exchanged a few blows for fun.

"Excellent! Now, no using it with anyone but Dad or myself until you get some practice. Don't let James talk you into fighting him with steel, keep to the sticks with him. He'll try to goad you into it, but no matter what he says, you resist, hear me? You aren't ready yet, and he might not account for the shorter length compared to his."

"Yes! Thank you, Michael!" Tristan said, his eyes shining.

"It was Dad's idea, go thank him. Don't blame me if you get a hand chopped off," Michael said. There was no need to say how much raw talent he saw in Tristan, but he watched the boy handle his new sword with great pride. Even James's teasing came from a place of admiration for his younger brother's efforts, though Tristan didn't see it that way. Michael was confident that with a real sword in hand, Tristan would catch up to his peers.

Arms crossed, Thomas viewed the exchange from a distance. He had held his youngest back from using steel as long as he could, reluctant to admit it was past time. He could do so no longer. Tristan was far better than he knew himself, and his father could see he was more than ready. Nevertheless, his heart squeezed at the idea of Tristan fighting for his life in battle. These visions haunted Thomas's dreams, and he muttered a rare prayer that no war would come anytime soon.

As winter abated, Thomas made plans to leave for the mountains. Michael and Tristan were far from eager to depart, both preferring the comforts of the home they had at Altair. But neither of them considered breaking up the family, although they would have been welcome to remain at the castle. And this year, Ethan would be joining them. He claimed there was much to gain through the practical experience that might present itself. In truth, with the family reunited, Ethan had no desire to be apart from the others once more.

Tristan was very sorry at the prospect of leaving Christiana. She had a deep, irrepressible core of sweetness that had endeared her to him over the winter months. They were devoted to one another, and he would have faced dragons for her, had they existed. Tristan hugged her fiercely before he left, missing her already. As they rode down the lane, Christiana waved goodbye, blinking back a few tears.

"The dear boys. I do hate it when they leave us," Charlotte murmured. "I had hoped Thomas might change after finding Tristan, but it appears not to be. I fear you will miss him, even more than the others."

Christiana sighed, yet her eyes sparkled. "I will, but they'll return in the fall. And someday, when we marry, we'll never be parted again."

"Marry Tristan? Good heavens, child, the things you say!" Charlotte laughed outright, though truth be known, the idea pleased her more than she would admit.

Christiana smiled to herself.

# Chapter 15

# A Golden Summer

*Dear Christiana,*

*I'm sorry I have not written more this summer. We are deep in the Shadowlands. Courier opportunities are few, and we get little notice when we have a chance to send anything. Also, James teases me something awful that I write to you at all. Tonight I volunteered for first watch, so I can write by firelight as late as I want and no one will think the worse of me if I'm tired in the morning (and James won't see me at it). The moon is rising, and I can hear the echoing calls of wolves in the far distance.*

*I've been forgetting to thank you for smuggling the small chess set into my things when we left Altair. It took me some time to narrow down the giver. I knew James wouldn't have dreamt of it, and Dad grumbled it was a waste of packing space. But he said it with a smile, and as he's pulled it out to play many times, I'm not worried. Ethan declared he hadn't, and as he is the very soul of sincerity, I could never doubt him. I thought it was Michael for a long time, but he only regretted not thinking of it himself. Therefore, I must conclude it was you. We play in the evenings, and I hope you will find me a better player, which no doubt was your intent, as I have been told you let me win last winter. I denied this, but after losing all summer, I'm beginning to wonder.*

*It is beautiful here in the mountains. They're green and full of odd plants we never find on the coastlands. Ethan spends his days gathering and studying the medicinal ones, and Dad tries to teach me which ones are edible, with no success. I do see their loveliness, and if I had any gift at all in drawing, I would try to capture it for you. Alas, as you know, I have not an artistic bone in my body. Of course, I could write volumes, but I'm afraid time and paper do not permit. I'll do my best to describe it all to you when we see each other again.*

*I turned fourteen in June. Ethan and I had a riot celebrating our brief twinship. Also, since my birthday, Dad has started to let me go scouting with him or Michael. It isn't as exciting as I thought it would be, but I'm glad to be helping beyond taking care of the horses. Speaking of which, Dad's horse had a nasty infection in a hoof and nearly had to be put down. I managed to bring Marley through it. Dad was ridiculously pleased. He's very fond of the beast and offered to buy me a new horse, but I won't be parted with my dear Dun. He whinnies his greetings to you and begs you to tell Cook to plant more carrots in the castle gardens this year, please.*

*I must finish this. I'm sorry. I miss you, and while I love the wilds of summer in the mountains, I look forward to the quiet pleasures of winter and playing chess with you. Although I suspect you won't go so easy on me this time.*

*Affectionately,*
*Tristan*

Tristan shuddered awake, gasping and wet at the shock of icy-cold creek water being poured over his head. James hooted with laughter as he tossed an empty bucket aside. With a curse, Tristan jumped to his feet and shook the water off. He barreled into James headfirst, knocking his much larger brother backward through the tent flap. James twisted him over, pinning both his arms with one hand.

Michael strolled by with an armload of firewood, laughing. "That's what you get for sleeping in. Goodness knows I tried to wake you, but you wouldn't budge."

"I was tired because I had watch!"

"You had the first watch," said James, still restraining Tristan with ease. "Plenty of time to sleep afterward, but Ethan told us you stayed awake long past, writing. What were you doing, composing poetry to Chris? *My darling Christiana—*"

"Shuddup!" Tristan gurgled under the weight of his brother.

"If I let go, are you going to try to land me again, or will you settle down?"

Tristan grappled a moment longer, but James started tickling him. Tristan's anger dissolved into outraged cackles as he laughed and cursed his brother all at once. With a war cry, Ethan launched himself at James, who released Tristan in his surprise. Together, the two of them tackled their oldest sibling, throwing a few punches and tickling him in turn.

Michael strode away, rolling his eyes, and hailed Thomas, who was leading his great chestnut stallion.

"You off?"

"Yes, look for me by sundown."

Tristan extricated himself from the pile and came trotting up. "Dad, you sure you don't want company?" he asked.

"No, son. You chatter far too much, and this needs to be a quiet ride." As Tristan's face fell, Thomas chucked the boy's chin affectionately. He knew Tristan was uneasy when he or Michael rode out alone; those old fears of abandonment always seemed to lurk beneath the surface. "I'll be back before you can miss me. Keep an eye on James. I leave you in charge of him."

Tristan laughed at this before heading off to care for the horses. Thomas's gaze followed the boy. He remembered the angry, frightened lad who had stood before him last summer, and it gave him great delight to see his youngest son happy. Michael caught his eye and grinned. "You're such a pushover with him."

Thomas rumbled a bit and mounted his horse. "Like you're not. Watch over things, Michael."

Tristan fed and watered all the animals, checked a hoof bruise Dun had picked up two days before, and ensured they were all content. His duties finished for a time, he was wandering back to the main camp when a whoop distracted him. He spun about in the direction of the sound with a good idea of what he would find.

Sure enough, there he was—Ethan crouched in a mass of ferns, swooning over some plant. Tristan shook his head, knowing what he was in for if he continued to approach his brother, but he did it anyway.

"Tristan! Look at this! *Monotropa uniflora*! Isn't it stunning?"

Tristan knelt on the damp earth. While *stunning* wasn't the word he would have chosen, he had to admit it was the oddest plant he had ever seen. He whispered when he asked, "What's it do?"

As Ethan babbled on about it, using words like *saprophyte* and *anodyne*, Tristan smothered a laugh, for plants and medicines brought out his brother's talkative side. Unfortunately, only their father had any comprehension of what Ethan was saying on the topic, and Thomas wasn't around to interpret for him that day.

Ethan's excitement subsided as he fondled the plant, and Tristan wondered if his brother had forgotten he was even there. He retreated, eliciting a warning from Ethan not to trample on any patches of the weird discovery that might be lurking about. He watched his step and returned to camp.

In the heat of the day, Tristan headed to the tent he shared with Michael, who was talking to himself. Clothing and other sundry items lay in neat piles beside a canvas bag, waiting to be packed. Instantly, Tristan went on the alert. He sauntered over and sat on the ground, watching Michael sort through his things.

Michael hid a smile, for he knew what Tristan had on his mind. On occasion, Michael left camp to get the word from local villagers on what was happening in the region, and he had promised Tristan could come along on a foray sometime.

"When are you leaving?" Tristan asked.

"Day after tomorrow. Dad and I need to sort out how we can manage the camp with four men—er—people."

Tristan almost squirmed with excitement. "What town is it this time?"

"Caldwell."

"Small village?"

"Actually, it's quite a decent size for this part of the country. Several taverns and inns. A few shops. Livery. It might even have a church." Waves of anticipation seemed to roll off Tristan, yet the boy remained impressively nonchalant. Michael stifled his desire to laugh.

"How far is it?" asked Tristan.

"Two-day ride. I'll be gone about six days altogether."

"That's an awful long time to be on your own."

"And what a relief it will be, some silence after all your chatter." Tristan looked hurt at this comment, and Michael roughed his hair hoping to take the sting out of his words.

"I suppose managing the camp with four men will be hard," Tristan commented, flicking an invisible speck of dirt from his pants. "Imagine how difficult it would be with *three*."

"Impossible," stated Michael.

"Surely not!"

"Think about splitting the watch at night? And if two people went scouting, that would leave one to keep an eye on camp. No, most would say it couldn't work with three men."

"Right." Crestfallen, Tristan rose to his feet and turned to go, but Michael continued speaking, albeit in a louder voice.

"Then again, Dad and I worked it out one time, how it could be done with three people." Out of the corner of his eye, he saw Tristan freeze. "Good thing too. I'm going to need some help in Caldwell. Too much for me to handle—" Michael broke off when Tristan attacked him with a hug. "And I'm not packing your stuff! You take care of your own things!" he exclaimed, knowing full well he would end up doing all the packing. *Pushover indeed*, Michael thought, grinning.

The sun was sinking below the tree line when Thomas returned to camp. He cracked his neck, looking forward to resting before the fire. Tomorrow he would need to write a report so Michael could send it from Caldwell. Sammanon forces were on the move, and he feared they were preparing for war. It bothered him to have so little control over the situation out here in the mountains. His job was to report and let the higher ranks work it out. But Andrew valued his thoughts, and Thomas wanted to analyze things further before composing his letter. He hoped Michael or James would also lend their thoughts on the enemy's movements.

Laughter and the clash of blades reached Thomas's ears, and he let loose a contented sigh. It had been a good summer thus far. No major injuries to speak of, no problems with the locals, nothing to put a dark mark on their memories. Maybe it seemed more golden since it was the first summer with all his boys together. It had been pleasant not to hire strangers to fill out their numbers, even if they could have done with one or two more men.

By dusk they were all spread out before the fire, poking into their stores of food for a bite because no one wanted to cook. Ethan yammered about the plant species he had found until Tristan talked him into a game of chess. James leaned back against a log, polishing his sword and whistling. Catching the tune, Michael began humming along. Soon, he and James were singing some of the tavern songs they had picked up in their travels.

The moon rose fat and yellow. Chess was set aside, and Ethan joined the others in singing. Tristan contented himself with a day-old biscuit and made his way between Michael and his father. He lay down and gazed at the stars with a quirk of a smile on his lips, wondering what Christiana was doing. He hoped Caldwell had a shop where he could buy more parchment.

Fireflies glowed in the darkness. Wolves howled, but the hunting had been good, and they preferred to keep their distance. Thomas looked around at all four of his boys, happy and safe.

Yes, it had been a very good summer.

## Chapter 16

# Return to Altair

The Thatchers' winter return to Altair was joyous, and Christiana was in the stableyard before they had finished dismounting. She flew at Tristan in raptures, hugging and kissing him before leaping at Michael, leaving Tristan breathless and grinning. He had become used to her excesses and was delighted to find she had not changed.

That winter was mild, and the entire Kavanaugh clan came to Castle Altair to stay for several weeks. Tristan assumed James would relish the extended opportunity to nettle Cate; instead, he disappeared for hours at a time. Thomas rumbled his concerns about any mischief his son might be creating in town. As for Cate, they rarely saw her either, for she appeared to prefer spending most of her time in Christiana's room, or so everyone assumed. But during the dinner hour when the families were together, the quarrelsome duo had them all in fits of laughter over their witty sparring.

The other Kavanaugh daughters fawned over every male within striking distance, forcing Ethan and Tristan to hide in their rooms to avoid them. Between this and Cate monopolizing Christiana, Tristan had no strong love for girls that season.

"Why must they all hang about? I can't leave my room without one of them popping out at me," he complained to Michael one evening as they readied for bed. "And Cate is years older than Chris. They can't have much in common."

Michael chuckled as he tugged off his boots and tossed them aside. Tristan made a show of gagging over the smell.

"Cate's the same age as James," said Michael. "She and Christiana have more in common than you realize. And would you want to be around those sisters if you were Cate? And Christiana doesn't often see any girls closer to her own age other than her cousin Rachel. You haven't met Rachel, have you? She's a charming girl, you would love her."

"The last thing we need here are *more* girls."

"You might not think that way in a year or two." Michael swatted Tristan to move aside as he rummaged in his wardrobe.

Tristan scoffed with disdain but paced the floor. "You said Rachel's another cousin?"

"Yes and no. She's Christiana's cousin on her father's side. No relation to us that I'm aware."

"Pretty?"

Michael caught the too casual tone in Tristan's voice and realized with a start Tristan wasn't perhaps quite as dismissive of fairer sex as he let on. This was a first, and Michael was intrigued. He closed the wardrobe and leaned against it, thoughtful.

"Oh, yes. I would even say she's lovely. It's funny we're not related, because she looks a lot like Mother. She's taller but has the same coloring, the same sweetness. Christiana visits her every summer. She used to come here for Christmas but hasn't in a few years now."

Tristan threw himself onto Michael's bed, pretending to not care much. Michael noticed him brooding and sighed to himself. He remembered James going through this phase and hoped Tristan wouldn't be as difficult. Michael turned his back to the boy, for once making an effort to pick up his cluttered space and sort his many books.

Tristan watched him for a moment before venturing to speak again. "Michael?"

"Hmm?"

"Didn't you want to court Cate at one time?"

Michael paused for a fraction of a second before continuing with the books. "I can't believe you remember that. Well, I did for a short season. Rather thought it was obvious we weren't a good match. I could have pressed it, and some men might have, but I had no desire to force her affection."

"She was mad not to want you!" Tristan proclaimed.

Michael looked up, grinning. "Why thank you, Tristan. I appreciate the solidarity, although based on your comments I suspect you wouldn't have wanted us together."

"Well..." Tristan scratched his head. "I didn't like the idea of it, to be honest. But I want you to be happy."

"I'm very happy. Look, I'll admit I'm not as settled as I should be. Of course, I have options. I could go to Lockhart Manor and start a new life there. And yet, that's not what I want either. I don't know what I want. But never think I'm not happy."

"Did you ever tell Cate how you felt?"

Michael frowned. He had hoped he had changed the subject. "Not in so many words."

"In any words?"

"Now, Tristan," Michael said with an air of superiority. "I believe I know a bit more about women than you do."

Tristan couldn't argue this point, but he wasn't sure how Michael thought he knew more about women. Certainly he never socialized with any ladies aside from Charlotte or Mariah Kavanaugh. Tristan fell back across Michael's bed.

"Women are more trouble than they're worth," he said, groaning in exasperation. Michael laughed and returned to his books.

A few days before Christmas, Tristan happened to be walking past the common room when the sound of voices stopped him. Recognizing the deep tones of Andrew and his father, Tristan was about to pop in to say hello when Andrew said something that made him hesitate.

"Do you think Her Grace has anyone in mind for Christiana? She'll be fifteen next September. How old was Charlotte when she wed? Eighteen?"

"Nineteen, but she was betrothed for years before."

"Well, she has some time, I suppose, although people will be expecting an early marriage. At least a betrothal soon. There were rumors of her considering—"

"There were always potential complications there, as you well know. What if, by some strange movement of events, he actually ends up at Woodraven? Imagine how Charlotte would feel if, after all these years of contending against King Holden, her daughter left for Woodraven."

"I've heard Stuart MacClaren has reached new heights in his ambitions. He has his heart set on uniting the MacClaren and Reynard families."

"I wish him luck," Thomas said dryly. "Charlotte would sooner her daughter wed the fishmonger's son than Gerald MacClaren. I agree most will be expecting Christiana to marry young. Of course, given the queen's less than happy marriage, she might not follow as expected."

Andrew laughed. "True, and since when does Her Grace ever do what is expected?"

Thomas made a noise that might have been a snort of agreement. The scent of tobacco wafted from the doorway. Andrew must be quite invested in the conversation to be smoking. With an affectionate smile, Tristan envisioned Andrew taking a long drag from the cigarette before speaking again.

"Well, no question Lawrence was an entitled ass and a troublemaker. I don't know how his father convinced the old king to agree to that marriage. And then to die the way he did, who would have seen that coming?"

At this, Thomas muttered something low and incomprehensible. Tristan forced himself to tiptoe away. He had no idea girls were betrothed at such a young age. Why, Christiana was a mere child! He tried to imagine her as a married woman and laughed aloud. Ridiculous!

"Pity the poor husband trying to manage *that* one," Tristan murmured. He set about amusing himself by imagining what kind of man Christiana would marry. But then his grin faded. The prospect of her leaving Altair with some stranger made him uneasy. Lost in these thoughts, he failed to see the large object in his path until he stumbled back in shock. A huff of surprise came from Prince Justin.

"Tristan! Are you all right? I'm sorry." Justin reached with a long arm to help him up.

"I'm not sure if you're the one to be apologizing," Tristan groaned. "It seems you caught me woolgathering."

"I should say so," Justin said kindly. "I'll see you later."

Tristan was about to turn the corner when a thought struck him and he called out, "Justin, ah, Your Highness..." He fumbled for words, for he was never sure how to talk to the future king. Unlike James, he had spent almost no time with Justin on his own.

"Come on, Tristan, don't do that royal stuff with me. I'm sick of it all." Justin scowled.

"Right. I've wanted to ask you for some time. You've been to Woodraven. What's it like?"

The young prince seemed taken aback. "Woodraven? Why would you ask me? Your father grew up there. He can tell you far more about it than myself."

"I'm sure he could, but he doesn't care to talk about it. He won't say why. Is it that bad of a place?"

"Hmm, I don't have much time. Come with me to the library, and we'll talk on the way. What do you know of Aquila's history?"

"Not as much as I should," confessed Tristan. "They didn't think it wise to teach me while living in the Shadowlands. I'm trying to catch up, though."

"Well, we'll need to keep it simple for now. In the distant past, there was a king of Aquila whose younger brother sought a kingdom for himself and landed the throne of Woodraven. His descendants rule there to this day."

"Does that mean you're related to the current king of Woodraven?"

"Only in the vaguest sense." Justin laughed at the notion. "We're talking several hundred years ago. The blood is so diluted I couldn't even begin to tell you the exact relation."

"You would think Woodraven wouldn't be that different from us."

"True, but the entire personality of the country is quite different from Aquila. The Woodraven throne was taken through violence, causing a rift between our countries, and since that time we've grown apart. I sympathize with your father's reluctance to talk about his background. A man of his excellent character would find little to boast about being from there. It's a rough, ill-ordered society."

They arrived at the library, and Justin traced his fingers along the spines of books, murmuring almost to himself. "In Woodraven there are no churches, no priests, few places of learning. Certainly no abbeys. They appreciate cleverness but not education and embrace a sort of rustic exuberance. The people celebrate the strength of the sword arm, which has led them to be the great metalsmiths of the continent."

"They're still our allies, aren't they?"

"Oh yes! They keep to themselves as much as they can, but they are no friends of Sammanon, and they know we must align together for the safety of our borders. You'll see a few battalions in the wars. However, they retain the bulk of their army at home to protect themselves should Aquila fall."

While talking, Justin had been removing books one at a time, inspecting the titles and replacing them on the shelves until he found what he sought. "Here you are. This book is a good primer on our history, and you'll find enough in it on Woodraven to interest you as well."

"Ah, thank you!" Tristan leafed through the pages.

"You do know you can take any book from here?" asked Justin. But Tristan's nose was already buried in the tome. Justin snorted.

"Good heavens, you're as bad as Christiana. You should ask her about Woodraven. She's read more than I ever will."

"Except you've been there. You've met King Holden!" Tristan countered.

"It was nothing to get excited about. Trust me on this one."

Tucking the book under his arm, Tristan moved to leave the library when a thought made him stop. "Justin?"

"Hmm?" The prince kept his eyes on the shelves before him, still scanning them for the book he needed.

"Are you excited to be king someday?"

Justin whipped his head around and gave Tristan a sharp look. His eyes shadowed, he dropped his gaze to the floor and muttered, "Not particularly."

Everything about the prince's reaction warned Tristan not to pursue the topic any further. He thanked Justin once more and walked back to his room, his thoughts wandering again. By the time he was in the old corridor, Tristan was thinking of the queen's unhappy marriage and her dead husband. He remembered Christiana's response to seeing her father's grave the previous winter, and the cryptic comments Thomas had made concerning the man.

Ethan's door was open, and Tristan poked his head into the room. His brother was sitting on the floor, quill in hand and ink bottle nearby. Surrounding him were piles of journals and papers, with bits of browned and dead plants everywhere.

"Er, is it safe to come in?"

"Yes, yes. Sit here." Ethan gestured vaguely at a chair. Tristan stayed on his feet, wary of crushing a dried leaf. He leaned against the doorframe. Not for the first time, he admired Ethan's dedication to his chosen profession.

"What's going on here?"

"Cataloging the plants I found over the summer."

"Don't forget the weird one, montropoli-something."

Ethan narrowed his eyes. Seeing that Tristan was sincere in his efforts, he laughed and returned to his journal. "Good try. And yes, I have it. Thanks."

"Ethan, you've lived in Altair your whole life, haven't you?"

His brother nodded as he thumbed through the journal, seeking a specific entry. "More or less."

"Do you know how Lawrence Marchant died?"

Ethan looked up in surprise. "The queen's husband? Of course I do. Don't you?"

"How could I?" asked Tristan in exasperation. "I was gone for years, remember?"

"Oh, right," Ethan responded. After a moment's consideration, he shrugged. "I suppose there's no harm saying, everyone knows. He killed himself."

"What!"

"Yes, it was a tremendous shock too. Hung himself in his own chamber."

At this, Tristan did sit.

"That's awful," he whispered. "Oh, Chris..."

Ethan's whole demeanor drooped. "She was his favorite too. They were very close. She was six, or was it seven? I don't remember."

"Why would he have done such a thing?"

"I don't know. I'm sure Dad does, but you can see why he won't talk about it, at least with us."

"What won't Dad talk about?" Michael asked, coming through the door. Both younger brothers jumped at his entrance.

"Tris was asking about Prince Lawrence and how he died."

"Do you know why he killed himself, Michael?"

"I do not, and it was an awful business from what I understand. Nothing for casual conversation."

"I just wanted to—"

"No! That's enough on the topic," ordered Michael. Tristan and Ethan exchanged glances. Their brother rarely put his foot down, but when he did, he was immovable. At their looks, he forced a smile. "I think Christiana has been trying to find you, Tristan. She was in the Great Hall the last time I saw her."

With a jerky nod, Tristan got up. Michael grabbed his arm but gentled his hand at the sight of the sweet innocence in his brother's eyes. "Don't dwell on dark things, Tris. It serves no purpose."

"Yes, Michael," Tristan said.

"Good lad." Michael smiled and gestured to the door. As he watched Tristan trot away, he suppressed a shiver.

The Kavanaughs left after Christmas, wanting to be home before the worst of winter arrived. With the holiday festivities over, everyone settled into their usual routines. For the first time, Tristan worked with a sword master, the same as the other training men of the castle. These sessions were a source of frustration for him. It seemed that as soon as he mastered a particular parry or slice, half a dozen more were introduced to him. Meanwhile, James had grown larger and more enthusiastic than ever, and there were some great sparring matches that winter, especially between him and Justin. Even with his conflicting thoughts on fighting, deep down Tristan was jealous of his brother's abilities.

"Oh, do stop complaining and train more!" Christiana exclaimed when she had enough of his bellyaching. "Yes, he's had years and you're behind, but do you think you'll catch up with all this moaning about? Why don't you ask Michael for extra help?"

Expecting a sympathetic ear, Tristan was cut to the quick by her comment, and he sulked for days afterward. Nevertheless, before the week was out, he approached Michael asking for additional lessons.

It was almost spring before Tristan defeated Christiana at chess. She had been relentless all winter, encouraging but challenging Tristan at every match. The moment he proclaimed "checkmate" in triumph, a look of utter confusion swept over her, followed by the flush of embarrassment.

Tristan leaned over the board, his dark blue eyes twinkling, to whisper dramatically, "Shall I lose for you next time?"

Michael had been watching them play and thought Christiana might overturn the board in a fury. Then that impish smile of hers flickered as she whispered back, "Never."

# Chapter 17

# Snowfall

*My dearest Chris,*

*I should have written more this summer, but my letters would have been a continual complaint about the bad weather, bug bites, and the short tempers of five cantankerous men. I've never seen so much rain, and it has turned into a freezing sleet unseasonably early. You can imagine what sort of mood that has put Michael in. He and Dad are bickering about it already. James and Ethan ignore them. I hate seeing the two of them at odds. I'm inclined to side with Michael, but I also see something has been bothering Dad these past few weeks. Last summer he saw unusual patterns in the Sammanon army behavior, and they are still at it, but he holds it all to himself. He's determined to get to the bottom of it.*

*We are well, if you discount the endless round of colds and sniffles cursing us all. Ethan's store of medicines is almost depleted between sickness and minor injuries. Game has been scarce, and the wet spoils what food we have. We're all feeling the bite of hunger more than usual, which isn't helping our mood.*

*I expect the first snow any day, and I pray this is the last letter I send by courier before I'll be back myself. I miss the castle, my bed, and good food. Most of all, I miss your company, and I look forward to a long winter. I will even take morning sessions with the sword master without complaint if it means I'm home with you. Please give your mother my most affectionate greetings and tell Justin I'll be ready to spar this winter.*

*Your ever faithful,*

*Tristan*

Tristan shivered as he rode Dun through a great snowdrift. At last he understood why Michael hated to be in the mountains when the snows came. The cold made them all miserable, and the wolves were growing aggressive, approaching their camp for the meat they hung high in the trees. Yet here they were in the ranges a month after they should have left. Deep drifts aside, Tristan preferred to be out in the snow rather than at camp, where tensions between his father and Michael stung his peace-loving spirit, and the atmosphere even colder than the frigid weather. They had begun their annual feud about leaving the mountains weeks ago when the first frost descended. Now winter was fully upon them, and both men were always tetchy.

It had not been a pleasant summer. Everything had gone wrong. Horses went lame, injuries or illnesses plagued them, and it never stopped raining. Tempers were short, and the increasing rumors of war had put everyone on edge. Ethan appeared to be the only one unscathed by the moodiness of the group, but even he was subject to the occasional bout of melancholy. Tristan had fallen into a perpetually gloomy state of mind. It had been weeks since his last letter to Christiana, when he had hoped they would be traveling east. He had run out of parchment and could write no more letters.

"We won't be out here much longer," he said to Dun, hoping he spoke the truth. "Soon we'll be at Altair, with warm fires and soft feather beds. And a grand bed of straw for you, eh, boy?" He patted his horse's neck, and Dun gave a nicker of approval. Tristan wondered if Christiana was anxious because they were late returning this year. He had thought of her often and missed her companionship more than he cared to admit, even perhaps to himself.

At least he had been allowed to go scouting on his own. Although Tristan knew neither Michael nor his father would ever send him out to do anything blatantly dangerous, these expeditions filled him with a certain amount of pride. Today no specific danger lurked, but the clouds were heavy with snow, and the sound of wolves howling in the distance was enough to give any boy the satisfaction of potential adventure close at hand.

This ride was nothing more than a wide sweep, a perimeter check of the whole area, and Tristan maintained the protocols he had been taught. It was crucial to know how to avoid being tracked in the thick snow, which showed every step. Taking all the precautions wasn't necessary and would lengthen what was already a long ride for the day, but Tristan appreciated the opportunity to practice, and he had nothing better to do. When he reached the snow banked stream, Tristan guided Dun into the shallow water and rode upstream for a mile before crossing to the other side. This he did multiple times as they rose farther up.

He exited the stream near a particular cleft that allowed him to circle to the peak of the mountain. Tristan rode higher and higher until he came to a crevice that hid Dun well. Here he dismounted to climb the final, short ascent on his own. Tristan was huffing by the time he hauled himself onto a small outcropping that commanded a wonderful view of the valley to the west. Catching his breath, Tristan gazed upon the land and stumbled a step or two in shock.

Yesterday James had been here and reported nothing. Today, a sizable army camped below, and multiple campfires were scattered over several miles. He confirmed the sun's location, not wanting the light to reflect off his small spyglass. The sun hid behind a sheen of snow clouds, so he lay on the rocky ledge and studied the landscape. Tristan had an excellent memory for numbers but didn't try to count the people; even with his glass, it would be difficult to get anything accurate. Knowing the number of fires, tents, and horse ties would provide far more pertinent information. More importantly, the flag flying over the camp confirmed they were Sammanon forces. For a good half hour he lay there, muttering everything he needed to remember.

His horse whinnied below, and Tristan froze. Dun was usually quiet and not prone to making noise unless a stranger came near. A few seconds later, Dun gave a restless snort. Another mount must be close enough for the wind to cast its scent, and it was a horse Dun didn't recognize. Tristan stood and surveyed the camp one more time to ensure he had missed nothing.

Tumbling pebbles and stones caught his attention, and Tristan jerked his head around. About fifty yards away he spotted a sentry on rocky cleft, with a drawn bow. Before Tristan had a chance to register the sight, the arrow struck, and he was thrown back from the lookout point onto the rocks below. Dun squealed at his sudden appearance. The snow cushioned Tristan's fall, but he was overwhelmed by a searing pain so sharp his vision momentarily went black. He cried out as he struggled to grasp what had happened. A long shaft protruded from high on his left shoulder. Blood dripped into the snow, melting it with its heat. Between the sight of blood and the violent agony, a wave of nausea rolled over him.

With a toss of his head, Dun whinnied louder than ever and stamped his hoof. Tristan willed himself to think. Sentry. He was out of the sentry's line of vision, but how long would it take for the soldier to find him? Tristan had to move fast.

He floundered to his knees, bewildered to see his hands shaking as if he had the palsy. Tristan tugged at his woolen scarf, gathering it around the protruding shaft to staunch the bleeding, embarrassed to hear himself whimpering. He shoved a large handful of snow into his mouth to smother his cries.

Tristan moaned as the throbbing in his shoulder intensified. He thought of trying to hide the evidence of his blood, but it didn't matter. The trampled snow would give him away. As he staggered to Dun, Tristan had a moment of pure terror when it occurred to him there was no possible way he could mount his horse. He floundered through the snow to a fallen tree. It seemed an eon before he could climb to its crest. Sobbing, he called for Dun and hauled himself onto the horse.

Catcalls and yells sounded in the distance. Tristan knew he had to hurry. Another wave of torment caused him to slump against Dun's neck. As soon as it passed, he urged Dun around to the other side of the mountain.

Tristan groaned. He had ridden hours to get to the lookout point. Cutting through the woods would be faster, but he didn't dare. He had to follow the protocols he had practiced earlier, only this time it wasn't a drill. Now they held life and death in the balance. Not just for himself, but also for his father and brothers. A horse's neigh came from a distance. Tristan clenched his teeth against the torment, muttered a quick prayer, and rode downstream as fast as he dared.

The journey was excruciating. For an hour or two, Tristan lived with the constant terror of discovery, and dim crackles of broken branches or a faraway splash of water did nothing to lessen these fears. But there came a time when silence fell in the woods and thick flurries of snow swirled around him.

His mind strayed. A damp chill consumed him. He wondered why he was so wet. Had he fallen into the stream? It took Tristan far too long to conclude it wasn't water. His stomach sickened at the sight of his clothes drenched with his own blood.

He kept riding, increasingly confusing which side of the water he was on. He had lost all sense of direction. His vision dimmed and blurred, every bone shook and ached, and he bent over Dun's side to vomit. Dun gave a low nicker and Tristan mumbled, "I'm all right, boy. Jus' need Dad."

A wolf howled, and the distant answering calls made Tristan's head swim. In a last breath of consciousness, Tristan grasped a long strand of mane and wound it securely around his right hand. He fell across Dun's neck, giving the horse his head. Dun stopped and snuffed the air before picking his way through the forest.

# Chapter 18

# The Black Arrow

The shadows were lengthening in the snow, and the sun had fallen behind the top branches of the trees. Michael paced to the southern edge of the forest and back again, trying to quell his growing anxiety. He wandered to the fire circle, where he had absent-mindedly left his sword, and picked the weapon up, only to jam the tip into the ground in frustration.

At midday he had been annoyed, assuming Tristan must be wasting time on the mountain trail, but now his anger melted even as the cold grew worse. Nearby, Thomas was staring into the hills. When their eyes met, both knew what the other was thinking. Tristan should have been back hours ago.

The crunch of snow sent Michael spinning around to see James, who had been scouting along the creek.

"Anything?" Michael asked.

James shook his head, dispirited. Thomas caught the exchange and stalked off.

"Where is he?" Michael muttered, kicking at a rock.

Ethan, who had been sorting the medicine chest nearby, made a small, anxious sound. "It's not like Tristan to keep us worrying. He wouldn't do that. Something's happened."

"You're right. We should've been out there searching long before now. What was I thinking?" Michael groaned and marched to the horses, where he discovered Thomas saddling Marley.

"You going?" Michael asked.

"I can't stay here waiting."

"I'll come with you."

"You sure?" Thomas looked off into the hills again. "Odds are he'll ride in after I'm gone. No sense in us both heading out in the cold."

"Give me a moment."

Thomas nodded and continued to lead his horse.

As soon as Michael grabbed the halter of his bay, someone called Tristan's name. Relieved, Michael strode back to camp ready to shout at Tristan for causing them all to worry. The angry words died before they reached his lips, for a wild-eyed Dun stood riderless and near the tents. Ethan and Thomas were kneeling in the snow beside a limp figure while James worked to soothe the horse. Michael ran to them but skidded to a stop upon reaching the others. Tristan was shaking and white-faced, with a long, black arrow piercing through his shoulder. Cradling Tristan in his arms, Thomas listened as the boy mumbled something that Michael couldn't make out.

"James, take the horses and get some water on the fire," Thomas commanded. "Ethan, bring me everything we'll need." Thomas looked at Michael, his expression grim. "Sammanon encampment, on the northwest side of the mountain."

"That can't be right. James was there yesterday and saw nothing." Michael's heart pounded, torn between anger and deep concern.

Thomas surrendered his son to Michael, who carefully shifted Tristan up to a sitting position, supporting the boy from behind. Shivering hard, Tristan moaned.

"Is there anything else I need to know?" Thomas urged Tristan, rubbing the boy's cold hands between his own palms.

"We can't wait to do this?" Michael rasped, knowing the answer before he even asked. Their survival depended on Tristan's answers. He jerked his cloak off and wrapped Tristan in it.

"No. Don't fuss, Michael," Tristan muttered. An absurd wave of fury overtook Michael at his words.

"Don't fuss? You have an arrow sticking out of your shoulder, and you're covered in your own blood! Why would I fuss?" His voice rose, but he tempered it when Tristan winced. Michael held the boy closer, fighting off tears. "I'm sorry," he whispered. "I'm upset."

Ethan hauled over his wooden medicine chest and handed Thomas a large pair of shears they used for trimming horse hooves. The sight had Tristan groaning, but it was better than trying to break off the tip by hand. Thomas snapped off the pointed end protruding from the back of Tristan's shoulder. "This is a big one, but untouched as far as I can tell," he murmured, examining the arrowhead before tossing it aside. Ethan had been prepping a needle and thread, while Thomas sorted through clean rags and handed some to Michael. "Be ready to help staunch it." Using his teeth, he uncorked a bottle of whiskey and poured some over Ethan's hands and his own, grunting at the liquid's potent smell. He gave a few more rags to Ethan, who placed himself in position behind Tristan near Michael.

"You'll need to brace him," Thomas directed Michael. To Tristan he said, "Son, this is going to hurt like the devil. Do you want me to warn you or no?"

Tristan hesitated before answering. "Tell me."

Until that moment, Thomas had been methodical, even brisk, but now the mask dropped. He cupped his son's face. Tristan attempted a feeble smile in response that almost broke his father's heart. Inhaling, Thomas took hold of the arrow shaft with hands that trembled.

"Dad, wait," Ethan said. "Let me do it."

"What?"

"It's going to hurt him, yanking it out. I don't want you to have to do that. I'm trained for this too. Let me. Please."

Ethan gazed at his father, his eyes steady and calm. Thomas released a shaky breath and switched places, coming around behind Tristan.

Ethan grasped the arrow shaft and looked at his younger brother. "Ready, Tris?"

Tristan nodded, and Michael tightened his arms to hold the boy even as a cold sweat broke over his own body.

Ethan removed the entire shaft with one swift motion, and Tristan cried out before he succumbed to a dead faint. All three men worked to staunch the blood that had begun to flow from both sides of the wound. With the arrow gone, they could remove Tristan's jacket and clothing, exposing the ravaged shoulder. Michael let out a shaky breath at the sight and Thomas patted his arm in sympathy. They both kept pressure on the wound while Ethan cleaned and stitched it, moving at a speed Thomas knew he could never match.

"How bad is it?" Michael demanded when Ethan finished. A tight smile passed over Ethan's face.

"He'll be well enough in a few months, barring infection. Couldn't have hit a better spot, if it had to happen. An inch down would have shattered the bone. Two inches farther, and he would have bled to death.

There's an important artery right there, and if it had been cut, he would have been dead in minutes."

"Ethan..." Thomas warned, raising an eyebrow.

"I could have done without knowing that," Michael muttered through a clenched jaw.

"Sorry." Ethan flushed. "This just nicked the top of the collarbone and tore up the muscle. It'll probably give him an ache or two in the cold weather forty years from now, but otherwise he'll be fine. Let's get him to the tent."

They bedded Tristan down under a heap of blankets in the canvas tent he shared with Michael. Ethan volunteered to sit with Tristan so the others could rest. Outside, James had fresh coffee brewing. Thomas sat on a log, and Michael collapsed on the frozen ground at his feet with a groan. James handed out mugs of coffee to them both and disappeared into the tent with a mug for Ethan. When James returned, Thomas hauled out more whiskey and poured a dollop into each of their mugs. They sipped their hot drinks in silence until Thomas reached over to touch Michael's shoulder.

"I'm sorry, Michael. This was my fault. I should have listened to you. If we had left weeks ago, this wouldn't have happened."

"No, let's be fair. Tristan discovered important information we would have missed if we'd been gone already. Your instincts keeping us here were right. I only wish we hadn't let him go alone. I can't bear to see him hurt."

"It won't be the last time."

"No," Michael whispered. "It won't."

Thomas kept his eyes on the tent where Tristan was resting. He dragged a weary hand over his face before telling Michael about the troops spotted in the mountains. "This is a large encampment. What are they doing up so high in the Appalachia at the onset of winter?"

Michael leaped to his feet, startling both Thomas and James, and kicked snow as he paced before them, muttering to himself. He darted a look at Thomas and raked a hand through his hair before taking a deep breath.

"Why do we go on with this, Dad? Why do we continue to live such a rootless existence for no purpose?"

"No purpose?"

"I had hoped when we found Tristan you would consider a different life. You went into border work with the hope of finding your wife and sons. We're together, and we know what happened to Mother."

"What's your point?"

"Your *son* was shot by a blasted arrow! He could have died! All because we come out here every summer and—" Michael stopped, dismayed to find himself close to tears. Thomas glanced at James with a slight jerk of his head.

"I'll go...check on the horses," James muttered, and he slipped away.

"Sit down, Michael."

"I want answers."

"I know but sit."

Michael huffed and settled himself beside Thomas, who filled both their mugs with more coffee.

"How many times have we prevented another war with the work we do?"

Michael shrugged. Thomas leaned forward, his forearms on his knees, warming his hands with the mug. He sat that way for a spell, staring into the fire before speaking in a husky voice.

"You ask fair questions. I'll try to explain, but I'm not sure I can. War is messy and bloody, and yet there's a sense of clarity to fighting. Aquila has never gone to war to conquer. They've been wars of defense, which makes them seem worthy of the price. Peacetime, however..." Thomas took another sip of coffee, drumming his fingers on the mug. Michael sat straighter and waited.

"Some men can handle seasons of peace. Take Andrew, for example. He can manage his estate and has many things to keep him occupied. He has a wife and children as well. I have no estate, no wife, and my sons are mostly grown. I have no daughters. Sometimes I think if I had daughters...But no, I was blessed with four exceptional sons, and that is an entirely different matter."

Thomas met Michael's gaze, his expression distraught.

"I hate war. I hate seeing men and boys slaughtered. And knowing someday those will be *my* sons out on that field, facing death..." Thomas paused, anguished. "I can do nothing to prevent war at home. However, out here I've seen what can be accomplished. We've delayed war several times, more than a decade, far longer than the normal span. I promise you, even after today, the mountains are safer than a battle. At least our work has bought you boys some time. It won't be long now before war arrives on our doorstep. Ethan will be safe enough as a healer. James has learned how to fight as well as any man. Anything can happen in war, but I think he'll come out of it. And I never worry about you. Tristan—I don't know." Thomas swallowed hard and heaved a shuddering breath, the deep love for his sons breaking past his usual stoicism. "We'll see. I wish he was older."

"Dad," Michael groaned. "I'm sorry, I didn't mean—"

"I know, son, and all is well. Anyway, what else would I do with my life? Even my position in court has no official status, and there are those in power who would oppose my obtaining any real military influence."

"Is this because of your father, or is there something else you haven't told me? Charlotte could—"

Thomas held up his hand. "No doubt the subject of my father, for those who know, is an issue. And I would argue my close friendship with the queen is not always helpful. Those accusations of being a social climber and rising above my appropriate station as an illegitimate son, and all that. Then there were those rumors when Lawrence killed himself. I must be careful to never put Charlotte in a compromised position to secure anything for myself."

"Your father *did* claim you."

"You think I would use the name of that man for my own gain?"

James wandered into view. "Is it safe to come back?"

"Get over here," Michael said, rolling his eyes but smiling. James plopped next to Michael with a heavy sigh.

"Dad? Are we sure Tristan got away clean? He was out cold when he arrived, barely in the saddle. He mumbled about keeping to the protocols, but at some point Dun made his own way here. Plus, they came in from the north instead of the south as usual."

"Yes, we'll need to leave at first light."

"Can Tristan even travel?" Michael asked.

"He'll have to." When Michael started to protest, Thomas persisted. "Would you rather we remain here to be killed when a scouting party finds us? Because I don't think we can handle more than a dozen scrub soldiers. Less if they're decent swordsmen. Also, we can't build much of a fire after this. We need to go."

Michael remained silent, knowing the truth of the words.

"It will be painful for him. I'm sorry about that. We'll keep him as comfortable as we can. I'll see what I have to dull the pain. You two get packing. I'll join you after I check on my boy."

Thomas pushed through the tent flap to see Ethan holding Tristan up for a drink of water.

"Can I have a moment?" he asked. Before Ethan slipped out, Thomas touched his arm and gave it a gentle squeeze. "Thank you, Ethan."

Ethan peeked back at Tristan. He shifted closer to his father and whispered, "He's really hurting, Dad. More than he'll admit."

"I know. We're packing and leaving at first light. Better get to work."

As Ethan left, Thomas knelt beside Tristan's bedroll.

"You must be in a great deal of pain, son. I'm sorry."

Wincing, Tristan croaked, "Not too bad."

"No question you are a Lockhart. As stubborn as Michael." He tugged a small bottle out of his pocket. "Here, try this. I want to see if it helps."

After Tristan drank, Thomas piled the blankets over him, tucking his son in. "You need to stay warm. It'll be freezing tonight. The boys and I will be busy packing. We have to get out of here, so we'll hit the trail tomorrow."

"I'll be all right." The boy took hold of his father's hand. "Don't worry about me, Dad."

A rush of emotion came over Thomas. He didn't want Tristan traveling, and Thomas carried an enormous burden of guilt that his son had been hurt. He had to clear his throat before replying, "I know you're strong, far stronger than the rest of us. And I'm proud of you."

Tristan's face brightened. "Truly?"

"No father could be more proud. Try to get some rest. I fear the journey will be hard on you."

Tristan cuddled under the blankets and closed his eyes. Thomas left the tent, cursing whoever had fired that arrow on the mountain.

The next few days were a misery for them all. Tristan tried to ride, but it was soon evident he couldn't stay on a horse even as steady as Dun. Thomas berated himself again and again for their predicament, however he remained stoic as he settled his youngest in the saddle in front of him. He sensed Tristan flinching with every bad step his horse took, but the boy never uttered a word of complaint.

Ethan and James broke through the snow, hoping to bear the brunt of the worst drifts and missteps, with Michael staying near to watch Tristan with his father. The boy's face was white, his eyes dim and inward. At times, Michael would take a shift riding with his brother. He held Tristan close, loath to hand him over even to Thomas when they dismounted.

They were out of the mountains when Tristan developed the fever. Michael prayed it was a sign of healing, but by the next day they could all see angry red streaks when Ethan cleansed the wound. They were passing small villages now and debated whether to stop or push on to Altair. In the end, they decided to continue their journey. Hard though it might be, Tristan would do better with the medicines the city could provide. Plus, the cold had become cruel, and none of them wanted to be trapped in a western village if a blizzard caught them.

By the time they reached Altair, Tristan was delirious.

# Chapter 19

# Shifting Sands

A soft hand brushed against Tristan's cheek. He cracked his eyes to see his mother leaning over him. Tristan mumbled, "I've missed you, Momma."

A feminine laugh washed over him, and lips pressed to his forehead.

Tristan's eyes flew open. At first, his vision remained clouded. He made out a girl sitting near his bed. She seemed a stranger, but he felt like he should know her. Her copper-gold hair spilled out of its bindings, and her green eyes shone. Whoever she might be, Tristan thought she was lovely, with such delicate features. She reminded him of the stories his mother would tell him of the sea fairies. It took Tristan several seconds to recognize her.

"Chris?" he gasped.

"Yes, are you mad? Who did you think I was?"

"I'm not—" Horror struck Tristan when he realized she was sitting *on* his bed, not near. What's more, he didn't have a stitch of clothes on him. Blankets aplenty, and he was well covered, but *definitely* no clothes. Panicked, he pawed at the blankets, bringing them up to his chin and wincing at the sharp pain shooting through his left shoulder. Christiana's sweet laughter bubbled forth, and Thomas came in, his face showing relief.

"Ah, there he is. Thank you, Christiana, would you mind...?"

With a last pat to Tristan's head and a giggle, Christiana left the room. Thomas's eyes followed her before sitting on the bed. Tristan shifted his position, relaxing in spite of his throbbing shoulder.

"How are you feeling?" asked Thomas.

"Very confused. When did we get to Altair?"

"A few days ago. What do you remember?"

"I'm not sure, to be honest. Bits and pieces. Us riding?"

"You were already having difficulties traveling, and then your injury showed signs of infection." Thomas inhaled a ragged breath. "I thought..."

Tristan noticed the exhaustion and deep lines etched into his father's face. His throat clogged thickly when he tried to speak. "I'm sorry I worried you, Dad."

"Shhh, you did nothing wrong. I'm thankful the fever broke. I wasn't sure it would, but Ethan is a fine healer." Thomas lit up with pride. "I had no idea how skilled he was already. I think he saved your life."

"Where is he?"

"He's been awake watching over you for days. I convinced him to go rest once we knew you were in the clear."

"I bet Michael has been worked up."

His father smiled at that. "You can't imagine. In fact, I should tell him you're awake. James will be relieved as well."

"Did you report to Andrew what I found?"

"Yes, and he appreciates the information. It could be important. Also, Michael and I have talked and...we won't be going back to the mountains. We're done with that."

"Really? We can stay here all year?"

"Until war comes, at least." Thomas searched Tristan's eyes. "Is staying here something you would like?"

"All of us here at home?" Tristan sighed as he sank into the pillows. "Yes."

Thomas started as a wave of guilt swept over him at his son's obvious satisfaction. Before he could say another word, the door to Michael's room slammed open. Wild-eyed, Michael peered at Tristan. Since Tristan was obviously on the mend, Michael took it upon himself to berate his brother for being such an idiot to allow himself to be shot by an arrow. Tristan could only reply with a wobbly grin before Michael had him in a tight hug.

Tristan chafed over his slow recovery. Christiana did her best to amuse him, but he couldn't shake the sense that something had changed between them. Never before had he given much thought to Christiana's appearance. Now Tristan would catch himself gazing at her and blushing furiously as his imagination wandered. Nevertheless, she was as charming and impulsive as always and while he remained bedridden, he looked forward to her visits.

But as winter progressed, Michael noticed a change in Tristan's behavior. He was edgier, moodier, with his typically cheerful disposition slipping in and out. Michael couldn't put his finger on it. Thomas claimed he saw nothing, but Michael didn't quite believe him. It was more than the usual aggravation of a boy his age. Tristan was especially unpredictable around Christiana, from laughing with her over some nonsense the two had concocted, to brushing her aside to tramp alone in the snow.

Michael thought Christiana had to be aware of it too, but she seemed undeterred by the boy's moodiness. Tristan always bounced back with such apologetic sweetness no one could stay angry with him. Still, Michael had a nagging feeling that Tristan and all his confused emotions would boil over sooner or later.

He didn't have to wait long.

One evening in late winter, they gathered in the common room as usual. Tristan was deep in a book while James and Christiana plotted a secret attack from the other side of the room. After a whispered consultation, Christiana leaned over the sofa from behind and plucked the book from Tristan's hands. Laughing, he made a lunge for her, pulling her down with him as they bounced off the sofa and onto the floor with a thump.

Michael couldn't help chuckling as he watched Tristan try to wrestle her into submission. He was much stronger than he looked and careful not to hurt the wild child he had on his hands.

Between laughter and the ache of his healing shoulder, Tristan quickly grew breathless. James tackled him from behind, and the two brothers romped before James knocked him flat on his back. Michael rolled his eyes when Christiana leaped onto Tristan's stomach. Tristan chortled as Christiana tickled him. She knew all his tender, ticklish spots and dove in without mercy.

Charlotte called, "Christy dear, do get off Tristan. You are positively barbaric."

"C'mon, Chris," Tristan panted mid-laugh. "My shoulder hurts, and I'm not your horse. Get off me."

Christiana giggled and paid no heed. Tristan stopped laughing. She was far too close, too near. Her hair fell over his face. Feelings he had been fighting to suppress for weeks threatened to overwhelm him.

"All right, Chris, enough!" Tristan was terrified of his own thoughts, wanting to take her in his arms and...he shoved the girl aside. "Get off!"

Tristan scrambled to his feet. The room fell silent. Christiana sat there, stunned. Everyone gawked at Tristan, who appeared disoriented.

"Stop it! Just stop it, Chris!" he spat out. "We aren't children anymore, you can't—you just can't—"

"What in the world?" asked Charlotte. Thomas stood and stared at his son, who was always gentle with Christiana.

"I'm sorry. I'm so sorry, I didn't mean..." Tristan gasped and gulped for air. "Are you hurt?" he asked Christiana. She shook her head, but tears filled her eyes. The tears undid him. Tristan ran his hand through his shaggy hair and mumbled another apology before stumbling out of the room.

"What was that?" James asked, perplexed.

Michael helped Christiana to her feet and hugged her. "He didn't mean it, sweetheart."

Her expression showed hurt bafflement. "What did I do?"

"You didn't do anything," said Thomas.

"I'll go talk to him," Michael muttered, wondering why in the world he was volunteering for this one. He had a feeling he knew the problem.

"Please don't be angry with him," Christiana pleaded. "It wasn't his fault. He asked me to stop, and I didn't."

Michael offered a kind smile. "I won't. I promise."

He found Tristan sitting on his bed, face buried in his hands. Michael spoke his name, not wanting to startle him. Tristan moaned without lifting his head. "I am so, *so* sorry. I don't know what came over me."

"Yes, you do." Michael patted his arm. "I think we've all seen this coming."

"What do you mean?"

"Come here." After tugging the chairs closer together, Michael sat down. "Let's have a talk."

The boy let out a low groan before faltering over to the chair. Michael spoke in a soothing tone. "All will be well. Tell me what happened."

Tristan didn't meet Michael's gaze. "Ever since we got back this winter, it's been different. She isn't the same. Or I'm not the same. I want..." Unwilling or incapable of saying more, Tristan fell silent. He looked at Michael, his dark blue eyes wide with intense curiosity. "What's it like to be with a girl?"

Michael started in his seat. "How the blazes should I know!"

"To kiss a girl, I mean!" Tristan flushed, horrified at what he had implied.

"Bloody hell!" Michael stared at his brother, realization dawning. "Are you in love with her?"

Tristan jumped to his feet. "What? No! How can you ask such a thing? That's—that's absurd!"

"It's not absurd!"

"She's nothing but a child, and—"

Michael dissolved into amused cackles at Tristan's description of Christiana. What he had thought would be a mundane conversation about clarifying the burdens of burgeoning manhood was becoming more interesting by the moment.

"Stop laughing!"

"You are *babbling*, Tristan! Listen to you. A child—she's *three* months younger than you!"

Tristan opened his mouth but clapped it shut again without speaking.

Michael wrangled with his thoughts. "You must apologize to Christiana. Regardless of your feelings about her in any other way. She is family, and I know you care about her a great deal. You must clear the air between you."

"What am I supposed to say?" Tristan's voice pitched higher.

Michael stood and waved his hands. "Stop being melodramatic. I don't think she'll need an explanation. Tell her it wasn't her fault and you're sorry."

"It *wasn't* her fault!"

"That's what I said!"

They stood glaring at each other, Tristan fuming. "Is that all, *sir*?" he asked in clipped tones.

"No, it is not!" Michael snapped. Tristan flinched. Michael sighed, trying to rein in his temper and not smack the boy on the head.

"No," he repeated, gentling his voice. "Listen. I'm sorry you've been struggling with these feelings. You should have talked to me or Dad long before, we might have been able to help. As it is, you are correct. You two are not children anymore. Christiana should know better at her age than to act like such a little hussy."

Tristan, whose anger had softened with Michael's first words, flamed again, and his voice rose even higher. "She's no such thing! How dare you insult her that way!"

"I was joking. You know I would never mean that," said Michael. "But you are very quick to defend her."

"And why wouldn't I? She's sweet and precious, and I won't allow you to—" Tristan choked on his words, his face growing pale.

A long silence followed, and Michael nodded, at last understanding. He opened his mouth, but Tristan stopped him with a shake of his head.

"Michael, please," he whispered, blinking back tears. "Please don't."

"What are you afraid of, Tris?" Michael asked. Tristan looked everywhere but at Michael, unable to speak. A great love for the boy overwhelmed Michael. He cleared his throat and placed his hands on the boy's shoulders, startled to realize Tristan was almost as tall as he was. "Apologize to Christiana. Make things right between you. I know you too well. It will eat you up if you don't. She's an important part of your life. Trust me, you do not want strife between the two of you."

Tristan slumped, and Michael gathered him into a warm embrace, thankful he didn't resist.

# Chapter 20

# Man Talk

Tristan managed to stay calm until he reached the door to the common room, then his heart started to pound. He paused, raised his eyes to heaven, and blew the air out of his cheeks. Upon entering the room, he groaned inwardly at the sight of his father sitting by the fire, reading. At least his brothers were gone. Tristan wasn't sure he could attempt this if James had lingered. Charlotte and Christiana were deep in conversation, but they stopped speaking when he entered.

"Your Grace. Father." He nodded to each, fidgeting. Thomas arched an eyebrow at Tristan's use of the word *father*, the name the boys reserved for formal gatherings. Choosing to ignore the imploring look his son gave him, Thomas returned to his book. Tristan strode over to the ladies, hoping he didn't appear as terrified as he felt.

Christiana shot off her chair in an instant with tears in her eyes. "Tristan! I'm sorry! I didn't mean—"

He blanched when he saw she had been weeping. A desire to hold Christiana sent a rush of warmth to his face, and he was grateful when her mother interrupted.

"Sit, Christiana. Tristan has come to speak, and we must allow him to do so. Please do learn to conduct yourself with some restraint." The queen's tone was kind but brooked no argument. Christiana dropped her gaze down to her hands, twisting them in her lap.

Tristan gulped some air. Christiana had broken into his thoughts, and he couldn't remember what he had been about to say. He glanced once more at his father, but Thomas had not stirred. After an awkward moment of shuffling about, he knelt on one knee.

"Your Grace, I behaved terribly a short time ago. I fear I have offended you as well as others present. I do beg your pardon."

Thomas snorted from behind his book, but beyond that there was silence.

"Get up, Tristan. Kneeling before me is ridiculous." The queen spoke as though she was fighting back laughter. "You're acting like you were about to be led to the executioner's block! And apologies to me are un-necessary. I thought your actions perfectly correct, given my daughter's behavior."

Tristan leaped to his feet and grinned, but he sobered when he looked at Christiana. Her eyes were red, and there were fresh tears on her cheeks. He wondered if Charlotte had been severe with her.

"Chris?"

He stepped toward her, suddenly shy. She averted her eyes. Tristan sank on both knees before her, but with none of the grandiosity he had demonstrated before her mother. He took both of her hands in his, marveling at how small they were. Christiana continued to keep her gaze lowered. Tristan's throat caught, and he found himself close to tears. When he managed to speak, his voice was not much more than a whisper.

"Chris? Dearest Christiana, I'm sorry. You are the last person I would ever want to hurt. You did nothing wrong, I swear! I was..." He choked as he wrestled with what to say. "Chris, the thought of causing you pain is awful. Please forgive me. I couldn't endure it if I thought you were upset with me."

Christiana lifted her bright green eyes to his. Tristan forgot anyone was in the room beyond the two of them clutching each other's hands. How long they remained that way, staring at one another, Tristan didn't know. His father coughed, and the spell broke. Christiana smiled, and Tristan forced a laugh, releasing her hands. Waving at them both, Charlotte urged them to go wash for dinner and ushered Tristan out of the room. He did as he was told but quite sure he couldn't eat a bite.

"You mean he actually knelt before Charlotte!" Michael hooted with laughter, almost falling out of his chair.

He often strolled to Thomas's room late in the evening, where they had a drink or two and talked after everyone else had gone to bed. When they were on the road, such privacy was impossible, but over the years it had become a ritual for them when wintering at the castle. On this night, Thomas had taken great delight in telling Michael about Tristan's apology, punctuated with outbursts of laughter.

"I shouldn't laugh. I'm sure Tristan was sincere in his approach, however, the boy does have a healthy streak of melodrama. He gets it from the Lockhart side." Thomas winked at Michael, who laughed again.

"Poor Tristan, he's in for some difficult times ahead, I'm afraid. I mean, we all know—well, everyone except Tristan it seems—Christiana has been sweet on him for years."

"Tristan is a handsome lad. I've seen village girls notice him, but I thought he was oblivious. Now I wonder," Thomas mused. "I will admit there was something between them today. The start of his apology to Charlotte was a superb performance of abject humility, and I swear he enjoyed it. But when he saw how upset Christiana was, he fell apart."

Michael didn't respond for a moment, for he had not told Thomas everything about his conversation with Tristan. He mulled over the complexities of lovesick youth. "I never want to have children." Michael moaned before chuckling. "I jest, but Tristan is an education."

"That he is. You've had the raising of him almost his whole life versus my few years. And you can hardly count when he was a babe."

Michael covered his surprise with a light laugh. "You trying to blame me?"

"Not at all." Thomas looked at Michael, pride and affection clear in his eyes. "I'm quite serious. I know I don't speak of such things often, but you are every bit as much of a father to him as I am. More so, in a way, with all the years in the Shadowlands. I can't tell you how I envy the extra time you had with him. You've done an excellent job with Tristan. He'll be a better man because of your influence."

"I appreciate that." For once, Michael was at a loss for words. Trying to sort through the emotions flooding his heart, he shifted the tone back into a jovial one. "I simply passed on what I've learned from you. Come to think of it, I don't recall you teaching me anything about girls. I had to figure that out on my own. I guess we made the same mistake with Tristan."

"I'm sorry you had to deal with that. Had I known Christiana was the issue, I would've taken care of it myself. Although heaven knows I'm no expert on that topic. But I'm sure you did a better job than I would have done."

"Oh, I doubt it. At one point I thought I was going to knock him to the floor. He called me *sir*, the impudent pup!"

Thomas burst out laughing. "I wish I had seen the two of you bellowing at each other. It must have been a sight to see! He's feeling his oats, that's for sure. It's a tough age. Almost a man but not, the responsibilities growing but not the privileges. At least I can trust Tristan and his sense of honor. Unlike that wild redhead I sired."

"James isn't bad, and you know it." Michael smiled into his drink. "He wouldn't touch a girl inappropriately any more than Tristan."

"I'm not sure. I worry what will happen when he's in an army camp and the whores descend upon him."

Michael shuddered. "What *will* you do with the boys if war comes?"

"If?" Thomas sighed. "You know it's a matter of time."

"I know."

"James will fight. He's of age, I can't stop him." Thomas overrode Michael, who had tried to interrupt. "Ethan will serve with the healers and surgeons. He should be safe there."

"And Tristan?" Michael tensed.

"Tristan is a problem. He won't like being left out. Otherwise, I would keep him holed up here. He'll be sixteen in June. We know there will be boys his age—boys even younger—fighting. You don't suppose we can convince him to stay here?"

Michael thought of Christiana but shook his head. "He'll want to be with us."

"That's what I thought. I'm thinking courier. It's not perfect, but safer than the front, and he's an excellent rider. It's the best I can think of for him."

Michael nodded, still unsure. There was a long pause before Thomas spoke again.

"You joked about not wanting children. Do you think you will ever marry?"

"Haven't had much of a chance, have I?" Michael retorted. "We've spent years wandering around for months on end. It's no life for courting a woman, let alone a wife and children. Maybe I can think about it now if we're going to stop roaming about like gypsies."

Taken aback by Michael's tone, Thomas sipped his drink before responding. "I never knew you felt that way. You didn't have to keep working with us. You could have settled at your estate or here in Altair. It's not too late. Charlotte can find a place for you, a position deserving of your rank."

"That's not what I—I don't want that. I just meant, I like the idea of staying in one spot for at least a year. Get a feel for what having a real home is like."

Thomas flinched as he heard the echo of Tristan's words from weeks ago. Home. He had wanted nothing more than to escape from his own home growing up and had never considered all these years *home* was the very thing his sons needed.

"I'm sorry."

"It's fine, Dad."

Thomas fiddled with his glass, trying to marshal his thoughts. In an attempt to ease the conversation onto safer ground, he gave a light chuckle. "Whatever happened between you and the Kavanaugh girl? I know you were sweet on her."

"That might be overstating it," Michael said with a laugh.

"Henry Loeffler's daughter is—"

"Are we really doing this? And Maggie's taller than I am."

"How about Lord Tilney's—"

"What's come over you? Besides, she's betrothed."

"I want you to be happy. And she's not. She broke it off over the summer."

Michael blinked and sat straighter. "She did?"

"She's lovely."

"I hear she's a handful," Michael mused, but a sparkle came into his eye.

Thomas winked. "Might be fun."

"Well, perhaps."

"Maybe after we return from our trip south you can pay her a visit."

"Tell me again why we're going down there? You promised we were through with this."

"It's a few weeks in early summer, that's all."

"Lord MacClaren has his own people. Why can't he take care of this?"

"You know why. And it's complicated. MacClaren knows things. About my family. I would rather not rock the boat and do him this favor."

"You can't keep that secret forever."

"I know. I'll have to tell James soon. At least before the war. But let's not go back to that. How about a toast? To Lord Tilney's daughter?"

Michael laughed and raised his glass.

Michael watched Tristan and Christiana with a new perspective over the next few days. He hurt for the boy struggling with his feelings concerning the winsome girl who had long ago endeared herself to Tristan's heart. For Michael, it was bittersweet to see Tristan on the verge of manhood and going down a road he couldn't follow.

One evening when winter was tiptoeing into spring, Michael sat in the common room writing at the desk while Tristan had settled down with a book. Despite making a great show of wanting to sit alone, he huddled in the corner of the large sofa rather than taking a chair. When Christiana entered the room, she sat primly on the chair opposite the sofa with her own book. At first, Tristan seemed relieved she had kept her distance. But the boy's eyes flitted up with increasing frequency. He shifted in his seat, restless. Eventually Tristan spoke.

"See here, Chris."

"Hmm?" Christiana responded without taking her eyes from her book. Michael stifled his laughter. Tristan tried again.

"Do come here and read this passage. It's quite interesting."

"I will in a moment, perhaps," she replied, still not looking up. "You can see I have a book already."

Tristan snorted and returned to his book with a kind of sad bafflement showing on his face. Michael was torn between feeling sorry for Tristan and the battle to suppress his own amusement. Christiana tossed her book aside and walked over to the sofa. Unexpectedly, she nestled against Tristan and tugged the book out of his hands.

Tristan gazed at her. A soft tenderness showed in the boy's eyes that Michael had never seen before, and his own laughter died away. Tristan adjusted his position and tentatively stretched his arm around Christiana's shoulders, bringing her closer. Michael hoped he could hold that picture in his mind for the rest of his life—her head resting on Tristan's shoulder, and his head bent to hers, glossy dark hair blending with burnished gold.

His heart aching with both joy and an odd sense of loss, Michael left the room.

# Chapter 21

# The Degenerate Age

With the arrival of spring, Tristan found himself easy with Christiana again. He couldn't say what had changed, for there remained a tumult of confusion whenever she came near him. Yet, somehow, he gentled his temperament. Her feelings were his priority, and he restrained himself lest he do anything that might hurt her.

On one of their last evenings together, Ethan brought Brother Daniel with him from the abbey. This caused great excitement, for Brother Daniel was a storyteller of renown. In his early thirties, the monk was dark of skin with a clean-shaven head and unnaturally tall. The quiet man declined to dine with them, preferring a simple meal of soup in the kitchens.

After supper, everyone gathered together in the common room. Brother Daniel stood in front of the fireplace and surveyed the group. When his eyes fell upon Tristan's face, he froze, staring at the boy. Tristan himself only had thoughts for Christiana just then, for she had plopped herself down next to him and snuggled close, her head resting on his shoulder. Brother Daniel jerked his gaze away from Tristan and began to speak.

"I shall tell you the story of our history, which begins with the Degenerate Age."

At these words, an appreciative murmur filled the room. Almost everyone but Tristan had heard this story before. Though not long, it was one of Brother Daniel's best.

"From the moment of creation, the children have warred against their Father. This has always been the struggle and the curse. Even after the Great Sacrifice of Heaven, the children continued to stray. The stories of the Ancient Ones are complex and murky, for much was lost in the Second Fall. We know they created beauty and strife. Patterns emerged, patterns of birth and death, of peace and war. The same patterns, over and over through millennia. Always they sought their own greatness, always the vanity of the children. Yet the power of the Great Sacrifice held sway in the world, and if the children had but remembered the Father, they would have been saved. Then came the Degenerate Age.

"The Degenerate Age knew no Father. They denied the Great Sacrifice. Babel was a legend to mock and surpass as they built cities beyond all that had been seen before. Instead of seeking the restoration of the Father's glory, they sought their own greatness.

"They learned a powerful magic and with it commanded light and movement. They studied the art of flight. In a single day, they could travel hundreds of miles without the use of horses. Their magic could create beauty, yes, but it was surpassing dangerous—a sorcery that enabled them to build cursed weapons which could lay waste to entire cities, entire nations. They defiled creation with this power. The magic pulled them from the Father and into themselves. They grew to believe themselves to be the source of that power, equal to the Father.

"We do not know how the Second Fall began. Was it the Father wiping clean a desecrated creation, or their own magic that overwhelmed them? We do know there were plagues, famines, and wars. They rolled over and over each other like the waves of a great ocean. Relentless. Without mercy. Soon, few remained.

"Their power had relied on their numbers. Alone, they became as animals, retaining their soul and intellect but living in chaos. Flung back to the very dawn of time, they lived a tormented life, with memories of a past that no longer existed and hope for a future no longer theirs to claim. Still, the Father watched out for them. For a Remnant remembered the Great Sacrifice.

"The surviving children struggled, but their numbers increased. A few, precious few, had the foresight to gather up their knowledge and store it as best as they could. Some had a keen understanding of what should be saved and sorted through it carefully. Through these we retained some vital histories, some crucial intelligence, some tattered threads of knowledge. They had great learning of the body but relied on medicines too far beyond the reach of their ability. The wisest among them reignited ancient paths to healing through the plants, whose vitality had never forsaken us, even when we abandoned them.

"Our worship renewed, without the splintering to weaken the whole. Knowledge crept back, with warnings from the past. The chaff fell from the grain.

"The years crawled by. Cities crumbled, although their ghosts remain. Creation healed, but with scars from the Degenerate Age, which had sought to control it all. Rains fell, rivers swelled, and dams burst, rearranging the land. The seas crashed, and the retaining walls that held the waters captive became as dust. Ships no longer sailed the world, leaving all isolated and without voice.

"Years and years and years passed. Far too many to count, too many with no testimony. The children grew in number once again, and villages, cities, kingdoms emerged. To tell of the lost millennia alone would take years. What we know is every century that passes, every year—nay, every day—brings us closer to the great restoration. We see signs of the Rising. Ancient creatures long thought extinct are being restored to the land. The glory of the Father is returning to the world, though most cannot yet understand it. Eden will be renewed, for the day is coming when kings will be gardeners and not warriors. Kings who heal, not destroy. Indeed, some believe the seeds of these righteous kings are beginning to take root."

At this point, Brother Daniel sat, and silence filled the room. Tristan, who had never before witnessed formal storytelling in Altair, looked around, expecting something to happen. Michael indicated for him to remain silent. Brother Daniel rose and spoke once more.

"I take up my tale again with Aquila, the Great Eagle, and Altair, City of the Star. Aquila and Woodraven spread their wings and rose together. The realms were closely linked, with the ruling families intermingling, keeping them in a separate but peaceful alliance. The many small kingdoms of the south rested safe in the shadow of these mightier nations. For hundreds of years, peace and joy reigned. However, peace in this world is the grand illusion, and the splintering began again. Three men fractured our history, altering our course forever.

"For in those days there were two sons of the king in Aquila. The first was the heir, noble and strong. The second loathed his brother's position, for he had a black heart. This dark prince gathered armies and rebelled. Failing, he removed himself from Aquila instead of accepting the forgiveness of a generous brother, vowing vengeance and destruction. He took his forces west over the mountains, a feat unheard of then.

Some say he struck a bargain with the Evil One, giving him eternal rule. Others believe he passed, as we all must, but his seed had already been sown. Generation after generation arrived, holding the same black heart, the same thirst for blood, and the same name—Sammanon. This name has remained an evil to the people of Aquila.

"Many years would pass until his numerous children would return to inflict themselves upon us. In those days we did not know what Sammanon would become, and the rebellion was considered a minor interruption to the tranquility of Aquila's history. Then came the rise of Mohan."

At these words, Thomas rose and paced about the room. Tristan noticed Michael shooting furtive looks at their father but had no time to wonder why.

"Again, a second son of a king chafed at his position and wanted a kingdom to rule. Any of the southern kingdoms would have accepted Mohan, for he was a great man, but he did not desire the small and inconsequential. He could not force himself upon the throne of Aquila, for even he dared not aim so high. In those days, the Woodraven king was weak. Mohan gathered his own armies and conquered Woodraven with promises to leave their king as ruling steward. The foolish king gave himself up only to have his head struck from his body. Mohan stole the throne for himself, and his seed rules Woodraven to this day.

"Thus began a new era in our alliance with Woodraven, our brother, strange and uneasy. We abhor its rule, deny its heritage, reject its morals. Likewise, they have remained the jealous brother of the glory of Aquila. It is due to our mutual survival against Sammanon that we endure our discordant union.

"The last rebellion of the sons is well known to our people. Good King Emery defied tradition to break the law of elder inheritance, choosing instead to pass the crown to his younger son, Tristan. This proved to be wise, for Edmond was rash and impetuous, viewing the throne for his own gain and not for the good of the people. Tristan was gentle, compassionate, and wise, though some feared he would be too weak for the travails of leadership. But he had a backbone of fine steel and would prove to be fierce for his beloved country.

"Passed over, Edmond rebelled as did his ancestors and threatened death for the throne. Tristan, however, was one of the Faithful, and in all things tried to reflect the Great Sacrifice. He found it unbearable to see his people armed against one another and offered his life for the sake of theirs. He walked out to meet his rebellious brother, unarmed and facing death bravely. But then something unexpected happened. Edmond's love for his brother was more than his love of power. Would that Mohan and Sammanon had known how to love so well! For in the moment Edmond raised his sword to strike down his brother, he cast it aside and fell to his knees, begging forgiveness. The brothers embraced and wept. The blood of the people was spared, and Tristan lived.

"This, as we all know, began the reign of Tristan, a great king of Aquila. The years of his rule were some of our brightest. Edmond removed himself from court, content. With years, he grew wise and great himself, establishing the noble House of Lockhart. Edmond never again pursued the throne, seeing Tristan as his better in all things."

Tristan stared in amazement at Michael, who gave him a sheepish smile. At last, he understood why his brother had always refrained from discussing his true family name of Lockhart. If King Emery had allowed his eldest son to rule, Michael himself might now be king. With a shock, Tristan realized he and his brothers were also descendants of Edmond and King Emery through their mother. Distracted by these thoughts, he didn't notice the room had gone silent again. Brother Daniel stood still, his face altered, rigid and stiff. He spoke in a cold monotone.

"But the story is always being written. The future becomes the past, and the past informs the future. Aquila, the Great Eagle, is locked in a deadly battle of destiny. Decades of war with Sammanon, tensions with Woodraven, and the disjointed kingdoms of the south—all these threaten her survival. You here tonight—the Royal House of Reynard, House of Lockhart, and yes, the House of Thatcher—you all have roles to play. Young and old. Especially House Thatcher."

Michael shifted in his seat. This story had been passed around Altair for years, but it usually ended with the reign of King Tristan. And never had Michael heard of the House of Thatcher, a name indicating the status of nobility. He glanced at Charlotte, who was studying the storyteller through narrowed eyes. Thomas's quiet agitation ceased, and he stopped pacing to stare at Brother Daniel, who continued speaking in the same distant voice.

"Three sons of Aquila rebelled. I see before me three sons of Aquila who may mend all. Three brothers with great destinies, should they accept them. For there is always a choice. The eldest is already on his path. Time will tell if the waves break for him. The second's fortunes are hazy, for his destiny is tied with the others. And the youngest...ah, the youngest." Brother Daniel looked intently into Tristan's eyes. Icy shivers ran up and down the boy's spine.

"Oh, young Tristan, son of Aquila, son of Woodraven, son of King Tristan's own noble heart. You have stumbled upon an ancient tale. You will wage war against your destiny. But if you can bear its burdens, the circle will come round to you. You must—"

"Be quiet!" Christiana cried out, leaping to her feet.

Almost everyone jumped at the interruption. Brother Daniel and Tristan remained unmoved, their gazes locked on each other. A long silence followed before Brother Daniel swerved his glassy eyes to the princess, and he paced deliberately toward her. His own connection broken, Tristan shook his head to clear it.

Brother Daniel stepped closer and closer to Christiana, so near he could touch her if he chose. With a hoarse whisper, Brother Daniel spoke. "Never fear, little one. You too will help mend the breach. Your destinies are tied and intertwined forever."

Tristan sprang up and shoved Brother Daniel back. "Enough!" He clutched Christiana in his arms, his heart pounding with a terror he couldn't identify.

Thomas strode forward as Brother Daniel sank to his knees. The man knelt there, rocking and holding his head. Michael grabbed both Tristan and Christiana and dragged them from the room with James following.

"What was that?" James demanded, but Michael had no answer. Instead, he raised his eyebrows questioningly at Tristan. The boy walked a short distance from the others with Christiana, holding her, stroking her hair, hoping to soothe her.

Tristan had never held her like this before. As he wrapped his arms around her small frame, there was an unfathomable sweetness in the embrace. He caught a whiff of her hair, and his heart galloped faster. In that moment, Tristan knew he would do anything to protect her. Christiana tried to smile, but her lips trembled.

"Don't fuss," Tristan whispered. He cupped a hand to her cheek and leaned his forehead against hers. "Ghost stories, that's all."

Charlotte came into the entry hall, seeking Christiana. She exhaled with relief upon finding her.

"Well, this has been an unexpectedly eventful evening. Thank you, Tristan, you were very gallant. Christiana, dear, let me take you to your room." Charlotte disentangled her daughter from Tristan and led her away. Tristan was reluctant to release her and continued to watch Christiana until she disappeared from his sight. He rejoined Michael, who had been observing them with great interest.

"What happened back there?" Tristan demanded.

"I have no idea."

"That man is a monster!" Tristan would have said more, but Thomas joined them.

"Ethan is escorting Brother Daniel to the abbey. How are you?" Thomas asked Tristan.

"I'm fine." In truth, Tristan felt strangely weak and exhausted, but he chose to ignore it. "I'm just worried about Chris. She was terribly upset. What's going on, Dad?"

"Brother Daniel is from the family of Luminarium. Light Seekers. They are said to have the Sight. I don't know. I never believed in it before, and yet tonight was unusual." Thomas hesitated, as though weighing each thought before speaking. "Don't be angry with Daniel. He had no control over what happened, nor does he have any memory of what he said."

"It's always a fun, lighthearted evening until death and mayhem starts happening," James muttered. Michael chuckled, but Tristan didn't see the humor in it. They all made their way through the castle to their own corridor and Tristan remained deep in thought until they reached the door to his room. He followed his father and Michael into the chamber, with James on his heels.

"Those things he said about Sammanon. Why has no one alive today ever seen their king?" Tristan demanded. "Do they even have a king? What if he did strike a deal with—"

"Maybe it's a ghost king," James whispered dramatically as he passed through to Michael's room.

"I know it's not a ghost king!" Tristan yelled after him. "But are they normal? The Sammanon people? No one has ever been to the other side of the mountains and come back to tell us."

"You're right, Tris. All these stories of our armies fighting them were lies to cover up the fact that they were actually hideous demons." Michael cuffed Tristan on the head. "Don't be an idiot. I've lived among them, remember?"

"But you were still on our side of the mountains."

Michael scoffed. "They're flesh and blood, the same as the rest of us."

James emerged from Michael's room, holding the Lockhart sword aloft. "I hear they turn to dust once you stick them with this sword."

"Give me that!" Michael made a grab for the weapon, huffing in exasperation. "And they do *not* turn to dust."

James cackled. Frustrated and struggling for words, Tristan tried again.

"Brother Daniel said—"

"Don't get caught up with the mystics, Tristan," Thomas said. "I've seen what happens to those kinds of men. You'll be seeing magic on every corner if you go down that path. Those days are long gone, if they even existed, which I doubt."

Tristan froze. His gaze snagged Michael's before he shifted his eyes to the Lockhart sword, remembering the tingling sensation the first time he held it. Whatever had happened that day, it wasn't something he could explain. Michael caught his look and sobered. Exasperated with the whole affair, Thomas put his hands on Tristan's shoulders, his face stern. "This isn't a fairy tale, son."

A few days later, the Thatchers gathered to depart for their trip to the southern reaches of the kingdom. Queen Charlotte and Christiana came to the stableyard to see them off as usual. Christiana had been subdued since the storytelling, and Tristan did not want to leave her.

They each said goodbye to Christiana and the queen, but before he mounted Dun, Tristan broke away. He ran back to Christiana, catching her in a strong hug.

"I'm sorry I've been such an ass all winter," he whispered. "You mean the world to me, you know that?"

After a slight hesitation, he kissed her cheek. Her face lit up with a smile Tristan knew would stay with him in the weeks to come. All too aware of the dancing joy in his own heart, he sauntered over to Dun and jumped onto his horse.

Michael leaned over from his saddle and grinned at Tristan. "Nice move, Tris," he whispered.

"Oh, hush up, Michael."

However, Tristan couldn't help but grin back.

# Chapter 22

# Monsters in the Willows

The morning sun was already casting off heat as they rode from Altair. Tristan's thoughts remained at the castle, and hours passed before he grasped the fact that they were heading south and not west, on a road he had never been on before.

"Where are we going again?" Tristan asked, surprised. They all stopped and stared at him.

"You have got to be joking," James proclaimed. Ethan laughed, and Michael rolled his eyes. Tristan thought his father couldn't decide whether to be amused or exasperated.

Thomas kicked his horse into an easy trot and called out, "The southern border."

"The southern border? And, why? I forgot." The others ignored him and rode on, and he had no choice but to follow. Michael brought his horse alongside Dun.

"I knew you'd been in a daze these past few weeks, but c'mon. We've been talking about this for a while. There's been trouble with some roving gangs in the south. It's not clear if they're invaders from the

Shadowlands or…" He slanted his eyes at Tristan, unwilling to say the rest.

"Rounders?"

"Maybe. But there are no reports of people being forced further west."

Tristan shifted in his saddle. "And what are we supposed to do about it? Sail in with our army of five?"

"What we always do, Tris." Michael sighed wearily. "Watch, listen, report. I suppose if they are vagabond thieves we might take them on ourselves, we'll see. Otherwise, we stay out of trouble and do the usual."

Tristan had no memory of packing and wondered if he had the right clothes for summer in the south instead of the cooler mountain ranges, but he didn't dare say a word about it. Michael cut into his thoughts.

"I checked your bags and made sure you had packed properly. It was clear you weren't in your right mind."

Tristan glared at Michael. Given the circumstances, he decided to let it pass. Rather, he asked, "Why us? Anyone can do that."

Michael remained silent for several minutes before speaking. "Listen. James knows this. I'm not sure if Ethan does, but he will, so I might as well tell you. War is coming again, and soon. It's been building up for a year or more, and I expect we'll be fighting before too long. This is something we can do to stay productive without going too far. At least until we know what's happening."

Alarmed, Tristan glanced behind them. "Is Altair safe?"

"By which you mean, is Christiana safe? Yes, of course she is, are you daft?"

"Well, I don't know! You say war is coming, what am I supposed to think?"

"It doesn't just magically pop up at Castle Altair without anyone noticing!"

Tristan grumbled to himself. After some thought, he peeked over at Michael riding beside him, looking every inch a warrior. Curious, he ventured to ask, "Have you ever fought in a war?"

"For a short time. I fought in the last one, toward the end." Michael hesitated, considering his words. "I was about your age now. Things were already winding down, and I didn't fight long. It was after that war that we left Aquila to head south. Although training in the Sammanon army was no joke. Might as well have been at war. And by the way, James has never fought in one. Don't let him tell you any stories to the contrary."

"Did you grow up wanting to be a soldier like James?"

"Not particularly, although I always enjoyed the training."

"Then why?"

"Why did I learn to fight? Why do you learn? Being a soldier isn't about glory and honor as much as duty. We have to protect our land, our way of life, and protect those we love. Our brother's motives are good, and I do believe James will make an excellent career soldier, but it's not what he thinks it is. He'll find out soon enough. War is a nasty business."

"Will I have to fight in this war?" asked Tristan.

Michael studied the boy with love and pride. Tristan had grown over the winter and lost the ungainliness of youth. His rich baritone ranged deeper than before, though it still cracked on occasion. He sat straight-backed on his horse like a young centaur, his hand resting on his sword hilt. Tristan would never be very tall, but he was strong and handsome, with those intelligent deep blue eyes and shaggy hair that was always too long. A prince among men, Andrew had said years ago.

"Not if I can help it," Michael said grimly.

They discovered the first signs of distress near the southern border. Frightened villagers spoke of violence and thievery, farmers told of barns set on fire, and everyone seemed spooked.

"Why are we even here, Dad?" James asked one night as they gathered before the fire. They had picked up a flagon of ale at a nearby village and were having a quiet celebratory drink in honor of Tristan's sixteenth birthday. "Isn't this MacClaren territory? He must have his own people to take care of these things."

Tristan caught his father and Michael exchanging a look so subtle he wasn't sure anyone else noticed. However, Thomas only said, "We go where the queen commands."

"Anyway," James said, "at least it doesn't sound like Rounders."

"Why?" asked Ethan.

"Rounders are kidnappers. They work fast and don't bother with all this nonsense. These are thieves, and destructive ones at that. But nobody has gone missing. Dead, yes. Missing? No."

"Death and destruction, that's all. What a relief," murmured Tristan. Michael started to laugh but sobered too quickly, and unease skittered down Tristan's spine.

"What are you two grumbling about?" Tristan demanded as he and Michael led their horses to the lake for water. They had already packed camp and hoped to hit the trail before the full blast of the July sun was upon them. They were all ready to move, or so Tristan thought. But Thomas and James were bickering as they dug into their bags, searching through their equipment.

"Girth strap broke," James muttered when Tristan asked. "Trying to find the stuff to fix it."

"The saddle repairs? They're right over—hold up, I'll show you." Tristan handed Dun's reins to Michael and located what James needed. He examined the strap. "This is going to take a while."

"I don't want to lose the morning," grumbled Thomas.

"We won't," Michael said. "Tristan and I will go ahead. We'll scout the path around the lake and find the next campground, and you three can catch up with us later. What do you think, Tris?"

"Doesn't matter to me. Our horses are ready to go. Whatever Dad says."

Thomas thought for a moment. "Fine. Stick to the trail we already mapped out. We'll be along as soon as we can."

"Ethan, want to come?" Tristan called out to his brother, who was crouched at the lake's edge, talking to a plant.

"Ah, no. I'm going to..." Ethan's voice trailed off as he stroked the plant, whispering to it. Tristan caught Michael's eye and restrained himself from laughing out loud.

"Right. Let's go."

They mounted their horses and with a wave goodbye to the rest, Michael and Tristan set out. After some time of riding in silence, Michael ventured to say, "I haven't seen you write to Christiana. Funny, because we have almost constant access to couriers down here. You could write as much as you want."

"I don't know what you're talking about," Tristan said haughtily.

"Don't dodge."

Tristan groaned and kicked a rock. "I'm not sure what to say to her."

"You parted on what appeared to be excellent terms." Michael's voice held a hint of a chuckle.

Tristan shrugged.

"C'mon, Tris, you always miss her. I've seen it every summer. I'm not James. I won't tease you about it. Not much, anyway."

"I know. Thanks for that."

The trail passed through a dense willow thicket. Since the lake lay nearby on the left, they veered right. The weather had turned funny, with a thick fog cutting through the morning sunshine. They both dismounted, and Tristan led Dun along a narrow path, with Michael and his horse following behind.

"You're not sleeping at night. Haven't for weeks, even back at Altair. Thinking of her?"

"Nothing gets past you, does it?"

"Not with you anyway." Michael grinned. "What is it, Tristan? Can't you tell me?"

But Tristan was leaning over the damp ground. He pointed to a set of hoofprints in the earth.

"A few hours old." Michael surveyed the area. All seemed peaceful enough. "I don't think it's anything to worry about, but let's stay alert."

They continued along their makeshift path with Tristan in the lead and ignoring Michael. After a few frustrated attempts to get his attention, Michael bent and picked up a nice, round stone. He lobbed it at Tristan's back. His brother swore and glared at Michael with fire in his eyes. Michael gave him such a pointed look that Tristan burst out laughing.

"What do you want me to say?"

"We were discussing a beautiful young lady."

Tristan groaned. "The truth is, I don't know if I'm even good enough for her."

"Not good enough for her! Whatever gave you that idea?"

"Well, her family…" Tristan mumbled.

"You're a Lockhart," Michael said stoutly. "That's more than enough."

"*And* a Thatcher. Dad's a bastard, you know."

Michael cringed at the word. "Don't say that. And listen, there are things about Dad you don't understand. You're right, he's a—still, he's not unacknowledged. Dad knows who his father is, and his father has claimed him." Michael huffed with frustration. "I shouldn't even be talking about this. However, I can assure you there's nothing to make your suit inappropriate, if that's what you want."

"What if she doesn't care for me?"

"Now I know you're daft."

Tristan snorted and continued to lead the way. He stopped without warning, and Michael almost walked into Dun's rump. Tristan's voice floated back to Michael, soft and quiet.

"I love her, Michael."

"I know," said Michael. He forced his tone to stay light. "Just figuring this out?"

"No, I've known for a long time." Tristan's words dropped so low Michael struggled to make them out. "A very long time."

Tristan resumed walking. Dun nickered and tossed his head. Michael was too distracted with Tristan's declaration to notice, but Tristan gave his horse a thoughtful pat. A few moments later, Dun whinnied. Tristan stopped and rubbed his muzzle. This time Michael's face landed in Dun's whisking tail.

"C'mon, Tristan, quit stopping in the middle of the trail!" he called. Tristan didn't respond. Instead, he whipped his head around, trying to peer into the fog.

"What's—"

"Quiet, Michael!"

The sight of Tristan grasping his sword hilt made Michael's fingers twitch for his own. Dun pawed the ground and nickered again.

"Shh, Dun, don't talk," Tristan whispered, patting Dun. He called over his shoulder at Michael. "There's a horse nearby. One Dun doesn't know."

They both stiffened at the snap of a branch. The fog was thicker than ever, and it distorted the sounds around them. Another snap, this time from the opposite direction. They looked at each other. Michael drew his sword, and Tristan led both horses a short distance farther into the willows before rejoining his brother.

"To my back," Michael whispered. Tristan shifted his position. His heart pounded as he checked for his dagger and unsheathed his own sword. Fingers trembling, he gripped the hilt so tightly the whole weapon shook.

Trying to ease Tristan's fears, Michael quipped, "How's your shoulder these days?"

"Not bad. Glad I'm not left-handed."

Another crackle of a willow branch to Tristan's right.

"The fog. I can't see anything." Tristan was ashamed to hear his voice shaking. In contrast, Michael sounded steady, even casual.

"Don't worry. Use your ears, not your eyes. Deep breaths. If there's only one or two, let me handle it."

The ambush came so fast Tristan didn't have time to register the hulking shadow before it attacked Michael. He hung back, watching their blades flash before another figure raced toward him. A glimmer of steel flashed. Tristan swung his sword up, blocking the strike. The impact sent tremors along his arm. The fear left him, and his focus sharpened.

His opponent was a hooded behemoth of a man, and Tristan fought purely on the defensive.

Tristan found his rhythm, but the beast slipped into the fog. Lowering his sword, he saw Michael alone as well, breathing hard and staring into the willows. His brother swung around to look Tristan over.

"I'm good," Tristan panted.

Out of the mist, the large man attacked Michael, and a smaller swordsman slashed at Tristan. Also hooded, this fighter moved much faster. Tristan struggled to match his opponent's speed, and his heart thrummed with fear. He leaped from a vicious sideswipe, lost his footing, and fell.

The man's sword came straight at him. He rolled, and the blade stabbed dirt before it was jerked up. The enemy struck again and again at Tristan, who could do no more than block with his own sword while still on his backside. He cried out for Michael in a panic as his sword was knocked away.

With a yell, Michael barreled into the man. He drove his blade into the fighter, then kicked his body to the ground. Rushing to Tristan, Michael hauled him to his feet.

"Are you hurt? Tell me!"

Tristan gasped for air but waved a hand to indicate he was fine. Two bodies lay before them, and blood trickled down Michael's head.

"They're toying with us," Tristan wheezed.

"Yes," he said grimly. "I'm not even sure how many—"

An arrow whizzed so close to Tristan's head that a wisp of air blew across his temple. He dropped, dragging Michael with him, but not before a second arrow passed through Michael's right shoulder. Bone crunched, and Michael screamed.

Tristan crouched on one knee. A hooded archer stood at the edge of the thicket. Tristan yanked his dagger free and threw it with all the strength he could muster. The archer howled and slunk back into the willows. Tristan turned to Michael, who was struggling to sit.

"Michael! Can you—" Michael's eyes widened. Tristan spun in time to block a downward strike. He leaped to his feet and stood over Michael.

The hooded man laughed with derision, and Tristan's knees grew weak. He was a joke to them, waving his shiny sword. He didn't have much strength left. But when Michael moaned in pain, he renewed his grip on his weapon.

Tristan charged, twisted left and brought his sword around. The hooded foe blocked the stroke and drove his blade at Tristan's gut. Tristan jumped aside and parried. Their swords clashed multiple times. Tristan slipped. Taking advantage, the villain slashed his blade across Tristan's waist. He gasped and doubled over.

Clutching his hand to the wound, Tristan heaved a breath at the rush of hot blood seeping between his fingers. The man strode forward with his sword raised. Tristan tried to straighten but flailed and sank to his knees, his vision blurred. The clash of steel rang in his ears. Michael stood on his feet again, fighting left-handed. There was a strange, wet sound followed by a rending groan. Then silence. Tristan's sight cleared in time to see Michael fall once more.

Cold rage consumed him as Michael lay struggling in the damp grass. The hooded man raised his blade for a killing strike. A feral wrath unleashed itself. All Tristan knew was a wild urge to protect at all costs. He clenched his jaw and launched himself from the ground. The man swiveled on his feet, but it was too late. Tristan's sword had pierced him through, and with a savage twist, Tristan brought him down.

# Chapter 23

# The Last Homecoming

Tristan stood, shaking in his passion. With a harsh sound in the back of his throat, Tristan yanked his sword out of the man, who collapsed at his feet. He held his blade high, but no more attackers emerged. All was silent except for the steady drip of the fog. He remained still, staring at the body. His cold anger subsided, replaced by a paralyzing fear that he had killed a man. A horse galloping in the distance interrupted the silence.

"Tris...Tristan..."

Tristan staggered to Michael, dragging his sword along the ground. He wanted to throw it far, far away but didn't dare in case more marauders were lurking about. He kept a tight grip until he sank down beside his brother. Michael's eyes were dazed.

"Are you hurt?" Michael choked out.

"I don't think so. I'm cut, but it's not bad. Let me look at you." There was wetness and a growing pain on his left side, but Tristan paid no attention to it, focusing instead on his brother. His deepest concern centered on the arrow that had passed through Michael's shoulder, shattering bones along the way.

"I'm sorry you had to kill him...that will be hard for you," Michael said in a low voice, strangely breathless. Tristan said nothing, not wanting to think about that yet. Instead, he focused on working out what he should do next. Michael desperately needed care, but Tristan didn't know if he could get his brother on a horse. A thick, wet cough interrupted his thoughts even as he registered the pooling of blood at his knees. He raked his eyes over Michael.

"What's happening?" he whispered. Tristan jerked aside Michael's torn clothes and shrank back in horror. A long, deep wound gaped there, blood surging with each breath Michael took.

"Oh, dear Father in heaven," he breathed. "I've got to staunch this."

Michael protested as Tristan yanked off his tunic and ripped the linen into several pieces. It was filthy, but he had nothing else. He pressed some cloth against the wound as his father had taught him, gulping as it soaked through. He traded the piece for another, and soon it too dripped with blood. Tristan's hands shook, and panic overtook him.

"Michael, I can't stop the bleeding!"

"Tristan...come here..."

Tristan shook his head. Michael clutched his arm and with surprising strength pulled him closer.

"Tristan, I haven't much time. I want...need to say something."

"What do you mean you don't have time?" Tristan's voice rose. "We'll find the others and get you home."

"Shhh, be still. I don't think I'll be going back to Altair."

"Stop it." Tristan would have jerked away, but Michael held him fast. "You're going to be fine. I just need to go find Dad."

"No. They could be hours behind us. Don't go. Please...let me talk to you, while I can." Michael heaved a strangled breath and the hold on Tristan's arm loosened. Tears filled Tristan's eyes and fell down his cheeks. He gripped Michael's hand.

"Tristan, I'm sorry I won't be there for you. I've been looking forward to seeing you grow up...to see what kind of man you'll be." Michael's breaths were coming in gasps. "I know...you..."

"Please, Michael," Tristan whispered. "Keep fighting, don't leave me."

"I don't want to. I'll try to hold on, but I don't think..." He took a ragged breath. "Christiana. I see her..." Michael's gaze dimmed as his eyes drifted over Tristan's shoulder, a hint of a smile on his face. "I see her with holly berries in her hair. Coming to you. Wearing a bridal crown..." His eyes closed.

"Michael!" Tristan pleaded, and his brother's eyes opened again, trying to focus.

"Tell Dad he's been the very best of fathers. James...Ethan. Good boys, good men. But you, Tristan..." He raised his hand to Tristan's face, bringing him closer until their foreheads were almost touching. Tears spilled out of his own eyes. "I love you so dearly, my brother, my son...Tristan, you have been the joy of my life. Never forget that. Promise me."

Tristan sobbed. "Don't give up. Michael, I can't—I can't live this life without you. Not again."

"Yes, you can. And know I'll be proud of you. I will. So proud. Even if you can't see me watching." Michael's voice was growing fainter. His hand fell from Tristan's cheek, leaving a bloody track behind to mingle with Tristan's tears. A violent shudder went through him, and he groaned, kicking into the damp earth helplessly. With a cry, Tristan gathered Michael into his arms, holding him, cradling his head, ready to defy even death to take him.

"Michael, don't. I love you too much. Don't go."

"I'm trying, Tris."

"Stay with me, Michael, please stay with me."

"Tristan, don't be afraid." His words were no more than a murmur. "I'll be waiting for you, where I'm going. It won't be very long, not really..."

Tristan held Michael as time crept by. His own wound seeped blood, the hurt increasing. His thoughts grew sluggish. The fog lifted, and rain tapped around them. The willow thicket offered shelter from the scattered raindrops. Michael whispered Tristan's name once more before falling silent.

Time became meaningless. In his stupor, Tristan noticed inconsequential things. The lapping of the water on the lake. The smell of summer rain. A snail crawling along the trunk of a willow. Voices. He fumbled for his sword and held it up, his arm trembling, as a large man burst through the thicket right upon them.

"Tristan! No...Michael...oh no. Dad!"

More voices. Tristan knew he couldn't fight them all off again. Hands pried the sword from his hand. A voice he had always loved said his name.

"Tristan, son..."

"Dad...oh, Dad," Tristan mumbled. "Michael's hurt. You need to..."

Thomas was silent a few seconds before speaking hoarsely, "He's not hurting anymore, Tristan. He's gone."

Tristan knew the truth even as he continued to cling to Michael. His vision cleared enough to see his father bent over Michael, weeping. James knelt nearby, staring and frozen in his grief. Ethan's arms wrapped around him from behind, his sobs shaking them both.

Later, when Thomas tried to draw Tristan away from the body, he fought against the hands wanting to separate him from Michael.

"Tristan, you're hurt. We need to look at that wound."

"Don't take me from him."

"Tris, you're bleeding and—" Ethan pleaded.

"No."

"Son, please." His father's voice broke. "I can't lose you too."

Tristan sighed and released Michael into Ethan's gentle hands. Ethan lifted Michael's head from Tristan's lap and laid it on the ground, pulling a blanket over him as tears fell. With another hesitation, Tristan submitted to being led a few yards away by Thomas. With a moan, Tristan sank to his knees. James cried out his name, aghast at the sight of blood covering his brother's torso.

"Don't worry, the blood's not mine," Tristan said. He shivered. "Why's it so cold, Dad?"

Thomas grimaced. "Enough of that blood *is* yours. James, fetch the whiskey and start a fire. Ethan, help me here."

James rushed off, and Ethan searched for supplies in various bags. Thomas eased Tristan back against his chest, holding him steady.

"This feels familiar," Tristan mumbled. He flinched and cried out when Ethan poured some whiskey over the cut, then fell silent.

The wound stretched long across Tristan's body and had bled profusely, but it was a relatively shallow cut. Ethan stitched the injury while whispering an unbroken murmur of encouragement the whole time. Tristan never made a sound, even when his fingers clawed into the dirt.

When Ethan finished dressing the wound, James helped Tristan clean himself of the blood as best as possible with water warmed over the fire. They all rested and drank whiskey-laced coffee before deciding what to do next.

James nodded at the bodies of the slain men. "Did Michael kill them?"

"Most of them." Tristan wobbled to his feet and looked them over before spitting on one. "He was mine."

His father started in surprise, but no one said anything. James and Thomas studied the dead men, confirming they were strangers. They followed a few tracks until they disappeared in the grass.

"Should we hunt down the others?" James asked his father in a hushed voice while keeping his eyes on Tristan. His brother stood some distance apart from the rest, leaning against Dun and searching through his saddlebags.

"No. It's been hours, and the rain would have washed whatever trail remained."

James nudged Thomas and jerked his head toward Tristan. He was stumbling about, examining the bodies and muttering to himself. Ethan stood with him, watching anxiously over his injured brother. Thomas called out, "Tristan. What are you doing?"

Tristan didn't answer. Instead, he kept circling around the site of the fight, increasingly agitated. Thomas reached out to his son, but Tristan smacked his hands away, searching the ground. "My dagger. I forgot. I threw it during the fight, but I can't find it."

"Son, it's—"

"It was your dagger, Dad! The one you gave me. The dagger. Michael taught me how—" Tristan choked and gulped for air.

Thomas knew this wasn't about the knife. He gripped Tristan's shoulders. "I don't give a damn about the dagger. Remember what I told you? If it saved your life, it did its job."

Tristan gasped, breathing hard, his eyes filling with tears. "Dad..."

Thomas crushed Tristan to his chest, holding him tightly, fighting off his own tears. "It's all right. Tristan, my precious son, it's all right."

A sob shuddered through Tristan, but he didn't weep. Thomas held him for a long time before leading him back to sit again before the fire. All the while, Ethan was pacing.

"What is it, Ethan?"

Ethan took a deep breath and asked the question they had all been putting off. "What do we do with Michael?"

A long silence followed.

"We'll take him home," Tristan said.

James shook his head. "Tristan, we're at least a week's ride from Altair. We can't—"

"We will take him home," he repeated with a firm note of authority in his tone no one had ever heard before.

Thomas studied Tristan and cleared his throat. "James, go to the village we passed through yesterday. We need something to carry the body. A cart and a box, a coffin. Whatever they have that works. Have it filled with wood shavings or moss. Maybe a sturdy cart horse or extra mule too."

James made a move to rise, but Tristan stopped him with a hand on his arm. "Be careful, James. There may be more of those men out there." James looked into his brother's shadowed eyes and surprised Tristan by embracing him. Tristan grunted from the pain in his wound, but he hugged James anyway.

After James left, the three remaining set about disposing of the bodies of the brigands, tossing them into the lake. Thomas urged his youngest to rest, but Tristan refused. The moon had risen when James returned with all they needed.

Each of them took turns saying goodbye. Tristan sat by Michael for a long time. In the end, he brushed aside his brother's dark hair, kissed his brow, and whispered, "Until the Rising, Michael. For evermore."

For two days they traveled, and Tristan chafed at the slow pace. When they reached the town of Freestone, they stopped overnight. It had a military outpost, and Thomas requested a visit with their captain. In short order, a small military unit was at their disposal, with fresher, stronger horses and a better wagon. Before the group left the town, a courier was sent ahead to Altair with a letter for the queen.

Throughout the entire journey, Thomas kept a close eye on Tristan, even in the midst of his own deep grief. The boy hardly slept. He never ate more than a bite or two and talked only when necessary. Tristan was locked down within himself, rebuffing everyone's attempts at consolation.

The weather remained fine, and the roads clear. Thus, not many days later, the young Lord Lockhart came home to Altair for the last time.

When they arrived at the castle, the whole group was exhausted and weary with sorrow. Tristan feared he couldn't dismount Dun without falling flat onto his face. As it was, he did tumble to his knees, and Ethan had to help him up. Tristan leaned against his brother.

"Tris..."

"I'm all right. Tired. I'll rest when this is over."

Ethan met his father's eyes, and they exchanged worried looks. Charlotte rushed out of the castle to Thomas and took him in her arms, weeping. Thomas shuddered in her embrace. She caressed his cheek, whispering words for his ears alone. He nodded and left to speak to one of the men with the wagon. Charlotte tugged Tristan close.

"My dear boy," she said.

Tristan relaxed for a fleeting moment, recalling the sensation of being mothered. He disengaged himself and asked in a low voice, "Where's Christiana?"

"She's not here, Tristan. I'm sorry. I've sent her a letter, and I have hopes she will return soon."

Tristan's heart collapsed.

"It doesn't matter," he lied. "We need to keep going and dig—"

"Men have already dug the grave. I hope that's acceptable?"

"Yes. Thank you, Your Grace."

They buried Michael late morning, and the waters of the sea were poured over his grave. Then, after a quiet word to Ethan, Tristan disappeared.

# Chapter 24

# The Chapel

Every summer, Christiana left Altair to see her cousin Rachel for several weeks at the Marchant estate of Oakwood. The two girls were as close as sisters, and the visit helped pass the time with Tristan and his brothers away for the summer months. Christiana was also one of the few people who could tolerate Rachel's father. A cruel man, Barfius Marchant had lived his life bitter over the death of his brother Lawrence years before, snuffing out both their dreams and ambitions. Lawrence had loved his daughter, however, so Barfius did attempt to make her feel welcome. Christiana had been at Oakwood for a week when Charlotte's brief letter sent her reeling.

Christiana fell to her knees weeping, not to be consoled. Dearest Michael! Darling, handsome Michael, who had always been sweet and kind to her. How could he be dead, gone forever? Her mother had given her no details but urged her to return to Altair as quickly as possible.

Her heart already torn asunder, she thought of Tristan and a fresh outbreak of tears overwhelmed her. Tristan, who loved Michael, how his heart would break! What would this do to him?

The princess of Aquila was not one to allow grief to consume her. She far preferred putting her sorrow into action. She made plans to leave at once, but Rachel pleaded with her to wait until morning. Christiana at last agreed, recognizing the folly of traveling by night. She and her guards were up and riding before dawn, cutting a day-long pleasure ride in half with her furious pace. When her men urged her to rest, she spurned them. She was healthy, young, and an excellent rider. Why would she stop for momentary weariness?

Christiana arrived at the castle and ran for the corridor where the Thatchers lived. No one was about. She flew up and down stairs seeking someone, anyone. The murmur of voices caught her attention, and she rushed into the common room, panting. There, Thomas and Ethan stood, talking in hushed tones. James sat staring at the fire like one turned to stone, as if by moving he might shatter. Thomas's weary face brightened somewhat when she entered. Christiana walked straight into his big, strong arms and wept as he enfolded her.

Wiping her eyes, she scanned the room. "Where is Tristan?"

"I'm not sure," Thomas said thickly. "He disappeared after the burial, and no one has seen him since."

Ethan had stood aside at her arrival and now spoke in his usual soft voice. "Tristan's in the chapel. He told me he was going there and didn't want anyone to follow. I think he would make an exception in this case."

Thomas nodded and looked at Christiana. "He's shut us out, but maybe he'll talk to you."

She kissed Ethan on the cheek, blinking back tears at the sight of his red-rimmed eyes. Before leaving the room, Christiana slid her arms over James's shoulders and dropped a kiss on the top of his head. That seemed to break the spell he was under, for he rose and clutched her close.

Christiana hugged James as he struggled to restrain his own tears. After a few sweet, whispered words, she broke away.

Before the chapel, she stopped, unsure of herself. Nevertheless, she yanked open the heavy doors, breathing in the familiar scents of wax, wood polish, and incense. The space held candles but no windows, and it took a moment for her eyes to adjust to the light. At first, Christiana thought Tristan must not be there, for she could see no sign of life in the chapel. Then, a flicker of movement caught her eye. With his dark hair, he blended into the shadows. Christiana steadied herself and padded down the aisle to slip beside him.

Tristan was not kneeling but seated on the edge of the hard bench. Body rigid, head bent, and eyes shut, he gripped the rail so tightly his knuckles were white. Christiana sat helpless in the face of his anguish. He made no sign that he was even aware of her presence. She moved to leave, surprised when his hand grasped hers.

"Don't go." His voice sounded hoarse. "Please."

Tristan shifted his position. He continued to hold her hand but didn't move his head or open his eyes. "You know?"

"Yes. Tristan…"

Tristan let out a ragged breath and swiveled to see her better. His expression was bleak, and his eyes—but she couldn't look into his eyes. Without hesitation, she threw her arms around Tristan and held on to him, as though pulling him to safety from a black, endless precipice. Tears spilled down her cheeks. "My darling Tristan. I'm sorry, so terribly sorry. Oh, Michael! I loved him too. Sweet, sweet Michael."

At these words a shudder went through Tristan, and he resisted her embrace. He opened his mouth and shut it again without speaking. Christiana wept all the harder, and this pummeled through his last defense. He broke, falling into her arms with sobs that shook his entire frame. As he had feared all the long days on the road to Altair, once he discovered how to release the grief locked up inside of him, he couldn't stop. They clung together, each crying their heartbreak out to the other.

When Tristan could regain some measure of self-control, he wiped at the tears on his face. The corner of his mouth tilted in a hint of an embarrassed, shaky smile.

"I'm sorry."

"Don't be silly."

He took her hand in his again, relaxing against the back of the bench in his weariness before shifting.

"Where did you come from?"

"I was at my cousin Rachel's in Oakwood. Mother wrote what happened. The letter arrived last evening, and we were on the road before dawn."

"When—what time is it?"

"The noon bells were tolling when I entered the city."

"And you left Oakwood this morning? You shouldn't have done that, Chris. You shouldn't have ridden that hard."

"Of course I should have! You needed me."

Some emotion Tristan didn't understand flooded his heart. He enclosed her in an embrace of his own. "Yes," he whispered into her hair. "I did need you. Thank you."

Christiana said nothing more but nestled closer. She remained still beyond brushing the tears that continued to fall. The chapel was peaceful, with the wind moaning as it wafted through the rafters, causing the candles to flicker. The subtle, honeyed scent of burning beeswax was soothing.

Ever since that terrible day, Tristan's heart had been encased in ice. Even his body held a constant chill. Yet Christiana was warm in his arms. If she had bothered to restrain her hair at all, the bindings had loosened, and he buried his cold fingers into the golden strands. He rubbed his cheek against the silkiness, and without a thought, brushed his lips to her hair. Tristan held her closer, as if wanting to protect her bright and precious spirit from the darkness that always seemed to lurk in the shadows.

He kissed her hair again, and before Tristan even knew what he was about, he was holding her face in his hands and kissing the tears on her cheeks. Then his lips met hers for the barest whisper of a kiss. Their foreheads tipped together, and he swallowed hard.

"Don't stop." Her warm hand caressed his cheek. "Please, don't stop, Tristan."

Their lips met again and again, tender and light. A soft warmth stole over Tristan. After the wretched coldness within his soul since Michael's death, he surrendered to this gentle thaw. With a shaky sigh, he buried his face in her copper-gold tresses.

"Christiana." He intoned her name as if in prayer. "My dearest Chris. Thank you for coming back. I was lost without you."

Christiana snuggled against him, both content to remain in the quiet space. Tristan relaxed in her arms to the point of dozing, so that when she withdrew from him, he felt confused and almost bereft.

"Darling Tristan, you are dreadfully weary. Let me walk you to your chamber."

Tristan wanted to resist, but at her urging he rose to his feet. They met Thomas outside the chapel doors, waiting. Seeing Tristan on the verge of collapse, Thomas reached out to support his son. He mouthed "thank you" to Christiana before speaking aloud, "Why don't you get some rest? You've had quite a journey yourself."

She nodded, kissed Tristan's cheek, and made her way to her own part of the castle. Thomas half-led, half-carried a stumbling Tristan to his room. He helped his son undress and put him to bed with Tristan mumble-chattering all the while.

"Christiana is the sweetest girl, Dad."

"Yes, she is." Despite his own heartache, Thomas smiled. He had stepped into the chapel and left at once, giving the two time to themselves.

"Dad?"

"Yes?"

"I killed him. That man."

Thomas stiffened at his son's words. When he could speak, his voice was gruff. "I know. You had to."

"I don't mind so much that I had to do it. But I wish I hadn't *wanted* to kill him. Because I did. I wanted to cut him down, to slaughter him. After what he did to Michael."

"We'll talk about it later," muttered Thomas, his heart shredded.

"It's going to hurt a long time, isn't it? Michael."

Thomas struggled against the tears threatening to consume him. "Yes, son. A very long time. Go to sleep now."

Tristan sank into the pillows and was soon snoring. Thomas watched over Tristan even after he slept, clutching his son's hand. Sobs overcame him, and he shoved a fist into his mouth to keep quiet, weeping brokenly in the silence.

# Chapter 25

# Mourning and Grace

Tristan awoke confused and disoriented. He had no sense of time. The gray light coming through the window could have been early morning or twilight. Some remnants of a violent dream tugged at his memory, and his heart raced. Without thinking, he pushed himself into a sitting position and clenched his eyes shut as the room spun about. The fiery pain across his waist returned along with all the aches in his body. Everything flooded back, and he slumped, pressing his head into the blankets to keep from screaming out his grief. He remained there for some time, willing his heart to slow and trying to quell the brokenness that consumed him. He wanted to run to Michael's messy chamber and berate him for leaving him alone in the world.

Except he wasn't alone. His beloved father lived a few doors down the corridor, James and Ethan were here, and Christiana...

Ignoring his protesting body, Tristan rolled out of bed. He stood staring at the door to Michael's room before teetering to the wardrobe. Lifting his arm for a sniff, Tristan grimaced. He opened his mouth to yell a humorous comment about his stink to Michael, then bit his lip until he tasted blood.

The cool waters of the bathhouse soothed his body, even as dressing and grooming himself soothed his spirits. The growing darkness told him night was falling. Everyone would be in the common room. He was drawn there, like a moth to a light, but not confident he wanted to see anyone yet. Tristan blew air out of cheeks before opening the door. They all expressed surprise at seeing him. Thomas half rose at his appearance in the doorway, eyes full of concern.

"I'm all right, Dad," Tristan murmured, indicating with his hand for his father to remain seated. He eased himself onto the sofa between Ethan and Christiana, putting his left arm around her. His heart skipped a beat when she laid her head on his chest. Somehow the aches in his body lessened with her warmth beside him.

But it wasn't right. They were quiet, feeling the irreplaceable loss of someone they all loved. Tristan caught James's eye, the painful awareness passing between them. Beside him, Ethan slumped, burying his face in his hands. Tristan rubbed Ethan's back in a comforting gesture. He then squeezed Christiana when she brushed tears from her cheeks.

"None of that," he said gently, "or you'll get me started again, and James will never let me live it down."

James chuckled at those words, but the weak laughter gave way to silence.

"Are you hungry, son?" asked Thomas.

Tristan shook his head. "I'll beg some food off Cook later if I need a bite."

Justin slipped into the room and looked around to take in everyone. His eyes met Tristan's, and Justin offered a slight dip of the chin in acknowledgment before moving to Thomas. He placed his hand on the older man's shoulder and whispered into his ear. Thomas nodded his appreciation at Justin's words. Justin crossed over to James and sat near his friend.

All this time, Charlotte had been seated next to Thomas. To Tristan's surprise, she took his father's hand in her own. Then again, they had been friends for many years.

The room was a quiet haven. Just the occasional crackle of the fire as they held their vigil. Tristan pressed his lips to Christiana's hair, reassured by her presence. He almost drifted off to sleep several times before he shook himself and stood.

"It's been a long day. Many days. Doesn't feel like I slept at all. I think I'm done." On his way to the door, he reached out to Thomas, grasping him by the shoulder. "Don't get up, Dad. I'm good, I promise."

"Let me go with you," Christiana offered. She caught hold of Tristan's hand, and they left the room together. At the foot of the sweeping staircase that led to the family rooms, Christiana kissed his cheek and turned to leave.

"Chris, please," he croaked, not releasing her hand. He pulled her into a nearby alcove before kissing her. Both yearning and shy, it was a gift for Tristan to hold her close, to stroke her hair and caress her face. But to kiss her—oh, to kiss her! Her lips moving with his was unspeakably healing. After several kisses, he released her with great reluctance.

"You should go on to bed," he whispered. Yet she made no effort to leave. Tristan sighed, not wanting to be apart from her either. He bent to kiss her once more, and rubbed the tip of his nose on hers, bringing a smile to her face. A door slammed somewhere nearby, and they both jumped. He nudged her, and she flew up the stairs as Thomas came into view.

"Tristan? You're still awake?"

"I'm going to bed soon."

"You look feverish. How is your cut?"

As a matter of fact, Tristan had quite forgotten his wound in the last few moments. Now it twinged painfully. But his father had been so anxious for him, Tristan couldn't bear to cause him more worry. And he suspected his injury wasn't why he appeared flushed. "It's healing. G'night, Dad."

Tristan entered his chamber and stood there, lost, these wild, strange fluctuations of emotions wearing him down. He crossed to Michael's closed door and rested his head against the wood, toying with the latch, fighting off tears, terribly alone in his grief. A thought struck him. He wiped his eyes and straightened. He knew at least one other person was suffering under the weight of this far more than himself or his brothers.

A few minutes later he knocked on his father's door, holding two brimming mugs of ale. Thomas's eyes brightened at the sight of his youngest.

"Dad, would you care to have a drink with me?" At Thomas's surprised face, he rushed to explain. "I know you and Michael would spend the evenings together sometimes, and I thought...I don't have what you like here, just some ale."

His father's expression gentled. "I would enjoy that very much."

They sat in the chairs before the fire with their ale. Tristan lifted his mug.

"To Michael?"

"No. To my remarkable boys. All four of them."

Tristan smiled at his father even as he swallowed past the ache in his throat. After taking a drink, Thomas settled back.

"So. You and Christiana, eh?"

"C'mon, Dad..."

# Chapter 26

# Prelude to War

The summer days slipped past as the brothers struggled to heal their hearts. Many times, Tristan could be found in the chapel, wrestling in prayer over Michael's death and his own role in the skirmish. Ethan often sat with him, offering his quiet support. In contrast, James disappeared for long stretches at a time, riding alone over the countryside or locked up in a room with Thomas, where they talked over many things regarding the future. The awareness of war on the horizon remained a shadow over them all.

Tristan ached for Michael with a fierceness that physically hurt, and there were days he had to force himself to leave his room. In the sunlit hours he could manage his grief. Having never spent any time at Altair during the summer, Tristan explored the seashore miles away from the castle. Christiana remained with him always. With the prospect of separation looming over them, they viewed every day together as precious. On rainy days, the two would seek out an isolated place in the castle to be alone. They were the sweetest and gentlest of lovers, for Tristan was prudent in the care of her. To him, Christiana was a treasure he must not tarnish in any way. They tried to keep their courtship a delightful secret between the two of them, which naturally meant everyone was aware of their relationship and smiled among themselves.

But the nights were a despair for Tristan. Plagued by dreams, he would wake crying out, drenched in sweat, with the clash of swords in his ears. He took to wandering the castle in the late-night hours, afraid to sleep.

While prowling about the corridors one night, unusual sounds drew his attention—a series of strange thuds and the occasional clink of steel. He doggedly followed the noise, almost convinced he was going mad until he arrived at the courtyard. There he discovered James practicing with his sword in the moonlight. Tristan watched him work from the shadows. Shirtless, his brother dripped sweat; he must have been at it for hours. James stopped, wiping wet hair from his eyes.

"Still not sleeping, Tris?"

Tristan shook his head before comprehending the question. "How did you know I wasn't sleeping?"

James shrugged. "Ethan knew you weren't and told Dad, who mentioned it to me."

"I thought you practiced in the mornings?"

"I've been doing both, in the mornings with the master, and at night alone."

"How can you do that?" Tristan said, astonished. Sword work was exhausting, for the body *and* mind.

"Well, I haven't been sleeping either. This helps."

"And Ethan must not be sleeping, if he knew I wasn't." Tristan tried to keep his tone light, but then his voice dropped low. "I don't even want to think about what Dad is going through."

James blinked up at the stars, fighting to maintain his composure. "I know. You can't imagine how many times I've gone over that day in my head. If only I had been with you two, maybe I—"

"Don't say it."

"Sorry. You know what's odd, though? We haven't had a single word about anything wrong down there since we left. You would think the attacks would have continued, but nothing."

"Maybe we killed them all."

"Seems like there should have been more of them based on the reports we had. And you said one rode off."

"I don't know what I said, James. I was distracted."

James looked at him with sympathy. "I'm sorry you had to go through that alone."

"You sound like Dad."

"And that, young Tristan, I will take as the highest of compliments." James's tone shifted, and he grinned. "Now, if you care to pick up one of those extra swords over there, we'll have us some fun."

"C'mon, you *can't* be serious. Since when do I ever find it fun sparring with you? Besides, I'm exhausted."

"Yes, I know, that's why I'm going to make you do this. Once I began practicing at night, I started sleeping better. Besides, between your shoulder and your last injury, we haven't sparred in ages. Hop to it!" He smacked Tristan's backside with the flat of his sword, and his brother yelped.

"That's not funny!"

James's eyes narrowed. "Get the sword, or I'll do it again. I mean it, Tris."

When Tristan hesitated, James popped him even harder. Tristan grabbed the sword and held it defensively. James laughed with a glint in his eye. "Come on, little brother. What if Chris had been with you that day, would you have let her fight for you? She can best you with a bow—you ever try your sword with her?"

"Shut up, James!" Tristan's dark blue eyes flashed. He twirled the sword in his hand, getting a solid grip. James tensed, but the words tumbled out.

"I bet your sword doesn't even rise up to the—"

Tristan bellowed and gave in to the violence with a rush. Their blades crossed and rang out. Too late, James discovered this wasn't the same Tristan from a year ago. Something wonderful and new was at work here.

Tristan had become a swordsman.

He was raw and unpolished, fighting on pure rage, but Tristan was well on his way to being a worthy foe at last. Tristan fought much like Michael, agile and fast. James deflected a sideswipe and Tristan spun about, doing an unusual parry and ending with his back against James's chest.

Tristan threw his head, hoping to butt it hard against his brother. James staggered a step to the left, an inch shy of a broken nose. He muttered an oath, done messing around with his berserk younger brother. He rained a few blows at Tristan, who defended them admirably. In the end, he had Tristan on his knees gasping for air, and even James was breathing hard with a fresh sheen of sweat on his face.

"Blazes, Tris. You're better than I remember," he wheezed.

Tristan glowered at him, panting. "I was taking extra lessons too—from Michael."

At this, James's taunting eye gentled. He dragged his brother to his feet. Tristan spat some blood on the ground and glared at James, who clapped him on the shoulder. "You'll do. Drink some ale and go to bed. I bet you sleep tonight."

Tristan almost made it to the doorway when James called out, "Tomorrow night, little brother. Come again, and I'll teach you a thing or two even Michael didn't know. And Tristan? When fighting, lead with your head, not your heart. You need to learn to control that."

At those words Tristan wheeled around and stood tall. "Tell me, James. How many men have you killed?" His brother stared at him, speechless, and Tristan laughed without a trace of mirth. "That's what I thought."

Tristan stalked off with a growl. James slumped against the wall, his swagger gone. He hated pushing Tristan so hard after that hideous day. When James closed his eyes, he could still see Tristan covered in blood and clinging to their brother's gutted body. If Michael's death had shaken the foundations of his world, James believed it would shatter to dust if anything happened to Tristan. With Michael dead, James carried the burden to have his brother ready. War was coming. And James would be damned before he lost Tristan too.

In his chamber, Tristan had a long gulp of ale before crashing into bed. He didn't stir again until morning, when he awoke sore and aching. But the next night and every night thereafter, he joined his brother in the courtyard.

Used to the quiet days of winter when unpredictable weather limited travel, Tristan was surprised by how many people stayed at Altair in the summer. Gone were the cozy gatherings in the common room; the

Great Hall became the focal gathering spot. Men and women dressed in finer clothing, with more saturated colors and artfully woven fabric. The castle was packed, and the city bustling.

Christiana's cousin Rachel also came for a visit. Everyone hoped she would stay for good, as life with her irascible father had become unbearable. James and Ethan already knew Rachel, although it had been several years since she had last visited Altair, but Tristan had never met her. A thoughtful girl with dark hair and calm, gray eyes, she reminded him of his mother. Rachel was so kind that Tristan held her in high regard and never begrudged her time spent with Christiana.

The leaves were taking on a tint of gold when a rider came to the castle bearing news Sammanon had invaded the western border near Grodine. Everyone had already gathered in the Great Hall for the evening meal, and the room exploded into pandemonium. Despite his wish of being a soldier, James grew somber. No one observed Ethan casting a wistful look at Christiana's raven-haired cousin, whom he had long fancied in secret. He had wanted to spend more time with Rachel before war broke out. Thomas thought of his sons and groaned in his heart. War always seemed to be inevitable, yet he had hoped for another reprieve.

Tristan caught his father's eye and longed to comfort him, but he spied Christiana leaving the hall in the midst of the tumult. Conflicted, he glanced once more at Thomas, not sure where to go. With a sad smile, his father nodded his head in the direction Christiana had gone.

Tristan fought through the crowd. His attention snagged on Charlotte sweeping away, surrounded by military men. Justin followed her, his face pale and strained. Tristan was out of breath before he finally wormed his way out of the hall. Christiana had disappeared, but after a few minutes he found her sitting on a bench in the courtyard. It was quiet there, with a cool evening breeze blowing through. He sat next to her and took her hand in his.

He soaked in the peace of the night. The stars were hidden behind clouds, and the scent of incoming rain filled the air. He shivered in the chilly wind. Autumn was upon them, and this change in weather would soon alter the leaves of the countryside into brilliant gold, orange, and red hues before falling dead in winter.

"You'll be leaving, won't you?" she asked. He didn't speak, and Christiana choked out a sob. There were tears in her eyes, and Tristan wrapped his arms around her. He stroked her long hair.

"I love you," he whispered. "I don't want to go, ever. But..."

"I know."

With one hand at the back of his neck, she brought his lips to hers. Their kisses had always been tender, gentle—but the coming separation made them both hunger for more. Her mouth opened to his, surprising Tristan. Hesitant, yet increasingly eager, he kissed her with a growing passion, and she responded. The taste of her intoxicated him. Tristan ducked his head, heart pounding, startled by the intensity of his desires.

"Chris, I mustn't." His voice shook. She understood and kissed the tip of his nose, breaking the tension and causing him to chuckle. He gathered her close, and together they waited for the coming storm.

The day before the fighting men of the castle were to leave, Tristan tried to pack but only succeeded in making a mess. His father had insisted anything he forgot could be found at the camps, but Tristan liked to know he had everything he would need.

Without thinking, he called out, "Michael, can you—"

Tristan stopped and yelled in frustration, pounding his fist into the wardrobe. He cried out as a bloom of pain surged up his arm, and he struck it again out of angry stubbornness. Defeated, he slumped against the wall, massaging his hand, mired in dark thoughts. Weeks ago, they had been safe and happy, ready to make a home at Altair. Now Michael was gone, and the war would tear their family apart once more. Tristan felt lost and betrayed.

He looked at the door to Michael's room, open and welcoming in the past, now closed and locked. Tristan hadn't entered the room since Michael's death, but fumbling with his aching hand, he unlocked the door and stepped into the chamber. It smelled of books, leather, and...something indefinably *Michael*. He crossed over to the bed and sat, recalling all the times he had spent in this space, laughing and talking with his brother. Tears stung his eyes.

"Michael..." he whispered, voice cracking with grief. Heart-scalding anger burned in his chest. "Why did you take him! Wasn't Momma enough?"

The silence was deafening.

Tristan sat straighter and rubbed his face. He rose from the bed and spun around once. It was then that he saw it. Michael's sword leaning against the wall. The Lockhart sword, the source of not a few legends, passed down from King Emery himself, and rumors whispered it had been forged centuries before.

Someone must have brought it in soon after they returned. Dazed, Tristan crossed to the sword, and his fingers tingled as he unsheathed it and held it up to the light. The sword was lighter than he remembered. Tristan wondered if someday he might be worthy enough to carry it. For now, he hung it over the mantel in his own chamber.

Tristan stared at the sword for a long time, lost in his memories.

The last of the castle soldiers gathered in the stableyards before sunrise. A heavy fog had descended, and the thick smell of autumn danced around them all. Tristan shivered in the mist, thinking of that final day with Michael. The horses blew, clouding the air further with their breath. The creaks of saddles and rumbles of men filled the early morning. Many of the soldiers had left over the past few days, including Prince Justin. They would meet again at the camps later. James was already in his saddle, impatient to be gone, but Tristan and Ethan hung about until the call to mount.

Tristan's attention was caught by the sight of an older man standing on the battlements that loomed over the stableyard. A lord of some kind, he wore a fine but weathered brocade tunic and a cloak lined with fur, his steel-gray hair falling past his shoulders. What gave Tristan pause was the way the man stared at Thomas Thatcher, who stood nearby conversing with the queen. Never had he seen such hatred in a man's eyes.

"Ethan, who's that?"

Ethan followed Tristan's gaze and grimaced, muttering, "Lord General MacClaren."

Tristan took another cautious peek and beheld the eyes now trained on him, and he shuddered at the bitter expression. The old man spun away and disappeared.

Thomas left the queen's side and gave Christiana an affectionate, paternal hug before making his way across the stableyard. Ethan shyly said goodbye to Rachel and hugged Christiana. There were enough people milling about that Tristan restrained his impulses when he stepped forward to bid farewell.

"Princess Christiana," he declared with a teasing smile that hid the tumult of his heart.

"I have a gift for you." Christiana placed a small bundle in his hands. "Open it later."

Tristan slipped the parcel into his pocket and grasped both her hands in his. He opened his mouth to speak, but no words would come. He ached to hold her. Instead, he settled for kissing her cheek. "You'll be in my prayers, every night."

"And you'll be in mine," Christiana whispered.

Tristan approached Queen Charlotte, and she surprised him with a warm embrace. "My dearest boy. Take good care of yourself."

"I'm scared," he confessed as she held him.

She put him at arm's length and looked straight into his eyes. With a tone of authority she said, "You would be a fool if you weren't. No matter. I believe you will find a great well of courage when you need it. After all, you are a Lockhart *and* a Thatcher. Remember that." She winked, and he grinned, remembering their first meeting.

Horns blew, and a voice cried out, "Men of Aquila!" With a rush and swirl, the random squeal of a stallion's challenge, and cheers from all those gathered, the great cavalcade moved as one. The standard of the golden eagle flew high from the spears of the men. Tristan's heart couldn't help but leap as the mighty band spilled out of the stableyard and into the streets of Altair.

Tristan had his foot in the stirrup of his saddle when Christiana cried out his name. Before he had turned completely, she was there, throwing her arms around his neck. For a second he froze, then his own arms encircled her slight frame, crushing her against him. Their words tumbled over each other.

"Please, please come back to me, Tristan!"

"I will, I promise. Oh, Chris…"

They kissed each other with abandon, not caring who watched. How long they stood there, Tristan did not know. He only knew her—her lips, her touch, her hair threaded around his fingers. He fell to earth at the sound of his father's cough.

"I love you," he whispered. He kissed Christiana on the forehead. "Go back to your mother now."

Tristan refused to look back until he was on his horse with his father nearby. Thomas opened his mouth to speak to Tristan when a flat voice interrupted his thoughts.

"That was quite a demonstration."

Shifting in his saddle, Thomas noticed Lord MacClaren on his horse, just a few yards away. The man stared at Tristan with steely eyes before spurring his animal and riding off without another word. Thomas continued to watch him, and his gut lurched. He shoved aside his unease to drag his attention over to Tristan, who was gazing at Christiana with such longing, Thomas smiled in spite of his misgivings.

"You can stay here, son," he urged. "I won't think any less of you for not going."

Tristan hesitated before muttering, "No, I can't. Not when I have something to fight for."

He met his father's knowing eyes, and a grin spread across his face. "Besides, you need all the help you can get keeping an eye on James." He jerked his chin toward his brother, who was chuckling over the young lovers. Tristan groaned, knowing James would tease him mercilessly later that day, but he had no regrets. The remaining men were leaving, and Tristan blew Christiana a kiss before he cantered off to join the others.

"I love him, Momma. I can't let him go," she said, clinging to her mother's arm.

"I know, sweetheart, but you must. Their job is to go and fight. Ours is to let them. We lead from home. It has always been this way."

Christiana stepped away from her mother, watching the last rider on a small dun-colored horse disappear beyond the bend. She shook her head, whispering to herself, "No. It won't always be this way."

# PART II

# Chapter 27

# Preparations

With such large groups moving slower than a single rider could travel, it took two weeks to reach the easternmost army camp. Ethan and Tristan stayed together the whole time, while Thomas and James mingled with various groups. Tristan encouraged his brother to join the healers if he preferred, but Ethan shrugged and said, "I would rather be with you. Time enough for all that later."

Tristan gave him a grateful nod. Ethan's devotion to his family had always endeared him to Tristan, and he appreciated his brother's steady presence even more since Michael's death. In truth, Ethan was often overlooked and received less attention from the soldiers surrounding them, but he never seemed bothered by this. Altogether without ego, he was happy to serve and possessed a quiet confidence Tristan admired and wished to imitate.

On their final evening together, they all gathered around a fire. Thomas gazed at his sons, longing to take them back to Altair unscathed. He cleared his throat.

"James, Tristan has to travel as light as possible. He's going to make base camp with Ethan, but if he winds up at your camp, let him crash with you."

James smirked. "How can I do that if I have a girl with me?"

"James, I swear...but that reminds me. Listen, you're grown men." Thomas hesitated, looking askance at Tristan before nodding. "Yes, all of you. I can't tell you what to do anymore, but I implore you not to mix it up with the camp prostitutes. They have heaven knows what kind of diseases, and trust me, you don't want to be dealing with that."

"Dad!" Tristan was scandalized. Aghast, Ethan's jaw dropped, but James guffawed.

"You think I'm serious, Dad?"

"Sometimes I don't know, James. Remember, you were all raised to be decent and high-minded. Don't bring yourself down to the rest of this rabble. Be good men, strong men. Be leaders. And if you see anyone, *anyone*, mistreat a woman, whore or no, you deal with it. Hear me?"

"Speaking of women," Ethan said, turning to Tristan. "What did Chris give you? You never told us."

Stricken, Tristan searched his pockets, and James hooted with laughter. "She's going to love that you forgot about her present. I can't wait to tell her."

Shooting James a dirty look, Tristan was relieved to find the cloth-wrapped bundle. He unwrapped a small gold medallion of St. Michael. It glimmered in the firelight. The great warrior angel was holding his sword up in victory, a dead serpent writhing at his feet.

"Oh, Chris," Tristan murmured, his throat tight.

"Can't say the girl doesn't know you," James said as he reached over to squeeze Tristan's shoulder, all teasing gone from his face.

"I miss her already."

"She's worth missing, I think."

Tristan slipped the medallion over his neck. He fingered it in silence until he could speak again. "I've heard that when a soldier loses an arm or a leg, they still feel it later. Their bodies remember, somehow. We were at a tavern one time, and there was an old man who complained his foot itched even after being gone for twenty years. That's how I feel about Michael. I keep thinking he's right next to me, and I find myself wanting to ask him a question or tell him some nonsense Chris said..." Tristan's mouth hung open, but no more words came out. He buried his face in his hands.

They were all silent a moment before Ethan nudged Tristan. "What would you say to him if he was here?"

Tristan mumbled, "Oh, I don't know."

"Sure you do. C'mon, tell us. Even if it's silly. I bet he's here anyway, listening to our conversation turn mawkish and getting exasperated with us."

Tristan raised his head. His eyes were moist, but he gave a short laugh. "I would ask him why he let me forget that book I was reading. It's there by my bed. I can see exactly where it is if I close my eyes! Who knows when I'll get a chance at it again? He made sure I packed the right things."

Ethan chortled, and even Thomas had to smile. James launched into a decent imitation of Michael. "Now really, Tristan, if you weren't spending all your time mooning about the castle over Chris, even you could have packed your own things for once."

They all burst out laughing. One by one they told some of their favorite stories of Michael, tentative in the beginning, but with increasing enthusiasm. For the first time outside of his precious moments with Christiana, the cracks in Tristan's heart started to heal.

James left in the morning to report to his captain. His eyes glinted with mischief as he and Tristan said their farewells. "Keep up with the sparring practice. I look forward to testing you the next time I see you."

"I'll make sure he does," Ethan assured James. Tristan made a show of grimacing, and James chuckled before reaching out to both his brothers and pulling them in together. He held them close.

"Take care of each other, boys," he said in a husky voice. He left them without another word but waved from his horse before riding onward.

Ethan and Tristan would remain at their current camp on the eastern reaches of the army. Thomas breathed a sigh of relief. Though at some point Ethan might be required to move closer to fighting, for now he was safe. And he could keep a close eye on Tristan.

Thomas led his two remaining sons to their tent. "Listen, Tristan, you'll be riding all over the place, but try to end up here as much as possible. I trust you with Ethan far more than James."

Tristan laughed. "James likes to rile you. He's not bad."

"Now you sound like Michael," Thomas said with a wan smile. "See here, I have a chainmail shirt for you. It's the lightest I could find at the armory, and even still, it may take some getting used to. Wear this always, Tristan, please."

Tristan fingered the metal shirt. "What's this for? It can't be heavy enough for swords?"

"No, I'm hoping you don't need to block the point of a sword. This is for arrows. They're your greatest danger as a messenger. Put it on and let's see it."

Tristan had never worn chain mail, and it took him a few tries to get it on, but with Ethan's assistance he managed it in the end. Thomas made one or two adjustments before stepping back, satisfied. "You'll do. Don't be an idiot, Tristan. Be brave but use your head. Don't volunteer for the most dangerous rides, at least not until you've more experience. Stick to riding between camps. Or better yet, take messages to Altair. I've a suspicion you would like that."

Tristan couldn't help grinning. "Yes, sir."

"Good. I'm hoping Christiana will be motivation enough for you to stay safe."

All three left the tent and walked to a hitching rail where Marley waited, saddled and bridled. Without warning, Thomas tugged Tristan into a vast bear hug. "Be careful, son," he said gruffly.

"I will, Dad, I promise." Tristan's eyes pricked. "And I'll see you as often as I can."

Thomas eased him aside while clearing his throat. "I'll hold you to that. Ethan, come here." He embraced Ethan, fighting off a wave of emotions.

"I'll watch after him, Dad," whispered Ethan.

"Watch out for yourself," said Thomas. "You'll do well with the healers."

Thomas forced himself to mount his horse. Tristan released the bridle, and Ethan stepped forward, throwing his arm around his brother's shoulders. Thomas wished he could lock in the memory of them both standing there, happy and healthy, before he yanked on his reins.

"Damn Sammanon, and damn this war," Thomas muttered as he drove his heels into the flanks of his horse.

Within the week there was a gathering of scouts and couriers to judge their riding proficiency. They all had to run a difficult course, but the various obstacles were no issue for Tristan and Dun. At the end of the long day, the prospective riders lined up to be assessed by the officer in charge. Tristan peered at the captain as he approached each rider, dismissing some and approving others. A short, dark-skinned man with a barrel chest and mischievous brown eyes, Captain Stephens paused when he reached Tristan.

"Your name?"

"Thatcher, sir, Tristan Thatcher."

"One of Commander Thatcher's boys, aren't you?"

"Yes, sir, the youngest."

"Does he know you're here?"

"Naturally, sir."

"Rather short. How old are you?"

"Sixteen, sir." Tristan suppressed the urge to roll his eyes, for Captain Stephens wasn't much taller. Men of Aquila were not tall as a rule, but when everyone else in his family towered well over six feet, Tristan was used to being on the receiving end of surprised looks over his height. And his father had assured him he had a few more inches to go.

Captain Stephens discerned his frustration, and his own eyes twinkled. "Don't mistake me, I like my riders on the small side. Makes them faster. You were good today. Be ready at sunrise for the morning dispatches. Come to my tent tonight and we'll go over your route."

He angled away from the others and said in a conspiratorial whisper, "Bring a tankard. I have my own keg of ale."

The crisp fall weather fell in defeat to winter, and Tristan wondered at the reversed life he was leading, out working in the cold and wet instead of lounging near one of the many hearths at Castle Altair. The landmarks were so altered with the winter snow, one almost had to relearn all the routes.

"I'm glad you're well out of this, Michael," he muttered one day as he led Dun out of a deep drift they had broken through. He continued to ache for his brother, but he laughed out loud thinking of how much Michael loathed being in the snow. He studied the sky, where more clouds were gathering. "Bet you're chuckling to yourself up there."

Tristan thus far had seen no fighting. Indeed, very little had occurred beyond some minor skirmishes. Most of the current work centered on preparing for the battles sure to come in spring. Tristan's workload was light, which afforded him time to see his father and James with some regularity.

He made frequent trips to Altair over the winter months, and these were delightful evenings sitting by the fire with Christiana and Charlotte, telling army stories and exchanging news from Thomas. Tristan and Christiana played chess or took turns reading aloud from a well-loved book. Charlotte would leave them with a smile, and Tristan recognized the honor of her trust in him regarding her daughter. Sometimes dawn found the sweethearts on the sofa, snuggled together and dozing before the dying embers on the hearth. Tristan would depart the castle tired but with a full heart.

The mild spring winds were blowing, and the snow was melting when a veritable army of women fell upon the camps. Tristan realized with

distaste these were the camp whores. He had seen a few here and there over the winter, but those were more mistresses than prostitutes. Even if they didn't quite earn the respect of a wife, at least they kept themselves to one man. These fresh additions were different.

Tristan dipped his head politely when he crossed paths with any of the girls, but otherwise, he did his best to avoid them. To his consternation, the younger lasses went out of their way to bump into him. Tristan was young and handsome, and kind to any woman no matter her status. Consequently, the girls flew to him like bees to honey. After a few weeks, he was on friendly terms with a number of the wenches, but they had all learned he was a hopeless case.

Along with the women, new tensions rose across all the camps in the area. The men were cantankerous, and speculation about upcoming battles heightened the sense of anticipation. James rode in to see his brothers as often as he could. All too soon, the day came when he warned them it would be his last visit for a while.

"They expect the first real battle in the next week or two, and once the fighting starts, there's no telling when I'll get time off again."

"Are you frightened?" Ethan asked.

James scoffed, but at Ethan's insistence he grew serious. "To be honest, I don't know if I'm scared? More than anything, I want to make Dad proud and bring honor to the family name."

Ethan gave a snort of a laugh. "Oh yes, we must uphold the honor of the noble House of Thatcher!"

James went stiff and glared at his brother. His mouth opened as though he was about to respond but seemed to reconsider. Tristan, who had been pondering James's words, spoke up. "Do you think I should be fighting too? Instead of being a courier?"

Ethan exchanged a startled look with James, who was quick to answer. "You? Absolutely not. We don't want you out there, Tris. Let's not have more than one of us risking his life at any given moment." James winked, but Tristan shivered.

# Chapter 28

# Roadside Adventure

"You should consider acquiring another horse, Tristan."

Thomas had come to the far eastern camp, impatient for a certain dispatch from Queen Charlotte, and stopped to linger with his youngest son. They were leaning against a crude rail fence, watching the couriers' horses in the paddock.

"Et tu, Brute?" Tristan grumbled with a baleful glance. But it was quickly followed with a grin, for his father was one of the few people who would catch the reference. He was rewarded with a hearty laugh from Thomas.

"You know I think Dun is an excellent horse. But look at him. He's wearing down too fast with all the riding. I don't mean you should replace him. Just get another horse to trade off on trips. With battles picking up again, you'll be riding hard every day. I fear it will be too much for Dun alone."

At his words, Tristan studied Dun. He calculated his age and figured Dun must be about twelve, maybe fourteen. Not old by any means, but perhaps his father was right. Tristan berated himself for not having seen it before.

"If you find a good horse or even two, let me know," said Thomas. "Don't let cost be an issue. Do you need any coin?"

"No, sir. I still have the gold you gave me last time. And all the times before that."

Thomas laughed. "I appreciate your thriftiness, but don't be afraid to spend some coin on yourself. Anything you need, tell me."

"Thanks, Dad." Tristan gave his father a curious look. Thomas frequently complained about the exorbitant cost of some things like coffee, but the truth was he never had need of gold and was always more than generous with his sons, often slipping them bags of coin on the sly. Tristan wondered where the money came from. To the best of his knowledge, his father had no blood ties remaining in Woodraven and no legal connection to the Lockhart estate.

"Dad? Who did the Lockhart title fall to?"

Thomas blinked at the question. "Whatever makes you ask?"

"Just curious. I never heard."

"Since Michael died without an heir, it's up to the queen to decide. I suspect the title may come to one of you boys, since you're grandsons of Edward Lockhart." As Thomas spoke, his eyes drifted away, lost in memories. Then he cleared his throat and redirected his attention toward Tristan once more. "Mind, I don't know. And she might not make a decision for a few years. Michael's steward has remained at the estate and is more than capable of dealing with it until someone is chosen."

Tristan forced a laugh. "Can you imagine James as Lord Lockhart?"

"No, it won't be James."

At Thomas's somber tone, Tristan's laughter was cut short.

"Why not? He's the eldest, it would be reasonable."

"True, but that won't happen," said Thomas. Ignoring his son's attempt to break in with more questions, he added, "I'll tell you some other day. But James will never hold a title in Aquila."

Before Tristan could say another word, Thomas turned the subject back to a new horse.

As Tristan approached the courier tent one morning in May, Captain Stephens called out to him. The officer bounced on the balls of his feet, fidgeting.

"Thatcher! C'mere, lad. I have a delivery for Altair. And Tristan," he lowered his voice, "this must be given to the queen herself."

Tristan's gaze dropped to the missive. It had a red feather stamped on it.

"You might run into trouble along the way. Be careful. And stick to the main roads."

This comment intrigued Tristan. The road to Altair had become so mundane he had taken to learning alternate routes to relieve the boredom. He wondered what trouble could be found this far east.

As he readied Dun, he noted again his faithful horse seemed thinner and his coat dull. "After this run I'll give you a good rest, boy," he said, spending an extra moment rubbing him. "I'll borrow or buy another one until we get your gloss back. But you needn't be jealous. You'll always be my top man, I promise. That's my lad." Dun nickered and thumped Tristan's chest.

For a single rider on a good horse, the ride to Altair could be made in a week, barring problems. As Tristan knew it would be, the first day on the road was dull, all forest and dark under the trees. Several hours into the second day, he slowed Dun to an amble. He loved this section of the road with its rolling, grassy plains and scattered pockets of forest. The weather was beautiful, with a clear blue sky and mild temperatures. And yet...

He reined Dun to a complete stop, standing in the stirrups for a better view. It was too quiet. The birds should have been making a clamor, but they were silent. The hairs on the back of his neck rose.

An arrow thudded into the ground about fifteen feet ahead. It flew so far past him he couldn't believe any decent archer had been aiming for him. When a second arrow struck the ground beside them, Tristan determined that was quite enough and urged Dun to a run. More arrows rained all around them, and Dun squealed as one sank into his haunch.

As they ran beyond the reach of the archers, a small band of horsemen appeared on his left, another on his right. The group on the left fell behind, allowing the other group to direct Tristan north. They were herding him. He tugged hard at the reins, swinging wide until he was headed south again. Both groups were back on his tail. From this new angle, a bright light flashed in his vision. The sun reflecting off armor. Against the backdrop of a patch of forest half a mile off, he made out an encampment far southeast flying the eagle of Aquila. Tristan gave a shout of victory.

"Come on, Dun!" he yelled, aching for his poor horse, who was running as fast as he could with an injury. Dun huffed as he strained to race faster. They neared the encampment and the horses behind them split apart, circling the camp. With a final burst of speed, Dun flew through the tents, and a few men cheered them on. Tristan yanked him to a halt and fell over the horse's lathered neck, blowing hard. An uneven hitch in Dun's gait had Tristan twisting to inspect the arrow in Dun's rump.

Thankful to see it wasn't deeply embedded, he looked around with a relieved grin on his face and froze.

Stern-faced soldiers surrounded him. Several had arrows on the string and others had their swords drawn.

Tristan raised his hands and called out in a clear voice, "Messenger with Aquila's army. I'm on my way to Altair."

The men exchanged glances but otherwise didn't move. Tristan fought his growing bafflement until the two groups of horsemen who had been chasing him rode into camp. The silence grew more ominous. It dawned on him, too late, that these men were no friends of Aquila. He swore under his breath.

An officer strode into the circle and yelled in exasperation, "What are you men doing? You think this boy is going to kill the lot of you? Put down your weapons. And I told you archers not to strike him or his horse!"

Tristan considered urging Dun to run for it and tensed. The officer grabbed Dun's bridle.

"Easy, lad. Don't try to be a hero," he said amiably.

"How did Sammanon forces get this far east?"

The surrounding men erupted in guffaws.

"Sammanon forces? Didn't you see our standard? No, lad, these are good men of Aquila before you. Some of the best, I think. Now, get off your horse."

"No."

The officer's lips quirked, but his voice remained firm. "Get off, boy. We won't hurt you, and it seems to me your horse needs attention."

A quick survey of his surroundings told Tristan he had no choice, and he dismounted Dun. As soon as he hit the ground, the officer took hold of his arm while passing the reins to another man. Dun tossed his head and his ears swept back as he watched Tristan being dragged from him. He charged and the men leaped to the side, shouting. These men were not horsemen, Tristan thought with some disgust. Dun lashed out with his hooves. Tristan marveled at his energetic rebellion, injured as he was, and put aside the notion that his horse might be getting too old for this work. Dun broke away, weaving his way through the camp to freedom.

"Oh, let him go," the officer said when his men looked at him, helpless. He rolled his eyes at them. "The letter will be in the satchel anyway. Hand it over."

Tristan hesitated while his mind raced. His fingers twitched on his sword's hilt.

"Don't do it."

With a sigh, he handed over the satchel. The captain nodded.

"You're a brave lad. And more important, you're smart. What's your name?"

"Thatcher."

"You're Commander Thatcher's youngest, yes?"

Tristan saw no point in lying but wondered how he knew. "Yes."

The men muttered among themselves. The officer grunted and jerked his head toward a soldier.

"Bring him to my quarters."

His tent was spacious and well-ordered. They passed a table spread over with maps and other papers. Tristan craned his neck to get a glimpse, but the soldier urged him past it with narrowed eyes. However, the officer appeared amused by it all. He tossed the satchel onto the table and sat on a small wooden chair. Once settled, he dismissed the soldier.

"Alone at last. Captain Marcus Wylie." The man held his hand out to Tristan, who made no move to take it. "You've never heard of me?" At Tristan's silence, a shadow of sadness passed over Wylie's face. Then he smiled. "So, you're Thomas Thatcher's son. I know—knew—your father very well. Knew your cousin Lockhart, too. You remind me of him. He was a fine man, terrible shame about his death."

Wylie sifted through the satchel, removing the letter with the red feather and breaking the seal. His eyes dashed over the script. Frowning, he waved the letter. "What is this?"

"I'm just a messenger, I don't read what they give me." Tristan kept his tone mild, but Wylie gave him a piercing look. He held the letter open before Tristan. The words were nonsense, and Tristan shrugged. "Perhaps it's a code?"

Wylie stared at Tristan, who didn't blink. He sighed as he tucked the letter into his tunic. "I'm sorry about this."

Before Tristan could decipher those words, Wylie struck him hard across the face. The surprise of it made Tristan cry out. Wylie stepped close and muttered, "My apologies, lad. If it didn't seem like I roughed you up a bit, the men would be after you, and they would be far, far worse."

Tristan wiped some blood from his nose and scowled at Wylie.

"Good men of Aquila, eh?"

Wylie started before laughing. "Well, perhaps that was overstating it. They aren't Sammanon's creatures, at least."

"Who are you?"

"We're a faction of the army who believe the leadership is flawed, and we are striving to set things right."

"By betrayal?" Tristan demanded.

"Ah. Well, we have tried to make our voices heard through the usual channels, but to no avail. Further action must be taken. Anyway, this is of no import."

"I beg your pardon, but it is of great importance to me."

"Perhaps." Wylie considered Tristan for a moment. "Hand over your weapons, lad."

Tristan hesitated after unsheathing his sword. "Sir, my brother—Lord Lockhart to you—he gave this to me. It was my first sword and he…" Tristan fought the sudden tightness in his chest. He had long since outgrown the smallish weapon but had been loath to give it up yet. Understanding dawned in Wylie's eyes.

"I promise it will be returned in due time. You must understand, I can't let you walk out of here armed." Wylie confiscated the sword and called for assistance. In Tristan's ear he whispered, "Act defeated, lad, if you know how, which I doubt. Don't stir up my men with defiance. Trust me on this."

The same soldier from before reappeared, and Wylie handed Tristan over to the man. "Tie him to that big oak south of camp. And I want it clear he is to be left alone, you hear me?"

Tristan most definitely did *not* trust the captain and was far from defeated. But after taking a good look at the men watching him exit the tent, he considered it wise advice and hung his head, stumbling as he was led to an oak grove about thirty yards outside of the camp. The soldier bound him to a young sapling and left him. Tristan settled himself against the trunk of the tree, thinking. Escape was imperative, however that would have to wait until the cover of darkness.

It was a long day. At sunset a soldier let him loose long enough to eat a hunk of bread and gulp some water. Afterward, he was allowed a marginal degree of privacy to do his business before the soldier tied him up again. Tristan decided to get some sleep before attempting his escape. Thankful that he had inherited his father's ability to sleep anywhere, he was soon snoring.

When Tristan awoke under a rising half-moon, he guessed it was close to midnight. Trees surrounded him, blocking a clear view of the camp, but the flicker of firelight sometimes danced into his vision. He worked on his bonds, getting a feel for the cords and how they were tied, surprised his captors had done such a shoddy job. His feet were loosely bound, and even the ropes around his wrists were not very tight. In truth, Tristan felt a touch disgruntled that he didn't pose more of a threat, until he recalled something Michael had said to him long ago—*there's nothing wrong with being underestimated*. He almost laughed, remembering. It took some time, but Tristan was patient and snorted with contempt when he worked his hands free and made quick work of the remaining knots. He lurched to his feet and swayed, his muscles cramped from the long hours in one position.

Heavy footsteps approached. The snap of a twig. The sound sent Tristan rearing back up against the tree. Flashbacks of that day in the willows sent his pulse racing.

"Thatcher? Where are you, lad?"

Tristan didn't respond, quiet other than his thumping heart.

"I have your sword. You're welcome to it."

Tristan clenched his teeth and came out from behind the tree. Captain Wylie stood in the shadows with Tristan's sword in hand. His hands were lowered in a submissive gesture. "I was going to cut you free, but I see you've already taken care of that yourself," he said with a trace of wry humor in his voice.

"Why?" Tristan asked warily.

"What good are you to me as a prisoner? You're a messenger doing your job, I have no objections. Not to mention I wouldn't dream of antagonizing your father. That would take a braver man than I."

Tristan warily reached for his sword. "As long as I keep my mouth shut?"

"On the contrary, lad. I'm letting you go, hoping you'll tell Queen Charlotte what I said. Every word. I want solutions, and that requires attention. There are ways to defend Aquila without always resorting to war. But it takes time, money, and self-sacrifice. Look at what your father has done on the border! He doesn't want to fight this war."

"My father is no coward!" Tristan exclaimed. To his surprise, Wylie grinned.

"No, indeed he is not. He's one of the most courageous men I've ever known. Think to yourself, if you know him at all, why did he spend years in the mountains, even after he found you? Yes, I know your family history, Tristan Thatcher. Your father could have been a general, yet he's spent his life in the shadows. Why?"

Tristan was silent. This exact question had plagued Michael—the continued work in the Shadowlands, the relentless drive that pursued his father and his refusal to play court games. Wylie startled Tristan by grabbing his shoulders, almost shaking him.

"He's done everything he could to prevent the wars from ever starting! Catch problems early, find solutions before death and destruction! Consider this, lad. How does your father feel about these wars? Seeing good men slaughtered in this endless cycle? Teaching young men to kill? Generation after generation lost to our land. They weaken our armies until one day there will be none left. Can you understand?"

Tristan remained silent, knowing all too well what his father thought.

Wylie released Tristan and paced. "We should be strengthening our borders. Show we are a force to be reckoned with. Or if you want war, why not be the aggressor and attack Sammanon for once, instead of sitting back and waiting for the ceaseless barrage?"

"You're mad!"

"Am I? Perhaps. Maybe I've spent too many years watching men like MacClaren enjoy their health and wealth until war is inevitable and they send off other men's sons to die. Do you know MacClaren keeps his own people at home, sending mercenaries from the southern kingdoms to fight here instead? Saving his own army. Don't you find that interesting?"

Tristan found himself drawn into Wylie's words, despite his initial resistance. "Why would he do that?"

"That, my young friend, is the question." Wylie let his words hang in the air before muttering, "It's getting late. Go, and tell them what I said. Tell the queen everything I told you, understand? *Everything*. Now, take your sword and go. And Tristan? Your one weapon was exposed and ready for anyone to confiscate. Boots. A hidden weapon is a valuable possession, and a soldier or brigand doesn't always check the boots."

Tristan knew Wylie couldn't see his sudden grin in the darkness, but he ducked his head anyway. However, he sobered with Wylie's next words.

"Farewell, Tristan. It was a pleasure meeting you. You are your father's son, which is the highest compliment I can pay to any man. I'll leave you with one word of caution. Many people are aware of your affection for the young princess. Be careful, lad. And I'm sorry again about striking you."

And with that, Wylie melted into the darkness.

# Chapter 29

# Jericho

Tristan awoke with a start and sat bolt upright, disoriented. He had been sleeping so hard he forgot where he was. After leaving Wylie, he had crept through the woods for most of the night. In the gray hours before dawn, he discovered the perfect place to hunker down and get a short sleep in a shallow depression under a fallen tree.

Seeing the sun shining through the trees, Tristan crawled out of his hiding spot and stretched, his stomach growling. He always ate light on the road, but yesterday's morsel of bread seemed a long time ago.

"Wylie could have at least given me a waterskin," he grumbled. Tristan looked around, resigned. Nothing for it, he commenced walking, wondering about Dun. There was no telling where the horse had gone after his wild performance. A few times Tristan whistled to see if Dun might show himself, but to no avail. Otherwise, he kept quiet and worked his way east.

Tristan skirted the edges of the main road until near sunset. He was ravenous and considered setting up a small snare. But he balked at the idea. It would take too much time with no guarantee of catching anything quickly. He had a better chance of begging for a bite at a farmhouse. Tristan muttered a prayer of thanks when he came across a stream to slake his thirst.

For days he walked east. Often he gained a rest by a passing farmer taking him a few miles on a wagon. With his money packed in saddlebags and wandering somewhere with Dun, he couldn't buy food, but occasionally someone would offer a small roll or a chunk of cheese. By the time he arrived in the city of Altair, he was tired and bedraggled but exuberant. Given his appearance, complete with a scanty beard, he had some trouble getting past the castle guards. He was almost to the Great Hall when Christiana came rushing down the stairs and into his arms.

"Tristan, I've been so worried!"

"Whatever for? You can't have known I was on my way!"

"When Dun showed up without you, and hurt, I didn't know..." She pressed against him, and he didn't understand her next few muffled words. He held her out at arm's length.

"Dun's here?"

"He arrived two days ago. He was positively wild, but George managed to calm him."

Tristan started laughing. "Of all the horses..."

Seeing Christiana still shaken, he squeezed her tight. "I'm fine, love. Don't fuss." His reassurances dissolved into kisses, and he had to tear himself away. "I need to see your mother. As soon as possible."

"Yes, she'll be down in a moment. Or will you come up?"

Tristan followed her into the queen's chambers. He had never been in any of the private family rooms before. They entered an airy chamber that was part sitting room and part study, with a large desk dominating one corner. Charlotte swept in through another door as they arrived and embraced Tristan.

"My dear boy, what a mess! You can't imagine the tumult Dun has caused. Are you harmed?"

"Not at all, but tired and hungry as a bear."

"I'm sure you are, dear. There's food on the way."

Both Charlotte and Christiana fussed over him before allowing Tristan to tell his news, tugging off his boots over his protests and urging him to the fire. Despite the embarrassment, he enjoyed the attention. As he settled in and waited for his food, he told them of his adventure on the road. Normally impassive, the queen jumped at what Wylie had said regarding Lord General MacClaren but recovered herself.

"He's becoming bolder," she murmured. For a fleeting moment Tristan wondered whether the queen was referring to MacClaren or Wylie. She broke her reverie with a sharp question. "Are you sure about this?"

"Yes, ma'am."

"And you've told me everything? Think. Even the smallest detail in these situations can matter."

"Tristan's tired, Momma, and hungry."

Charlotte relented, for Tristan did appear weary. "It's a shame Wylie got the letter."

Tristan cackled. "Not quite. Hand me my left boot." He leaned forward to catch the boot from Charlotte. Smiling, he pulled from the depths a worn, stained letter stamped with a red feather. Christiana gasped and clapped her hands.

"Urgent news for you, Your Grace." Tristan bowed grandly. "Wylie said no one ever checks boots, and he was right. Even he didn't. I'm sorry for the stink."

"Good heavens! What letter does Wylie have?"

"A fabrication. Several months ago I had Ethan write some nonsense in code, his hand is far better than mine, and we made it look as official as possible. Whenever I've had a hint of danger on my rides, I stuffed the real letter in my boot and left the fake one in the bag. Stephens was so jumpy about me riding, I knew this was one of those times. Granted, I shouldn't have been such an idiot to be caught, but at least the code will keep them occupied awhile."

Charlotte studied Tristan before a laugh escaped her. Then she grew serious once more. "Tristan, I'm going to ask you to do a hard thing. You must not tell anyone about your conversation with Captain Wylie, do you understand? Don't say his name. You may speak of your capture and escape from brigands, but nothing more. Not to your brothers, not even your father."

Tristan frowned. He had never withheld anything from his father, but Thomas himself had impressed upon his sons to always abide by the queen and her commands. He nodded his assent with reluctance.

"Thank you, dear boy. I know I can rely on your discretion. And Christiana, the same goes for you. This must not leave the room. Don't write of it to your brother."

"Yes, Momma."

Tristan no longer cared about the queen's odd request after the tray of food arrived. The queen had retreated to her desk, and after a sheepish apology to Christiana, he dug in. There was hot spit-roasted chicken with fresh bread, spring grass butter, honey, and a tankard of ale. As soon as his eating slowed and he drank the last drop of ale, Charlotte called to Tristan from her desk.

"Why don't you go down to your room rest while I write a reply?"

"For a bit? He'll be staying for the night at least!" Christiana interjected. Her face fell when he shook his head. Tristan understood her disappointment, for he wanted some time with her too.

"I'll stay until the letter is done, but I've been gone too long, Chris. I have to get back as soon as I can. And I'll need a fresh mount. I doubt Dun can make the ride yet. He needs a good rest anyway."

Charlotte spoke without looking up from her writing. "Christiana, take him to the stables and show him Jericho. If you like him, Tristan, he's yours to keep. Your father wrote you were on the lookout for a second horse, and George thought he might be a good choice for you."

"You're too generous, I—"

"Shush, dear, I'm writing."

Tristan knew better than to argue, so he relaxed on the sofa. He was warm, well fed, and drowsy with his sweet girl's head on his shoulder. When Charlotte declared her letter done, he tugged his boots on with great reluctance. She handed him several letters, and he took his leave of her. Christiana walked with him to the stables. There he was reunited with a very happy Dun.

"There's my good lad! How are you, boy?" Tristan exclaimed as he inspected his horse. He was pleased to see Dun's injury healing and said as much to George, the head stableman.

"Aye, give him a few weeks and he'll be as good as new. I'll send a groom with him to the camp. I hope ya like the horse I found for ya. It'll be better for this ole lad if ya could have another mount, as yer father said." George led him to a different stall. "This, young Tristan, is Jericho."

Tristan's eyes widened, and Christiana giggled.

"He's gorgeous," he whispered. He stepped into the stall, eyeing the tall, red bay stallion. Jericho had a deep chest, long legs, and strong haunches. Tristan's mouth went dry. Jericho was built for speed and more. With his height and large bones, he wasn't just a riding horse or a mountain scrub. He was a *warhorse*. Far more horse than Tristan had imagined owning for a long time.

"Jericho," crooned Tristan, and the horse turned his bright, intelligent eyes on him. Holding out his hand, he let Jericho snuffle him. The ears pricked back and forth. With a snort and a step forward, the animal thumped his large head against the boy's chest. At Tristan's laugh, George chortled.

"He's not cut and very spirited, but he's no real vice, young Tristan. Ya'll have no problem handlin' the likes of him, the way ya are with the beasts. Barely four year. He should be grand for ya."

A slow smile spread across Tristan's face.

"I can see I've made ya happy."

"Very happy, thank you, George."

"Good lad. I'll return to my work and will send Dun to ya soon."

Once George left them, Tristan grinned at Christiana. "I'm smitten, Chris. Is he truly mine?"

He looked the horse up and down, felt his legs, checked his mouth, murmuring horsespeak all the while. Jericho seemed to approve, his eyes fiery but soft. When Tristan reached for a bridle, Christiana cried out in dismay.

"You aren't leaving yet!"

"I must, it's been days past when I should have been back. If Dad's heard I've been missing this long, he'll be frantic."

Her jaw set in that stubborn way he knew all too well.

"C'mon, Chris, you want to let him think something's happened to me? I can't do that to him! Not after last summer."

"But you must be exhausted!"

"I am, and what's more, I hate not having time with you." Frustrated, he glanced around the stable and brightened before grabbing her hand. "Come with me!"

They climbed into the hayloft, stifling their laughter until Tristan playfully flung her into the hay, causing her to giggle aloud. He put his arms around her.

"Be quiet, or someone will hear us. Just a few minutes." He kissed her. Another lengthy kiss and she buried her face into his neck, giggling harder.

"Will you stop?"

"Your beard tickles."

"There's hardly anything there! Now shush, or I'll—" He rolled over her with a fervent kiss of longing that led to another and yet another. His latest adventure had made him bold, and her fire matched his. Her fingers tangled in his hair, and he loved the way she encouraged his kisses.

Tristan held her body against his own while his head swam with the closeness of her. Christiana's mouth was honey to his lips, and he couldn't get his fill. He didn't care that he dangled on the edge of a dangerous precipice. His kisses wandered from her mouth, trailing along her neck. The heat of a reckless passion demanded more, but a quiet voice in his heart urged caution. Every fiber of his being wanted her and the voice grew in strength.

The loud squeal of a horse from below brought him back to himself, flushed and excited. Tristan stared at Christiana, startled at his own behavior.

"I'm sorry," he said, panting. "I shouldn't have—as tired as I am, I didn't think—"

"I know," she whispered, bringing her hand to his cheek in a soothing gesture.

"You do stir my blood, Your Highness," Tristan said with a rueful smile as he put some space between them. Tristan propped himself up on one elbow, thinking how lovely Christiana looked nestled in the hay.

He chuckled but sobered almost at once, gazing at Christiana with such tenderness it made her ache to hold him. Tristan brought his hand to her cheek and stroked it. "More so, you stir my heart, you know that?"

She leaned into his caress. "How I do love you, Tristan."

Tristan swallowed hard. "When this is over, I'm never leaving you again. Not to the mountains, not anywhere. If you'll have me, my sweet Christiana." He bent to her with a whisper of a kiss that grazed her lips.

"Stay here with me. Please, Tristan."

"I can't. Dad—"

"Go tell your father you are safe and come home. He'll be happy knowing you're here, out of danger."

"I don't think so. Yes, he wants his sons safe, but that doesn't mean he would be happy with me hiding from it all either. Not really."

He flopped back into the hay, sighing, and rubbed at his eyes. They were itchy from lack of sleep. She cuddled against him, her head on his chest. He marveled at the delicious warmth of her lying alongside him. He couldn't fathom what he had done to win her heart, but he would never cease striving to deserve her. "It's not the right time for us anyway."

"How can you say such things?"

"I want to be worthy of you, Chris. Truly worthy. Loving you isn't enough, at least not for me. As much as we jest, you *are* the princess of Aquila. Do you believe anyone would think my work as a messenger boy is enough?" He couldn't help the touch of scorn that colored his tone.

"Your work *is* valuable, Tristan. Think of what you did!"

"Perhaps, but no. It's not enough. Sometimes I feel guilty, loving you this way. I don't deserve you."

"Stop," she said, raising her head to kiss him.

"Deserve you or not," he whispered, "I do love you. Someday..."

She lay down again, and he stroked her long hair, unbound as always. They remained still for some time. It was warm in the hay, and gentle nickers floated up to them. Tristan caught himself dozing several times and knew he would be snoring hard if he stayed much longer. He forced himself to sit.

"You need to go?"

"Yes, I'm sorry."

He made a show of saddling the tall Jericho, punctuated by laughter from them both. When he mounted, he asked, "How do I look?"

Her eyes sparkled, for Tristan sat taller on the giant beast. "Impressive," she said flirtatiously, "but I like you better on the ground with me."

"Until next time, my love." Tristan's gaze drifted down the lane to the city gate, and he shivered for some reason he couldn't explain. He shook his head to clear it and leaned from his saddle to kiss his girl one last time.

Tristan stayed off the main road on his return trip, using the hidden trails he had learned over the winter months. He ran into no trouble, but the route took longer, and he was anxious to get back to camp. Nevertheless, they had made excellent time. Tristan couldn't believe how fast the new horse could go, but Jericho also had a hard mouth that needed work. Dun moved at the lightest touch of the reins, whereas Jericho required a constant grip. When he rode up to the courier station, Tristan slid out of the saddle with a bone-deep weariness, many days past when he should have been back.

"Tristan! By the faith, I thought you were done for!" Captain Stephens gasped at his appearance. "What happened to Dun? And since when do you ride a charger?"

Tristan gave Stephens a summary of his adventure. After a chuckle over the coded letter, the captain grew serious, saying, "It might not be a bad idea to implement on a regular basis."

"Not too regular. We don't want anyone getting wind of it," Tristan said. He accepted a mug of ale from Stephens with a nod of appreciation as he handed the queen's letters over. The captain's eyebrows shot up when he saw one was addressed to him. He opened it and sat, sipping his own ale. His eyes darted to Tristan once in surprise before returning to the letter.

Tristan noticed, but before he could question Stephens, his jaw almost dislocated with a tremendous yawn. "My apologies, sir. I'm done in, to be honest. Would you mind getting word to my father that I'm safe? I need rest and food, or I would go to him myself."

"I will. Ho! Groom! Come take care of this man's horse."

Tristan hung back, surprised. Most of the couriers cared for their own horses. But Stephens took it a step further.

"This is Thatcher, our top man. I want his horses to be cared for at all times. You hear?" The groom bobbed his head and led Jericho to the nearest pen. Stephens slapped Tristan on the shoulder. "I'll send your message to Thomas, don't worry. Get a good rest."

Bemused, Tristan had a troubling suspicion he had just been promoted.

# Chapter 30

# Tavern Gossip

Tristan's rides to Altair had come to an end.

Wylie's men had withdrawn and hidden themselves in some mysterious new location. This made the Altair road easy and safe once more; a good route for breaking in fresh riders. War now raged in earnest, and as one of the more experienced couriers, Tristan was needed for more dangerous rides.

Watching new riders take over the Altair route filled Tristan with envy, for he had no idea when he would see Christiana again. The prospect of being parted from her indefinitely made him gloomy. They wrote often, and Tristan reminded himself of the many summer months he had spent in the mountains. Those times had offered rare chances at mail, so this was better in some ways.

Captain Stephens held his breath every time he sent the youth out. He admired Thomas Thatcher, but word was the man held a particular soft spot for his youngest son. Stephens suspected the commander would personally see to his miserable death should anything happen to Tristan, and he had no desire to test this notion. However, time and again, Tristan proved himself worthy of the challenge. He had a knack for weaving around pockets of battle. He knew the terrain and his horses well and would choose which horse to ride based on the job at hand. If the ground was rough or he had to dodge enemy camps, steady Dun was his first choice. When circumstances demanded pure speed and boldness, Tristan could be seen flying across the meadowlands on Jericho. He soon gained a reputation for being fearless and was in high demand for the most dangerous rides, much to the disappointment of his father.

Though Tristan rarely found himself exposed to the worst of the fighting, it was harrowing at times. He would often come upon a field after a battle, forced to pick his way over dead men and the mangled corpses of once-beautiful horses. Tristan shuddered at the cries of the wounded and the blood streaming over large swaths of war-torn earth. But more than anything, the smells were what got under his skin. Between the stench and the carrion birds, Tristan could locate the site of a battle from miles away.

A few weeks after his last ride to Altair, Tristan heard rumors Captain Wylie and his company had been captured, and Wylie was to be hanged for sedition. He never dared ask anyone if the stories were true, fearing it would open a tangled conversation he had sworn to keep secret. Some nights when sleep failed to come, Tristan would recall the words of Captain Wylie and wish he could talk it over with his father.

*My dearest Chris,*

*I'm due to ride, but Stephens is giving me a few moments before sending the latest courier to Altair. Your last letter made my heart dance even as it made me blush. I plead with you to send no such letter again. For one, it could be intercepted. But more to the point, it caused me to lie awake half the night considering your words.*

*To tell you how much I miss you would take pages, and I must be off. Greetings to your mother. Tell her I spoke with Justin not long ago, and he is quite well. Please keep James and my father in your prayers as they fight for us all.*

*I love you so dearly and hold you in my heart.*

*Always yours,*

*Tristan*

The boys had been surprised to see Thomas enter the war as a commander, one step below general. He had resisted a higher placement for years, and Charlotte almost had to issue a Queen's Command to force him to take the position. He accepted with great reluctance, but his sons were proud of the recognition. Although Tristan endeavored to see his father whenever he could, there was never time for more than a quick word. Through Tristan, the family maintained near-constant communication. He often carried notes between them as he traveled among the various camps.

James quickly gained a reputation as a bold, reckless warrior and deadly with a sword. Unsurprisingly, he had been promoted to captain soon after his first battle and seemed to always be in the worst of the fighting. His brothers quaked at his fearlessness. They spent many long nights awake after rumors of a battle, waiting for the lists to see if James's name was among the dead.

The three brothers did their best to see one another whenever they could. Michael's death and the war had made them closer than ever. That is not to say they were without strife, and Ethan frequently played the role of peacemaker between James and Tristan. Nevertheless, the brothers loved each other with a fierce devotion. When Ethan and Tristan were shifted farther west into the primary camp, it was an occasion of great joy for all three to be close to each other once more.

Soon after acquiring Jericho, Tristan admitted to Ethan he looked forward to seeing James's reaction. He was not disappointed.

"I see you finally got a real horse!" James said with deep admiration. "He's a handsome boy. What happened to the pony?"

Tristan glared at James, but Ethan jumped into the conversation before he could respond. "Took an arrow in the rump. Tristan got Jericho on his last ride to Altair. Dun's well now, and he's been riding both."

"What happens later with this beauty? Will you have to send him back to Altair?" asked James, walking around the young stallion. Jericho recognized a kindred spirit and tossed his head, showing off.

"He's *mine*, James. Don't get any ideas. I'll use them both, it'll be better anyway. Dad told me I should have two horses, and he was right. All the riding has been hard on Dun."

"Tris, you know I'm teasing about Dun. I'm glad he wasn't seriously hurt. Do let me have a ride on this one, a little roundabout. Please?"

With a dramatic sigh, Tristan handed over the reins.

It was new for Tristan and Ethan to be in the thick of the fighting army with thousands of soldiers surrounding them. James thrived on the chaos, but his younger brothers yearned for the quiet of Castle Altair.

A few weeks after Ethan's eighteenth birthday, a lull in battle came, and the brothers grabbed the opportunity to be together. They wandered over to the rustic tavern that had sprung up in a matter of days last spring. It was large and packed full of customers happy to spend a day or two away from dying on the field of battle.

Waiting for the barman, Tristan eyed a table of Woodraven soldiers off to themselves. "Those Woodraven men are enormous! Do they all grow so big there?"

James grunted in response.

"That must be where you and Dad get your size," Tristan continued. "Ethan too. Well, he's tall at least. Why couldn't Dad have passed that on to me?"

Ethan chuckled and looked from James to Tristan, exaggerating the height difference with his gaze. Tristan playfully punched James, who seemed bent on ignoring him.

"What do you think of those Woodraven men? How do they fight?"

"Why are you asking me?" James snapped. "I'm no expert on Woodraven."

Both his brothers stared at him, and James shifted. He forced an apologetic smile. "You're the youngest. Maybe Dad's blood was running thin by the time you came around."

Tristan rolled his eyes, causing James to smirk. His grumpiness dissipated, and he sprang for the first round of ale. They settled in a dark nook, happy to be together.

"James, question for you—aah, this is excellent ale!" Tristan said with relish after gulping some down, and James laughed.

"Yes, but it's powerful stuff, be careful. I hear they age it in whiskey barrels."

"I can tell!" Tristan gasped, wiping some foam from his mouth. "James, where does Dad get his money? I've been meaning to ask you for ages and keep forgetting."

James dropped his eyes and fiddled with his mug. His brothers exchanged significant looks. James coughed. "I'm not sure what to say."

"What do you know?" Tristan demanded. "Does he still have some family in Woodraven?"

James raised his hands. "It's complicated, Tris. He might be waiting until you're older to talk about it."

"I don't see what age has to do with it!"

"Have it out with Dad!"

"Perhaps," Ethan inserted with a sly grin, "he has a rich mistress."

All three burst out in a fit of laughter. Good humor restored, they spent the next half hour amusing themselves with guesses concerning the source of their father's money. Soon they were cackling, trying to outdo each other with wilder, crazier notions. As they joked, a nearby table filled with a large group of soldiers, and one of them arrested James's attention.

"See there," he said in a low voice. "That's Gerald MacClaren, old Lord General MacClaren's son."

The name MacClaren alerted Tristan, and he peered over at the table.

"That's the younger MacClaren?" Ethan asked. "I've heard of him but didn't know what he looked like."

Tristan took a long sip of ale, thinking of Captain Wylie. "Andrew Kavanaugh hates Lord MacClaren, and from what I hear, the feeling is mutual."

"No love lost between him and Dad either." James winked at his youngest brother. "Gerald there is a piece of work. He's a braggart and a bully. Mind you, that's half the men here. Supposedly, he's rough with the camp wenches. An incredible swordsman, though, one of the best I've ever seen. Look at him, Tristan. He's massive, but I tell you, he's also more agile than you would assume. A lot of men his size think they can throw their weight around with a sword, but he has true skill. I would love to see you matched against him, your speed against his strength."

Tristan shuddered after sneaking another peek. MacClaren was a hulking beast of a man. "No thanks. He would have me down in a minute flat."

James hooted. Tristan scrunched his face, thinking. Something about the younger MacClaren tickled Tristan's memory, although he couldn't recall ever meeting him. Perhaps it was his previous glimpse of Lord General MacClaren that made him think so.

The men at the other table continued laughing and talking about women, and Tristan tried to block his ears from their vulgarities. A shift in their conversation caught his attention, and he shushed James, who was telling a story about his most recent battle.

"I did hear the princess had a conquest of the heart. Someone in that family, what's-their-names. The ones who raised Lockhart?"

Tristan hunkered on his bench, thankful they had chosen a table in a dark corner. James, on the other hand, always intrigued by gossip, tried to angle his body into a position to hear better.

"Thatcher? What a joke! It was a sorry day when that interloper came to court. Father's been trying to drive him out for years."

These comments were nothing new to the brothers after months in the army. Thomas Thatcher elicited extreme opinions from the military and nobility, ranging from devoted respect to disdain. These opinions trickled through the ranks until they reached the boys, and they were used to it.

MacClaren continued. "I'll concede Captain Thatcher is a fine fighter. Even Father has been impressed with his sword arm. It was rumored long ago the queen intended to pair him with Princess Christiana, and I can see why they thought—"

James let loose a snort before smothering it, but he couldn't entirely contain his mirth after the suspicious glare Tristan shot him. Shaking with suppressed laughter, James raised his hands in a helpless gesture at Tristan.

"—the other two aren't even fighting. Well, one is a healer. But then there's that runt of a younger brother. Wherever did they dig him up?"

The humor left James's face. There were guffaws, and one of the men rose to refill a few mugs. A man at the table made a comment the brothers didn't catch. MacClaren responded with a sneer. "Oh, he's young, I suppose. Still, when you have fourteen- and fifteen-year-old lads wielding swords, what does he mean by traipsing around on a horse? A glorified messenger boy at that age. Father would be ashamed to have such a coward for a son."

Tristan blushed. Rising to his feet and gripping his sword, James raised his eyebrows at Tristan as though demanding permission to engage. Tristan shook his head, and Ethan yanked at his arm. James sat back down, releasing the pommel of his sword. He shoved his mug aside and raked a hand through his red hair.

The beer fetcher had rejoined the table, and MacClaren jostled him while speaking in a conspiratorial tone. "I'll tell you something few others know. Queen Charlotte and Father arranged it years ago, but it's been kept quiet. The Houses of Reynard and MacClaren will be joined when the war is over. The princess and I have been good friends for years, and let's say I've visited Altair quite a bit these last few months and been greeted with open arms."

There was an enthusiastic response to these words, and toasts were given. MacClaren emptied his mug and urged the others to do the same. Soon after, the crowd dispersed.

Tristan sat as though turned to stone, his face drained of all color. It couldn't be true, he knew in his heart, and yet...It had been months since he had been to Altair. Had things changed? Was he being pushed out of the way for another, more worthy suitor? But no, Charlotte had encouraged their courtship. He thought of that day with Christiana nestled in the hayloft, and the sweet warmth of memory washed over him. No, he must not lose faith in that. He must not lose faith in her.

Ethan placed his hand on Tristan's arm. "Don't think about it, Tris."

"You should have let me run a sword through him," said James.

"Don't be such an ass," Ethan snapped in a rare show of temper.

Choosing to ignore the comments about Christiana altogether, Tristan clenched his jaw. "He's right, though, isn't he? About me not fighting. People say I'm a coward?"

James winced. "In a way, yes. That's how some may see it. But listen, it doesn't matter. Dad doesn't want you fighting, he's told me this a hundred times. And it's not only about keeping you safe. He was really broken up about what happened that day. I'm not talking about just losing Michael. Dad hated that you had to kill a man, young as you were."

"If it makes any difference," Ethan added, "Michael didn't want you fighting either. If anything, he felt stronger about it than Dad."

"Of course he did. Michael would have wrapped me in wool batting if he could have." Bitterness laced Tristan's words, and a tight ball formed in his chest. "It was a year ago, you know. Last month."

Always unsure how to handle Tristan in these moments, James flapped his hands at Ethan, who moved to Tristan's side of the table and put his arm around his brother's shoulders. "Michael didn't think you weren't capable. He was very proud of you, he told me days before he—He loved you, Tristan, and wanted to protect you more than anything."

Thinking of his final minutes with Michael, Tristan nodded, his throat aching. "I know he did."

"And so does Dad," insisted Ethan. "And not just you. He loves all of us, much more than he can ever say. Don't you think if he could stop James from fighting, he would?"

Tristan offered a strained smile. "I doubt even Dad could manage that."

Relieved that Tristan seemed to be moving past his angst, James urged them all to get another round. The afternoon continued, and Tristan joined in the conversation as much as ever. But Ethan watched him closely, a little seed of worry taking root in his mind.

# Chapter 31

# Before the Storm

After the brothers left the tavern, James grabbed Tristan's arm, steering him along the camp road without a word. Distracted by an amusing story Ethan was telling them, Tristan let James take the lead until they reached the sword master's training ground. The air was dusty and thick with the sound of clashing swords.

"Oh no!" Tristan groaned. "I've been practicing, James, I swear it, but no."

James turned to Ethan, who affirmed Tristan's claim. "It's true. I've seen him at it."

"Excellent. I expect to see improvement," said James.

"Have a round with me first!" Ethan volunteered with unexpected eagerness. "It's been a long time, and I'm out of practice."

"Sounds good!" James said, his eyes brightening. He didn't get a chance to spar with Ethan as often as he liked. "Don't run off, Tristan, or I'll find you."

Tristan grumbled, knowing it to be true.

"Where is your sword anyway?" demanded James.

"In our tent."

James swore and grabbed Tristan by the arms, giving him a shake. "*Never* leave your sword behind, you hear me?"

"Are you daft? I didn't think I would need it to drink an ale!"

"I don't care if you're going to the privy! You can't—" James huffed a deep breath, and Tristan drew back, startled at the intensity in his brother's eyes. Lessening his grip, James roughed Tristan's hair, his voice softening. "Sorry. I just don't ever want you to be caught unawares. You hear me?"

Heat flooded Tristan's face. Even Ethan had his sword strapped to his side. His brothers continued walking to Jarvis, the sword master. Tristan saw James pointing in his direction. Jarvis laughed and began walking toward Tristan.

"What is James up to?" muttered Tristan.

Jarvis approached Tristan, holding out his hand. "I see Captain Thatcher here now and then, but I've yet to meet you, lad."

Tristan introduced himself, and they stood against a fence rail, watching the others. Ethan rarely sparred with James, so it was always a treat to watch them face off. They were well matched in height, however their physiques and approaches to fighting were quite different. James's technique relied on his muscle and heft, whereas Ethan used even the biggest war sword in a way that was almost like dancing.

"Here we are, lad," said Jarvis, breaking into his thoughts while waving over a young soldier. "Your brother said you are a decent swordsman, why not have a round with Thorne here? He's fresh and eager. You best him, he'll learn from it, and if he gets the better of you, well, no shame. The boy's not bad. Thorne! Come over here."

Tristan was about to object but shrugged and took the sword Jarvis held out to him. He swung it a few times before nodding to Jarvis.

Thorne and Tristan acknowledged each other, and their swords went up. Tristan fought on the defensive, getting a feel for the soldier's fighting style. It took seconds to see Thorne would be no challenge. Thinking this must be some trick by Jarvis, he pulled back and glanced around. Jarvis showed no trace of humor on his face. Shrugging it off, Tristan disarmed his opponent in less than a minute.

He shook hands with Thorne, who looked shamefaced. Jarvis eyed Tristan before barking out a name followed by, "Try another round, lad?"

Tristan agreed enthusiastically. Fighting James was a game of mental and physical exhaustion but sparring with Thorne had been enjoyable. And it felt good to be doing something other than riding. He nodded at the new candidate Jarvis led to him.

"Paddy here, he's older. He'll test you, lad. He's heavier and seasoned. Don't fuss if he lays you out."

Tristan sized up the new fighter, and their swords flashed in the sunlight. Jarvis's assessment proved to be accurate. This man was a solid fighter. What's more, he knew how to throw his weight into his strokes. But Tristan had years of experience fighting bruisers like this with James, and his brother was far more skilled.

He grinned. Learning to fight had always been a necessary survival skill, not an exercise to be enjoyed. But this was *fun*. Tristan wondered if knocking back a couple of ales had loosened him up, because he could do this for hours. Paddy tripped over a stone and stumbled a few feet, allowing Tristan to take advantage with a peculiar upthrust that sent the other man's weapon flying.

Hearing his name, Tristan whirled around to see Ethan beaming at him. Tristan laughed and ran his hand through his mop of sweat-soaked hair. James clenched the hilt of his sword. He narrowed his eyes and stalked up to Tristan.

"Right. My turn. Here!" James tossed Tristan a steel helmet. Tristan gaped at his brother. They had never used proper armor when crossing blades, just bracers and a hardened leather tunic covering both their front and back. James donned his own helmet and called out, "Let's see what you got, *little* brother."

Tristan gritted his teeth, gauging his approach. James would expect him to take the defensive. And if he wanted them to wear helmets, his brother was planning to be merciless. Tristan stared at the helmet, wondering if he dared launch it at James and make a run for it. With a sigh, he tugged it onto his head.

James made his move, but Tristan was ready and threw himself into the fight instead of taking the defensive. James huffed in surprise. That fraction of a second gave Tristan the narrowest advantage. Recovering, James blocked Tristan's attack and swung his own counterstroke.

"Watch your feet!" Ethan warned. Tristan jumped as James swiped at his legs. Another stroke came near his head, and he dropped and rolled. Jarvis chortled and yelled, "You're not supposed to kill the lad, Cap!"

Tristan popped up with a handful of dirt and threw it at his brother's face. Enough got through the helmet, and James recoiled, blinking hard. Both brothers backed away from each other. James snickered. "Going to play dirty, are we?"

At his laughter, a shot of anger went through Tristan. He loved James and would do anything for him, but he would *not* lose to him this day. Nevertheless, he kept his temper reined in.

Tristan spun, shifting his grip from two hands to one to maximize his reach. Their swords swung so fast and hard, Tristan wasn't sure if he could prevent himself from actually striking his brother. James gasped for air. Tristan's own chest burned, but he pressed on. The blades locked, and they swayed together. Tristan growled through clenched teeth, "Enough?"

James held on for a moment longer and, with a stubborn jerk at the locked swords, assented with a grunt. They broke apart. Tristan ripped off his helmet, heaving gulps of air and dripping sweat. James yanked his off as well, and the two brothers circled each other like young bulls until James barked out a laugh.

"Yes!" he yelled. "Yes, Tristan! I knew you had it in you!" He threw one arm around his brother, hugging him. A warm glow filled Tristan. James had always been difficult to please, so to hear words of praise was an unexpected surprise.

Tristan muttered, "I'll get you next time."

"I hope so, Tris, I truly do." As they turned, they both stopped short at the sight of a small crowd that had gathered to watch, and there were cheers of appreciation for the day's entertainment.

"What a show, men!" Jarvis said. "That's about as exciting as it gets around here."

"I'm going to regret it tomorrow," James groaned as he stretched out his arm. Tristan grinned at him, thinking the same.

Jogging up to Tristan, Jarvis jabbed a finger at him. "You, lad! Hell's bells! What are you doing riding for the couriers when you could be out there fighting? We could use a sword arm like yours!"

Tristan froze. He dropped his head before handing Jarvis his sword. "Thanks for the loan." Without another word, he left the training ground.

"What did I say?" Jarvis asked. Ethan and James looked at each other, worry in their eyes.

Sure enough, Tristan's muscles were sore that night, and he paced the tent trying to stretch them out.

"Even my bones are creaking," he complained to Ethan.

"I'm sore myself," Ethan admitted. "I need to be practicing more. It's ridiculous to be this worn out from the little I did."

"Yes, but I fought three men. *Three.*" Tristan thought of Thorne and amended, "Well, two and a half, anyway."

Ethan laughed. "I know, and you were great. The pain is but fleeting. By the way, when you were springing for the second round of ales, I think you missed James talking about Justin."

Tristan, trying to massage his shoulder blade against a tent pole, shook his head. "I must've. C'mon, Ethan, don't you have anything for this?"

"Let me see. Anyway, Justin fell apart in that battle near Maris last month. Has Chris written about it?"

"No, I would have remembered that."

"This balm should work. Come here and sit." Ethan rubbed some of the goop onto his brother's shoulder and worked it into the muscles. His voice dropped lower. "Rumor is Charlotte is furious, calling him a disgrace."

"I don't get it. Justin is a great fighter. And the stuff you're using reeks."

"It's the herbs." Ethan shook his head. "Justin *spars* like a great fighter. There's a difference between sparring and actually fighting, you know that."

Tristan flinched. He knew all too well. He thought about his time with Justin over the years. The prince had always been a bit of an enigma to him. James and Ethan knew him much better—they had grown up alongside him for much of their lives. "That's good, thank you. What does James think?"

"He stood up for Justin, but I have a feeling he's conflicted about it. You know how loyal he is. For him to even be talking about it says a lot."

"Hmm. Do you need me to rub some on you?"

"No, I'm fine."

Tristan crossed over to his own cot while easing his shoulder up and down, amazed at how much better the muscles felt already. He didn't know what Ethan used to make that stinky balm, but it was magical. Kicking back, Tristan watched his brother wipe his hands on a rag.

Ethan glanced up, and a smile quirked on his face. "Why are you staring at me like that?"

"You're really good at this." Tristan waved his hand at Ethan's chest of various medical supplies. "Did you expect to be working for the army when you decided to study medicine?"

Ethan grimaced. "No. I hate it. All I wanted was a quiet village life, caring for the sick. Helping midwives if they need it. Or maybe work with the brothers at the abbey studying the plagues. That said, I'm glad I can be useful here."

Tristan lay on his cot, only to pop up again. "I'm not going to be able to sleep. I think I'll take a walk and see if that helps. Want to come with?"

Ethan considered but shook his head.

"Right, I won't be long."

Tristan walked along the row of tents, breathing in the fresh night air. He grinned, recalling how he had bested his big brother. Sure, Jarvis called it a draw, but they both knew who had won. Tristan longed to tell Christiana about it. He almost spun around toward his tent to start a letter. Then he remembered what they had overheard in the tavern and kept walking, the enjoyment of the day fizzling.

His thoughts wandered back to Ethan's words. If Justin had been frightened going into battle, Tristan didn't blame him. He would have to fight someday himself, whether in this war or the next, and the thought filled Tristan with dread. It wasn't a fear of dying so much as the horror of killing. Tristan had killed one man, and that had terrorized him. It required several long talks with his father and the Altair priest to manage his feelings having done that. Tristan knew killing in self-defense wasn't the same as cold murder. But to fight in war...to willfully slaughter...Tristan shuddered. He understood too well the heat that raged in a man's heart when battle fell upon him, how it could consume everything else, and hated knowing that shadow lurked in his own soul.

Tristan mused over something his father told him long ago, when Thomas had begun to think of his future. He had been young to be planning so far ahead, Tristan had thought at the time. Now at seventeen himself, he understood what his father meant. Tristan knew what he wanted in life. He longed for quiet evenings by the fire with a book and Christiana by his side. To bury his hands in rich, dark soil, planting for the future, or to start his own stables with the best bloodlines he could find. He had never been like James, who thrived on adventure. All he had ever wanted was a sense of home. To be still and keep those he loved safe. But deep down, Tristan suspected the sweet moments he savored had a price. He feared they must be earned with violence and bloodshed in the name of duty.

A scream shattered the night, breaking Tristan out of his reverie. The occasional screech from a woman wasn't unusual in the camps. Some wench getting a slap, he thought, a sour taste flooding his mouth. The cry pierced through the dark again—a frantic, terrified wail. Tristan could see no one else about. The night was young. Many men would be carousing at the tavern or before their own fire circle. Another scream burst forth but came to an abrupt end. Tristan shifted his direction toward the source of the sound. He hustled around a tent, bumping shoulders with a large man coming from the opposite side.

"Watch it!" Tristan growled. The man grunted and kept going. Tristan tried to get a look at the man's face, but it was hooded and hidden in the shadowy darkness. Tristan's gut clenched. He considered following the man until a moan interrupted his thoughts. Forgetting the man, Tristan jogged around the tent. A girl huddled against a nearby tree. She held up her hands defensively, sobbing. Tristan knelt beside her, making no attempt to touch her.

"Don't worry, lass, I'll not hurt you," he said. The girl had been beaten into a bloody mess, and his temper boiled, but he kept his voice low. "Who did this to you?"

Her eyes were enormous with fear. The shuffle of a footstep crept up behind him, and Tristan whirled, chiding himself for once more not wearing his sword.

"Who's out there?" called a voice.

"Thatcher, and who are you?"

"Tristan?" A dark-skinned youth came out of the shadows, and Tristan recognized Murphy, Captain Stephens's nephew and a fellow courier. He sighed with relief to see a familiar face.

"Murph, get over here. There's a girl who's been hurt." Tristan turned his attention back to the girl. "We'll not harm you. Let's get you to your feet, yes?" She hesitated, so he continued with, "My brother is a healer. He can clean you up. You won't have to go to the regular medical tent."

At these words she relaxed and allowed him to help her stand. Murphy and Tristan walked alongside her until they were close enough for Tristan to call out to his brother.

Ethan let out a sound of disgust over the sight. Tristan knew it was in reaction to whoever had done such violence, but the girl shrank away. Ethan saw his mistake and lowered his voice, urging her to come into the tent for care. She clenched her hands and fresh tears streamed down her cheeks. Tristan huffed in exasperation. "Would you want to go into a tent with three strange men after this?"

"True," said Ethan. "Well, my girl, we'll set you up out here." While Ethan worked on the battered woman, Murphy and Tristan stood aside.

"Who do you think did this?" Murphy asked.

"I don't know, some nasty piece of work getting his kicks off preying on the helpless."

Murphy nodded. "Do you mind if I scoot out of here? I was going to meet some fellows for a drink. You want to join us?"

"No, I'm off to bed after we're done with this. I have a ride tomorrow. Thanks for your help. Tell the boys I said to have one for me."

"I'll do that. G'night, Tristan."

Tristan rejoined Ethan when he finished his work. The girl stood on trembling legs, and Tristan asked her, "Would you like me to walk you somewhere?"

She wouldn't meet his eyes. "No. But thank you."

"Why won't you tell me who did this?" Tristan sighed at her silence. "Right. Well, be careful. Hey, what's your name?"

The girl paused before whispering, "Nancy."

The brothers watched her slip into the shadows.

"How bad was it?" asked Tristan.

"The beating? Bad enough."

"You know what I mean."

"What do you think?" Ethan gave him a grim look before pushing his way into the tent.

Tristan followed him, imagining Christiana in the same scenario, and his stomach twisted. "Poor girl," he muttered.

"They're used to it. They're raped almost as often as they are paid."

"What happens if—"

"You don't want to know, Tris."

The brothers sat, each lost in their own thoughts. Tristan thought the girl might have been pretty. It was hard to see through the bruises and terror. He fidgeted with the blanket on his cot.

"Ethan, have you ever thought of...being with a girl?"

Ethan didn't move other than his eyes flashing up to meet Tristan's, then a wry smile of understanding crossed his face. "Yes. Of course I have. But I wouldn't. That's not the way I want it to be. Or the way I think it should be."

Tristan lay back on his cot. He remembered kissing Christiana in the hayloft and wondered when he would see her again. Staring at the canvas ceiling, he had a sudden thought.

"Ethan, do you think James—"

"Not going there, Tris."

"Right. What a day," said Tristan as he rolled over. He was asleep in minutes.

Chapter 32

# Gathering Clouds

S omeone was shaking Tristan awake, and he didn't appreciate it.

"No," he stated firmly.

"Tris, c'mon. Something's happening," said Ethan. Tristan heard the strain in his brother's voice and sat, rubbing his face. Men were yelling nearby, and he caught sight of torchlight through the canvas of their tent.

"Whas happenin'?" he grumbled.

"I don't know. You're a bear to wake up," said Ethan.

An angry voice shot out from the dark exterior of the tent. "Thatcher! Get out here!"

The brothers gaped at each other, and they both stepped out of the tent. Three or four thugs tackled Tristan to the ground and bound his hands. Ethan launched himself at them, throwing one man off his brother, but a different man struck him down and kicked him in the gut.

"Stay out of it!"

Sucking in air, Ethan rolled and pushed himself upright in time to see the men towing Tristan along down the row of tents. Murphy stood nearby with a stunned expression on his face. Ethan flung him against a tree. "What did you do?"

"Nothing! I swear! I was out for a drink, and some fellows asked what happened with the girl. Next thing I know, those men are out for blood. I told them Tristan didn't do anything, but they ignored me."

Ethan let Murphy go, thinking rapidly. It had to be a misunderstanding, a mistake with a straightforward solution, and yet... "Get your uncle." When Murphy continued to hang about, useless and frightened, Ethan bellowed at him. "Go!"

After Murphy left, Ethan dressed and belted on his sword, his hands trembling. Seeing Tristan dragged away, shirtless and barefoot, had shaken him to the core. Ethan had finished buckling his boots when Captain Stephens called his name.

"What the devil is going on?"

Between Ethan and Murphy, they told Stephens the whole story. He remained calm, but Ethan could sense anger beginning to simmer.

"This is ridiculous!" exclaimed Captain Stephens.

"Will you help me?"

"Yes, certainly. Clearing this up shouldn't be difficult."

"You didn't see them. I'm scared of what they may do if we can't stop them."

Stephens studied the young man, thinking. He didn't know Ethan well. No matter. Ethan was Tristan's brother, and that was good enough for Stephans. He whipped around to his nephew.

"Ride out, Murph. Find Captain Thatcher or Commander Thatcher, and bring them here."

"Lord General Kavanaugh as well, if you can locate him," Ethan put in. Captain Stephens's eyebrows raised at this, but he nodded to Murphy, who took off running.

"You boys have friends in high places," Stephens said as they walked together.

"You don't know the half of it," Ethan muttered.

It was easy enough to find Tristan. A crowd with torches had gathered near the tavern. Soldiers had been at the drink all day, and a dangerous atmosphere coursed around them. Ethan was relieved to learn Tristan had been taken to a large tent nearby. Stephens and Ethan forced their way through the men. Two soldiers barred the entrance, but their stance weakened at the sight of Captain Stephens.

"Move it!" Stephens boomed with authority. He winked at Ethan as they passed into the tent, whispering, "Sometimes it pays to be an officer."

Tristan stood with his hands bound and two soldiers on either side, holding him by both arms. His face was pinched and frightened, but a wobbly smile appeared at the sight of his brother.

"Ethan!" Tristan cried out. One of the soldiers struck him, and he didn't say another word.

"What's going on here, Mallory?" Stephens asked the officer in the tent. "I know you're MacClaren's flunky, but this is reaching high, even for you."

"He's Lord General MacClaren to you, *Captain*. Thatcher raped and beat a prostitute."

"That's a lie!" Ethan cried out.

There was a slight wheeze, and Ethan spun around to see Stephens laughing.

"I'm sorry," he said, holding up his hands. "That's the funniest thing I've heard in weeks. Tristan Thatcher! Accused of rape and...and by the faith!" Stephens slapped Ethan on the back, guffawing so hard he struggled to get the words out. "That boy wouldn't even look at a woman without her permission, much less harm one. Oh, that is rich!"

Mallory glanced around, flustered and scowling.

"I'm sorting this out, Stephens, and I don't need your help. And I sure don't need *him*." He jerked his chin in Ethan's direction.

"Where's the girl, Mallory?" asked Stephens.

"Who knows, but I don't need her."

"You don't need her testimony?" The laughter left Stephens's face so abruptly Ethan wondered if it had been real. In the blink of an eye, Stephans was nose-to-nose with Mallory, speaking with a hoarse intensity. "Listen. I don't know what's going on here, or what MacClaren has on you, but Thatcher is *my* man. He's the best courier we've got and, what's more, you will release him at once. If you do not, you'll be calling up the fury of his father and some very important people. Trust me when I say that you do not want that hanging over your head. Take my advice and let's move on."

Mallory's face flushed, and he licked his lips. His eyes darted about and he stiffened.

"Get out," he growled. "Fifty lashes in the morning. Frankly, I wish it was worse, but she was only a damn whore."

Tristan went white, and Ethan could see him shaking.

"Please," Ethan pleaded, all the anger gone, "don't do this. I was there. I saw the girl and dressed her injuries—" Ignoring Ethan, Mallory walked over to his prisoner and yanked out a dagger. Before anyone could react, he struck Tristan hard across the head with the hilt. Tristan sank against the men holding him, and Ethan cried out. He made a lunge for his brother, but Stephens grabbed his arm, restraining him. Mallory fixed his beady eyes upon them both.

"Shut up," he snarled. "Get him out of here."

Ethan fought to reach Tristan, struggling against Stephens, who shoved him through the exit, declaring, "We're doing more harm than good here." Outside the tent, Stephens gazed into the night sky. "We have a few hours. Let's see what Murphy can do."

Tristan awoke with a throbbing head and terribly thirsty. He couldn't move his arms, and the more he slid back into consciousness, the greater his consternation. He was surrounded by utter darkness. A suffocating terror overtook Tristan, and he forced himself to breathe. Memories of the night flashed past him. He was tied up, that was all. Not the first time. *Probably not the last*, he thought, his humor edging toward hysteria. Tristan took another deep breath and hoisted himself up to sit against a tent pole, trying to wrestle his tangled thoughts into submission.

Raping a prostitute. The idea would be funny if it wasn't sickening. A mirthless laugh escaped his lips, but that made his head ache even more.

He thought of Christiana and jerked at the ropes again, gripped with anxiety. What would she think when she heard about this? He tried to calm himself. After all, he hadn't done anything wrong, and the truth would come out. This was one of those bizarre misunderstandings he would laugh about later. Still, the scandal of it all. He adjusted his position, careful not to jar his head. Ridiculous or not, his sense of unworthiness preyed upon him. Being thought of as a coward. His father's lack of an honorable family name. Tiny arrows of poison shot through his mind.

But if this was just a misunderstanding, why had he been left here, bound? He closed his eyes and prayed, longing for the quiet of the Altair chapel.

A sharp light pierced his vision. Before his eyes could adjust, someone yanked Tristan to his feet. "What's happening?"

"Whipping. Fifty lashes."

Shocked, Tristan reared back. The soldier cuffed him on the head in the same spot where he had been struck hours before. His knees buckled, and the world spun around him. The soldier half-dragged him outside to a pole and tied his hands above his head. A crowd gathered nearby, murmuring. It was a different group from the night before. Those men had been hostile, whereas these soldiers were half asleep and confused. The Thatcher brothers were well liked by most of their comrades, and Tristan saw many faces he knew with baffled expressions. Some loud voices broke the silence, and he thought he recognized Ethan.

"Ethan!" Tristan cried, frantic. Ethan yelled out his name, followed by the sound of a scuffle. Tristan heard nothing more and struggled against the bonds that held him, craning his neck to find Ethan. The pounding in his temple returned. He clenched his eyes shut only to open them and see a hairy bear of a man towering before him.

"Pittman," the man grunted. He leaned against the pole and began speaking as if he were a farmer discussing crops with his neighbor.

"Ach lad, there's an art to a good army whippin'. It ain't like your floggin's you might have seen. You don't want to kill the man, unless it's death by whip." Pittman dug a knife out of his pocket and picked under a dirty fingernail. "It takes a great deal of know-how to do it proper. See, I can go easy or go hard. You use different whips, flogs, cat-o'-nine, depends on what you want. I start slow and see what a man can take. Build up to just the right amount of pain. You soften the skin and muscles, see, before you cut 'em. Bruise 'em real good."

Pittman studied Tristan, who was already in a rank, cold sweat, his heart thundering.

"You're a likely lad. I'll try not to work you over too much. To be frank, I don't care for harlots, nasty things. Fifty lashes, hmm, well...I'll not bleed you for the first dozen or so. Will hurt, mind, but less damage."

Tristan was trembling hard, and he feared it could be seen by the crowd. He told himself to get a grip. Pittman offered a shaft of wood, indicating Tristan should bite it. He shook his head in refusal. The whipping was shameful enough. Tristan thought he should at least bear it with courage. A few cheers rose from the men.

Pittman chuckled. "You're a brave lad, to be sure. Still, you might wish you hadn't done that."

"Get moving, Pittman!" someone called.

Pittman waved a hand at him, tolerant in his patience. He heaved himself away. "Here we go, lad."

Tristan squeezed his eyes shut and braced himself for the blow. When it came, he grunted but didn't cry out. He had been cruelly belted many times as a child at various jobs after Michael was taken. Surely he could handle this. Tristan tried to take long breaths and focus on something, anything.

Christiana floated into his mind. Thinking of her, the shame of this—how could he ever face her again? He choked down the fear of losing her and tried to shift the direction of his thoughts.

The lash struck harder.

Michael. Michael had been flogged. He had said it wasn't too bad, but Tristan had seen the scars. Michael must have stretched the truth there...An image of Michael dying in his arms flashed through Tristan's memory and he gasped.

Pittman paused, and Tristan wondered why until the next strike. Pittman had switched to a different whip. The end of the lash sliced into him. Pittman broke the pattern, and without the ability to predict when he would be hit, Tristan couldn't brace himself, making it difficult to control the pain. Silent no more, he groaned with every strike, losing track of how many were left.

"Pittman!" Mallory was small, but he thrust the bearlike man aside as if he were a puppy. "Stop going soft on this one! I want him hurting!"

Mallory picked up a long whip and sank it deep into Tristan. Tristan screamed that time, the shock of it was too great. It cracked again and again. He sagged against the pole, dispassionately watching drops of blood falling into the dust at his feet. Once, twice more, and his insides were heaving. Another stroke and he would give in to the darkness and be thankful for it.

Mallory stalked to the pole and yanked Tristan's head up with his hair. "You will not faint on me," he growled. "You will feel *every* lash strike."

With great effort, Tristan held his head erect, his dark blue eyes flaming sapphires. In a fit of reckless fury, he spat at the man. Mallory slammed his head against the pole, and Tristan slumped, pinpricks of light in his vision, consciousness fading. Blood ran down his neck. It tickled. The crowd murmured, and with an odd whimsy of humor, Tristan thought they sounded like a hive of angry bees.

Again and again, the whip snapped. The crowd was shouting now. He wished they weren't so loud, it made his head ache. He found his feet and forced himself upright, legs quivering, readying himself for the next strike. The whip cut into him with such heavy intensity his whole body shuddered. More yelling, much closer. First one person and then several people were bellowing at each other somewhere nearby.

"Please, be quiet," he whispered. Tristan spiraled into a black void, never to return. Someone sliced the rope holding him upright, and he was falling, plunging...

"Tris, oh Tris, those bastards. It's all right, I have you, you're safe."

James's brawny arms supported Tristan and held him close as he transferred the weight of his brother to Ethan. Voice thick with emotion, James muttered, "Get him out of here."

"Be careful," Ethan said, low.

"I can take care of myself. Go!" James bounded into the fray where several men, including Andrew Kavanaugh, were in the middle of a violent argument.

# Chapter 33

# Repercussions

Ethan maneuvered Tristan to their tent and laid him on his cot. He swore harshly as he looked over his brother.

"Didn't think you knew that word," Tristan slurred with a hint of weak laughter.

"Be quiet, Tris. You're in shock and talking foolishness," said Ethan, recovering his usual soft tone as he pushed down the desire to weep. His brother's torso was slick with blood, and he shuddered so hard even the cot trembled.

James burst into the tent, wiping at a bleeding lip with a satisfied air before groaning when he saw the full extent of the damage done to Tristan. He hung back at first, unsure what he could do to help. Tristan whimpered as Ethan cleaned a vicious cut. Wincing at the sound of his brother suffering, James slipped past Ethan. Kneeling by the cot, he brought Tristan's head to rest on his own shoulder. Ethan could hear the two whispering to each other while James supported Tristan with a gentleness Ethan had never before witnessed in his warrior brother.

"I think I'm done," Ethan said after a long, tense hour. When Tristan didn't speak, he inhaled, alarmed, but James shook his head.

"He's been out a while, it was too much." His voice low and strained, James remained on the ground, holding Tristan and stroking his hair. Ethan had not seen James so distressed since Michael's death. He knelt beside his older brother.

"James?"

"I never told you. Right before Michael...we were talking about the war, and I promised him. I promised to watch over Tristan if anything happened to Michael. And I didn't—" James couldn't go on, and he brushed at his eyes.

"No one could have seen this coming, James. And no one is a better brother. To both of us," whispered Ethan. The reference to Michael cracked his professional façade. He had been able to set aside his emotions at Tristan's mention of it being a year ago the previous day, but now...faced with the bloody stripes on his brother's back, Ethan swallowed as renewed grief struck him full force. Fighting the tightness in his chest, he cleared his throat and tried to refocus on the present.

"I know it's ugly. The bruising will be excruciating for a few weeks, but that'll pass. Mallory is a weak little mouse of a man. It could have been much worse. If I'm careful, I might be able to minimize the scarring. Several of those cuts are nasty. I'll have to watch them for infection."

"How many hits did Pittman get in before Mallory took over?"

"I'm not sure. I was fighting his men, and they knocked me out."

"His head has blood on it."

"I know, but the bleeding's stopped, and I need a break."

"Are you all right?" James eyed Ethan with concern, noting for the first time how exhausted and battered he looked.

"Better than Tristan."

"That's not what I asked." When Ethan shrugged, James grimaced. "I bet you worked all yesterday and never got any sleep. You're done. Hand me what I need, and I'll clean his head. Rest a few moments."

Ethan hesitated. James was not known for his compassionate doctoring. Exasperated, James insisted, "Come on, Ethan, I can handle that much. You were awake all night, and who knows what's coming next."

Considering the point, Ethan gave his brother everything he needed. James eased Tristan's head to rest on the cot and set to work. He moved more slowly than Ethan would have, but his hands were careful. Afterward, he helped Ethan with his own minor injuries, interrupted by the occasional huff of laughter from them both at James's clumsy efforts. When Ethan finally batted his hands away, they fell silent.

The brothers huddled in the tent without talking much. Ethan was desperate for sleep but remained watchful. James stood near the tent flap, his hand on the hilt of his sword. When a bull's bellow echoed across the camp, they both knew it was what they had been waiting to hear.

"You dare take a whip to my son!"

"Dad's here," Tristan whispered, and the others jumped, not knowing he had regained consciousness.

"I'd better make sure he doesn't kill anyone," James muttered, slipping outside. He hadn't been gone long before Thomas blazed into the tent, seeming twice as large as usual and spitting fire. James appeared in the entrance saying, "Got him before he ran his sword through Mallory. I'm going to wait outside for Andrew." Then he withdrew.

The flames died when Thomas knelt beside Tristan and moaned.

"Tell me everything," he rasped as he examined the cuts. At these words, Stephens and Andrew Kavanaugh arrived. Together, Ethan and Stephens told their end of the story.

"Let me get this straight," said Thomas with barely contained fury. "Mallory held no trial, sentencing Tristan to fifty lashes without any proof? How does MacClaren justify the behavior of his captain?"

"Lord MacClaren was there," Tristan mumbled.

"What?" said everyone at once.

"Before Ethan came to the tent, Lord MacClaren took Mallory aside and they had some words. He looked right at me."

White-faced, Thomas turned to Andrew. "MacClaren *knows* Tristan, and if he saw the boy and didn't stop Mallory...He told me Mallory did this on his own. Where's the girl?"

"We don't know, she's disappeared," said Ethan.

"Dad..."

Thomas crouched beside Tristan's cot. "What is it, son?"

"I'm sorry. I didn't mean to shame you with this, on top of everything else." Tristan's voice broke. Thomas shot a confused look at Ethan, who grimaced.

"He needs rest."

"I'm sorry," Tristan moaned.

"Shh, be still. You could never shame me. I'll be back soon." Thomas jerked his head, indicating for Ethan to follow him, and they all left the tent.

James had overheard everything while waiting outside, pacing. His eyes held an unusual hardness. "We need the girl. Cutting Tristan free and starting a brawl didn't end this."

"You and I will go see if we can find the wench. Come with us, Stephens. Andrew, can you keep the peace until we figure things out? Ethan..." Thomas's gaze flitted back to the tent, his expression bleak. He tried to speak, but no words could move past his clogged throat.

"I'll take care of him, Dad."

"I know you will," Thomas muttered. "Thank you, son." He squeezed Ethan's shoulder and walked off with the rest.

Ethan sat on the ground next to Tristan's cot and rested, with his back against the wooden frame. He wondered if he dared sleep.

"You awake, Tris?" he whispered, not wanting to wake him if he slept. Tristan mumbled some words he couldn't decipher. "Can I get you anything?"

"Water, please."

Chagrined he had not offered water, Ethan helped his brother sit in order to drink. The movement was painful, but once settled, Tristan drank deep gulps of water. He leaned against Ethan when he finished and said, "You look awful."

Ethan stared at Tristan. His eyes were closed, but he had a weary smile on his face. A gasp of laughter escaped from Ethan. It was a soft chuckle at first but grew in volume, the tension of the previous hours releasing. Tristan tried to join in with a weak laugh of his own until it turned into a yelp. Their laughter faded, and Tristan groaned. Ethan tsked at his brother, helping him lie down again.

"What am I going to tell Chris?" Tristan asked, his voice trembling. "How can I ever face her after this?"

Any remaining amusement drained from Ethan, shifting into a desire to weep. "You'll tell her the truth, and she will believe everything you say. But we've got a while to worry about that. You're not traveling to Altair anytime soon. Try to rest. I'll not leave your side, I promise."

Crying startled Ethan out of sleep and he rubbed his eyes. He had dozed off on the ground with his head on Tristan's cot. Tristan was awake and wincing as he tried to peer outside. Ethan stumbled out, shocked at the darkness cloaking the outdoors. Several men with torches were coming his way, and he withdrew his sword.

"Don't take another step," Ethan warned, but Thomas's face appeared in the light. Behind his father were James and Stephens dragging Nancy, who was sobbing hysterically. "What did you do to her?"

"Nothing yet," Thomas growled. They dragged the girl into the tent.

"Look!" James shoved Nancy closer to Tristan. "See what they did to him!"

"James!" Ethan forced James aside and took the girl's arm.

"Let her be," Tristan said, lifting his head. The girl sank trembling in front of him.

"Don't let them hurt me," she whispered.

"I'll do my best," Tristan said, grimacing as he tried to sit. Injured as he was, Tristan gave his oldest brother such a scathing glance that James shuffled his feet. He crossed over to help Tristan.

"I want her to tell us what happened, Tristan. We need to be sure your name is cleared."

"By terrorizing the poor girl? After what was done to her? Talk sense to them," Tristan said to Andrew, who had entered the tent.

"Little crowded in here," said Andrew as he took in the scene. "Out!" he barked at James and Stephens. James started to protest, but Andrew propelled him out of the tent. Stephens slipped out as well.

"Can you behave yourself?" Andrew asked Thomas, who assented with a growl. Andrew led Nancy to Ethan's cot and helped her sit. "Lass, this young man has been ill-used because he tried to help you. He *did* try to help you, didn't he?"

Nancy twisted her hands in her lap, tears running down her face.

"Child," continued Andrew, "please. His life may hang in the balance. We must have the truth."

Ethan looked from Andrew to his father. "What are you talking about?"

"There's a mob at the tavern working themselves up for a hanging as we speak."

"What!" gasped Ethan. "I don't underst—"

"Trial or no, Tristan was condemned for assault. Cutting him free didn't end this. We need this girl's testimony to clear his name."

Ethan knelt in front of Nancy, tears brimming in his eyes. "Please. I know you aren't used to kindness, but my brother—he's good and gentle, don't you remember? Let's try this. How about I say what we saw, and you confirm, yes or no. All you have to do is nod. Let's start there, yes? Tristan found you already beaten, and he brought you to me so I could help you."

The girl gulped and nodded. "It's true, these boys were kind to me," she said to Andrew. "They didn't do nuthin' bad. They tried to help."

"Why are you frightened?" Tristan asked.

"He'll kill me for sure."

"Who?"

Nancy shook her head, ignoring the question. "Who do I talk to? To help?"

"That's a good lass. No one will hurt you," Andrew assured as he led Nancy out of the tent, allowing James and Stephens to come in.

"What do we do about that crowd, Dad?" demanded James.

"Andrew has guards stationed around the tent. If we can make it for another half hour while the girl tells her story, all should be well. Stephens, I can't tell you how grateful I am for all you've done. Why don't you get some sleep?"

"Will do. I'll check on you in a few days, Tristan."

"And now, we wait?" asked Ethan, sitting on his cot and watching Stephens leave.

"Better watch it, Ethan, a girl's been in your bed," Tristan joked weakly, leaning against his father, who had sat beside him.

Ethan rolled his eyes. "Very funny, Tris."

Thomas put his arm around Tristan's shoulders, taking care to avoid his wounds, and kissed the top of his dear boy's head. A sigh escaped Tristan.

Andrew returned after escorting Nancy to the tent in the woods that she shared with some other girls. She had done as needed, speaking before himself, Lord General MacClaren, and Captain Mallory. Tristan had been officially declared innocent of any wrongdoing. Still, Andrew's voice was sour when he spoke.

"I don't understand what's happened here. He's kept his hands clean on this, but MacClaren relished having an opportunity to go against a Thatcher, even young Tristan. This will come to a bitter end someday, Thomas, mark my words."

"But not today," Thomas whispered, his gaze sweeping over his sons. Ethan had long ago collapsed and slept on his cot. Slouched on the ground with his head resting on Tristan's cot, James snored. He had one protective hand on his youngest brother while the other gripped the hilt of his sword. Tristan moaned softly in a painful, light sleep. Yet they were all there, and for that Thomas was thankful.

The next morning dawned peacefully enough, given all that had happened. Ethan dressed Tristan's wounds, listening to James whistle a tune outside as he heated water over the fire. Someone called out, and the whistling stopped, followed by voices in low conversation. James came into the tent with Andrew and Thomas, refusing to meet Ethan's questioning eyes. Andrew looked distraught, and Thomas's face was ashen.

"What is it?" Ethan asked. Tristan propped his head up on his arms, fatigued with pain and lack of sleep.

Thomas cleared his throat. He tried to speak but couldn't. Andrew stepped forward.

"Nancy. The girl. She and Mallory were found dead outside of camp. Both their throats were slit."

# Chapter 34

# Shadows in the Dark

Tristan's convalescence continued, albeit it was a slow and painful process. Authorities cited Captain Mallory as the officer ultimately responsible for the flogging, but with him dead, Thomas could go no further to extract justice.

The battle lull had passed, and the war returned with violence. Thomas and James had to leave. Left alone to work with the healers and care for his brother, Ethan did the best he could, but Tristan still spent many stuffy, hot days in the tent alone. Ethan would return after long hours of work to find his Tristan listless and irritable. It was a miserable time for them both.

Tristan was almost dozing when he heard Ethan clamber into their tent.

"I'm trying to sleep," he grumbled. When Ethan didn't respond, he dragged his head up from his cot and froze.

A girl stood in the tent, peeking outside through a small gap in the tent flaps. Tristan gasped with astonishment, and she whipped around to face him with wide, frightened eyes. For several seconds they stared at each other. With a trembling hand, she brought her finger to her lips, her expression entreating. Tristan nodded, but after a week of painful boredom he was bursting with curiosity. Groaning, he hauled himself into a sitting position, and the girl shrank into a corner. Tristan gave her what he hoped was a reassuring smile and lumbered to the entrance of the tent to peer outside.

"No one's out there," he said as he thumped back to his cot and sank down upon it.

"You sure?"

Tristan watched the girl take another look for herself. She was quite stunning, with dark hair rippling down her back like a waterfall, snapping black eyes, and rich olive skin.

"Bad man?"

"Ain't they all?" she retorted waspishly.

Tristan sighed. "I hope not."

Her own curiosity getting the better of her, the girl stepped closer. Examining his exposed wounds, she frowned. "You seem safe enough. You're the one who helped Nancy, ain't you?"

"I tried."

Without warning, she knelt before him and put a hand on his knee. Her voice dropped low and husky. "Thanks for not calling out."

Tristan shifted his leg away. "Ah, I have a love."

"So do a lot of men, doesn't seem to stop them," she responded with a mischievous twinkle in her eyes.

"I suppose that's true, but that doesn't apply to me. Besides, I wouldn't anyway."

"You sure about that?" She looked him straight in the eye. He tried to move even farther and winced.

"You still painin'?"

"You could say that. In fact, I may need to lie down again. My apologies."

Tristan was surprised when she helped him adjust his position onto his stomach. Bending his arm at the elbow, he propped his head upon his hand, knowing he would regret it. A terrible crick kept creeping along his neck. The girl plopped to the ground in front of him. She showed no signs of leaving anytime soon. This didn't bother him, although he wondered what would happen if Ethan came home to a prostitute in their tent.

"What's your name?"

"Thatcher. Ah, Tristan."

"Foster. Lucy," she said, an impish smirk overtaking her face as she imitated him. "Tell me about your girl."

Tristan's cheeks burned, and he dropped his gaze. Lucy's smile disappeared.

"You don't want to ruin her precious name talkin' about her to the likes of me?"

He shifted on the cot. "No! That isn't it at all. It has nothing to do with you. I'm afraid I may have disappointed her with something...that happened."

"If you don't sleep with whores or other girls, and you don't beat her, I would say she has a good thing, and she knows it." She shrugged. "You're a right handsome catch. Nice voice also, just low enough, it has a rumble to it. You can tell a lot about a man by his voice."

"I suppose you would know," he murmured, thinking her definition of a good man might have a little left to be desired.

"Good voice for singin'. Do you ever sing?"

"I do not, and never ask me to try," he said, for he was *not* a talented singer. His family always teased him when songs broke out around the fireside, for he sang everything lustily off-key. James would often snicker that such a fine baritone had been wasted on someone with an awful ear for music.

Lucy laughed in response. The sound carried not a hint of a girlish giggle. Instead, it pitched low and husky like her voice. Sounds outside the tent hushed her, and she rose to take another peep.

With her back to him, Tristan couldn't stop himself from looking at her. She was tall, almost his height he guessed, with a full, lush figure. Everything about her spoke of ripe womanhood. He felt his cheeks heat again and averted his eyes, his mouth gone dry. When he dared to glance up, she was watching him.

At that moment Ethan burst into the tent, mumbling about some tonic he had forgotten. He stopped, gaped at the sight of Lucy, and immediately spun on his heel to leave.

Tristan couldn't stop himself from grinning. "Ethan!"

Ethan crept back in.

"Lucy, this is my brother Ethan. Ethan, I was assisting Lucy escape a...friend she did not wish to see."

Perhaps hoping his brother would make up for Tristan's lack of interest, she turned the full blast of her charm on Ethan. Tristan almost laughed. Poor Ethan was no match for a girl so entirely self-aware of her own appeal. Ethan blushed and his eyes dropped, but he greeted her like a gentleman. An awkward silence followed.

"Well, I'd best be goin'," Lucy said brightly. "I have business to attend to."

Ethan went all the redder thinking of her *business,* and the girl offered him a wink as she left. He followed her with his eyes until she was gone and then stared at Tristan with wonder.

"Tell me everything."

As the days crawled by, Tristan's body healed but nightmares slithered into his sleep. For months they had been absent, but now they returned with a terrifying force. Tristan would wake screaming, drenched in a cold sweat.

*A shallow grave.*

*The crack of a whip.*

*Hooded monsters in the fog.*

*A village on fire, his mother screaming.*

*Michael...*

Ethan learned to act quickly when Tristan started moaning in his sleep, shaking him awake before the dream hit its crisis point. Neither of them slept well.

The war had picked up its pace, with battles to the west and north of them. Tristan's frustration with his inability to work was acute. He had been rendered useless for the one thing he believed he could do well. Captain Stephens took time to visit Tristan and tried to convince him that he was needed with the couriers, but left shaking his head. He had seen broken spirits before.

While Ethan worked, Tristan paced the tent alone, his bruised and battered body aching. His mind felt chaotic, disconnected from any stable anchor. Others showed their support with words of encouragement. Prince Justin sent him a brief note from his own army camp miles away.

And then there were the letters from Altair. Christiana pleaded with him to come home, but that only made him feel worse. Although Tristan longed for her sweet voice and gentle touch, he struggled under such a burden of shame that he couldn't write. His secret, dear dreams of a life with her were falling to pieces, and he had not the strength to pick them back up.

Ethan tried to help him however he could. He gave Tristan some potent medicine to make him sleep, but it made the nightmares worse. Frustrated with his own inadequacies in handling the situation, Ethan feared the darkness Tristan had experienced throughout his young life was gathering into a black cloud he could no longer banish. He watched his brother slide further and further into the abyss, desperate to help yet unable to reach him.

One tenuous thread held Tristan to the surface. For months he had ended his day with a prayer for Christiana, and in this he never failed, no matter how bleak his thoughts or exhausted his body. Ethan could hear Tristan whispering as he lay in bed, the same words, night after night. *Father, I entrust she who is dear to me into thy never-failing care and love...that thou do for her better things that I can desire or pray for...* The love fairly throbbed in Tristan's voice as he prayed for her, and a lump would come to Ethan's own throat, his heart aching for his brother.

The wounded who survived on the field were brought by slow wagons from the battlefields farther west. Often the wagons would be full of dead upon arrival, the flies and stink rising. Ethan would work himself to the point of collapse to care for those he could. One crisp afternoon he hit such a state of exhaustion, he feared doing more harm than good in his stupor. Leaving the medical tent, he muttered a prayer of thanks that at least the heat had broken, and a hint of fall teased in the cool breeze that washed over him. He staggered toward his tent, but he skidded to a halt at the entrance. Jericho stood tethered, saddled and bridled. Ethan eyed the horse, not comprehending. He shook his head, blinked, and looked again. Jericho snorted at him. Now fully awake, he burst into the tent.

He found his brother sitting on his cot with full saddlebags on the ground. Tristan was dressed and appeared as though he had washed. The beard that had begun to emerge in the last few weeks was shaven clean. Ethan chastised himself that he had not realized how thin Tristan had become. His cheeks were gaunt, and there were dark circles under his eyes. Nevertheless, Tristan took one look at Ethan and shook his head. When he spoke, his voice was heavy with concern.

"You look awful, Ethan."

"So do you. I'm just tired."

"I know. You work for days and nights on end, and when you do manage to get to bed, I destroy your sleep." Tristan paused, then added, "I'm leaving."

A sudden, nameless fear took hold of Ethan. "Wha—what do you mean?"

"I won't be gone long."

"Tell me where you're going, at least."

Tristan coughed out a strange laugh.

"I can't tell you because I don't know. I need to get away for a few days, to be alone."

"No, that's precisely the problem, you've been alone too much. You aren't yourself. You should go home to Altair and see—" He faltered at the flash in Tristan's eyes, which seemed to dare him to say more. Ethan took a deep breath. "She loves you, Tris. Nothing has happened that will change her mind."

"Everything has changed," Tristan muttered. "I don't even know if Altair is home anymore."

Ethan tried to calm the growing panic in his heart. "Did she write—"

"Ethan, stop!" Tristan stood in a rage, but seeing Ethan's stunned face, he did his best to tamp down his fire. "I've changed. I'm broken. Don't you see? I have to find my way back. Find a way to deserve her again. Again! As if I ever did to start. Maybe she was always a gift I could never keep."

"She loves you," Ethan said again stubbornly.

Tristan slumped, the fury flamed out.

"At least let's talk to Dad first," Ethan pleaded.

Tristan embraced his brother hard, with a fierce love. Ethan had never given up on him, not even after all these miserable weeks.

Ethan whispered, "Don't go, Tristan. Please."

Tristan blinked, fighting off tears. He coughed and retrieved his saddlebags. "Dun's with the courier horses, they'll take good care of him until I come back. I won't be gone long, I promise."

With those words, he was gone. Ethan sat on his cot in a daze, trying to make sense of what had happened. Oddly, he felt better knowing Tristan had left Dun behind, for his brother would never abandon his faithful horse. Exhausted as he was, Ethan gathered parchment and a quill to write a letter to his father.

As Tristan rode out of the encampment, he sat straight and strong, despite his aching back. He knew others were watching him, but he didn't turn his head to the left or to the right. That is until he passed a girl with long black hair heating soup over a fire. When she looked up and beamed at him, he almost stopped Jericho to speak with her. In the end, he kept riding, driven into a future unknown.

# Chapter 35

# Regrets

Christiana fingered a bundle of letters tied with a ribbon, fighting off tears. It had been weeks since she had heard from Tristan. Letters from his father and Lord General Kavanaugh had arrived for her mother, who read them aloud to Christiana. As usual, Thomas had stuck to the hard facts of the event, although one could discern his deep feelings on the matter. Andrew, on the other hand, held nothing back in his letter.

Charlotte had been livid with Lord General MacClaren but restrained in her response to the whole affair, infuriating Christiana. She did not comprehend her mother's behavior and had engaged in several rousing arguments with her, demanding action, all to no avail. With the long silence from Tristan, her temper soon dissolved into fear. So when word reached her that a rider with the army had arrived, she hoped for fresh news, perhaps even a letter from Tristan. She rushed down the stairs but slowed to a stop.

A young man waited in the entry hall, and for one terrible second she didn't recognize him. When she did, her face went white. They stared at each other wordlessly. Then she was with him, wrapping her arms around his neck while he embraced her.

"I didn't do it, anything they may have told you, I swear..." he choked out. She shushed him with a tender kiss.

"I never thought—My sweet Tristan, what they did to you—" She kissed him again. He knew he shouldn't, told himself it would make everything worse, but he responded to her kiss with a feverish intensity. He stopped, ducking his head. She rested her warm hand on his cheek. Tristan squeezed his eyes shut, placing his own hand over hers, pressing it closer. At her gentle urging, he met her gaze.

"I'm not staying."

"I don't understand. You're not leaving, I won't let you."

He stood there, unable to speak.

"What is it, Tristan?"

"I'm no good for you. Even knowing the truth—Chris, I don't think people believe I didn't do it. They see me as someone who would—I can't be with you. I'm so ashamed. Don't you see?"

Christiana remained motionless, watching him. Her stillness unnerved Tristan, and he gulped for air.

"I wrote you a letter, but I couldn't send it. I knew it wasn't right. That I needed to tell you, to see you one last time."

"One last time? What do you mean?"

Tears filled his eyes. "I'm not coming back, Chris. You need to—there are many better men for you. Men with names, men with family, not the son of a Woodraven bastard."

"How can you say such things about your father!"

"I love my father! But in the eyes of the world, he's...it's the truth. And with this, people see me as a whore user, a man who slices girls when he's done with them like trash. They were already calling me a coward! How can I bring this shame upon you?"

"Who dared call you a coward?" Christiana cut in, but Tristan kept talking, knowing if he didn't say it all now, he would never get the words out.

"It's time for me to fight. I've talked to Andrew, and he's going to assign me to one of his cavalry battalions. Maybe...maybe I can find myself again. Maybe someday I can believe I deserve you. I don't know. I need to know you're free to find someone else to love and not be tied to me if I can't find my way back."

Christiana's breath caught in a little sob, and Tristan pulled her against him, his own throat clogging with tears. He breathed in the scent of her hair, wanting to hold on to the memory forever. Tristan's heart broke into a hundred pieces. "You deserve a better man."

She shook her head against his chest, crying. "I deserve a man who loves me! A man I love! And that has always been you. Please, Tristan. Stay here with me. This isn't you speaking, not truly. Stay and talk to Momma."

They clung to each other before he drew a ragged breath and broke from her embrace. He kissed her forehead, whispering, "May the Father keep you, my love." His heartbreak complete, he turned to go.

"Tristan!" she cried out. He staggered, falling against the wall. If she came to him now, he would never be able to leave. Seconds dragged by. When Tristan didn't feel her touch, he straightened and left Christiana weeping in his wake.

Thomas could hear his sons yelling at each other from what seemed a mile away. By the time he made it to the tent, James and Ethan were almost at blows. James must have crossed some line, for Thomas had never seen Ethan this angry. Sure enough, Thomas stepped between them just as Ethan was about to land a solid punch on his brother.

"Stop it! What has gotten into you two? Ethan, I'm shocked at this behavior. And you—" He cuffed James on the head. "Get a hold of yourself. You're both acting like idiots. In the tent!"

As soon as they were inside, James started again. "Some guardian for Tristan you've been! How could you let him go? After everything he's gone through, what were you thinking?"

"Be quiet, James," Thomas growled, shoving James onto one cot and Ethan to the other. He stood between them, arms stretched out to hold them in place. "No one has done more for Tristan than your brother."

"I will not be quiet! My brother—"

"*Our* brother," snapped Ethan.

"He's out there somewhere, and no one knows where he is!" James rose halfway to his feet, and his voice broke. "Maybe you don't remember what it was like to lose him, Ethan, but I do! And I will not lose him again!"

Ethan clenched his fists. "What was I supposed to do? Strap him to his cot? You try stopping Tristan when he gets his mind set on something! I tell you, it's not so easy!"

"Shut up, the both of you!" Thomas bellowed.

"What's going on?" asked a soft voice. All three turned. A young soldier stood at the tent entrance. Rather than exclaim over his sudden appearance, they stared at Tristan as if he were a ghost, for he had changed since they last saw him.

His groomed hair was cropped, shorter than any of them ever recalled seeing it. He wore immaculate, clean trousers and a linen shirt. His boots were polished. Most striking was the long riding duster in rich burgundy, which brought out the faintest hint of red in his short, dark hair. A new longsword hung at his side. Still too thin, he had at least some color in his face. He held himself relaxed and easy, even if sadness lingered in his eyes.

"Where did you come from?" James asked.

"Lawnwood, and before that, Altair."

"Did you see Chris?" Ethan demanded.

"Yes."

Thomas had been studying him and spoke in a strangled voice. "You're dressed like a soldier."

"I am one. Mariah helped me get sorted out with the clothes. She sends her love to you all. I told Stephens. He was disappointed, but he understood. I'll be working with Andrew's cavalry under Commander Martin. Not for another few weeks, though."

"You haven't been trained to fight from a horse. It's not what you're used to."

"I know."

"Dammit, Tristan!" Thomas exclaimed. "You don't understand what I'm saying. Fighting on horseback, it's different. It's—"

"I'll learn, Dad," Tristan insisted. He searched his father's eyes, pleading for understanding. Instead, Thomas spun away. Tristan glanced at Ethan, who shook his head.

"Is that a sword by Hillyer?" asked James, eyeing the weapon.

"Yes. It was time for a new one."

"Who's Hillyer?" Ethan looked confused.

James leveled a rather lofty gaze at Ethan. "Only the best sword maker in Aquila. That must have cost you, Tris."

"A bit."

James nodded his approval, his good humor returning. "And who cut your hair?"

"Ah, one of the girls here."

"Do they include that in their price?"

"James!" Ethan glowered at his oldest brother.

"What?" he asked innocently.

Tristan rolled his eyes and snorted. He approached Thomas and touched his father's back, feeling the muscles tense. Tristan cleared his throat. "Would you mind if I had a word with Dad? And please try not to kill each other outside. I prefer you both alive."

As he spoke, his lips quirked, hinting at his first smile in weeks, but it faded as his brothers left him alone with his father. Tristan winced, knowing he was doing what Thomas had always feared. He stared at his father's back and fidgeted before turning to sit on his cot. "Can you please talk to me, Dad? You're like a mountain, standing over there."

Thomas rumbled but sat on the cot opposite Tristan.

"You're disappointed in me," Tristan stated. Thomas shook his head.

"No, I could never be disappointed in you, Tristan. Never. I'm disappointed in the circumstances that have led you to this point."

"You knew I would have to fight sooner or later."

Thomas shrugged. "These wars can be brief. Some have lasted a few months with years in between. I was hoping to delay the moment, to get past this one at least."

"I'm sorry, Dad. You know how much I hate causing you to worry."

"Well, I would be a poor excuse for a father if I didn't worry." After a long pause, Thomas added gently, "What happened at Altair, son?"

Tristan stiffened and averted his eyes, but Thomas caught the powerful emotion that passed through them. His heart bled for his boy.

"Oh, Tristan. I wish you hadn't. I fear you will regret it for the rest of your life."

Eyes shadowed, Tristan whispered, "Of that I have no doubt."

# Chapter 36

# A Flagon of Wine

The winter snows raged with a vengeance, and the fighting slowed. Battles still broke out, but on the whole, things became quieter. Some men went home for a brief spell. Others remained throughout winter, either duty or lack of family keeping them in the camp, where they had comrades and the ale continued to flow.

Two weeks before Christmas, Ethan and James were ready to ride to Altair. They planned to spend a few days at Lawnwood along the way. James was impatient to be off, his grumpiness increasing with every delay, but Ethan lingered. He had a new horse and used her as an excuse to put off their departure.

"What do you think of her, Tris?"

"She's the prettiest thing I've seen in a long time. I would love to breed her to Jericho someday."

"That's an idea," was all Ethan said, but he puffed his chest out with some pride that Tristan thought so highly of his mare. Then he sighed. He was unhappy about Tristan staying behind, but at least his brother seemed to no longer be shadowed by darkness, much to Ethan's relief.

"What can I say to change your mind?"

Tristan laughed, but to his brother it sounded hollow. "I'm fine, Ethan, I promise. You have a good time."

"You know Dad's going to have a fit when he sees you're not with us," put in James.

"Why else do you think I insisted Dad leave two days ago?" said Tristan. "He won't be able to do much about it by the time you get there."

Ethan stepped close to his brother. "It will break her heart not to see you, Tris. Can I give her a message at least? Anything?"

"No, but tell Dad...well, you know what to say better than I do. Get out of here, the daylight is wasting."

"I'll see you soon."

They started to ride until Tristan called Ethan's name. Ethan reined in, while James kept going. Tristan leaned against the mare and fiddled with her mane. Ethan waited. He could catch up with James later.

Tristan cleared his throat but didn't take his eyes off the horse's neck. "Tell her Merry Christmas for me. Maybe next year. And..." And what? That he dreamt of her nightly? That the world was a cold, dark place without her?

"Tristan?"

With a helpless shrug, Tristan muttered something incomprehensible. Ethan smiled and clapped his shoulder. "I'll pass it on."

Tristan watched him ride away and kicked at a clump of snow. "Why did I do that?"

As James had predicted, their father expressed dismay that Tristan had not arrived with them, but he seemed to understand. However, on Christmas he looked so forlorn without his youngest son, both brothers vowed to never let Tristan duck out again.

Christiana's disappointment was no less. She entered the Great Hall, searching the crowd, for many came to stay at the castle on Christmas. Catching Ethan's eye, she brightened until he shook his head. Christiana slowed her pace as she continued to wiggle her way toward him.

"He didn't come? Not even for Christmas? How have I angered him?"

Ethan stared at her, wondering how on earth Tristan had made such a mess of things that Christiana believed he was angry at her. He drew her into a corner, and Rachel came with them, hovering like a protective shadow.

"Anger him? Chris, he loves you. I know it. He's almost pulled himself out of the pit and just needs time to work things out." And he told her what had passed between them as he had left the camp. "He wanted to say more, much more. I know he did. Tristan prays for you every night, I hear him. Please don't give up on him."

"I will never give up on Tristan," she said before disappearing into the crowd. Rachel started to follow her, but Ethan caught hold of her hand. She paused, her eyes wide with surprise.

"Rachel, what can we do about those two? Maybe we could conspire together."

She spun her head around, trying to find her cousin. Redirecting her attention back to Ethan, she stepped closer, thoughtful. "I'm sure we can come up with some sort of plan."

"May I...may I write to you, perhaps?"

Rachel's cheeks went pink, and her thumb brushed over his palm. Ethan caught his breath.

"I would enjoy writing to you very much, Ethan." With a nod, Rachel slipped after her cousin.

Ethan told himself it was only to help Christiana and Tristan, yet somehow for the first time in months, his heart beat with hope.

On Christmas Eve, Tristan walked through the snow, listening to the men carousing as midnight crept closer. He and Stephens had spent the previous hour having a quiet ale together. Tristan took a meandering route to his tent, watching soldiers make merry. He wasn't unhappy exactly, but he did miss his father and brothers. Most of all, he tried not to think of one green-eyed lass with long, unbound hair.

A feminine voice called his name, the tone a striking contrast to the men nearby. Lucy appeared out of the darkness and ambled alongside him. The two of them had seen quite a lot of each other since the day he had sought her out to cut his hair, for Tristan found her mischievous humor endearing in a camp full of ill-tempered soldiers.

"I have a present for you," she said with a flirtatious little bounce.

"And I have a feeling this is a present I must refuse."

"Don't be such a goose, I know the high-and-mighty Tristan too well for that. Take a taste of this, though." She held out a flagon.

Now, Tristan was an ale man and could wax poetic about the magic of hops and barley, much to the amusement of his brothers. Even Thomas could be reduced to fits of laughter over Tristan's expressive devotion. One quick sniff of the flagon told him this could *not* be ale. He hesitated, unsure if he wanted to try whatever she was offering. But since he didn't wish to be impolite, Tristan took a cautious sip. His eyes widened, and he blinked in surprise at the rich, red wine—some of the best he had ever tasted.

Lucy's husky laugh burst forth over his reaction, and her black eyes sparkled. Tristan glanced around and whispered, "Did you steal this?"

"Don't be daft. It's good, though, ain't it?"

"It's amazing. May I?" He gestured with the bottle, and she nodded. He helped himself to another drink, deeper this time. The warmth of the wine flowed through him.

"Makes me think of home," he said dreamily.

"And where is home, Tristan?"

"Altair. At least it was." Tristan shook himself out of his reverie and smiled at Lucy, offering the flagon. "Thank you, that was delicious."

"It's a present, I told you."

"What?" Tristan gasped. "I can't drink it all! I would be dead to the world in an hour. I'm not used to the stuff these days."

"Well then, we can share it. I'm not workin' tonight."

She gave him a droll wink, and he laughed outright. Sobering, Tristan considered her words. Truth be told, he was lonely and didn't want to spend Christmas Eve by himself, brooding about everyone celebrating at Altair.

"All right!" He grinned in a moment of reckless abandon. "But let's go to my tent. It's freezing out here."

They kicked through the snow arm in arm. Once in the tent, Tristan spread out a blanket and they sat picnic-style, passing the flagon back and forth. For the next hour they laughed and talked.

"My brother Michael would have loved this, he adored a good wine," Tristan murmured, trying to peer into the flagon to see the color. He couldn't remember the last time he had felt so fine.

"I've never met a Michael Thatcher."

"No, he's gone." Tonight, memories of Michael brought happiness more than pain, and a gentle warmth filled Tristan's heart.

"Was he killed fightin'?"

"You could say that, but not here. We were ambushed by some land pirates on the southern border, well over a year ago."

"I'm sorry," she said.

"Not your fault." He took another sip, thinking. A memory tickled at him, something James had said. Why had the thieving stopped after the skirmish? It was impossible those few men had been the ones causing the problems in the south. Tristan shrugged off the thought; he was weary of going over and over that day, and he wanted to be happy this night. Instead, he smiled at Lucy until he saw how close she sat beside him, and his stomach clenched. Tristan scooted a few inches, hoping to put some distance between them.

"What did he look like? You boys are so different. Sure you had the same father?"

Tristan laughed. "Yes, I'm sure. What's funny is Michael was actually my cousin. My parents fostered him from a young age. Yet he and I looked the most alike."

"Quite the handsome one then," she whispered. Everything about her seemed to soften, and Tristan went still. The sounds from outside faded away.

She reached out to him, placing her hand on his cheek. Her fingers trailed along the outline of his jaw, and a gentle tug brought him closer. He shut his eyes as her mouth met his. Tristan did not respond to her kiss, but neither could he bring himself to stop her. His breath caught as her lips moved. Otherwise, he remained frozen in place.

Lucy paused. His eyes popped open, and they gazed at one another before she leaned forward, her lips now on his neck. Tristan shivered at the warm breath of her husky laugh on his skin. A little involuntary moan escaped him.

Bringing one leg over him, Lucy eased herself onto his lap. Her lips continued to roam, and with trembling hands he pulled her more firmly against him. His breath came in quick gasps, and his heart skittered and raced.

"Why, young Tristan is made of flesh and blood after all," she whispered into his ear. He gave a short, breathless laugh.

"Never said I wasn't," Tristan rumbled as he rubbed his face against her neck, taking in her scent. She wore a rich perfume that made his head swim, but the echoing scent of fresh, sunny hay floated past. He pushed the memory back as far as he could and wrapped his arms around Lucy. Tristan relished the feel of her body against his own. It had been so long since—he wrestled that thought into submission. Her hair was beautiful, thick and cascading, and he fingered the black strands...but he saw copper-gold curls. His leaping, bounding heart stilled at the recollection. When Lucy brought her lips to his once more, he turned his head, not meeting her kiss.

"Lucy...I..." He tried to swallow.

She stroked his cheek. "It's her, ain't it? The girl you gave up?"

Miserable, he nodded. Lucy nuzzled against his chest. Tristan's arms remained where they were, holding her; however, the embrace had shifted from a burning heat to sweet affection.

Tristan kissed the top of her head. "Even if she wasn't in my thoughts, I wouldn't want it this way."

"Is it because of what I am?" she asked.

"A little, but not entirely. It's a sacred thing, at least to me, and I want to be wed beforehand. Definitely not what I want to do for the first time in a smelly tent with hundreds of men nearby. Still..." He tilted up her chin, forcing her eyes to meet his. "I've never been this tempted."

"Well, that's somethin'." She sighed, rising.

He grabbed her hand. "Don't go. Stay with me, please."

"Don't fuss, young Tristan. I think, though...I think I do have some business tonight. I had better get to work."

She left as Christmas bells rang throughout the camp. A rush of cold air flooded the tent at her departure. There were cheers and laughter from the men outside as they toasted the moment. Tristan missed Altair with an intensity that overwhelmed him. The siren call of home was almost irresistible to his weary young heart. He had a wild desire to mount Jericho and race to Altair. Race to *her*, catch her in his arms, and hold on to her forever.

He had been a fool to let her go.

Tristan drained what was left of the flagon. Dawn broke before he slept.

# Chapter 37

# Mousetrap

With the lessening of the snow, the war picked back up with a vengeance. The brothers continued to see each other as much as possible, but when the fighting was excessive, even Ethan and Tristan could go days without passing each other despite living in the same tent.

Ethan willingly gave himself to his work, where his fellow healers held him in high esteem. On days with heavy fighting, he spent his hours working under the weight of intense agony, always fearing he might see his father or one of his brothers brought in, bleeding his life away.

The night after Tristan's first battle, an exhausted Ethan had staggered to their tent to find Tristan sitting on his cot in shock, covered in blood. Ethan flew into a panic. Tristan stammered that he wasn't hurt, the blood wasn't his, and admitted he found the battle to be exhilarating in a way he had not expected. Then the excitement faded, leaving a frightened young man who had seen and brought about death, whose moralities were shattered. In the dark hours, Tristan finished his long day weeping broken-heartedly in the arms of his brother.

Ethan wept with him for all they were losing every day the war continued. He fervently prayed his sweet-natured brother wouldn't become like other soldiers he had met, with hearts of stone and dead eyes.

He was thankful to see his prayers answered over the following months. Tristan did not harden so much as he strengthened. He grew up, maturing into manhood while retaining his kindness and good humor, somehow finding his own way to cope with the hazards to his soul. No doubt he struggled, but by the time spring blossomed into summer, Ethan could see Tristan would do well.

Whenever the call to arms rang out, Tristan showed himself to be a fearless soldier, fighting with a relentless intensity; yet after a battle was over, he could be found praying over the dead and dying, be they men of Sammanon or Aquila. Tristan inspired deep admiration in his fellow soldiers, and it wasn't long before those much further up the chain of command began to take notice.

Both Ethan and James strove to protect their youngest brother as best as they could. If fighting on the same field of battle, James kept watch over Tristan far more than his brother ever knew. There were several times when Tristan's sheer boldness made James's heart leap to his throat, but he was also deeply proud of Tristan's exploits.

Ethan found solace in his correspondence with Rachel, and he treasured every letter he received. They carried a soothing whiff of home, and though no words of love were written between them, he often dreamt of her starry gray eyes. Together, they contrived to keep Christiana and Tristan connected. He faithfully sent Rachel letters with reports of Tristan, hoping she would pass them on to everyone at the castle. Her return letters were full of news about Christiana, which Ethan would read aloud.

Although Tristan acted exceptionally eager to listen whenever Ethan received a letter, he never spoke of Christiana. But at night, awake in his cot, Ethan heard the whispered prayer...*Father, I entrust she who is dear to me into thy never-failing care and love...*

Tristan sat huddled as close as he could to the fire, his wool cloak wrapped securely around him. A frigid blast had come through that morning, and it would be snowing soon. Despite the mutterings and complaints of the men near him, a palpable sense of hope hovered in the air. The Sammanon forces had been retreating, and many believed one more push on Aquila's part would end the war. Tristan wondered what life would be like afterward but buried the thought. "Survive this first, there's a good lad," he muttered to himself.

The wind shifted, and Tristan eased away from the line of smoke swirling at him. All he wanted was to see his family again. His battalion had pulled out of the main camp two months before, and he had not seen Ethan since. He ran into James occasionally but couldn't remember the last time he had his father. He missed Lucy too. After the Christmas fiasco, Tristan had been relieved she seemed more than happy to resume their friendship, and they had spent much time together, even if a subtle new edge colored their banter. But like the others, he hadn't seen her in months.

Movement caught men's attention. Commander Martin was roving among the soldiers and coming in their direction. At his approach, Tristan and the rest of the soldiers nearby began to rise to their feet, but Martin waved at them to remain seated. He tossed a log onto the fire, and Tristan watched mesmerized as sparks flew upward.

"Where's Farley?" Martin barked.

The soldiers all eyed each other until one of them piped up. "Ach, you know Farley's dead, Commander."

"Right," Martin grumbled to himself as though Farley's death were a personal inconvenience to his sense of order. "How long was he with us?"

"He served since the beginning, but captain for only one day, sir," Tristan said. Their battalion had an unfortunate history of captains not surviving.

"Well, that's inconvenient. All right, here we go." Martin grunted as he scanned the group of men. "Thatcher! How old are you, lad?"

"Eighteen this past June, sir." Tristan spoke through clenched teeth, cursing himself for speaking up about Farley. He had a very bad feeling about what was coming.

Martin cocked his head. "Good. You're Captain Thatcher now. Try to live more than one day, if you don't mind."

Tristan squeezed his eyes shut, wishing himself back in his featherbed at Altair. When he opened them again, Martin was already making his way down the line of fires. Tristan scuttled after him.

"Sir! Sir, I don't think that's the best idea. I know nothing about—"

"Meh, don't make a bother of it. Yell at the men, tell them where to go, stick the enemy with their swords. Try not to die. It's not difficult."

"But I—"

"Come on, Thatcher. It might be good for you. Just the sort of thing to awaken the manhood, know what I'm saying?" Martin grinned, for it was well known Tristan never had a girl in his tent.

Tristan grimaced and tried one more time. "You see, sir, my father wouldn't—"

"Are you defying my orders, *Captain*?" Martin stepped close, and since they were the same height, their noses were almost touching.

Tristan sighed in resignation. "No, sir."

"Be at the officers' meeting at dawn!" Without waiting for a reply, Martin sauntered off, his good humor restored.

Tristan ran his hand through his hair and groaned. "Dad is not going to be happy about this."

Tristan woke to fresh snow on the ground and couldn't help smiling while walking to the officers' meeting. Within an hour it would be a trampled, ugly mess, but he savored its clean beauty as the sky turned gold, sun glinting on the white.

He approached the meeting tent, but paused when someone yelled, "Tristan!" Before Tristan had time to respond, he was tackled into the snow by James. His brother hauled him back to his feet, and they hugged joyously.

"I almost didn't recognize you, Tris. Look at you, you're practically tall!"

Tristan laughed, giddy at seeing James. "I'll never catch up to you."

"Probably not, but..." James's voice trailed off, staring at his brother who seemed different somehow. Tristan's hair had long since grown back to its usual shaggy curls. Perhaps it was the light beard his brother sported? Whatever it might be, James approved. "What are you doing over here anyway? Running errands for Commander Martin?"

Tristan's happiness faded somewhat. "Ah, you might say that."

"Well, you better scoot before they catch you. They don't like when the lower ranks try to sneak into these things."

"Right."

A commanding voice called for James, and he grimaced. "I'm sorry, I have to go. Maybe we can get together after this meeting? See you soon."

"Real soon," Tristan muttered as he watched James enter the tent. He waited a few minutes before slipping in himself. Tristan huddled in a corner, unnoticed by most of the other officers there. To his dismay, his father entered, and James moved to greet him. They stood together near the front, and Tristan prayed they would not see him.

Different officers came forward and spoke, and Tristan had a difficult time following some of their talk. It didn't matter. He just needed to pay attention when it was Commander Martin's turn. The tent had filled, causing him to lose sight of his father, but several times Tristan heard Thomas's deep voice asking a question or giving an opinion.

Commander Martin started speaking, and Tristan stood at attention. Martin was a good leader on the field, even if he could be a bit of an ass. Tristan relaxed, relieved he understood everything, when Martin's familiar bark made him suck in his breath. "Captain Thatcher!"

Everyone looked at James, who had a baffled expression on his face. Martin searched the crowd, exasperated to find himself in a tent seemingly full of Thatchers. "Captain Tristan Thatcher!"

His father's head whipped around, and Tristan gulped as he wormed his way to the front. "Here, sir."

"This is Captain Thatcher's first day here. Let's hope it's not his last." Most of the men chuckled at the weak joke. "Thatcher, you understood what I said?"

"Yes, sir." Tristan was concentrating hard on *not* looking at Thomas. After Martin dismissed him, he slunk back to his corner. Tristan could sense his father's eyes boring into him. As the meeting ended, he resisted the urge to take flight.

Then Thomas stood before him, and he seemed extra massive in that moment, with his arms crossed. But his voice held a gentle rumble when he spoke.

"Captain, eh?"

"Yes, sir. As of last night."

"You must have made an impression on Martin."

"To be honest, I think he was running out of options."

"I doubt it. I've known Joseph Martin a long time, and he doesn't make these decisions carelessly. If he appointed you captain, he's seen something in you. I'm impressed, Tristan. Quite impressed."

Tristan had not anticipated this reaction, and a sudden warmth flooded through him. More than anything, he craved his father's approval, and he resisted the sudden impulse to hug Thomas.

As a matter of fact, Thomas was so proud of his son he could hardly contain himself. He had known James would do well as a soldier but had kept a tight rein on his expectations with Tristan. This promotion under Commander Martin was no small matter. However, concern tempered his pride.

"Try not to get yourself killed, son." Thomas shook his hand and winked.

Tristan grinned and left the tent happier than he had been in a long time. Thomas watched him stroll away. Exactly when his son had entered manhood, he wasn't sure, but the young officer carried himself differently than the boy he had been. The smile on Thomas's face faded, and he sighed. The upcoming battle promised to be brutal.

James caught his father's mood shift and nodded in sympathy as Thomas walked back in his direction. "I'll watch out for him if I can, Dad. But you know what he's like when he gets his fire up. There's no stopping him."

"I'm thankful I've bred no cowards, but must you both always put yourselves into the very worst of it?"

James chuckled. "That's what you get for having sons."

"I suppose." Thomas watched Tristan making his way to his own campsite. He mused to himself, "He's grown taller the past few months."

It was freezing cold and Tristan shivered, rattling the heavy chainmail he wore. Jericho blew steam from his nostrils. Tristan would have preferred Dun this day, but he knew his respectability went up when he rode the fiery bay stallion.

The clash of battle could be heard in the distance, for the Aquilan forces had snuck upon the Sammanon encampment during the night. In the gray twilight before dawn, they had attacked. Thus far, Tristan's men were in a holding pattern. The infantry and main cavalry had been fighting for hours while his own men remained on the edge of the forest, awaiting word to further decimate the enemy. If everything went according to plan, which it rarely did, their entry into the fight would be the last thrust to win the battle and end the war.

Martin had surprised him with this assignment, for it was a crucial one, and Tristan carried the burden of his new promotion seriously. It also meant he would arrive at the battle late. For hours they were surrounded by the noise of death. The strain of anticipation was wearing down on them, and some men were getting antsy. Tristan took a deep breath and rode to the front. At least he had a strong voice and knew how to use it.

"All right, men! I know you're cold. I know you're tired. We've been out here for a long time. And I know you're hungry—hungry to hunt these Sammanon devils and bring this war to an end!"

There was a general murmur of approval, but Tristan could see he needed to ramp it higher. He kicked Jericho into a canter and swept up and down the line.

"Now I've heard a rumor! They say this is the big one, and if we can drive these devils back one last time, we can go home. I don't know about you, but I want to be home for Christmas this year!"

This brought a rowdy yell from the men. Tristan fought to keep his face as stern as possible.

"When we get the word to move, I don't want men who are falling asleep! I don't want men who are thinking about their stomachs! And I sure don't want men who are complaining about the damn cold! I want men who are ready to ride the hell out of their horses, ready to ride those Sammanon brutes into the ground! I want you ready to spear them on your swords like meat for the fire! Men of Aquila! Do you hear me?"

Swords and lances were raised high, and there was a cacophony of cheers and yells. In fact, Tristan had roused them so effectively, he hoped there would be something left to stir them up again when they were told to engage. A rider raced toward them, distracting him. Tristan was stunned to see Commander Martin, haggard and bleeding. He rode from his men to meet with Martin and other officers gathering.

"Disengage, Thatcher! You aren't going in."

"What's wrong, sir?"

"The whole bloody thing is a mess, that's what. They know you're here, and the element of surprise is gone."

Tristan looked in the direction of the battle. "Surely we can—"

"I appreciate your determination, Thatcher, but that's the word." Martin jerked on his horse's reins, spinning the animal away. Tristan growled an oath.

"Martin, hold!" ordered Tristan. Commander Martin gawked open-mouthed at his captain. Tristan huffed in frustration. He knew he had crossed the line in how he had addressed his commanding officer. Fighting an onslaught of emotions, Tristan lowered his voice. "I mean, sir. Show me what's happening on the map. Please."

Commander Martin pierced Tristan with a glare that the younger man met unflinchingly. "You've a mouth on you, Thatcher. You need to learn to listen and obey."

Nevertheless, Martin lurched off his horse with a grunt and a jerk of his head for Tristan to follow him. He barked for maps and showed Tristan the lay of the land. The infantry had marched into the enemy camp hours ago and flushed the Sammanon soldiers out. Archers had laid waste to those on the edges, and the first cavalry came in behind the infantry to further crush the field. However, the Sammanon soldiers had regrouped with their backs to the forest, and several enemy battalions reinforced them from the surrounding foothills. The Aquilan army was surrounded. Meanwhile, word had filtered down of Martin's surprise attack from the hill, so the whole point of their ride was in ruins. They were expected and would be lambs for the slaughter.

Tristan groaned. Martin jabbed at the map. "Your father is right there, holding them together as best as he can, but the line will break soon."

Letting out a yell of rage and frustration, Tristan yanked off his helmet and slammed it to the ground. Martin chuckled, admiring the young captain's fire. He had long been watching Tristan, for his gut had told him the boy was an officer in the making. Seeing it unfold before him filled Martin with excitement.

Tristan willed his brain to work faster and think harder. He raked one hand through his hair and paced a few steps. Skidding to a sudden stop, he whirled around and stared at the map again. Tristan looked up, clenching his jaw. "I have an idea."

Commander Martin had already dashed away on his horse to find Lord General Kavanaugh when Tristan called for Riggs, a competent rider who had a good head on his shoulders. He and Tristan consulted for some time, resulting in Riggs removing most of the battalion. Tristan mounted Jericho and faced the few men remaining.

"Men! Some things have changed. Word is they know we're coming, and our gambit of surprise is foiled. Commander Martin wants us to call it off."

The men muttered at this news, but Tristan raised his hand.

"I've already told the good commander I refuse to back down! I say we will not go quietly. We will crush this army! We're setting a mousetrap for them, and they will regret the day they met Martin's riders! Onward Aquila!"

As the men cheered, Tristan turned Jericho toward the slope. He thought of Christiana, and a wave of grief swept over him at the thought that he might never see her sweet face again. But Tristan imagined his father at the bottom of the hill, fighting for his life. Heart pounding, he crossed himself and kissed the St. Michael's medallion before pulling on his helmet and drawing a shaky breath.

# Chapter 38

# The Battle of Hill Run

When Tristan's men burst from the forest and raced down the steep hill to the fighting, their job was clear—sweep in and kill as many Sammanon forces as they could and be a deadly distraction, allowing the Aquilan soldiers a chance to regroup and renew the army's strength.

It was a suicide mission, but Thomas Thatcher was down there in the thick of battle with his life on the line, and Tristan would do anything to save his father.

As they barreled toward battle, the standard with the golden eagle whipping in the wind, Tristan imagined himself less of an eagle and far more like a sparrow attempting to peck a lion. But it was too late to reverse course, and in seconds they were in the fray. As expected, their entry into the fight surprised no one, and a number of the enemy forces had separated to face them. The riders dodged around or rushed through them to join the thickest fighting in the center. They all had a target on their back, and every rider focused on inflicting as much damage as possible before most of them were unhorsed.

Jericho did not like being rammed against other horses. He kicked with such violence that Tristan fell against the horse's neck and almost lost his grip on his sword. The large bay threw his head back against his rider's face. An explosion of pain ripped through Tristan as blood dripped from his nose. Jericho plunged through the melee, and Tristan gave the horse free rein while he focused on the enemy, sword swinging. They tore through the battle and were soon in the center of the worst fighting. Abruptly, Jericho skidded to a stop and reared so high he fell backwards. Tristan's head struck the ground hard. His vision went black as he wrestled to stay conscious.

Sight returned and with it, chaos. His helmet had fallen somewhere, and he was surrounded by thunderous hooves. Tristan tried to stand, but the world tilted, and he dropped to his knees. He fumbled to his feet, slipping on the muddy slush. Everything snapped into focus as he blocked a sword coming at his head. With a snarl, he struck, sinking his blade deep into the enemy soldier.

He worked to take in his surroundings. The horses were scattering, and most of his men were fighting on their feet. Desperate, Tristan scanned the east and then the south, but the ridgelines remained empty. He wiped mud from his eyes and dived into battle.

It was madness to fight in such close quarters. A large, helmeted soldier swung at his sword, and shock waves thrummed up his arm. Tristan returned the attack with a bellow. When their blades crossed again, he was stunned to see the soldier jerk his weapon away. Mud caked any insignia, but a glint of red hair peaking under the rim of his helmet caught his eye. The man charged, sword raised, this time to block a spear aimed at Tristan's back.

Tristan stumbled onward. His fighting spirit waned in his exhaustion. Then he saw his father battling not too far from him. Blood ran down his face, but he was alive and engaged with two Sammanon soldiers. Tristan raced to Thomas and slid beside him in time to block a killing blow.

"Behind you, Dad!" he cried to ensure his own father didn't move to strike him by accident. Back-to-back, father and son fought. The surrounding enemy deepened. More and more, Tristan feared his plan had gone terribly wrong, and soon they would all be dead in the mud.

A joyous horn echoed across the battlefield, and tears sprang to his eyes. It called again and again. Tristan risked a glance toward the ridge-lines, but he was too thick in the battle to see far. But the cheers of men rose like a crashing wave.

Taller than most of the men surrounding him, Thomas spotted the long line of Riggs's horsemen flowing down the hill from the south, Lord General Kavanaugh's forces riding in from the east, and from the north came Prince Justin with his troops. If the Sammanon men had thought Tristan's small band was all that remained to challenge them, they were sorely mistaken.

The enemy did not retreat or give in at once. If anything, they dug in even harder in those last moments. The battle was a victory, yet far from over for those fighting. A spear crossed Tristan's sword, sending the blade flying. He made a desperate leap for it, feet slipping on mud. Trying to regain his balance, he was kicked to the ground. A hand grabbed his hair and shoved his face into the wet muck.

Tristan flailed and scrabbled his fingers into the mud, searching for some leverage in order to throw himself backward against whoever held him down. Winded from the fight, whatever energy he had left ebbed as he smothered. Tristan attempted a ragged breath, only to suck in water and mud. He gagged, forcing out what little air remained. His lungs burned and his head pounded. Movement slowed as his valiant heart struggled. Tristan was dying and could do nothing. He tried to get one arm propped under his head, while the other hand kept grasping, ever weaker. As the long seconds ticked by, everything staggered to a halt. His body convulsed once, twice. His hand fell limp.

Captain James Thatcher had engaged in almost every battle in the war since its beginning, and he could not remember one with this level of brutality and desperation. James had been among the first in the battle that began before sunrise, and as the sun rose they had been hedged in a tight circle by enemy fighters. When the small group of riders started their descent, the surrounding soldiers cheered, and James whirled in confusion to see what was happening. He swore as he recognized the bay stallion at the head.

"What the bloody hell are you thinking!" he yelled. Tristan's battalion should have called off its engagement. It was one thing to fight honorably but another to defy all common sense. James watched in shock at the mere twenty-odd horses careening down the hill. No force that size should be attacking. Then his canny military mind understood what Tristan was doing. He groaned, both alarmed for his brother and full of admiration for him.

When Tristan fell off Jericho, James tried to reach him, but the fighting was too intense. Over and over again, soldiers pressed him back. Much later, he had the most peculiar sensation when he crossed swords with a fierce, shortish soldier. James had stumbled back in confusion. It was hard to distinguish the fighter's face covered in blood and mud amidst the crush of humanity surrounding them, but something about the swing of his sword was too familiar. Instead, James chose to dive at an obvious Sammanon fighter rushing up with a spear in hand.

As reinforcements arrived, cheers broke out around him, and the Sammanon men made a hasty retreat. James found his father, who was bent double, panting.

"I'm too old for this nonsense," Thomas rumbled, swiping at a cut on his temple. James chuckled while trying to regain his breath. At the sound of the familiar laugh, Thomas raised his head and grinned at his son before his eyes narrowed. He spun around before looking at James again. "Was that you who had my back?"

"I just got here," said James. His father's face blanched, and James's gut twisted with anxiety. "Where's Tristan?"

"He was right here behind me!"

"Let's split up. Yell if you find him." James weaved through the men. Sammanon soldiers were being rounded up as prisoners, and of all the soldiers left standing, none were Tristan.

It had begun to snow once more.

"Where are you, Tris?" he muttered, resisting the panic that threatened to engulf him. There were wounded and dead all around, and he didn't know where to begin searching. Adding to his fears, the silent snow was dusting the scores of bodies lying on the ground, making it difficult to discern those still clinging to life and those already dead. James was running out of time. If the snow kept falling, he wouldn't be able to distinguish anything under the soft white mounds.

The crowds were thinning, and one large soldier hauled himself up from a crouch to stumble off. No other movement showed from the dead men surrounding him. Breathing fast, James wandered, unsure where to go. He picked his way over bodies and almost let his eye slide past a glint of light at his feet. James refocused to see the glimmer of a gold chain on the neck of a soldier sprawling face down in the mud. He took in the figure, and his heart pounded. He thought of calling his father, but he had to know for himself first. James knelt, placed a trembling hand on the shaggy head and knew it was Tristan. Tears glazed his eyes. James gently drew the body over, and his world shattered.

"Tristan, no, please no. Not you." James moaned, bending over his brother, heartbroken. Brushing away the blood and wet slush, he cradled Tristan to his chest as sobs ripped forth. "Not now. Not when it's all over. Come back, please come back, Tris."

In his anguish, he caught his father's gaze. Thomas's face drained of all color at the sight of his two boys, one hanging loose in the strong arms of the other. He wended his way to them, his feet dragging.

Clinging to the lifeless body, James wept. He struggled to pull Tristan upright, to hold him ever tighter, tears streaking through the blood and grime on his face. With shocking suddenness, his brother shuddered and coughed. Tristan coughed again, then retched up mud, and James reeled away.

Thomas took over, doing his best to help his son, who gagged repeatedly, attempting to expel the sludge. His hacking grew so violent that vomit soon mixed with the slop. Tristan convulsed as he strained to breathe, and James found himself whispering prayers for the first time since he was a child.

After the worst had passed, Thomas eased Tristan back to James before sinking into the mud, shaking in his relief. Tears still falling, James held his brother close as he muttered a final prayer of thanks. Tristan's dark blue eyes opened and he smiled faintly upon seeing James. Then his eyes closed again. He relaxed, knowing he was always safe in his brother's arms.

# Chapter 39

# Together Again

The Battle of Hill Run, as it became known, was indeed the final thrust needed to gain victory against Sammanon. Small skirmishes continued to break out, but everyone agreed even those would be over soon. Once again, Aquila had rid herself of the vile stink of her centuries-old enemy.

In the face of certain defeat, Commander Thomas Thatcher was praised for holding the forces together, while his son, Captain James Thatcher, was given an official commendation for his steadfast leadership during the battle. The men under Commander Joseph Martin, terror of the cavalry, were hailed as the winning stroke against the enemy. Lord General Kavanaugh and a common cavalry soldier named Riggs were lauded by soldiers as the heroes who saved them all in the last hour. And the entire army breathed a quiet sigh of relief that Prince Justin had at least one noteworthy act in the war.

And what of Captain Tristan Thatcher? Those who didn't know the situation saw his courageous charge as nothing more than foolish stupidity. But the truth spread from the soldiers of his battalion, and Commander Martin sent a letter of praise to the queen. Months later, stories would be told in taverns of the brave young captain who challenged the entire army of Sammanon single-handedly. Of greater importance to Tristan, had he known, the tale soon reached the ears of a tender heart who adored him still.

Tristan didn't care about honors or commendations. The war was over, and those whom he loved most were safe. His last battle had been harrowing, and he knew how close to death he had been in those final moments. He was content and thankful to be alive, and deep within, Tristan had discovered a glimmer of hope for the future.

Tristan pressed through the tavern throng searching for his brothers. The crowd was in high spirits, and as he made his way around the room, he was often stopped for quick greetings and comradely huzzahs.

Stephens clapped him on the back. "How's Jericho?"

After the battle, the big bay had been found pawing the ground and acting generally annoyed. Only when James tried to lead him from the field of battle did the horse's limp become obvious. Gathering around, they discovered a hot and swollen foreleg. Ethan had worked hours over the horse, and soon Jericho was on the mend.

"He'll be fine with a long rest, which he deserves," assured Tristan.

"Good." Stephans raised a mug, toasting Jericho. "He's a grand horse. I'll see you later."

James and Ethan waved from a table, and Tristan meandered over. They were already sipping ales, and a foaming mug awaited him.

"Thanks." He grinned and proceeded to drink almost half his mug in a single gulp. "This ale is the one thing I will miss. Isn't this crowd something?" When his brothers didn't respond, his heart rate accelerated. "What's wrong? Is Dad—" Tristan stood, anxious. There were still small skirmishes in the area. But James pushed him down.

"No, Dad's well. He was here but had to go. Said he'd see you tomorrow."

"Why the glum faces? This is a happy day! Cheers!" When his brothers returned his toast halfheartedly, Tristan gulped and set his mug down. "What is it?"

Ethan and James eyed each other, and Ethan looked away first. James cleared his throat.

"This, listen, we don't know if this is true or not. I mean, I was told it was true, but I don't believe it. Well, I did wonder. Anyway, Dad thought it was bunk, and I consider his opinion to be the important thing here."

Tristan arched an eyebrow at Ethan. "Am I supposed to understand what he said?"

"James heard a rumor today. Strictly a rumor, mind—"

Gaining courage, James interrupted him. "I heard an engagement would be announced by Queen Charlotte soon. For Christiana."

"Oh." Tristan stared at the table and toyed with his mug. "That's good. Wonderful. I want her to be happy."

"I don't think it's true," James insisted. "But we didn't want you to hear it from someone else and be caught off guard."

Listless, Tristan shrugged. They sat for some time in uncomfortable silence before Tristan risked a glance at Ethan. "Has Rachel mentioned anything in her letters?"

Ethan shook his head as James stared at him. "You've been writing to Rachel Marchant? *Our* Rachel?"

"Heaven help me," Ethan muttered. He raised his eyes skyward and his face flushed red.

Not catching the exchange, Tristan drained his mug and pushed himself from the table. "I need to start packing. You know it takes me forever."

"Tristan…"

He forced a smile. "I'm fine. Have things to do. I'll see you boys later."

Tristan strode through the camp. It was his own fault. He had been the one to end things, to tell her to find another man. Just when he thought he might have something worth offering…

Black hair floated in front of his vision, and before he knew it, Lucy had hooked her arm through his.

"Hello there, stranger," she said brightly.

His heart lightened a touch at the sight of her. "Well, hello. I've been watching out for you. Where have you been?"

"Getting things settled with the other girls. Have you grown? You look taller."

Tristan laughed. He had put on a solid two inches in the past year, and it pleased him very much she had noticed. Tristan suspected he was done growing but was happy with whatever he could get at this point. "Must be the boots. But maybe."

"Where are you headin'?"

"To my tent, to pack."

"You want company?"

Tristan stopped and studied her with such intensity, Lucy almost blushed. He had a hungry expression she had not seen on his face before, and her heart fluttered. But Tristan started walking again. "No, I had better not. It's hard enough without being distracted. You may walk with me to the tent if you like."

"And where will you be goin' from here?"

"I'm not sure, to be honest," Tristan hedged. "I might go to my brother's estate. I've never been there, and I'm curious to see it."

"I didn't know one of your brothers had an estate. Ethan or James?"

"Michael, actually. Lockhart Manor. I might—" But Lucy had stopped walking. "Anything wrong?" Tristan asked.

"I thought your brother was Michael Thatcher?"

"Oh, right, didn't I tell you? My parents fostered him. Although he went by Thatcher, he was born Michael Lockhart. Unusual, I know. Important name...I guess you've heard of it?" Lucy appeared as though she might swoon. She stepped back, her eyes large and scared.

"Lucy?" Tristan gently tipped her chin up, but she jerked away from his touch. "What's wrong?"

"I need to go."

"Wait! Where are you going after this? I want to see you again. Lucy?"

"Maybe Altair. I don't know. I'll talk to you later." And with these words, she lost herself in the crowd.

Tristan was knee-deep sorting through his belongings when Ethan returned alone.

"Tristan, honestly. Do you have to make such a mess of packing every single time?"

Tristan grunted in response. Then he looked up. "I had the oddest encounter with Lucy."

"Why does this not surprise me?" Ethan sighed. He sometimes worried about how attached she and Tristan had become, and he jealously guarded Tristan against any further heartbreak. But his curiosity was roused when Tristan told him about his latest conversation with the girl.

"And the Lockhart name upset her? I don't know, Tris. You could ask Dad, he knows the family histories better than I do. My guess is she didn't realize the relation before, and it surprised her to find you so well connected. How did this come up again?"

"She asked where I was going after this, and I told her I might go see Lockhart Manor."

"What is this? When did you make these plans?" Ethan stopped his own packing and looked sharply at his brother. Tristan avoided his eyes.

"Just thinking about it," he mumbled.

"Well, go to Lockhart Manor anytime in January, but you will be at Altair for Christmas."

"C'mon, Ethan—"

"No, you're facing this nonsense once and for all. I'm not going to live conflicted between never seeing you or never going back to Altair for the rest of my life, especially if..." Ethan went a little red.

"How's Rachel?" Tristan asked with an innocent air.

"She's well," mumbled Ethan. "Now clean your mess."

Within the week, hundreds of soldiers and officers were on the road. On the first day Tristan was in high spirits, far more than his brothers could remember in a long time. He chattered, sang tavern songs off-key, joked, and even challenged James to a short sparring session. But as the days passed, he grew quieter and more introspective, and they could all guess the reason.

On the third day, Thomas rode his horse alongside Ethan. "Son, can you tell me anything about this young lady Tristan talks about? Lucy, I believe?"

"Lady? I think you know what she is, Dad."

"I do. Should I be concerned? I ask because Tristan spoke of her several times yesterday. To be honest, he seems quite taken with her."

After shifting in his saddle to make sure Tristan wasn't in earshot, Ethan said, "I'm fond of Lucy. She's helped Tristan a great deal. I believe he finds her enticing, but I wouldn't worry about that yet. He's still very much in love with Chris. If he believes there's a chance of winning her back, I don't think you need to be concerned."

"And if nothing comes of Christiana?"

Ethan's hands involuntarily twitched at his reins. "There might be enough between them in that case. Tristan is a romantic soul."

Thomas smiled at this description of his youngest. "You know, I didn't always approve of the idea behind the match with Christiana. Charlotte and your mother had long laid plans to pair her with one of you boys. Consolidation of power by merging the Lockhart line into Reynard, they said."

Thomas could have said much more concerning bloodlines and family legacies, but he didn't. Instead, he added, "To be sure, Charlotte would never force Christiana to marry any of you if it had been against her wishes. And I've never objected as long as they love each other."

"You don't believe she is to be engaged to another?"

Thomas snorted. "Not at all. The queen won't give up her plans that easily, I can assure you. And I would be the first to know if that were true."

Ethan looked at his father, wondering at this statement.

"And what of you, son? Are you still corresponding with Rachel?"

Ethan reined his horse to a stop, staring at Thomas. "Are there no secrets in this family! Who told you? I swear, if James—"

"Charlotte told me months ago." Thomas laughed, but seeing his son's embarrassment, he sobered. After a minute of silence, he coughed. "Have any plans?"

"More dreams than plans, if that counts," Ethan said, blushing. "But that's a long way off."

"Her father's no gift, but he shouldn't be around much longer. If those dreams become a reality, you have my blessing. You deserve someone special, and Rachel is perfect for you. She's a sweet lass, and you could do no better."

A soft smile spread across Ethan's face. "I think so as well."

With a click of the tongue, Thomas urged his horse forward, and Ethan followed suit. In an effort to change the topic, Thomas spoke again. "I've heard nothing but praise from your colleagues. Some are proclaiming you to be the best of the healers."

"Nonsense. I was doing my duty, that's all."

"Well, I'm deeply proud of you. A father couldn't be more blessed than to have you as his son."

Ethan's heart filled with joy hearing this. "Thank you, Dad. That means more than you know."

"Now if we could get Tristan and Christiana settled, I would be a happy man."

"Forget old James, eh?"

Thomas grunted. "That boy. I don't know what to make of him. He has women on the brain, but I've heard nary a rumor all these years."

Ethan had, in fact, heard a rumor quite some time ago. He had also seen a half-written letter hidden in a pile of papers among his brother's things the week before. But other than a quiet chuckle, Ethan held his tongue.

As they entered the city of Altair, happiness and anxiety battled for Tristan's heart. Between the end of the war and the coming of Christmas, the city was jubilant. The sun was setting and candles twinkled in windows. There would be many days of celebration among the people, culminating with Christmas.

Tristan knew he had given up the right to call the castle home, but pure joy cascaded over him at the sight of the familiar outline in the darkening sky. Tristan glanced at Jericho, whom he had on a lead rope, and bent to stroke Dun's neck.

"Here we go, boys," he muttered. Dun nickered in response.

# PART III

# Chapter 40

# Secrets

The Great Hall thronged with people, and Tristan wondered how many would remain through Christmas. He spied the Kavanaugh family at one end and blew a kiss to Mariah. Tristan started to make a comment to James about how pretty the oldest girls were looking, but his brother had disappeared. In fact, Tristan had somehow become separated from everyone. Cursing his height, he stood on tiptoes and glimpsed red hair. He grinned at the sight of his father waving for him near the dais.

Tristan meandered through the hall, readying himself to see Christiana again. He was glad they had arrived with enough time to have a wash and dress in fresh clothes. Tristan had not felt so grand in over two years, with an embroidered tunic and a dark blue wool cloak. His hair had been brushed to a high sheen, and his boots were polished. He had debated keeping his scruff of beard, but in the end opted to shave. Tristan's only annoyance came from the need to borrow a sword for the presentation at court. His had been lost in the battle, and no one had come forward with it. He grumbled at the thought of some scrub soldier coming across a sword made by the great Hillyer and deciding to keep it for himself. Tristan made a mental note to ask Justin once he returned to Altair.

Officially, the prince had been delayed traveling home due to his lingering duties in the aftermath of war. But the rumor all over the army was that given the general perception he hadn't contributed much to the war and Justin was loath to face his mother.

Approaching the dais, Tristan couldn't prevent a soft chuckle. They would all be ceremonially welcomed by the queen as officers. He recalled the first time he had ever met her, with his clumsy bow, and hoped his courtly grace had improved in the years since.

The formality lasted about three seconds. He was introduced as Captain Tristan Thatcher, which he thought sounded rather splendid, but before he could bow, Charlotte had him in her arms.

"My dear boy," she said. "Such stories of bravery I've heard! I'm thankful you are alive and flourishing. How handsome and tall you are! Doesn't he look well, Christiana?"

Out of the shadows she came, and Tristan's heart stopped. He had always thought Christiana sweet and pretty, but she had bloomed into something ethereal. Her copper-gold curls were piled high, and her creamy skin shone in the torchlight. She kept her gaze lowered until she stood before him and lifted her emerald eyes to meet his own. His heart began beating again with a wild and irregular rhythm.

Tristan tilted his head in an odd little quirk of a bow. "Princess Christiana."

"Welcome home, Tristan," Christiana almost whispered, lightly kissing his cheek. He stood still, stunned, and all the grand ideas of how he would impress her with his exploits deserted him. Her eyebrows went up as he remained silent. Tristan blinked and leaned forward to return her kiss. He hesitated at her cheek, catching a whiff of her hair, and thought should he be struck dead on the spot, he would die a happy man. She moved on to greet Ethan, and Tristan was left bemused. All his feats, the work he had done, the bravery he had striven for—they all seemed paltry offerings now.

Tristan looked around the room in a daze and jumped when his eyes met those of Lord General MacClaren. The old man stared at him with cold hatred. Tristan shuddered at the memory of the whip's lash. He wove through the crowd and into the quieter entry hall. Even there, people milled about. Grumbling to himself, he stumbled his way into the courtyard. Fresh snow lay on the ground, and Tristan inhaled as he tried to compose himself, grateful for the cold, clean air sweeping into his lungs.

Whispers tickled his ears, and he started. Someone else occupied the courtyard. *Two* someones. Tristan peered into the shadows, where he saw a soldier clutching a girl close, kissing her with great passion.

Tristan blushed and wondered how many such reunions were happening as men came home from fighting. He knew he should leave them alone, but his curiosity burned hot, and he welcomed the distraction from his own confused heart. Though quite tall, the girl was dwarfed by the large man who held her with such tenderness. The man murmured soft words, but Tristan couldn't hear his voice well. The girl laughed, and the hairs on the back of Tristan's neck rose. He *knew* that laugh.

He edged closer, trying to get a better look. They were kissing again, and Tristan had to give them credit for their enthusiasm. He couldn't recall ever letting himself go with such abandon, and he envied the man. The couple paused, and the low masculine rumble of a *very* familiar voice made Tristan's eyebrows shoot up. He had to clap a hand over his mouth to stifle his surprise.

The girl whispered, "We should go inside before they notice we're missing."

"See you later?" the man asked with a tone of gentle yearning. Tristan gasped at the sound of their voices, so close, which confirmed all his suspicions. In a panic, he slunk deeper into the shadows, praying he wouldn't be seen. The couple strode arm in arm to the doorway, and after one fervent, parting kiss, the girl slipped inside. Her lover hung about for a moment, whistling a tune. Tristan stayed hidden, although a part of him wanted to tackle the man with a yell of triumph. But the soldier decided enough time had passed and marched through the doors, brazen as could be.

Tristan snorted and began laughing. Once he started, he couldn't stop, and tears ran down his cheeks. As soon as he thought he had it under control, it broke out again. He walked into the Great Hall with a grin, rubbing the chill out of his hands. The old habit of sharing laughter with Christiana drove him to find her. Tristan discovered the princess sitting beside Gerald MacClaren, and their heads were bent close to one another as they talked.

The merriment died in Tristan, and he made his way to his room, his mood darkening.

"Good evening, Rachel," Ethan said with a smile. She was as winsome as he remembered. "I've so enjoyed your letters this past year. They've been an enchanting diversion."

"Yours have been a delight for me as well, Ethan." Her cheeks were pink, and he hoped it was a good sign.

Ethan tried to speak, but the crowd shifted and jostled him, almost upsetting his goblet of wine. On his second attempt, the music struck up again the moment he opened his mouth. He looked around the room, desperate for a solution. In a fit of inspiration, he leaned toward her to whisper, "Would you like to take a walk? If it's not too cold?"

Eyes sparkling, she nodded. No one saw the pair slip out of the castle.

Near midnight, Christiana walked in circles in her spacious tower chamber. It had been well over a year since Tristan was last at Altair, and though his arrival had been expected, it had still shaken her. Ethan had written to Rachel everything that happened at Hill Run, and Christiana had wept, knowing how close she had come to losing him forever. But now—he had returned, safe and sound, and yet she knew not what to say to him. She made a small huff of annoyance at her own behavior in the Great Hall. Tristan must have thought her a foolish child after the way she had stood there, waiting for him to speak, hoping he would take her in his arms once again.

Always handsome, he was more striking than ever, with his dark hair and luminous blue eyes. Those eyes haunted her; they seemed to pierce into the very quick of her. When had he grown so tall? And that quiet confidence he had never shown before as he stood steady and strong when she approached him. If anything had been lacking before, he was complete now, her sweet Tristan, whom she loved with every breath she took.

That Gerald MacClaren! What right had he to monopolize her the way he had, the obnoxious prig. Christiana was well aware of the ridiculous rumors attaching the two of them. She wondered if Gerald himself had begun to believe them. She might have known his family since childhood, but surely he didn't think she would stoop to marry into the MacClaren clan?

Christiana scoffed at the thought but then gasped—what if Tristan had heard those rumors? What if he believed them? Agitated, she resumed her pacing, wondering where Rachel had gone. Her cousin had always been her confidante in all things, the one person to whom she could reveal all her heart, but Rachel had disappeared.

James had long since abandoned the gathering and was restless in his room, mired down with tangled thoughts of his own. When a tentative knock sounded on his door, he leaped to answer it, welcoming the distraction. He almost laughed at the sight of his brother who looked tired and harassed.

"Still got it bad, haven't you?" he asked with a teasing smile.

"About as bad as you, I'm guessing," Tristan countered. James gave him a penetrating stare, wondering what his brother was implying. Leaning against the doorframe with a grin of his own, Tristan asked, "Feel like sparring?"

"Hell, yes. Give me a minute."

Tristan rummaged about for a practice sword and in short order, both brothers were in the stableyard, their blades dancing in the moonlight. They took some satisfaction in releasing their mutual frustrations by pounding each other to pieces. Neither of them wanted to give in, and after an hour they were both ready to collapse. Tristan had brought a flagon of ale with him, and they passed the bottle back and forth as they slumped in an empty stall.

Tristan studied his brother from the corner of his eye. Their relationship had shifted since the Battle of Hill Run. Tristan couldn't say precisely what had changed, but the bond between them had strengthened. He was well aware James had saved his life on the battlefield. Though memories of that morning were hazy, what remained clear was James holding him tearfully, sobbing prayers of thanks that his brother lived. Tristan had been given a rare glimpse into his brother's heart and discovered that beneath James's seemingly carefree demeanor, there was a great depth of spirit kept locked and hidden away.

He had amused himself thinking how he might entrap James into a confession but decided it wouldn't be gallant. Instead, Tristan asked, "How long has it been going on?"

James stiffened and darted a look at Tristan before dropping his gaze. He took another swig from the bottle. "How long have you known?"

"I saw you two in the courtyard earlier."

"Oh. That."

"Yes, *that*. Really, my dear James, I had no idea you had it in you."

"You aren't the only romantic in the family." An unexpectedly sweet smile brightened his face. "I fell for Catrina Kavanaugh when I was fifteen years old. She slapped me for saying something, I don't even remember what. No doubt I deserved it. But in that moment, I knew Cate was the one for me. She was such a little wildcat back then. It took me a while to convince her, but I won her over."

"You *would* fall for a girl for slapping you." Tristan snorted. "But all the bickering over the years?"

"Just part of the fun, fooling everyone. We would sneak off, and—say, you know that alcove off the entry hall?"

Tristan laughed wistfully as memories of that very alcove were recalled in an instant. "All too well."

"Those stolen moments in that alcove, among others...I could fight a war for years on those memories. She's so bewitching, Tristan. Much more than you could ever realize behind that sharp tongue of hers."

"Why keep it secret all this time?"

"Well, I felt bad for Michael, he had a yen for her too. I didn't want to hurt him, but later, even after I knew Michael wouldn't be bothered, we kept it up. It was too much fun. I regret that now. I would've liked for him to know how happy we are. Or were." James fell silent, and the glow left his face.

"What is it?"

James stood and kicked at the hay.

"Are you engaged?"

His brother shook his head and jammed his hands into his pockets.

"Are you going to ask her to marry you?"

"I don't know, Tris. I would have been overjoyed to marry her two years ago, but the war interrupted everything."

"The war is over."

"It wasn't just the war. There are other things, things I—listen, it's complicated."

"And you can't tell me? I thought we were closer than this, James. I thought—"

"You want to show me how this is done? Let's talk about you and Chris. Because I would love to hear how that's going to work out."

Stung, Tristan slumped. He had no right to question his brother's romantic entanglements, not after the way he had messed up everything with Christiana.

James groaned and sank into the straw next to him. "I'm sorry, I didn't mean that, Tris."

Endeavoring to lighten the tone, Tristan joked, "And all that talk of girls and wenches over the years?"

James gave a small laugh. "Poor Dad. He has no idea. It's been fun to rile him, though."

They sat in silence. Tristan fiddled with the medallion around his neck. "Seems like neither of us is very good at this."

"I'll say."

"What are we going to do?"

"I don't know. But Tristan? I'm glad you're here."

"Me too. Thanks for saving me, by the way. I don't remember if I ever said anything."

"Thanks for not dying on me. I don't think I could have handled that." James threw his arm around his brother's shoulders for a rough side hug. He passed Tristan the flagon, and his roguish smile flashed across his face. "Of course, I'm still the better swordsman."

"The hell you are."

The brothers looked at each other, grinned, and picked up their swords once more.

# Chapter 41

# A Spark of Hope

Tristan awoke grumpy and irritable. In spite of his delight in falling upon his old featherbed, he had not slept well. As he dressed, Ethan strolled in, tired but happy. Tristan shot him a glare. "What happened to you last night? You wandered off and left me!"

"I didn't know I existed to entertain you," said Ethan.

Surprised at his tone, Tristan grimaced. "You're right. I'm a selfish cad. Sorry, but I did wonder where you were."

Ethan started to speak, stopped, and bolted the door.

"This must be good," mused Tristan.

"Rachel and I were walking."

"A bit early in the day, isn't it?"

"No, last night."

"What, outside? In this weather?"

"It wasn't bad. Actually, it was wonderful."

Tristan's eyes lit up, for whatever brought Ethan joy was a source of happiness to him. "You were *just* walking?"

"Well, I don't want to move too fast."

"Ethan, you move about as fast as a snail. You've been writing for a year, which I would say justifies a kiss or two."

"Yes, but our letters have never been about us, they've been...well, never mind. I suppose you're right though." He pondered the notion and fidgeted. A note of panic crept into his voice. "What if she was expecting me to kiss her and she's disappointed?"

"Rachel's not exactly a woman of scandal. My guess is she's happy with your pace. Keep at it, lad."

"Sorry about ducking out of the gathering though."

"Oh, it was fine. I had a good talk with James."

"Dad and I are going into town. You want to come with?"

"That would be perfect. Last thing I want is to be stuck in the castle all day. Stifling in here. All these people."

"Interesting." Ethan smirked.

Tristan rolled his eyes in exasperation at his overly perceptive brother. "C'mon, let's go."

The two were soon stomping through the fresh, fluffy snow to meet Thomas at the gate, with the occasional snowball thrown at each other. It was a beautiful winter day with a clear blue sky overhead, and Tristan enjoyed watching the various people as they walked.

"Where's the other one?" grumbled Thomas.

"I have no idea," said Ethan. "He disappeared after breakfast. Said he had some errands to do for Christmas."

Tristan snorted with laughter and tried to smother it with a cough. Ethan narrowed his eyes at his brother, who avoided looking in his direction. They had arrived at the marketplace when a feminine voice called out Tristan's name. Thomas noted the instantaneous joy that beamed on his son's face.

"Lucy! You're here!" Tristan trotted over and gave her an enormous hug, almost lifting her off her feet. "It's wonderful to see you!"

Tristan sobered as he turned toward his father, somewhat anxious about how Thomas would react to this introduction. "Lucy, may I introduce my father, Commander Thomas Thatcher? Father, this is Miss Lucy Foster."

A gentleman always, Thomas gave her a slight bow. She returned the gesture with a saucy little curtsy, which brought out an unexpected rumble of amusement from him. He understood how she might appeal to his son and offered her a warm greeting.

"I'm pleased to meet you. I've heard quite a bit about you from my son."

"Good things, I hope?" An uncertain smile flickered before she shifted her gaze back to Tristan. "I've been looking for you. Might we have a word?"

"Of course! Dad, I'll find you later."

Thomas bowed once more. "Good day, Miss Foster. It was a pleasure."

She blushed, glancing at Tristan. Thomas perceived the truth of the matter and sighed—the pretty young prostitute was indeed infatuated with his son. Thankfully, Tristan did not seem to notice. At least, not yet.

Tristan steered Lucy down a narrow street, almost laughing with genuine happiness. She was a delight to see again, pretty with her flushed cheeks and black eyes gleaming. "You've made me very curious about why you were seeking me out, but I'm glad you did."

"Tristan," she whispered.

"What's wrong?"

"Do you remember the last time we saw each other, what we talked about?"

"You mean my brother Michael?"

"His name—you said he was Michael Lockhart. Lord Lockhart, yes?"

"How did you—" Tristan paused, for her lips trembled. Tristan took a step closer, placing his hands on her shoulders. "What is it, Lucy?"

"In my profession, I hear things. Do you understand? I hear many things from many...different men."

Tristan dropped his hands and his happiness evaporated. He preferred to ignore what Lucy did for a living whenever he could.

"Your brother's death wasn't...Tristan, I don't know how to say this, and I'm frightened. Those men weren't some random ambush. They were after somethin', or someone."

"What do you mean? I told you, there were marauders in the area, and we were—"

"No! That was the bait, don't you see? Who asked your father to go south?"

"The queen, naturally. Lord MacClaren needed assistance."

"Why? Why would a lord need you when he has his own people?" Her eyes were darting about, watching every movement around them. "Find out, Tristan. Find out why."

"I don't understand?"

"Do it!" she hissed. "I need to go."

Tristan grabbed her arm. "Wait, Lucy—"

"Let me go! Please."

"Not until you tell me more!"

"Not here. I'm at Barley's Tavern, you can meet me there."

"On the western edge of town?"

"Yes. Now, I must leave."

She jerked her arm free and hurried away, looking around her as she went. Tristan stared after her, trying to make sense of her words.

Tristan wandered back to the castle, lost in thought. Why had they been the ones to travel south? Michael had passed it off as a way to keep busy before the war began. James had questioned the reasoning as well, and his father's answers had been vague.

His first instinct was to question Thomas, but he hesitated. He had no wish to reopen old wounds without reason, so he directed his footsteps to the one other person whom he hoped might have some answers. Half an hour later, he knocked on Queen Charlotte's door.

"Tristan! How delightful to have you visit. I've wanted to have a chat with you." Charlotte indicated a chair by the fire. "Sit, my dear boy. Tell me what came between you and Christiana last year."

Tristan was nonplussed. He had forgotten Charlotte's ability to take complete command of any conversation.

"Be easy, dear, I have no intention of berating you. I want to know, for Christiana tells me nothing of her heart. You were the one to end things, were you not?"

"Yes," he said shortly. To his surprise, she laughed.

"What nonsense got in your head I can't begin to imagine, for I've never seen a man more besotted than you are with my daughter. If I had ever doubted it, the way you looked at her yesterday would have told me all I needed to know. Tell me everything."

So he did. His belief that he was unworthy of Christiana, compounded with his shame from the whipping and accusations, his dreams of love shattering, and his longing for his dead brother. Tristan told her of battles and his renewed sense of worth, and his profound distress at killing others. He confessed his jealousy toward Gerald MacClaren and told her about Lucy and their friendship. In the end, he talked of Christiana and the deep love he held for her. Through it all, she let him speak uninterrupted.

"I think I understand you, Tristan," Charlotte said when he had concluded. "To start, I will relieve you at once in saying there is nothing between Christiana and Gerald MacClaren. And there never will be. As if I would marry my daughter into that family."

Tristan gave a silent prayer of thanks for that assurance. No matter what became of him and Christiana, he couldn't imagine his precious girl in the arms of that oaf.

"Regarding to your feelings of unworthiness, you should have known that as a direct descendant of King Emery and Prince Edmond, there is no imbalance between your stations. What's more, you are a grandson of Lord Edward Lockhart, and you and your brothers are all deserving of the title of lord. You are as qualified to marry Christiana as any man. Perhaps even more than you realize."

"But my father—"

"Your father!" Her gaze strayed to the window, and she seemed to be speaking more to herself than to Tristan. "Thomas Thatcher, you will be the death of me, you idiot man."

She turned her attention back to Tristan. "Never mind your father, this truth will come out soon enough. Let me make this very clear, Tristan. If I could pick one man for my daughter, out of all those down in the Great Hall who think themselves so fine, it would be you."

The spark of hope that had been flickering since the war ended came to life at her words. "Why me?"

"Because you love her. Oh, you're not perfect, and you've made mistakes. Giving her up was ludicrous. That was your hurt and damaged pride speaking. Please understand, I don't blame you after what happened. Still, you were rash. You would have found much comfort in her love when you desperately needed it. But putting that aside, what I see in you is a man whose love has always led you to think of her needs, not your own, mistaken though your resulting actions may have been."

Charlotte lowered her gaze and twisted the small gold band that she always wore on her right hand. "The man I married, I did not love. Nor did he love me. Ours was not a happy marriage. I had hoped, in time, to make it a fulfilling partnership at least. For a short while we did. Then even that became impossible. If I had been loved the way you love Christiana, ah! How different life might have been. Christiana has a position that entices many men to marry her, but those are not the men I want for her. Listen to me, Tristan. What a mother wants most for her daughter is a man of noble character who loves her beyond all reason. And in this, my dear boy, you exceed them all."

Tristan's breath caught at her words. His dreams seemed to be within his grasp, his future opening before him. However, he had to ask, "How do you know how much I love her?"

"Women see these things, don't try to understand." At this, Charlotte laughed, waving her hand as if it were a silly question. "Consider the pride in your heart, Tristan. Don't allow it to stand in the way of your happiness—or hers. Think on that."

"I thought perhaps you didn't approve. The letter to Captain Stephens...he stopped sending me to Altair afterward."

"That letter was one of commendation for your actions as a courier, urging him to use your abilities where they were needed most. Although I suppose it did have that unintended consequence. But I never meant to divide you two."

Tristan stood and paced the room. How much time had he wasted with his own stubborn pride? He paused, anguished. "I don't know if she even loves me anymore. What if I've ruined our chances for good?"

"Then, my dear boy," Charlotte challenged. "You win her back."

The little spark in Tristan's heart burst into a bonfire. Seeing the fire kindled, Charlotte nodded with satisfaction. She rose and glided to the mantel. There she traced her fingers over a small, ornate coffer.

"Now, I have something for you. I've wanted to give you this for a long time." Charlotte opened the coffer and withdrew a letter. With a sigh, she passed it to the young man who stood before her.

Tristan saw his name on the letter, and the handwriting...He looked up, startled. There were tears in Charlotte's soft brown eyes.

"Michael gave this to me not long before you all traveled together. He said if anything was ever to happen to him, to give this to you."

"But he's been dead for over two years," protested Tristan.

"He left instructions to wait until your seventeenth birthday. I had no desire to entrust an item this precious to a courier, and this is the first time I've seen you since you came of age."

Tristan circled the room, trying to make sense of everything. His thoughts whirled around Christiana, the queen's steadfast approval of him, Michael...

With the thought of Michael, his focus sharpened. He tucked the letter away, determined to keep his mind clear. When he turned again to Charlotte, his spine was straight and his voice firm.

"Your Grace. Why were we sent to the southern border two years ago?"

# Chapter 42

# Another Farewell

"Let me get this straight. Lord General MacClaren asked us to go south, and the queen refused? And Dad took us there anyway?"

Tristan grunted, trying to think. He had marched to Ethan's room from the queen's chambers, relieved his brother had already returned from town.

"That doesn't make sense," said Ethan.

"I know. MacClaren sent a letter outlining the problem, and since he knew we wouldn't be going to the mountains, he asked for our help. He claimed that sometimes local problems are handled better by outsiders, men without bias. Charlotte told him to take care of his own people."

"And Dad went anyway?"

"I got the impression he and Charlotte argued over it. In any case, something convinced Dad to go, and she wasn't happy with his decision."

"Must have been serious for Dad to go against Charlotte," Ethan mused. "She didn't say anything else?"

"She said I needed to talk to Dad about it. To be honest, I'm not sure if she didn't know or did but wouldn't tell me."

Ethan stared at his brother. "What's going on, Tris?"

"I don't know. But I might know someone who does. I'm going to the tavern to see Lucy. I will force the truth out of her if I must. Will you come with me?"

"Give me a moment."

Tristan hesitated as he passed through the doorway. "And Ethan? Make sure you bring your sword."

"What about you?"

Tristan offered a grim smile. "I know where to get one."

They made their way to Barley's Tavern, and Tristan was deep in his thoughts when he bumped into a large man leaving the tavern at a hot pace.

"Watch it," he grumbled and then stopped dead in his tracks, looking back at the departing figure. He was double cloaked and hooded, unusual in broad daylight, even on a winter afternoon.

"What is it?" Ethan asked.

"You ever have the sense that something has happened to you before? Like it's happening again?"

"I suppose."

"I have this feeling. I don't know...running into him." Tristan struggled a moment longer before giving up. "It's probably not important. Let's keep going."

The tavern was a low-class sort of place. No matter what she did for a living, Tristan thought Lucy deserved better than this. They were disappointed in their desire to meet with her at once.

"Aye, Lucy's here, but she's with a customer, you know?" The barman gave them a lecherous smirk. "If you're willing to pay me, I'll hold your place in line. One at a time, mind. She refuses to take on two."

Tristan flushed. Ethan rasped out, "We are not *customers*. This is personal business we have to discuss with her."

"Well, if you put it that way. Aye, I'll tell her you're here when she's done. It never takes long."

"That was disgusting," Ethan muttered after purchasing two ales and handing one to his brother who stood seething. "Calm down, Tris."

Tristan scowled upward as if he could see through the ceiling. "Why does she keep this up? I would give her a home. Keep her safe. I would give her everything she needs, anything at all. She doesn't have to keep doing what she does."

Ethan stared at his brother. "Maybe you should sit."

Tristan sat with an angry thump. Ethan was studying him as though he was some strange new plant specimen. He gave a light cough. "Are you saying what I think you're saying?"

"I'm saying," Tristan growled at Ethan, "I would take care of her. Not as a mistress, get your mind out of the gutter. As a...a..."

"A pet?"

Tristan snorted. "Oh, stuff it, you oaf."

Ethan laughed, and even Tristan started to chuckle. A high-pitched scream cut their laughter short.

"What the..." Ethan said, meeting Tristan's shocked eyes. Everyone in the room fell silent before another scream echoed throughout the building. The brothers jumped to their feet and ran up the stairs. Half-dressed girls and their customers spilled out of rooms, and a crowd gathered at a doorway. Tristan eased himself through with Ethan close behind.

"Father in heaven," Ethan prayed as he crossed himself. A groan wrenched itself free from deep inside Tristan. Blood was everywhere. Scattered on the walls, across the bed, dripping onto the floor. Tristan cautiously stepped toward the girl who was sprawled over the bed facing the opposite wall. The long, dark hair trailing down the bare back confirmed his worst fears. Tristan's hand raised to touch the body, but he stopped himself. Instead, he walked around the bed and beheld her battered face, frozen eyes wide open in terror. Tristan whirled away from the sight. Throat tight, he pleaded, "Ethan, please."

Ethan closed her eyes. Tristan dragged a blanket off the floor and covered the body. Kneeling beside the bed, he prayed in a hoarse whisper before slumping. A hand gripped his shoulder. Ethan muttered, "We need to talk."

"Who'll take care of her?"

"It's not like that, Tristan. They'll bury her with the paupers. Or burn the body."

"No...no, they can't." Distraught, his gaze swept over the women who were lurking in the hallway. "Who's in charge here?"

A middle-aged woman stepped forward, careworn but with kind eyes. "I'm the mistress."

Tristan rummaged in his pocket and picked out some gold. "Will this be enough for something proper?"

"Who are you?" demanded the woman. "You've never been serviced here before."

Tristan winced. "No, I'm a friend. Please? Is this enough?"

"More than, thank you kindly."

Tristan squared his shoulders and left. He was sick in the hall. Someone handed him a glass of whiskey, which he gulped. The alcohol hit his vitals, and almost made him sick again, but he managed to hold it down. Voices surrounded him, and Ethan's hand rubbed his back.

Tristan braced himself against the wall. "This is what happened to Nancy, remember? She talked and then someone killed her. The MacClarens are behind this. I don't know how, but they are."

"Gerald MacClaren was her last client."

"What! How do you know?"

"I spoke with the head woman while you were sitting with—the body. They all saw him leave the room. She took longer than usual to dress, so they sent one of the other girls to check on her. The woman said this wasn't the first time he's been violent with the girls."

"Why?" Tristan moaned. "Why would she allow him to meet Lucy? Any of them?"

"Money, Tristan. It's always going to be about money for these women. It's how they survive."

Tristan's eyes blazed. "He killed her, didn't he? She knew something about our trip south. About Michael's death. She wanted to tell me, but she was terrified. And he killed her. I swear, I'll do whatever I must to—"

"Tristan, listen to me. We have no proof. Even if he was here, no one saw him do this."

Tristan ran a hand through his shaggy hair. "What do we do?"

"We've got to talk to Dad."

"You're right."

They were both silent until they were outside walking the cobblestone street, and Tristan stopped in his tracks.

"Nancy."

"What about her?"

They were at the corner where Tristan had bumped into the hooded stranger, and it niggled at a memory. Right before finding Nancy, what had happened? "There was a man there, the night I found Nancy. A big man, like—" Tristan looked at Ethan in shock.

"MacClaren?"

"I don't know, I didn't see his face."

"We have to think this through, Tristan. What else do we know?"

"Somehow all these deaths are connected. Lucy, Nancy, Michael..."

"Don't forget Mallory."

"That's right! And Lord MacClaren lying to Dad about not knowing anything about my arrest."

Ethan grunted and began walking briskly. When he spoke again, he kept his voice low. "We need to be careful."

"I know. When we get to the castle, you go find Dad. I need to see Chris. She was with MacClaren last night at dinner. I want to make sure she's safe."

"All right, but promise me you will stay out of trouble until I get Dad."

"I'll do my best."

"That's not the answer I wanted," Ethan muttered as he chased after Tristan to the castle.

## Chapter 43

# The Bitter End

When Tristan entered the Great Hall, he was relieved to see the crowds were minimal compared to the night before. He suspected some were dressing for dinner or resting before the evening's festivities. Knots of people were conversing here and there, but there was space to walk unhindered. He caught James sneaking away with Cate trailing behind him. In spite of his tangled thoughts, Tristan wondered if they were heading for that alcove.

Tristan searched until he found her. To his dismay, she stood at the far end of the room talking to Gerald MacClaren himself. Even though Charlotte had reassured Tristan that MacClaren could never be a rival for her hand, Tristan burned to see her smiling at the man. Tristan steeled himself against silly, petty jealousies. In this crowd she was safe from harm, and he could watch over her from afar until Ethan brought their father.

Tristan had resolved to find a place where he could sit in the shadows when someone called his name. He spun to see Christiana standing before him. She hesitated, as if unsure of what to say.

"Where did you go to last night, Tristan? I was looking for you."

His heart leaped that she had noticed his absence, but he attempted to adopt his father's stoicism. "I had some things to do. I'm sorry we couldn't speak longer."

Christiana stunned Tristan by placing her hand on his cheek. "Did you break this?" Her thumb stroked the bridge of his nose.

Tristan's mouth went dry at her touch, and he gulped. "No. I mean, yes. In the last battle. Jericho threw his head against mine. He won."

"That sounds quite...exciting." She giggled.

Tristan choked out a laugh before MacClaren appeared. Christiana dropped her hand, her cheeks turning a rosy pink. "Gerald, may I introduce—"

"Yes, yes. I know Thatcher."

Tristan nodded curtly and would have left, but Christiana laid a hand on his arm and held him still, stating firmly to MacClaren, "Tristan is a captain, and military etiquette demands he should be addressed as such. He was the hero of Hill Run, did you not hear?"

MacClaren sneered as if he would rather die before treating Tristan as an officer. But Tristan's eyes met hers at these words, and some unspoken emotion pulsed between them that made his heart pound. He forgot everything except his desire to be alone with Christiana, to clear the air between them, to hold her, to declare his undying love... Impulsively, he choked out, "Christiana, might I have a word, please?"

She stepped toward him, but MacClaren caught hold of her hand. "You can go with Thatcher when we're done talking."

Tristan darted a sharp look at MacClaren. After what he had seen earlier, he did not want MacClaren to be agitated while Christiana remained so close. He did his best to plaster on an amiable smile. "Very well, I can wait until you are done."

"Wait all you want, she's with me this evening."

"Gerald, honestly," Christiana exclaimed, jerking from his grasp. "Don't be such an ass."

She came to Tristan, and all attempts at disguising his heart were forgotten. He took her hand, the pent-up love shining from his eyes for all to see.

MacClaren growled, watching the two. Before they had walked many paces, a dagger drove itself deep into a wooden pillar inches from Tristan's head. Cries of surprise came from a few people nearby.

Tristan pivoted, bringing Christiana behind him. He glanced at the dagger. Slowly, he took a firm grasp and yanked it out of the pillar. Tristan's eyes flashed up and settled on MacClaren with an icy stare. He tossed the dagger upward and caught it by the hilt. It seemed hours passed before he spoke, his voice preternaturally calm.

"This is a beautiful weapon. Too fine to be from a metalsmith in Aquila. Looks to be of Woodraven make. Where did you find such a piece?"

MacClaren's glare turned wary. "Who knows, picked it up somewhere."

"I'm curious. Is this the same dagger you used to kill Lucy Foster?"

"You're the one with a reputation for killing whores, Thatcher."

"I never said she was a whore. Funny you knew that."

Silence descended upon the Great Hall. Tristan passed the dagger to Christiana, the fingers of his free hand twitching at the hilt of his sword. Christiana caught the movement and sucked in her breath at the sight of the weapon hanging from his belt.

MacClaren gawked at Tristan before laughing again, but now an uneasy edge clung to the sound. "Ah, Lucy of the long, black tresses.

*Everyone* in the army knew her. Are you jealous, Thatcher? I know she was a friend of yours, except I heard you couldn't rise to the occasion."

Whispers went through the onlookers. To Tristan's dismay, Christiana came out from behind him and marched to MacClaren. "This is ridiculous. It can't be true. I've known Gerald for years, he could never do such a thing."

"Witnesses say otherwise, Christiana. They claimed he was the last man in the room where she was found dead." Tristan spoke softly, while his heart screamed for her to get away from the monster.

MacClaren recovered his bearings, and his eyes grew calculating. "I knew she was special to you, but I guess you didn't satisfy her or she wouldn't have come running to me. Or did you have dreams of marrying her, Thatcher? A bastard's son and a wench sounds about right. Yes, I sliced her a bit, but she was breathing when I left her. She had a mouth on her and needed a lesson."

"You didn't!" Christiana gasped.

"Don't make such a fuss, she was just a whore—"

Christiana struck his face hard with her fist. A few women in the crowd shrieked. MacClaren wiped a dribble of blood from his nose before savagely raising his hand to strike back.

"No!" Tristan lunged forward, unsheathing his sword in one fluid motion, his fingers tingling. The blade of the legendary Lockhart sword caught the light. There were murmurs from those who recognized it. Sneering, MacClaren drew his own weapon.

"Tristan, don't..." whispered Christiana.

In a flash, time slipped sideways for Tristan. The years of swordplay, sparring with his brothers, fighting the war, Michael's death...they all rolled into this one moment.

With a gentle push, Tristan moved Christiana behind and away from him.

The first stroke came before Tristan had established his footing. He slipped as he swerved and struggled to keep his feet under him while MacClaren threw his full weight into the sword. His power combined with his skill made it difficult to parry. Tristan found his balance and danced around MacClaren, deflecting blows and landing a few of his own.

Tristan dove under a sideswipe. MacClaren carried almost a hundred pounds more than his opponent, but Tristan was faster. He dodged and ducked, spun and struck, fighting with a style he had developed over the years, combining brutality and grace. MacClaren's sword sliced deep into his upper left arm. Tristan staggered back with a cry, gasping for air. He bent forward, his sword hanging limply from his hand.

MacClaren readied his sword for a killing blow, but Tristan lunged at his opponent. Eyes widening at the feint, MacClaren narrowly avoided being impaled by a last-second dodge.

Their blades locked until Tristan jerked his sword free. MacClaren stumbled back a step, and before he could regain his footing, Tristan barreled into his stomach. Together, they fell to the ground. Both their swords skidded across the floor. Tristan grappled for one, fingers flicking the pommel but coming up empty. Grabbing his feet, MacClaren dragged him a short distance. Tristan bucked and elbowed MacClaren's face, throwing him aside.

"Tristan!" cried Christiana.

He crouched on one knee as she tossed the dagger to him. Catching it, he adjusted his grip and threw it. MacClaren teetered as the dagger embedded itself into the upper half of his right arm. Tristan crawled, trying again to reach his sword. MacClaren yanked the dagger out. With a feral roar, he charged Tristan, dagger raised. Tristan fingered the hilt of his sword and swung it around, blade pointed up as MacClaren leaped.

MacClaren skidded to a stop at the point of Tristan's sword, the tip aimed at his gut. A small patch of blood appeared where the sword had broken the skin. They both froze, Tristan still on his back. He was breathing hard, and pain was shooting through his body. MacClaren, too, showed evidence of injury in multiple spots, although Tristan didn't remember landing a strike other than the thrown dagger.

A commanding voice boomed over the heads of the people. Soldiers entered the hall alongside Ethan and their father. Thomas had his own sword unsheathed. At his quiet word, soldiers took hold of MacClaren.

Tristan somehow got to his feet and walked on shaking legs toward Christiana. His sword rattled when his nerveless fingers let it fall onto the flagstones. Reaching Christiana, he cupped her face in trembling hands, speaking hoarsely. "Are you all right?"

"I'm fine."

They gave each other a long look before he kissed her forehead and wrapped his arms around her, murmuring, "Thank you, Father. Thank you." She was safe, and he knew MacClaren would never touch her again. No matter what came next, for this one glorious hour, she was his once more. He tipped his forehead to hers and whispered her name.

Loud voices intruded, and he glanced up in time to see Lord General MacClaren striding up to his son with a riding crop in hand. The younger man shrank at his father's approach. "Father, I—"

"You idiot!" Lord MacClaren growled. "Be silent or I'll kill you myself."

"But you told me. All of this, it was you—"

His father ripped the crop across his son's face three times. He slumped unconscious, with deep furrows of blood revealing the strikes.

Lord MacClaren whirled around to glare at Tristan and Christiana. He strode toward them, and Tristan shifted to stand in front of her.

"What is the meaning of this?" Queen Charlotte swept through the crowd. Lord MacClaren dragged his eyes away from Tristan and made the barest gesture of respect to Charlotte.

"I'm afraid my son has insulted Your Grace with his actions. I have rectified his behavior, and he will not return to this castle again while I am living. You have my word on this." Without permission to depart, Lord MacClaren left the Great Hall, gesturing to the soldiers to follow with the limp body of his son.

In the disorder that followed, only Tristan saw Thomas retrieve the dagger, wet with blood. He stood there, staring at it in shock, before his eyes rose and met Tristan's. After a long moment, his father's face hardened.

Tristan returned his gaze to Christiana. "Let me see your hand."

His breath caught, for it was already bruising over. He moaned at the sight. "You should have Ethan look at this," he said and brought her hand to his lips for the lightest kiss.

"You're bleeding." Christiana was trembling and tearful, seeing the blood dripping from his sleeve to the floor.

"I know, and it hurts like the devil." He grimaced.

Then they were surrounded by people, separated by questions and general chaos. James cuffed him affectionately, exclaiming, "Fighting Gerald MacClaren without me here to see it! What were you thinking?"

Tristan locked eyes with Ethan, and they fell into each other's arms.

"You could have been killed," Ethan whispered, hugging Tristan. "I told you to stay out of trouble!"

"Trouble found me," mumbled Tristan.

"Let's get you somewhere I can treat that cut."

Ethan gently tugged at his brother. Tristan resisted, looking for Christiana. Charlotte held her, and when his gaze locked onto the queen's, she gave him an almost imperceptible nod. Tristan relaxed. Knowing Christiana was safe, he allowed Ethan to lead him away.

# Chapter 44

# The Queen's Council

Tristan started limping as Ethan helped him to the common room. Ethan peered down, looking for another injury. "Did he cut your leg too?"

"No. A sprain," Tristan said through clenched teeth. "I think."

"Your arm hurting a lot?" Ethan asked.

Tristan grunted an answer. He sank onto the sofa with a groan and hissed in pain when Ethan propped his left arm up. Talking under his breath, Ethan poked around until Tristan yelped and growled, "Stop muttering about it, makes it seem worse. Talk in a normal voice or be quiet."

"Sorry, it's a bad habit, I know. I just noticed how it's all the way to the bone. This is going to hurt, Tris." Ethan nodded his thanks to the servant girl who arrived, bringing his bag of medical supplies.

Tristan gritted his teeth, a fresh sheen of sweat popping out on his face as Ethan cleaned the wound. A door creaked open. Ethan's eyes rose and dropped back to his work with a smile teasing his lips. A soft step, a whisper of rustling fabric, and then Christiana was sitting beside Tristan.

He beheld her with some confusion. "Chris, I'm a mess, you don't—" He interrupted himself with a small gasp of pain.

Christiana placed her hand on Tristan's cheek and easing his head onto her shoulder with a whispered, "Shush." She continued to stroke his temple while Ethan worked. Tristan nuzzled deeper into the crook of her neck and closed his eyes. Despite the intense pain, it was one of the most blissful moments of his life.

When finished, Ethan gathered his things. "I'll be back with a liniment for that sprain. For your hand too, Chris, it's bruising badly." Tristan raised his head, but Ethan could see he wasn't paying attention.

"Thank you, Ethan," said Christiana.

"It might take me some time to find what I need," Ethan said with a hint of a chuckle. "You two can rest here while I'm gone."

The door opened and shut, with the echoes of voices from outside flaring loudly before fading away once more. Tristan groaned as he shifted his position, uneasy as Christiana studied him. The silence grew heavier, and Tristan thought he might suffocate if he didn't break it.

"Chris, I—"

"No, Tristan." She placed her fingertips against his mouth. "I don't want to hear what you have to say yet. There will be time for questions later. And yes, I will expect some explanations as well. I think I deserve that, wouldn't you agree?"

"I just need—"

"Be quiet, Tristan. Be still." Her voice was kind but firm. "You talk far too much sometimes. I'm going to ask you one question, and I want you to nod or shake your head. Don't speak. Can you do that?"

Tristan nodded, wanting nothing more than to take her into his arms and kiss her.

Christiana removed her hand and contemplated him. Eyes sparkling with unshed tears, she asked with a quavering voice, "Tristan Thatcher, you have been and will always be the love of my life. But do you love me still?"

With a sound that was almost a sob, Tristan nodded once more, and they were in each other's arms. Tristan's heart bounded with joy as he kissed her. Her touch healed his tender wounds lingering within, her kisses sang of forgiveness for his many mistakes. She was a cool spring for his parched heart, and he drank her in. Between murmurs and whispers of their love for each other, they kissed again and again, neither wanting to stop.

They both failed to hear the soft knock on the door or the creak as it swung open. They were in a world entirely of their own making until his father's gentle cough broke through, a sound Tristan would have recognized in a hurricane. He froze, and Christiana shook with suppressed giggles as she buried her face against his chest. Tristan craned his head around to see Thomas peering out a window into the dark night as if there were no one else in the room.

Sheepish but regretting nothing, Tristan held Christiana close as he shifted his position. He adopted what he hoped was a tone of casual nonchalance. "Yes, Dad?"

"Ah! There you are, Tristan. Her Grace the Queen would like to meet with you and a few others about the events of today. If you are quite fit enough."

"Yes, sir, I'll be there."

"No need, the meeting will be here. You may stay...comfortable a moment longer." With a wink, Thomas left.

Tristan swore under his breath. "I wasn't ready to stop."

Christiana shook her head with a look that made his heart throb. "Don't think you're off the hook. There are still debts to be paid."

Acknowledging the truth of her words, Tristan leaned back against the sofa with a contented sigh, hugging her close with his good arm as she rested her head on his shoulder. He couldn't help dropping a kiss or two on her hair; otherwise, they remained quiet while they waited for the others to arrive.

A few people filed into the room, including all the Thatchers, Lord General Andrew Kavanaugh, and Queen Charlotte. Upon their entry, Tristan removed himself far into the shadows of the room, where he could watch Christiana unobserved, his dark blue eyes glowing with joy. Ethan joined Christiana on the sofa, and James sat enthroned on the chair opposite.

Facing the fire were Andrew and Charlotte, and Thomas stood near the hearth. Guards had been placed at the doors outside the room so the busy castle life would not spill over into this select gathering. Charlotte scanned the group, her sharp eyes catching everyone's attention before she spoke.

"I called this meeting in order to delve into the events of this afternoon. But before we begin, I know of at least one person here, likely more, who would enjoy seeing me wipe the MacClaren name from our map forever. I want to offer a word of caution. The MacClarens are an old family and a powerful one. We must be wise in this hour."

A long pause followed this pronouncement. Assured that her true meaning had been understood, Charlotte moved on.

"I would like to start with the events of today. Ethan has told me what occurred when he and Tristan discovered the body of the young prostitute at a tavern. Gerald MacClaren is known to be her last customer and was heard by many in the Great Hall admitting to cutting her. That said, there were no witnesses to his killing her. While I have no doubt of his involvement in her death, I'm afraid his position as a nobleman's son will outweigh the death of a prostitute. What I'm not clear on is why he killed her?"

James growled. "He's long had a reputation in the army as a brute to the girls. More than one of his regulars has shown bruises and black eyes after a night with him."

"Yes, but to murder in such a cold-blooded fashion? There must be a reason."

Ethan glanced at Tristan. His brother still lurked in the dark corner. It didn't matter, for the queen sought him out. "Tristan, you defended the girl's honor. Why were you at the tavern at all? For I know you too well to believe you were there for any business."

A dark chuckle escaped James. Everyone else remained silent as Tristan emerged from the shadows. The flush of his earlier happiness had faded. The long day and injury were making themselves felt, leaving him pale and wan.

His gaze flitted to Christiana before speaking, pacing while he talked.

"Lucy Foster was a camp follower Ethan and I knew from the war. She ducked into our tent one day to escape a rough client, and we became friends. I had told her I had a brother named Michael, and she assumed he had the same surname as myself. The last time we talked before our return to Altair, she learned he was in fact Lord Michael Lockhart, which frightened her. Then we ran into Lucy today. She urged me to look into who sent us to the southern border, which you may remember I asked you, Your Grace." Tristan wished with his whole heart he had not let her run off the way she did. He moved toward Christiana, desperate to be alone with her.

"I should hope so, since it was this morning," Charlotte huffed. "You think she had some fresh news concerning Michael?"

"It would seem. She indicated there might be a connection between those who requested our presence and the ambush that ended with Michael's death. I never got more out of her."

Tristan moved to retreat again, exhausted. But Christiana grabbed his hand and pulled him down to sit next to her.

"No more hiding," she said, as her eyes searched his with questions he couldn't answer yet.

"Wait, you knew Lord MacClaren was the one who requested help?" Andrew asked Thomas. "Why? How did he drag you into this?"

Thomas said, "Lord MacClaren knows things about my past. Circumstances that—"

"Ah," Andrew interrupted. Tristan looked curiously at his father, but Thomas refused to meet his gaze. Charlotte pushed back into the conversation.

"We agree the girl had information and Gerald MacClaren killed her for it. What else do we know?"

Ethan spoke up. "There was that business regarding Captain Mallory and the camp follower Nancy."

"I remember," said Andrew. "She was found dead, alongside Captain Mallory, after she helped clear Tristan."

"Are you implying Lord MacClaren killed one of his own men? That doesn't make sense," said Tristan.

"Your unjust punishment made a big stink," James mused. "Maybe Lord MacClaren wasn't too happy with the way Mallory handled things."

"It's not only that, James. Lord MacClaren lied," said Ethan. "He claimed Mallory acted on his own, but he didn't. MacClaren was in on it the whole time."

"And it was Lord MacClaren's men who continued to keep things stirred up. Tristan might have hanged if it were not for Andrew," Thomas reminded them.

"Your Grace—" Tristan hesitated, not sure how to ask his question. "On my last journey here as courier, there was an incident..."

Charlotte gave him a peculiar smile. "You may speak freely, Tristan."

"What Captain Wylie said that day, about Lord MacClaren—" Tristan saw his father and Andrew both start with surprise, but they remained quiet at a wave from Charlotte's hand as she spoke.

"Here is something you did not know, Tristan. Wylie was *my* man. He grew up in Lord MacClaren's territory, which enabled him to gain a position under him in the army, but he has always been loyal to Aquila. Everything that happened that day was planned. You being herded into his camp, the information he gave you. He chose you, knowing that as Thomas Thatcher's son, you would be loyal to the crown. Wylie orchestrated it to get information back to me as discreetly as possible. What you considered to be the rant of a madman was in fact information for me."

"He was a spy?" asked Tristan.

"Yes, and a good one."

"Why was he leading what anyone would call a traitorous faction?" Tristan huffed in frustration.

"That I'm not sure. I suspect MacClaren had become of aware of what he was doing, and Wylie was trying to get his men out of MacClaren's sight. But I never saw Wylie again to ask."

Thomas interrupted at last, agitation spilling out for everyone to see.

"You met Marcus Wylie? Why did you never tell me, Tristan?"

"I ordered him not to, Thomas," assured Charlotte.

Thomas ignored Charlotte's comment and ran a hand through his hair, looking unusually flustered. "Tristan, you should have told me."

"The Queen's Command," Tristan said, shamefaced. "Dad, I didn't want..."

Thomas gave the queen such a sharp look, Tristan could have sworn Charlotte blushed. But when he spoke, his voice was calm, if strained. "It's all right, son. You did as I taught." Thomas fell silent again before asking, "Did Marcus have a message for me? Anything at all?"

Tristan stared at his father in confusion. "Not that I recall." Thomas grunted and resumed his usual stoic expression.

"Marcus admired you very much, Tristan," murmured Charlotte. "He thought the coded letter was a brilliant move."

"Wylie knew it was a fake?"

"Not at first, but he figured it out quickly. The whole exchange amused him, I must say." The queen sighed. "He was a valuable man to me."

"And he died for it," Tristan said.

"Yes, he did. Lord MacClaren's flunkies captured him and moved on his execution before I could intervene."

"They seem to have a habit of doing that," muttered James.

Tristan bent forward with his elbows on his knees and held his head in his hands. Weariness consumed him. Scrubbing his face, he said, "There's something else. The day Michael was killed, I lost a dagger.

Threw it at the archer who shot him. I searched later but couldn't find it. Today, that dagger is the one Gerald MacClaren threw at me."

The queen looked at him askance, doubt clear in her eyes. "Are you sure? Daggers are common weapons."

"With respect, Your Grace, that particular dagger was not. It was a gift from Dad. Woodraven metalsmiths mark their pieces, and they never make the same weapon twice. I would have recognized this dagger blindfolded."

"You realize Lord MacClaren will claim his son found it somewhere." Charlotte scoffed. "I can hear him now saying Gerald picked it off a dead soldier on the battlefield. I believe we know the truth of the matter, but it must end there."

"What do the MacClarens have on us, Dad?" Ethan asked.

"Lord MacClaren has long desired my absence from court," muttered Thomas.

"You've said that before, but why? Where does the bad blood come from?"

"The queen and I have been close friends since I came to Aquila. Lord MacClaren has always been jealous of my perceived influence, even more after my marriage into the Lockhart family. To be clear, he wasn't the only nobleman who viewed me with suspicion and jealousy." Thomas looked at his sons. "Anna's health drove us south before the strain became too much and, well, you know how that ended. My work on the border kept me away from court for months at a time, allowing my enemies to rest easy, thinking my relationship with Her Grace had weakened."

"If what you say is true," interjected Ethan, "what has reignited their malice so pointedly in the last year or two?"

Thomas shrugged.

"There had long been a rumor of an arranged marriage between a Lockhart descendant and Christiana. Many assumed it would be James, being the eldest. However, that could never be. Lord MacClaren knew this, yet he chose to remain quiet but watchful. When a Light Seeker prophesied in this very room of an alliance between the Houses Lockhart, Thatcher, and Reynard, it may have inflamed him and made him desperate."

"I don't understand," said Ethan.

"Many of the old families in Aquila take the word of a Light Seeker quite seriously. Brother Daniel didn't suggest *any* alliance. He pointed to Tristan in a specific way. Not you, not James. Not even Michael, who would have been the most obvious choice with his bloodline."

"But why would that have led him to kill Michael?" Tristan asked.

Thomas crouched and put his hand on Tristan's knee, his voice gentle.

"Perhaps Michael was not their target."

For a moment, Tristan didn't comprehend his father's words. As their significance sank in, Tristan moaned. "No..."

Thomas continued. "I believe he wanted you out of the way. Especially by the time the war started, it was well known among the upper circles you were courting Christiana with the queen's full approval."

"It was supposed to be me," whispered Tristan. Christiana grasped his hand, squeezing it hard. Thomas shook his head sadly.

"Why else were you accused of what happened to that prostitute? No one who knew you would have dreamt of such a thing. Why were you rushed to a punishment that should have taken a formal military trial? And how were good soldiers manipulated into a mob demanding you be hung? Never has the mistreatment of a whore in an army camp been reviled in such a way. Lord MacClaren was pulling the strings all along, I suspect."

Andrew burst forth as angry as Tristan had ever heard him. "I fail to understand why we've put up with that family all this time! The MacClaren name is mud and has been for years. What tenuous hold does he have over you, Your Grace?"

"You think I tolerate them out of affection?" Charlotte asked with an edge in her voice. "I've always known their potential danger, but I would rather have them near me than turned loose and not know what is happening. For example, I learned Lord MacClaren is building a secret army for some nefarious purpose. Knowledge is power, and keeping the MacClarens within my reach is important."

"Where does this end?" asked James, fire alight in his eyes.

"It doesn't," Tristan said bitterly.

"What would you have me do?" demanded Charlotte. "Initiate a war with Lord MacClaren? Aquila has not engaged in a civil war since the death of King Emery, and I refuse to be the ruler to start one unless I have no other choice. We know Gerald's sins, and he is under his father's thumb. I think Lord MacClaren will do far worse to him than I ever could. And as for Lord MacClaren himself...No. We will wait and watch him carefully. But, Andrew, I want him out of the army."

"Done."

"Make it discreet. I don't want him to be in public disgrace. In fact, honor him for his many years of dedicated service. The last thing we need is to arouse suspicion and sympathy." Charlotte stood. "Well, this evening has given me much to consider."

Everyone rose to depart, but Tristan held up his hand. There were still many secrets in this room. Some he believed had been kept far too long, and he was more than ready for the weight to be lifted. He stood before his father and looked him in the eye.

"I held back my encounter with Wylie from you, and I'm sorry about that. It wasn't my choice. But for years you've been keeping things from me as well. No more secrets. It's time I know."

Thomas regarded him with some confusion. "What is it, son?"

"Where do you come from, Dad? I don't mean Woodraven, we all know that. Who is your family? And what of your past has MacClaren held over you? What's so awful you can't even tell your own sons?"

"Ah," whispered Thomas.

The queen gave him a sad, sympathetic smile. "Everyone present either knows already or should know, Thomas. Should have known long before today."

Tristan beheld an emotion in his father's eyes he had never seen before—something desperate and pleading. Thomas spun away and remained still. James stood and placed a hand on his back as they whispered together. Distraught, Thomas turned to face his two younger sons.

"I am a bastard, as you know," said Thomas. Everyone could see he was choosing his words with great care. "My father has not many heirs. He was forced to recognize me as his son years ago. By acknowledging me, and therefore my own sons, he guaranteed several options beyond his legitimate children that his line would continue."

Tristan steeled himself, frightened for some inexplicable reason.

"My father..." Thomas looked at Ethan, then Tristan, and drew a deep breath. "My father is Holden, of the House of Mohan, King of Woodraven."

# Chapter 45

# The Letter

Tristan stood there, unbelieving. Without knowing why, he lashed out at James. "You knew, didn't you? Didn't you!"

James nodded miserably.

"For how long?"

"Dad told me after Michael died, right before the war."

"That's more than two years ago! Of all the traitorous—" James tried to put his hand on his brother's shoulder, hurt astonishment on his face, but Tristan jerked aside, putting distance between them. "Get away from me!"

James sank into his chair, burying his head in his hands. "Oh, Tristan..."

"Don't be angry with your brother, he has burdens enough already," Thomas ordered. "He was obeying my orders not to tell you. The blame is entirely on me."

"Ethan?" Tristan swung around, almost pleading.

"I'm only just hearing this," Ethan said with quiet anger.

"Michael knew, of course. But why James and not the rest of us?"

"I wanted you boys to make your own futures, not hindered by my past."

"Dammit!" Tristan's voice rose to a yell, and he slammed his fist on the mantel before pacing across the room. "We are your *sons*! And you kept this from us?"

"Tristan," commanded Charlotte, breaking through his anger. He turned to see the queen standing. "Let your father speak, dear."

Once again, Christiana tugged at his hand. This time when he sat, she hooked her arm through his as though to hold him in place. This both annoyed and exhilarated him, but it succeeded in calming him down.

Thomas drew a chair closer to face Ethan and Tristan. "My boys, my precious sons, pride of my heart, hear me out. It was probably a mistake, I'll admit that. I grew up knowing him, he supported my mother and me. Even still, Holden didn't formally acknowledge me until your mother was carrying James."

"Mother knew?" Ethan asked.

"She did. And I carried a double shame of illegitimacy and knowing my blood flows with the blood of Mohan. For this goes beyond me. You, all three of you, are part of the royal House of Mohan, grandsons of King Holden. You are titled princes of Woodraven. King Holden has upheld that decree, for his own selfish reasons. He wants to ensure his bloodline will remain on the throne. I kept it secret all these years, even if there are some in Aquila who know it."

"Like Lord MacClaren?"

"Yes. You know how Woodraven is viewed by those who live in Aquila. Your mother and I raised you to be men of Aquila, no matter what might come later. Lord MacClaren discovered everything about my past, and he relished holding that knowledge over me. Understand, I had other reasons for not wanting this known. Queen Charlotte has long been my friend, supporting me for years. I did not want her to be abused for her trust in the illegitimate son of the Woodraven king.”

“I've told you many times, I do not need your protection!” Charlotte exclaimed, coming close to Thomas.

“You are my chosen sovereign. As a man of honor, I know no other way.” He gave Charlotte a look Tristan did not understand.

Christiana waved her hand in a confused manner. “What does this mean when King Holden passes?”

“Nothing for me. He and I agreed on that. And besides, their laws of inheritance are complex, far more than Aquila. Here the kingdom passes in a fairly orderly succession, but in Woodraven there are multiple scenarios that could play out. My sons are acknowledged descendants, and the priority goes to the eldest. With James as the first among the three of you, he had to know even if you two did not. I didn't want that burden on you so early in your lives. I hoped that by waiting, I would allow you to be free to make your own choices, not based on where you came from or your bloodline.”

“Except for James,” Ethan said, anger lacing his words.

“It may never come to that. And if it does, your brother has a choice and will always have one. That's a decision he'll have to make for himself. His is a different burden.”

“That's why you said he could never be Lord of Lockhart Manor?” asked Tristan. “If he holds a title in Aquila, he can never be...what, king of Woodraven?”

“Close enough. He would retain his status as a lesser prince, but the line to kingship would be cut off. Which is also why he could never marry into the House of Reynard. There is no clear path for James. Many things can happen to alter his destiny—deaths, alliances, betrayals.”

"Time will tell if the waves break for him," Tristan muttered, recalling Brother Daniel's words. He looked at his oldest brother, who had not moved since his own explosive rejection. He thought of what his father had said about the burden James carried and knew it must have been so much worse to carry it alone. And was this the reason he hesitated moving forward with his Cate? Shame filled Tristan to his very core. James had always been the very best of brothers, but Tristan had unleashed nothing but anger upon him.

"What I don't understand—forgive me, Dad, but I can't help thinking if this had been known, how different things might have been." Ethan sat stiff, clenching his fists, his normally soft voice raised. "What Tristan went through? Would Lord MacClaren have dared to raise the whip if the world had known of our connection? And Michael! Would Michael be dead if this hadn't been a secret to be held over your head?"

Thomas's eyes fell, and he shuddered. "I know."

"We *don't* know," Andrew said. "And your father's reasons for keeping it quiet were valid. Even before she was queen, Charlotte looked to Thomas first among her advisors and friends, and if his connections had been widely known at that time, the potential ramifications for the kingdom could have been devastating. You have no idea what the court was like in the early days of the queen's rule—the first woman to wear the crown in over two hundred years! This is about more than your family."

"Not to us," Ethan choked out, with tears in his eyes.

"Oh, my dear boys." Charlotte stepped forward to place her hand on Thomas's shoulder. In turn, he reached up and put his own hand over hers. She continued, "Michael knew the situation and accepted the risks. We all make mistakes, my dears. Your father has been required to make many difficult decisions in how to raise you over the years, and without your mother by his side. I can assure you, he has done the best he could. His love for you knows no bounds."

In the silence that followed, Tristan remembered James holding on to him after he woke from that bleak darkness on the battlefield. No matter what happened later, he knew without a doubt James had the noble heart of a king. There were tears in his throat when he called, "James?"

His brother raised his head, his eyes steely and cold. To have James regard him in such a way was a dagger to Tristan's heart.

"I'm sorry, James...I..." Tristan fumbled for words.

James's icy gaze melted at once. He stumbled over and enclosed both his brothers in an embrace, his arms shaking. "You don't know how hard it was to keep it from you, Tris. I wanted to tell you so many times. You too, Ethan. I hated it, every moment. I'm sorry."

Everyone had filed out of the room except for Christiana and Tristan. They remained seated on the sofa, grasping hands but not looking at each other.

Tristan grappled with the tumult of emotions raging within his heart and stared at the wall across the room. "Please tell me you didn't know."

"No. I did think there was something. A bigger story. But I didn't expect that."

"How's your hand?" he asked after a long pause.

"It's sore, but just a strain."

"Quite a punch for such a little thing. Remind me never to get you that mad at me."

"Who says you haven't?" she retorted. He chuckled at her words until she asked, "Who was she, Tristan?"

"Lucy?" Tristan sighed. "She was a friend. As much as you can be with a camp follower, I suppose."

"Was she...pretty?"

"She was beautiful. And also very kind."

"Did you love her?" Christiana asked tremulously.

"I cared for her a great deal. She...tempted me, at one point. I was lonely and found it hard to resist her. After the flogging...for a while there I thought I might be going mad, and she helped me find myself again." At last, he faced her. "But I've only ever loved one woman."

Her eyes filled with tears. Tristan repeated, "I have only loved you."

The tears spilled down her cheeks. "The day you ended things between us—you broke my heart! I loved you so much, and I love you still, but Tristan..." Christiana began weeping in earnest.

"Oh, Chris." Tristan pulled her to him. "I was a fool, Chris, a damn fool. After the flogging, I was so broken. I didn't even know who I was anymore. Ethan told me to wait. He said I wasn't myself and told me not to make rash decisions. And yet I did anyway. I see now how selfishly I behaved. Oh, my love, my dearest love..." Tristan's newly mended heart wanted to break into pieces all over again, but he held on to her, rocking her in his arms, and swore to himself he would spend the rest of his life making it up to her.

When Tristan woke the next morning, he lay in bed a long time, thinking of the last few days. Setting aside his exhaustion and pain, he had stayed up late with Christiana, and they talked of many things of the past even as they tried to recover their future. He knew he had inflicted deep wounds upon her heart. But she had forgiven him, and he was humbly grateful.

He walked alone to the castle graveyard. Sitting on the stone bench beside Michael's grave, he unfolded the letter Charlotte had given him the previous day. His vision blurred at the sight of the familiar, neat script splashed across the page, and he wiped at his eyes impatiently.

*Dear Tristan,*

*It's late in the evening, but I know you're not asleep, for I can't hear that snore of yours. You have been so restless these last few weeks. I suspect that's due to a certain young lady with green eyes and long red-gold tresses. It is winter at Castle Altair and the kind of night I like best, when the wind howls and blows the snow against the shutters, but we are snug inside. Although I have a good book beside me, I am drawn instead to write this letter.*

*Our lives are precarious things, Tristan. No one knows this better than you. Your father and I recently discussed the upcoming war, and it occurs to me our very breath can be ripped away without warning. I hope you won't ever read this letter, because if you do, it means I am gone, lost to you once again. But I want to be assured that I do not leave this world without a few words to you.*

*Do you remember—well, no, you don't, you couldn't, even if I've told you the story a hundred times—when you were born, I was the first to hold you? Mother's pains came on quickly, and you were early. Dad rushed to fetch the midwife (Mother insisted on not disturbing the servants in their sleep). I sat with her while he was gone, and thankfully you waited until they returned. When you came out, Mother told the midwife to put you into my arms, saying, "This is your precious little brother, the last of you, for I shall never have another. Watch over him, Michael." I looked at you, and I swear you smiled at me. My heart was stolen from that day onward. We didn't know then if you would survive. Thank heavens you did. What I don't think you know is Dad wanted to name you after me, but Mother proclaimed I must be the one to choose your name, and I did—Tristan Michael Thomas Thatcher.*

*Why did I burden you with the name of the great king? I often questioned that during our days in the Shadowlands. I always loved the stories of King Tristan and his brother Edmond. Names can have deep meanings, and I prayed you would grow to be as brave and noble and pure of heart as the king you were named for. I have no doubt those prayers have been answered.*

*I can see you shaking your head at me for I know you've been conflicted about fighting. Be assured it is not rooted in cowardliness, for you are braver than anyone I have ever known. But your heart is not meant to kill. Neither was King Tristan's, but he understood there was a time to fight and a time to sheath the sword. There is a time for both. I feel it in my very bones you will come to understand this as well. You'll find your way, Tristan.*

*For these reasons, and others, I want to pass on my sword to you should I fall in war. The queen may do as she will with my estate, we've discussed this. However, the Lockhart sword is destined for you. I can think of no one worthier.*

*This life is fleeting but beautiful! So much awaits you. I pray you know great joy. And when sorrows come, as they must, I am confident you will overcome them. You are much stronger than you believe. Stronger than I could ever hope to be.*

*And now I hear your booming snore echoing through the halls of the castle, and my heart is at peace, knowing you are sleeping next door. I hope to live with that sound thundering in my ears, keeping me awake for many years to come. Yet I'm compelled to say, in case I do not...*

*Tristan, I've always loved you as my brother, but having had a hand in raising you, I've received a glimpse of fatherhood and what it means to love a son. Nothing has brought me more joy than watching you grow up to be such a fine man and knowing I played a part in it. Know I love you dearly, and if the Father allows such things, I will continue to watch over you until we are together again. Until the Rising, for evermore.*

*Your brother,*

*Michael*

Thomas had been searching for his son all morning and discovered him in the castle graveyard. A letter lay open in his lap, and though his eyes were on the stone slab in front of him, Thomas could see his thoughts were miles away. Tristan turned at the crunch of footsteps in the snow.

"Permission to engage the enemy?" asked Thomas.

Tristan smiled, folding the letter and placing it in his pocket. He would share it with his father someday soon, but he wasn't ready quite yet.

Thomas sat beside him. "How often do you come here?"

"Not enough." Tristan gave his father a sidelong glance. "Dad, about last night, I'm sorry. I said some unforgivable things to you, and I regret them deeply. I don't know why I get so mad sometimes."

"You're a Lockhart and a Thatcher. Destined to be brave, stubborn, and hot-tempered." Thomas nudged him. "And I do recall assuring you it was safe to speak your mind to me. I'm sorry too, for not telling you years ago."

"No more secrets?"

"Hmm, secrets of state perhaps."

"You promise?" Tristan growled. Thomas snorted.

"I promise. How's your arm?"

"It hurts a lot. But it'll do."

"I can't decide," Thomas mused, "if that move yesterday was an act of supreme bravery or simply idiotic."

"I'm going for both," Tristan said with a grin, and they both laughed. Then Tristan's face grew serious. "What will happen with the Mac-Clarens?"

"You heard what Charlotte said."

"That's it? And the lives of two girls and Michael? Are the scars on my back a diplomatic mistake? Where's the justice here?" At the stricken look on his father's face, Tristan dropped his gaze. "I'm sorry, Dad. It's not your fault. Not Charlotte's either."

Thomas cleared his throat and reached for something in his pocket. "The big question now is, what of the girl?"

"There's always the girl," murmured Tristan, and a smile quirked.

"Do you remember this?"

Tristan's gaze lit with interest at the velvet bag his father held. "I wondered what happened to Mother's jewels."

Thomas dug into the bag with his large, roughened fingers. "Ah, here it is—your mother's wedding ring." Thomas withdrew a gold ring set with an emerald. The band had intricate filigree, and the years had not dimmed the stone's luster.

"I remember," Tristan said.

"Giving her this ring was the happiest day in my life, at least until you boys were born. Ah, well. It's silly to keep these things locked away. Perhaps you might find a use for it." Saying this, he placed the ring in Tristan's hand.

Tristan froze. He looked up at his father, who winked. Tristan beheld the ring with a new perspective.

"The stone matches her eyes," he whispered. With a shaky laugh he added, "I sure hope she says yes."

"There's one way to find out."

"I've made some serious mistakes. I hurt her very much."

"I know, son, and it's good to be aware of these things. But she has a forgiving nature, same as you. I trust it will work out."

"You do approve, I hope?"

"Would I have handed over your mother's ring otherwise? Yes, Tristan, I've known for a long time she was the one for you. I believe you will be extraordinarily happy together. A word of caution though. Be careful, son. Charlotte loves you, but that won't stop her from using you to achieve her ends. There will be challenges I don't think you anticipate, marrying into the Reynard family. It's a game of chess with real stakes, and Charlotte always expects to win. Don't let yourself be another pawn."

"I'm beginning to see that. Christiana is worth whatever comes." Tristan took a deep breath. "Life sure was simpler when it was just us men in the mountains."

"True, but women make it a hell of a lot more fun."

Tristan grinned and stood to brush some snow from Michael's stone. Thomas heaved a sigh. "I miss that lad more than I can say."

"Me too." Tristan choked out, thinking of the letter. "He was the best of us, Dad."

Thomas looked at Tristan and saw his bravery, loyalty, and steadfast sense of morality. He had been a delightful boy to raise, and Thomas very much admired the man he was becoming. "I'm not so sure about that, Tristan. I'm not so sure."

His son's eyes flickered to him, and a small smile teased the corner of Tristan's mouth. Together, they walked back to the castle.

# Chapter 46

# Stargazer

In the land of Aquila, Christmas Day was a quiet affair spent with loved ones and family. For those wealthy enough to have servants, the food was simple and served cold in order to allow their people a day of minimal labor. Everyone slept late after the rejoicing of the previous night. For it was on Christmas Eve when dancers gathered, fiddlers played, and banquets overflowed the sideboards.

The anticipation of the day began in the morning, with a crush of humanity in even the smallest village. Markets spilled over with sweetmeats and other delicacies. By the time the noon bells tolled, much of the crowd had dissipated into their homes in preparation for the night's revelries. In the winter twilight, music floated through the air—the sounds of a fiddle here, a penny whistle there, the clang of spoons adding a silvery percussion. As the first stars twinkled overhead, full merrymaking broke out in every city, town, and village. Roving musicians played for the couples dancing in the streets, taverns rolled out barrels of brew held back especially for this night, and long tables were set in the squares where people gathered to feast.

When the bells tolled midnight, the Faithful joyfully made their way to churches, and the laughter and music of those less inclined to worship drifted in among the rafters. No one minded, however, for it infused their services with the exultation the night deserved. After their sacred rites, families with small children hustled them off to bed with the promise of treats upon waking. Those with endurance would stay awake and celebrate until there were streaks of pink in the sky.

At Castle Altair, things were no different, if a touch more exclusive. Noble families who could travel the distance through the snow gathered in the Great Hall. There was no formal dining—tables were set with food and drink, the people helping themselves when and where they wished. Even the servants were permitted to celebrate whenever their duties allowed. It was not uncommon in the late-night hours for the revelers of the castle to spill over and join those in the stone-paved streets. There were storytellers, music and dancing, and tricks of illusion.

Nowhere else on remembered earth was Christmas celebrated with such fervor as in the land of Aquila.

"Oh, just do it and get it over with!" James exclaimed. "I'm tired of you moping around. It's been over a week."

The brothers had gathered in Tristan's room while he prepared himself for the evening, forever fussing and fidgeting with his appearance in front of the rather warped glass. Tristan let out an anxious whimper, and James stalked up behind him. Expecting more taunts, Tristan stiffened. Instead, James leaned close to his ear. "She's going to say yes, Tris." Their eyes met in the mirror, and Tristan smiled his thanks. James grinned back and left the room. He had his own plans for the evening.

Ethan stayed in his chair, content to rest easy by the fire with a mug of ale. "He's right, Tristan. Ask her." The only response he received was an explosive oath as Tristan yanked off his jacket and threw himself onto the opposite chair.

"I'm not going down there," he said moodily.

Ethan remained calm. "Yes, you are. And stop being melodramatic." For Tristan had let forth a mournful sigh.

Tristan gave him a dark look before he got up to try again.

When Ethan and Tristan entered the Great Hall, James called out, "Oy! Boys! Where've you been? Come taste this ale, it's that golden and pure!"

The brothers snorted and laughed.

"We'll be hauling him off to bed tonight," Ethan said.

"Hope you're stocked up on hangover cures."

The hall was a swirl of colors and light, and Tristan's anxiety tripped away in the merry atmosphere. It had been two—or was it three?—years since he had spent Christmas at Altair, and he'd forgotten the joyful gaiety. The floor had been cleared, with the long tables pushed back against the walls. The fiddlers were lively, and couples were dancing reels. Tristan spied Christiana already dancing with... "Look, it's Justin!"

Ethan smiled and left to greet the prince. Tristan murmured a prayer of thanks that Justin had come home at last, for Christiana had been worried he might not make it in time for Christmas. He had hopes for the evening and feared they might be squashed with Christiana fretful and anxious concerning her brother's absence. Now, Tristan's heart lightened considerably.

Justin waved and swung Christiana over. To Tristan, she was more beautiful than he had ever seen her, with her hair down and her cheeks flushed. Justin shook his hand.

"Thank you for taking care of that nasty business, Tristan. I'm sorry I wasn't here to help, but I'm glad to hear those MacClarens are getting what they deserve."

"We hope," Ethan said, voice low.

"If nothing else, it's clear to everyone they serve no one but themselves."

"Let's not talk about that tonight," Christiana insisted. "Dance with me, Tristan!"

He put his arm around her and twirled her before his ankle gave out. "I can't, this wretched sprain."

"I'll stay with you."

"Don't be daft, you love to dance, and you don't get to often enough. Take as long as you want, and when you're done, dance back to me. I'll be waiting."

She stood on her tiptoes for a light but enchanting kiss, and his heart dissolved within him. "You promise?" she whispered. He kissed the tip of her nose and prodded her into the throng.

"Sorry you can't dance with her, son," his father said. Tristan wondered when Thomas had snuck up behind him.

"It's all right," Tristan whispered as he watched her, his eyes shining. "As long as she's with me in the end."

Tristan wandered from the Great Hall and into the courtyard. He wondered if he would find any more sweethearting couples, but it was cold and no one lingered. He gazed up into the clear, star-filled sky. Tristan's thoughts drifted to Michael. The heartbreak of his death had mellowed over time into something more bearable; however, the events of the last week had brought it back into sharp relief. Michael had loved life at Altair, far more than the mountains, and Christmas had been his favorite holiday.

"I thought you said you'd wait for me?" Christiana stood in the doorway, her eyes twinkling at his startled expression from her sudden appearance.

Tristan held out his arm, and she nestled against him. "I'm sorry, love, I needed some air."

"Stargazing?" she asked, her voice muffled.

"A bit."

"No matter how happy he is, he's missing you too."

Tristan's arm tightened around her. She had done that a few times, seeming to read his mind. He buried his face in her curls, trying to compose himself, but the familiar scent of sunshine in her hair sent his heart racing faster.

"Chris, when we were apart—" She started to speak, and he placed his finger over her mouth. "My turn," he whispered.

"When we were apart, I mean, truly apart, the sun was so cold. Even in the height of summer when we fought on the field, the sweat pouring, my heart was frozen. The sun gave me no warmth." He tipped his hand under her chin, his voice hoarse. "I don't ever want to live that way again. Protect me from the cold, my love. Marry me, Christiana, and always keep me warm."

Christiana stood there in silence, staring at him until he gasped out, "Ah, please?"

She shook her head and then nodded.

"Is that a yes?" he asked, panic washing over him. But when she kissed him, he knew her answer.

Ethan was the first to spy the young lovers when they reentered the Great Hall. His face lit up, and he caught the attention of his father and brother, jerking his chin toward the door. They didn't have to look at her hand to see the emerald sparkling there. They didn't even need to see Christiana, aglow with love. The sight of Tristan told them everything as he protectively guided her through the crowd, his eyes burning with a fierce joy they had never seen before. After all he had gone through, the sheer delight on his face when she kissed him before everyone was enough for those who loved him best to know all would be well in the end.

# Chapter 47

# Ever Faithful

Tristan tossed on his bed and heaved a groan of frustration.

After many months of longing for his thick feather mattress, he had been delighted to sink into it upon his return to Altair last month. But lately his blood ran like fire through his veins, and he had a hard time sleeping. And eating, for that matter.

To be sure, he had only himself to blame. Placing his mother's ring on Christiana's finger had released unexpected passions. Cautious in the past, he was rendered almost incapable of restraint. No longer content with his lover's gentle touch or sweet kisses, his desires had taken an irreversible leap forward. He passed the waking hours exploring the snow-lined streets of Altair or riding Dun to the seaside cliffs. His nights were spent in a fever pitch of anticipation.

Now the wedding was upon them, and tomorrow she would be his. Decency permitted them to go only so fast, and they had rushed through the banns as quickly as the church allowed. With the war over, weddings were happening almost every day, it seemed. Tristan wondered if the kingdom would be bursting with babies by the end of the year. His cheeks flushed when he realized the direction his thoughts were moving.

Restless, he hauled himself from bed and threw open the shutters, inhaling the sharp, cold air. Christiana's windows were on the other side of the castle, and he had no way of knowing if she was awake, but he doubted it. He closed his eyes and envisioned her curled up in bed, soft and enticing. He longed to be with her, holding her close, feeling her warmth...

Tristan arrested his thoughts, but the damage was done. Although dawn wouldn't break for at least an hour, there would be no more sleep this day. He dressed and left the castle.

Tristan had become a familiar sight to the townspeople, and his wandering path through the city was marked by chuckles and winks. "Aye, the lad has it bad," and other similar comments followed after him. He suspected they found it all quite amusing, and he didn't care in the least. Walking was the safest way to pass the time.

When he returned at dusk, he wanted nothing more than to go to bed, alone for one more night. But he came home to a castle in joyous chaos, and he would not be allowed to sleep as soon as he would have liked.

Before he had even pulled off his boots, his brothers entered his chamber with Rachel. She bore a set of lethal-looking shears. Spying them, he threw his hands up in alarm.

"Oh, no!"

"Yes, Tristan." Ethan laughed, shoving him into a chair. "It is time to cut the locks. Your hair is ridiculous. Rachel could braid it."

Tristan spluttered, "You can't!"

"Who do you think you are, Samson?" James lay back lazily on Tristan's bed. "I can say with confidence you have no special powers tied into those messy curls of yours."

"Tristan, listen to me," Rachel said in her soft voice. "I promise it won't be as bad as you fear, and I know what Christiana likes. She loves your hair, but she doesn't want it longer than hers."

Tristan rolled his eyes, but she gazed at him with such sweetness he couldn't deny her. Rachel steadied his head, and the shears clicked close to his ear. He squirmed as he watched the hair fall. James passed him a flagon of ale, and he took a hurried swig before handing it to Ethan.

"Looking forward to tomorrow evening?" James asked, and Tristan almost choked and glared at his brother. James shrugged. "I meant the wedding. It's late in the day, isn't it?"

Tristan nodded, and Rachel tugged at a long strand of hair and ordered, "Be still! Or I'll take off an ear."

"I'm glad there's a feast tomorrow. There never used to be anything fun until Third Night. Charlotte has loosened that up," said James.

"Not much of a feast," Tristan said. "Just a simple feed for those at the wedding."

"Better than you taking the vows and disappearing." James ignored the look Tristan flashed in his direction with those words. "Is it true old King George started Third Night because he was so bawdy for his bride he didn't want to waste time feasting after the ceremony?"

"James, really," Rachel murmured.

"A rather indelicate way to describe it, although correct in the essentials," Ethan affirmed. "King George was mad for his wife, Constance, but she was an ardent member of the Faithful. As such, she made him wait until their wedding night. By that point he was too worked up.

He canceled the wedding festival and bedded her immediately after the ceremony."

"I'm thankful to King George," muttered Tristan, louder than he intended. James hooted with laughter.

Ethan gave them both an amused glance before continuing. "We don't actually know what night it was, but eventually they came out and the party took off. The guests had hung about, not knowing what else to do. The tradition caught on and, over time, people other than family stopped coming to the wedding itself and waited for the celebration after."

"There, I'm done," Rachel said. Tristan shot to his feet as though he were sitting on hot coals and ran to the glass. He had to look twice, for he could see no difference. A pile of hair lay on the floor, but no matter which way he turned, it didn't appear that different from what it was before. At least hair no longer hung over his eyes, and cool air brushed his neck.

"You're as vain as a maiden at her first dance, Tris." James laughed.

"I'm not! I'm trying to figure out what she cut."

"You *are* vain," Ethan asserted. "And she took off a lot. There was so much that it's still a shaggy mess even after being cut."

Tristan looked again and sighed with relief. He wanted to feel like himself on his wedding day, not like the time he had his hair cropped when he joined the army.

"It's perfect, thank you, Rachel." He kissed Rachel's cheek, causing her to blush.

"Hey now," muttered Ethan. Tristan shot his brother a grin.

"Well, well. Lady Tristan approves, that's something," James said, smirking.

"Indeed. That said, James, if you will sit yourself down, you are next." Rachel snapped her shears.

James's eyes went wide with genuine horror as Tristan gleefully threw him into the chair.

Tristan had a late dinner in his chamber, though he ate little. He paced his room, far too nervous to sleep. He gazed up at the Lockhart sword, returned to its place over the mantel, and wished with all his heart he could have a talk with Michael. Tristan thought of Thomas but suspected his father would be embarrassed to offer the kind of advice he sought. Spurred on by restlessness, he left to wander the castle. After half an hour, he found himself knocking on a door. Rachel answered.

"Tristan! Whatever are you doing here?"

"May I see her? Please? I won't be long."

Rachel hesitated before smiling indulgently. "Wait here, I'll ask." She shut the door. Tristan fidgeted, hearing the murmur of feminine voices, including the queen's laugh. A few seconds later, the door opened, and Christiana slipped out.

"This is very naughty, Tristan, you should—" Tristan drew her into a close embrace. There was no heat, no passion, just a quiet desperation to hold her in his arms, for the reassurance of her. She relaxed into him as though she sensed his need. He held her for a long time without saying a word.

At last he released her and skimmed his lips to hers. She refused to let him go until she gave him a proper kiss, one that sent his head spinning.

"I'll see you tomorrow." He gulped down the thickness in his throat to get the words out.

"Tomorrow," she whispered.

"How are you doing?" Thomas asked, peering into his son's face as they waited in the small chapel. Paler than typical, Tristan jittered on his feet.

"I'm hungry," Tristan muttered. "I haven't been able to eat much the last few days."

"Ah. Well, the ceremony is quick, and you can eat right after."

Tristan snorted as though he doubted it. Thomas chuckled and surveyed the chapel.

Family and a few old friends such as the Kavanaughs were the only ones there. He thought it a shame that Cate had never married, as she had grown to be a stunning young woman. She seemed quite changed from the sharp-tongued lass he remembered. Indeed, these days she was almost withdrawn. Thomas sometimes wished there had been some sort of romance between her and Michael. Perhaps then...*Best not think on that,* Thomas said to himself. He caught James shooting an odd look at Cate. Thomas wondered again why those two had never gotten along. How he would have enjoyed seeing them together, his son and the daughter of his oldest friend.

Thomas returned his gaze to Tristan. The boy seemed composed enough, but he suspected Tristan's outward demeanor was covering many turbulent emotions. He remembered his own wedding to Anna. What a winsome bride she had been! Nothing like Christiana, either in appearance or personality. Anna had been more similar to Rachel. His eyes darted to Rachel, and he delighted at seeing Ethan sitting with her, holding her hand.

Thomas sighed, thinking of his wife. His sweet Anna, so quiet and dear. She had not been his first love, and he had still been suffering the pangs of a disappointed heart when he began courting her. Yet how he had come to love her! Thomas closed his eyes and for a brief moment smelled the salty sea and sailing with her on their wedding night. He had not grown up near the water and made a mess of the whole thing, but later...

Murmurs from the people brought him back to the present. The queen had entered the chapel. Charlotte winked at him, and he almost laughed. How that woman loved to tease him, even after all these years.

When Christiana came into the chapel and took his hand, his heart stopped beating. She was exquisite in a dark red dress, her hair done up with a bridal crown composed of holly berries. His breath caught, his mind seeking out a memory of something...

Then the memory scattered. Tristan thought only of his bride, and he faced her full of happiness, his love shining in his eyes. His father had been right, the ceremony wasn't long. When the time came to kiss her, she gave him a mischievous smile that melted his heart. His hand rose to her cheek, and he nervously glanced around the room. She whispered, "Don't worry about them. It's just us, Tristan."

He heaved a breath and bent his head to hers for a soft whisper of a kiss. Tristan would have stopped there, but she kept him with her a second longer, demanding a little more. A chuckle rose from the pews—Tristan couldn't be sure if it was his father or James—and it broke them apart. Flushing, Tristan kissed her forehead and turned to the others, a grin spreading across his face.

It was a small crowd for such a decadent feast, with plenty of food for all, but Tristan found himself unable to eat more than a few bites. Getting through the ceremony had been one thing. Now another matter was straining his nerves. For his attention was increasingly focused on the hours *after* the feast.

How did this end? He had no idea how to bring it about. What did they expect him to do, yawn and declare it was time for bed? Leave, hoping Christiana tagged along after him? Or did he stand and boldly demand his new wife join him? The thought made him chortle despite his anxiety. He caught the eye of his father, who smiled at him with amused sympathy. Tristan's cheeks burned. By the faith, everyone knew! Everyone knew what was coming. There was no being discreet. He grasped at the nearest drink and almost choked on the rich red wine.

Christiana brought her head close to his, hissing in his ear, "What *is* the matter with you?" Tristan took another gulp, prepared for it this time.

He shot Christiana a look and stilled, his gaze arrested. She had removed the bridal wreath, but her hair was still up, and he very much wanted it flowing down. Without thought, he took her face in his hands and kissed her, and his courage grew with her kiss. He never heard the laughter as their kiss continued. Nothing else mattered. Everything centered on her, his wife, his dream come true.

In a fit of inspired bravery, he stood and cleared his throat. All the happy chatter died away. He avoided looking at James, who seemed to be on the verge of laughter. Ethan nodded encouragingly. Tristan raised his goblet to Christiana and said, "To my wife, my love, my sun. Thank you for loving me as you do. You are ever faithful."

Everyone drank to the toast. Tristan took her by the hand and led her from the table, calling over his shoulder, "Carry on without us, if you don't mind." There was a burst of surprised laughter, and the couple bolted from the room.

# Chapter 48

# Cherish

Not sure if they would be followed, they raced up the stairs, but the distant echoes of laughter faded. They danced and spun through corridors, snatching kisses at every turn and laughing until they entered Christiana's tower room. Far removed from the other family rooms, they would have all the privacy they needed here.

Tristan slammed the oak door shut, and Christiana slid in the bolt. He leaned over her with his arms outstretched on the door. Tristan guessed he loomed at least seven inches over her and rather enjoyed how tall she made him feel. Having her trapped against the door was a nice position for more kissing, and he undertook that endeavor with enthusiasm.

"All alone," he murmured, laughter still burbling up inside him.

"All alone," she repeated, giggling and growing breathless. "And we don't have to stop."

"No stopping." But a short time later he stepped back.

"You said no stopping!" she demanded, and he grinned.

"I would like to find someplace a bit more comfortable than standing here." Tristan glanced around. He had never been in her room before, so he wasn't sure what he would encounter. He certainly didn't expect such a large semi-circular chamber, and he was delighted by the number of mullioned glass windows making up the exterior wall. He suspected the room must be very bright on a clear day.

Tristan ignored the bed that in his imagination dominated the entire space. He wasn't ready to be quite *that* comfortable. But near the fire stood a substantial, squishy-looking chair that looked like it could serve his purposes nicely. He went to it, leading Christiana, and bounced down, pulling her onto his lap.

"There," he said with satisfaction, cradling her in his arms. "This is by far a superior position." She appeared to agree, and nothing more was said for several long, sweet minutes. Her hair was falling, and Tristan enjoyed snatching out more pins between kisses. Still, he needed to talk and thought it best to get it out of the way while he could.

"Chris..." Tristan found it hard to speak when his fresh young wife refused to stop kissing him. He tried again, lowering his voice in what he hoped was a decent imitation of his father's commanding rumble and said, "Christiana." She laughed, the minx. He turned his head, but she changed her kisses to delightful nibbles along his neck.

"Chris, please..." he pleaded before being rendered silent by her biting his ear. This was a new and wonderful approach on her part. At this point he gave up speaking, his priorities shifting into something far more carnal in nature.

"Were you going to say something?" she whispered, her breath in his ear.

"It's such a strange thing," he murmured.

"What, dearest?"

"To have spent so long not doing all the things I wanted to do with you, and now that I can, I'm not sure how to proceed." His lips traveled down one shoulder, delighting in the delicate slope of bone and flesh. She shivered.

"I do believe you are doing fine."

Her hair tumbled free and spilled over her shoulders, utterly enchanting him. Tristan nuzzled into her neck, burying his face in the long curls.

"Why do I smell the sea?" he whispered.

"Seawater. They blessed the room with it," she said, bringing her lips back to his.

He smiled at the thought and kissed her again, long and slow, even as his heart thumped faster. Without thinking, he blurted out, "You know, we don't have to keep going, if you don't want. In case you don't—you didn't—"

Christiana pushed her hands against his shoulders. "What is this you are saying?"

Pink-cheeked, he babbled, "I mean, we have all the time in the world. I'm in no rush, I can wait. I don't want you to be frightened—"

"Oh, Tristan, you sweet fool," she breathed, bringing his face to hers for a long kiss. Her kiss deepened as Christiana opened herself entirely to him, warm and melting. Caught up in a fever dream of delight, Tristan shivered as a wild joy pulsed through him.

His whole body came alive to her every movement, and when Christiana shifted her position, he was almost undone. One hand tangled in her hair while the other caressed her. Part of Tristan wanted nothing more than to give in to the desire that roused him, but he also wished to ensure his wife's own pleasure.

Waves of heat rolled over him, and he gasped, heart racing. "How are you feeling, love?"

"I feel," she murmured between kisses along his collarbone, "we should move to the bed."

Tristan gulped, his head spinning. "Chris, maybe we should wait."

"Tristan."

"I don't know how to do this," he whispered, frantic. She caressed one cheek, bringing her forehead to his.

"I don't either, but I'm sure we'll figure it out. Most people do." Christiana looked into his eyes, and Tristan saw uncertainty flicker in a sea of green. With a shock, he realized she was frightened as well, perhaps even more than himself.

"Just love me, Tristan. I know you can do that."

Tristan found his courage in the face of her fears. He stood with Christiana in his arms and carried her to the bed. They tumbled onto it with quick, nervous laughter, but kissing her, he knew she was right. All he needed to do was love her.

For Tristan, creation shifted, the polar axis crumbled, and his internal compass rearranged itself around her. Christiana forever claimed him, becoming his entire world, his epicenter, his own true north. They were both shaking afterward, shattered and reborn, holding each other in a tight embrace neither wanted to break. When they were quiet, his voice was thick with emotion.

"Do you remember the first time I kissed you? There in the chapel? I knew at that moment I would love you for the rest of my life. Not because of the kiss, but because you came back to me when I needed you most." Tristan swallowed hard, his emotions threatening to overwhelm him. "You forever hold my heart in your hands, Christiana Thatcher. Please, I beg of you, be gentle with it."

Christiana ran her fingers through his hair and caressed his face. "And do you not also hold mine?" Unable to speak, he simply nodded. With a kiss she whispered, "We'll hold each other's hearts, then, and cherish in the holding."

# Chapter 49

# Sea Song

After a restless doze, Tristan awoke to the delicious new sensation of his wife curled up against him, and a smile flitted across his face. She slept with his arm draped over her. He shivered and snuggled her even closer, dropping a feather-light kiss on the top of her head. She murmured in her sleep, and to his chagrin, she stirred.

"I'm sorry," he whispered. "I didn't mean to wake you."

She reached for him, bringing her lips to his. All his regrets at waking her disappeared as he kissed her. He was starting to enjoy this new delight when a loud growl issued from under the blankets. Her eyes flew open, and they both froze, stopping mid-kiss. Another rumble floated upward, and Tristan buried his face into the pillows while Christiana started giggling.

"Was that your *stomach*?"

He choked on his own laughter and nodded, refusing to lift his head from the pillow. Christiana sat and attempted to shove him over, but he wouldn't budge. Years of play had taught her all his tickle spots, and she set about it with great skill. Screeching unmanfully at the surprise, he bucked Christiana aside and dove on top of her, holding her wrists. She shrieked and wriggled under him until they were laughing even harder amidst energetic kissing. Tristan forgot his weight until she gurgled that he was squashing her. He rolled off, and they lay facing each other, panting between kisses. His stomach growled again, setting her laughter off once more.

"It can't be close to morning. How are you hungry already after the feast?"

"Ah, I didn't eat. At least, not much."

"Why not?"

Tristan flushed and nuzzled into her. At her urging, he mumbled, "I didn't feel like it. I was far too anxious."

Her incredulous expression turned gentle. "Anxious about being together?"

"Yes," said Tristan and then amended, "Not only the bedding, although that would be enough to terrify anyone the first time, I should think. I feared hurting you, and it was important to me to make you happy. But..." Tristan fell silent, thinking. The last few hours had been a revelation, stretching his mind and heart in ways he never expected. His very soul had been touched. "I love you. But more so, I love *us*. Everything about us, how we are together. What we've built between us over the years. I was frightened at the idea that being together...like this...might change us. I know, it sounds ridiculous now."

"No, it doesn't," she whispered. She moved against him in a way that made him catch his breath as she murmured, "Let your stomach growl. We'll take care of that later."

Tristan sank back on the pillow, running a shaking hand through his sweaty hair, and the cold air of the room hit him. He shivered and tugged up the tossed blankets, making sure to tuck them around Christiana, who lay with her head resting upon his shoulder. They were quiet for some time as she brushed her fingers over his chest. She sat, peering at him intently.

"Your chest hairs are red! Well, reddish."

He grinned. "I know. I couldn't escape Dad's red hair. People have told me there's glints of red in my hair in the sun. I don't know. It isn't as though I carry a mirror with me outside to check."

"You don't?" She smirked.

"I'm not *that* vain."

"Hmm." Christiana brushed her fingers over his cheek. "I've never seen you with a beard, just a bit of growth that one time. Does it grow out red?"

"No, it's dark like my hair. Takes forever for me to grow one too. I can go a week or more without shaving. But it's a nice full beard when it comes out. I grew it for a while in the army. I'm glad I don't have to shave every day though, like James. He's truly hairy."

"Yes, I know," she said absently, continuing to tangle her fingers with his chest hair. Tristan let that sink in and squirmed to sit up.

"Eh, how?"

"How what?"

"How do you know? About James?"

Christiana shrugged. "There's a peephole in the bathhouse. Rachel and I would sometimes watch you boys bathe."

"What!"

She giggled. "I have a brother, you know. It's not as if I had no idea what went on down there before tonight."

"But to—to peek—and Rachel!"

"And Catrina Kavanaugh, if she was in town."

Tristan spluttered something incomprehensible. Christiana lifted her head and eyed him. "I should point out I chose *you* and not either of your brothers. You might think on that for a moment."

The droll look she gave made him settle down, quite smug. "So you did." After a long pause, he cleared his throat, trying to sound as casual as possible. "Where is this peephole, exactly?"

"No, not telling." She kissed away any further thoughts about peepholes in bathhouses.

He sighed, happiness filling every inch of him. "I cannot deny it anymore, Chris, I must have it out. I'm madly in love with you."

"As you should be."

"That said, I must also confess that I'm *very* hungry. For *food*."

"I know. I think there's a hamper of sorts by the fire. You could see what's in it."

Tristan shyly pulled on his trousers, causing Christiana to giggle. He lumbered over to stir the fire with Christiana following, wrapped in a blanket. His eyes brightened at the sight of her. They dug into the hamper, and to Tristan's delight there were smoked meats, cheeses, fresh bread, and butter. At the bottom were several flagons of ale and wine. They both attacked the food with healthy young appetites sharpened by their many exertions.

"If I had known, I would have hung the ale out a window to keep cool," Christiana complained.

"Keep cool? Frozen, more like. Besides, it's cold enough in this room even by the fire. Why did your mother put you here of all places?"

"She didn't. I chose it."

Baffled, he cocked his head. A smile danced across her face that Tristan found adorable. She gestured toward the outdoors. "The sea, Tristan."

Without a word, Tristan leaped up and ran to the windows.

"Don't be ridiculous, darling, you can't see the water at night and there's a blizzard roaring. But when the weather is clear, the view is beautiful. That's why I chose this room, although I'll admit it's chilly in winter."

"Chilly!"

"Never mind, we'll settle in your room after Third Night where it will be much warmer. Come here."

Chewing a mouthful of bread, Tristan shook his head. "Are you sure you want to live in my room down in the depths?"

"Absolutely I do! I can't wait to live alongside your brothers."

Tristan sat back, brow furrowed, not sure what to make of this. Christiana saw his confusion and laughed.

"Oh, you should see your face! Listen, although I love my brother, Justin has never been around much. To be honest, I was rather lonesome growing up. Momma's wonderful, but she's always busy. I'm excited to have a real family near me."

"You won't have the sea," Tristan said wistfully.

"I'll have you."

"I fear I'll be a poor substitute. And it won't be as quiet, you know. Nor as private."

"As long as there is a sturdy bolt on the door, I'll be happy."

"You're a scandalous woman!"

"I am, aren't I?" she teased between bites of bread and butter. Tristan dropped his bread and leaned forward to kiss her with a sudden longing. Her cheeks went pink, and she prodded him with a finger. "Eat your food! I don't want to hear that stomach of yours growling the rest of the night."

Tristan chuckled and continued eating until he believed he could survive whatever came. Gazing at the fire, he stretched out his legs before him and leaned back on his arms. Christiana studied him appraisingly. Given his height and lithe appearance when dressed, one couldn't tell how strongly built he truly was. Never stocky, he was flush with long, sculpted muscles. Years of using a sword had given him a powerful upper body that tapered to a trim waist, flaring into well-muscled thighs from riding.

There were also the scars. The angry cut from the duel with Mac-Claren was healing, and the result of the arrow that struck him at fifteen was stark on his shoulder. The faded scar along his waist served as a permanent reminder of that horrible day in the willows. She couldn't see the whip marks on his back that would never be gone. Young as he was, he already had the battered body of a warrior.

Christiana shivered and slid over to him. Tristan put his arms around her, kissing the top of her head. Happy, he started to hum a tune his mother had taught him long ago, but he stopped, knowing it must be off-key. She whispered, "Is that 'Sea Song'?"

Tristan nodded. Christiana nudged him to continue. A little embarrassed, he hummed some more. She picked up the tune and sang softly.

*Oh, hearts entwined,*
*love sealed with a kiss,*
*bond made fast,*
*salt blessed;*
*tidewaters flow,*
*two merge to one.*

*Heart's blood, crashing,*
*past tidal waves*
*rush to me, come to me,*
*hear my love call.*
*Oh, hearts wrested,*
*love broken—*

"Don't sing the rest. It's too sad," Tristan whispered. They sat in silence again, holding hands in the firelit darkness. She relaxed against him in a way that stirred his heart with infinite tenderness. "Let's go to bed. It's late. And I've long dreamt of sleeping with you by my side. Shall we?"

It wasn't quite that easy. Tristan discovered that a simple goodnight kiss could stretch into another hour of wakefulness. He wondered if he would ever be able to sleep with her lying beside him. But as she stroked his hair, he melted into her arms and gave in to the night.

Tristan had fallen into a deep sleep and a long snore dragged out of him. Christiana giggled. Ethan had warned her about his snoring, but she thought he had greatly exaggerated the issue. She propped herself up on an elbow, regarding her new husband. He looked so very young and unspoiled. How had he fought in the war while retaining such a sweet nature? Then again, she remembered his face when he had seen the dagger. Watching him fight MacClaren had opened her eyes to a different side of Tristan, one that wouldn't hesitate to do whatever was necessary to protect those he loved.

Laying there, exhausted yet wide-awake, her thoughts wandered. Christiana had wanted to believe Tristan would be the lover she had imagined, but too many accounts of disappointed hopes had made her apprehensive. She had heard the whispered stories when married women gathered, tales of girlish giggles turned to tears when their supposed sweethearts became monsters in the bedroom. Often cruel, or indifferent at best, marriage would always be a gamble for a woman in her world.

She should have known that her darling Tristan would prove true. To be sure, it had hurt the first time, more than she would ever admit to him. But beyond the initial sting, she had perceived a hint of something that bordered on the edge of wondrous. Tristan had been so gentle, so ardent; she had been cherished and safe as he led her to joys previously unknown. Her love for him knew no bounds after the way he had given himself to her.

Sleep taking hold, she snuggled next to him, her hand lying over his heart. Remembering how she might have lost him, Christiana treasured the strong beat against her palm. Her breath caught with the image of his body trampled in a muddy field, and she gasped.

As if he sensed her distress, Tristan ceased snoring and rolled to his side, enfolding her in his arms. His lips brushed a kiss against her hair before he whispered, "My love." Tristan's breath steadied as he slept again, but no longer snoring.

Wrapped in love, sleep came to Christiana as well.

# Chapter 50

# For Evermore

Unlike the many days preceding, the morning dawned a brilliant blue. Tristan kept the fire burning, for the tower chamber was colder than ever. At one point, a spirited debate erupted concerning who was now the better chess player, which resulted in a game being set up on the bed. Neither of them played particularly well, distracted as they were making moves between kisses and tickles. One delightful wrestling match succeeded in toppling whole kingdoms to the floor. They had reset the game a second time when the knock came.

The intrusion startled them both. Over the past few days, they had forgotten anyone else existed in the castle, so wrapped up were they in their own sweet cocoon. Wearing a rumpled tunic already, Tristan hauled himself up while retying the drawstring of his bed trousers, which tended to slip. He unbolted the door, and Rachel stood there, with her eyes cast down and cheeks pink. Self-conscious, he yanked his trousers higher, and she blushed even more.

"Er, it's Rachel," he called to Christiana, thankful she at least wore a dressing gown. He rolled his eyes when the girls greeted each other as though it had been years.

"Your mother wanted me to remind you of tonight."

"Tonight? What time is it?" Christiana looked a little perturbed at Tristan, clearly implying he should know the time. He raised his hands in a helpless gesture.

"It's midafternoon," Rachel offered, before adding. "Third Night?"

"By the faith!" Christiana exclaimed, and before Tristan even knew what was happening, he had been herded out of the room, clothes and boots in hand, and urged to clean himself before the evening. Confused but content enough, he meandered through the castle to his room. He decided that a trip to the bathhouse was in order. But before he washed, he spent an inordinate amount of time inspecting the walls. Try as he might, he could not imagine modest, blushing Rachel taking a peek at a roomful of naked men. However, he could clearly see his own wife doing it, giggling all the while. And Cate! Just the thought sent a shiver of mortification over him. No, best not to think of it.

He never did find the peephole.

Tristan was puttering about his room, dwelling on certain memories of the last few days and fully embracing marital bliss, when a joyful yell interrupted his thoughts. Ethan dragged him to a chair and plunked him down as James forced a mug of ale into his hand.

"What was it like?" Ethan demanded.

Tristan chortled.

"Make him drink up, Ethan. Maybe we can pry it out of him bit by bit," James suggested.

"A gentleman doesn't tell," Tristan said with a superior air. "All I will say is it was better than anything—*anything*—you can imagine."

Ethan grinned, but James swore under his breath.

At their looks of surprise, he sighed. "Sorry. I'm happy for you, Tris. Truly."

James stared moodily into the fire and sat in the opposite chair. Tristan studied his brother and suspected he knew the reason why. He rose and dug into a dark corner of his wardrobe, seeking an old piece of velvet, folded and tied with a ribbon.

"I have something for you," he said, tossing the packet into James's lap. James grunted and his big hands fumbled with the wrapping until out spilled a long golden chain, from which hung a faceted garnet. It gleamed in the firelight, reflecting sparkles onto the wall.

"Well, this is lovely, but I don't think it's my color." James smirked. With considerable nonchalance Tristan sat and sipped his ale. Intrigued, Ethan moved to the arm of Tristan's chair and perched upon it.

Tristan nodded at the necklace. "Do you know what that is?"

"Jewelry."

"Brilliant. Do you know where it came from?"

His oldest brother shrugged.

"That was Mother's garnet necklace," said Tristan.

James's face softened, and he studied the necklace with an appreciative eye. Then he looked up, suspicious. "I thought Dad had all her things. Why do you have this?"

"Ah, well, that is a story. You see, this is the necklace I showed Andrew when—I can't believe you haven't heard this before!"

"I might have," James said. "It was a long time ago, Tris."

"Right. Why do you think a necklace would have helped Andrew know who I was? Just a necklace, nothing too exciting."

"Because Andrew Kavanaugh was once in love with our mother, and he gave it to her," Ethan said. James's eyes widened, and a sparkle lit itself in their blue depths.

Tristan waved at the necklace. "Granted, I've never asked for details, but from what I've gathered over the years, this necklace was a Kavanaugh family heirloom. Andrew let Mother keep it even after she married Dad. Insisted, really. I never gave this to Dad. You can imagine why." Tristan laughed and swiped the garnet from James. "Now envision the beautiful Catrina when presented with a long-lost heirloom as a gift. A *love* gift."

James's eyes grew wide with panic, and he jerked his head toward Ethan, who started laughing.

"Don't worry, I've known for months."

"What?" exclaimed both James and Tristan, and Ethan laughed even harder.

Tristan snorted and held up the necklace. "Do you want this?"

James gazed at the jewel but made no move to take it.

"What's the problem?" demanded Tristan.

"Woodraven."

Tristan remained silent. He didn't know what to say.

"Is she aware of your potential...inheritance?" Ethan asked.

"I keep no secrets from Cate."

"If she knows everything already, I'm not sure I understand."

"C'mon, Ethan. My future is dangling, unknown. I don't even know what I'm going to do with the war over. At least I knew who I was when we were fighting."

"You could always give it up," Tristan said. "The throne. You can stay in the army. You'll be a general someday."

"No. Like it or not, I am a grandson of King Holden, a prince of Woodraven. No matter our personal feelings on the topic, to deny our blood would be to deny our father, and that I will never do."

"Nobly said," Tristan whispered. He cleared his throat. "You don't even know if it will happen. And it could be years."

"What are your chances anyway?" Ethan asked.

"Of the throne? A sketchy third, maybe fourth in line. Of course, in that murderous country I could be crowned next week. Or never. There's no telling. Meanwhile, I wait. And my sweet Cate lives out the years watching everyone she knows marry, even her younger sisters. I don't want to live apart from her anymore, but how can I ask her to be tied to a man who can offer her nothing certain in life?"

"Couldn't you—"

"All I wanted was to lead the armies of Aquila someday. I was successful as a soldier, but I'm not sure how far I can rise in the military when this gets out. And Woodraven may never happen. I'm a man without a future. I am nothing."

"That's not true," said Tristan angrily.

"You will *never* be nothing, James," Ethan insisted.

Tristan nodded and waved his hand toward his oldest brother. "You are a prince of Woodraven, no matter what comes. That has to be worth a great deal. Plus, you are a Lockhart."

"And a *Thatcher*," inserted Ethan with a wink. "From the glorious House of Thatcher."

All three burst into laughter. When they subsided, Tristan leaned forward. "James, remember a few weeks ago? When you asked me how I would work things out with Chris? Well, I didn't do anything. I...I just loved her. And she loved me. It worked itself out. Don't let this

Woodraven stuff hold you back from Cate, not any longer. We'll figure it out together somehow."

"It's time, James," Ethan agreed.

"You don't get it—"

Tristan stood impatiently. "Who is this man before me? Not Captain James Thatcher, commended for bravery by the queen herself! Not the future king of Woodraven! This is a craven coward impersonating my brother. Will you take this necklace and ask the woman you love to marry you once and for all, or must I do it myself?"

James hesitated, then lunged for the stone dangling from Tristan's hand. He held it to his chest, his voice was thick with emotion. "Thank you, boys. I'll do it tonight. Heaven help me."

Tristan smiled at James with great affection. He had never imagined rooting for the Cat to be his sister, but he was all in now.

Tristan waited for his bride at the foot of the grand staircase and lit up when she came flitting down. "You're beautiful! And don't mock me, but I missed you."

"Thank you." She kissed him. "Are you ready for this?"

"Do we have to? I would far rather take you back to bed."

"Stop," she whispered with another kiss. "Later. I promise."

"On that promise, I shall endure whatever lies ahead."

"You love gatherings!"

"I do, if I can hide in a corner and watch everyone else. I don't like being the center of attention." He nibbled along her neck. She whimpered.

"Nonsense," she declared, making a countermove on his ear. She claimed victory when he moaned. "I've heard the stories. Three ales in and you'll be dancing on tables, singing bawdy tavern songs off-key."

"Ha! That is a vile, false rumor, and I deny every word of it." Their lips met, and after several minutes they might have indeed declared defeat for the evening had not a familiar commanding voice startled them.

"There you are! Come along, the gathering awaits." They broke apart, and Charlotte beckoned to them. "Do try to keep your lovemaking in the bedroom, dears, or at least a side corridor. Not the main entry."

It wasn't bad in the end. Tristan and Christiana were made to stand on a table with demands for a kiss. Tristan teased the crowd with a great spectacle of pleading with Christiana, even kneeling before her, but she shook her head, speechless with laughter. He called out, "A kiss? One kiss? That's all you need?" The crowd roared their approval.

Tristan turned to Christiana and took her face in his hands with an exaggerated show of longing, leaned forward, and pecked the tip of her nose. The crowd groaned and booed. After a great deal of laughter, Tristan whispered in his bride's ear, and she nodded, blushing. They kissed with an enthusiasm that would have rivaled any wedding couple, and everyone cheered, with a few wolf whistles thrown in for good measure. They were allowed to get off the table at last, much to Tristan's relief.

Things settled down afterward, and most of the attention revolved around Christiana. She was pretty and sparkling; Tristan could have watched her for hours. He caught sight of James gulping down an ale. Their eyes met across the room, and his brother gave Tristan a wobbly smile before reaching for Cate's hand and disappearing.

"It's ridiculous, what these women do to us," Tristan muttered. He jumped as Charlotte's voice rang in his ear.

"And yet I think you boys enjoy it. Is that James leading Catrina off? Has he worked up the courage to propose after all these years?"

Tristan gaped at her, and she winked at him, reminding him of her daughter. "Did you believe it was such a secret?"

"Well, I thought so," he rumbled, annoyed to realize he had, in fact, been the last to discover the truth. Other than his father. He looked around the room.

"Trying to find Thomas?" Charlotte asked. "He's in the common room. Do go fetch him, he's not feeling very sociable. He grumbled about needing a drink first."

Charlotte was correct, for he found Thomas with a tot of whiskey before the fire. Tristan thought his father had the right idea about how to spend the evening. At the sight of his son, Thomas brightened and stood.

"Tristan! Let me see you, son." He peered at Tristan, who couldn't help but start grinning, and Thomas laughed. "Ah, yes. You've the look of a man well bedded by his wife. I hope Christiana is happy?"

At this Tristan grinned even more and said, "Yes, sir, I believe she is."

Thomas chuckled and offered a drink, but Tristan held up his mug of ale. They sat in comfortable silence for some time, which Tristan finally broke.

"Charlotte was asking for you, by the way."

Thomas grunted and muttered to himself. Tristan made out the words "that woman" and "relentless," yet his father sounded more amused than annoyed. They continued to sit before the fire, hearing the gentle distant noise of the partygoers. Tristan loved few things more than sitting with his father in this way, but he did wonder about Christiana.

Thomas also reveled in the quiet contentment of the moment. His boys were safe, and Tristan's obvious happiness filled him with joy. When the door opened and his son's face lit up, Thomas didn't need to be told who it was.

"Hello there," said Christiana, dropping a kiss on top of Thomas's head. Thomas rose to embrace her.

"Hello, dear girl. Has this son of mine been treating you well?"

"He'll do," she said saucily, and Thomas laughed.

"First Momma sent Tristan in for you, and now me to fetch both of you."

"There goes the peace," sighed Thomas.

"Not at all. Come, my love." Tristan held out his hand to Christiana and plumped her onto his lap. She burrowed against him, and the three of them remained cheerfully together, with the occasional murmured conversation.

Even later, Ethan popped his head in with Rachel. Soon they were sitting on the sofa, holding hands. Before long, they were all laughing and telling stories. But the laughter came to an abrupt end when the door flew open. Cate and James swirled in, kissing passionately. For a second, Tristan thought they might tear each other's clothes off, their heat was so palpable. Christiana giggled.

They both froze, and James muttered, "Aw, hell."

Turning slowly, he saw both of his brothers with grins on their faces. Cate wore a stunning garnet necklace. With the happiest smile any of them had ever seen on his face, James bowed toward his father, who sat stunned.

"Father, may I present my future wife? I believe you may know her."

They all rejoined the party at last. Tristan retreated to a corner and watched all those he loved with great joy. Mariah and Andrew were laughing with Thomas, celebrating their families uniting. Cate and James were sitting together, her head on his shoulder, the ancestral garnet glowing as it hung from her pretty neck. From across the room, James gave his brother a grin. He was happier than Tristan had ever seen him. Somehow, Ethan had convinced shy Rachel to dance, and she was beautiful, reeling with her long dark hair flying. Then a pair of sparkling green eyes were before Tristan, and his own dear wife gave him a kiss that made his heart skip a beat.

"How many ales have you had?"

"Two. No dancing on the tables yet. How long will this go on?"

"Until dawn at this rate. We're allowed to leave after midnight. In fact, they will expect us to leave soon. They'll make merry while we are presumably making babies."

He leveled a look at her. "I can live with that."

She smiled at him mischievously and kissed the tip of his nose before going back into the throng.

Tristan roamed the party for the next hour, making small talk but watching Christiana out of the corner of his eye the whole time. Charlotte had long since retired, and once or twice he wondered where his father had disappeared to. Then his wife came bouncing to him as the church bells struck twelve. A cheer rose from the crowd, and they were practically expelled from the Great Hall. The doors slammed shut. It was quiet in the entry after the bright noise of the party. Christiana started to lead him away until he held up his hand.

"Wait. Let's steal a couple of cloaks and go outside."

Her eyes brightened at the prospect of an adventure, and she grew more excited when he led her, not to the courtyard, but out the grand doors to the wide-open lawn covered with untouched snow.

Distant shrieks and laughter reached a high chamber in the castle. Curious, a woman wandered to the window and looked down, smiling at the two figures playing in the snow far below.

"I do believe those children are mad!" she exclaimed, laughing. "Snowball fights, really!"

She watched them for a while, envying their playfulness and youthful vigor. When the larger figure dragged the smaller one into the drifts, she wondered aloud, "Surely they aren't going to bed one another right there in the snow? Look at them!"

A man came out of the shadows of the room, and a deep rumble of a laugh burst forth. His strong arm reached out for her. "Let's leave them to it. Come back to me, my dear."

"I shall do as I please, sir," she said primly.

"Yes, Your Grace," the man said, giving a low chuckle. Then, with an ardent kiss, he drew her into the shadows.

Tristan had thrown Christiana into the snow, laughing hard, and pounced upon her. But she tickled him without mercy until he was thrashing about, gasping. He managed to pin down her arms, and he kissed her. She kissed him back with such heat he wondered that the snow didn't melt into springtide.

"Take me to your bed, Tristan."

"Our bed," he mumbled mid-kiss.

He helped her to her feet and brushed the snow off. Giggling, they returned the stolen cloaks to where they had been hanging and ran through the castle hand in hand, laughing and chasing each other all the way to the long corridor and his old room. Tristan checked the fire and a gleam from the corner of his eye caught his attention. He glanced up at the Lockhart sword hanging above the mantel and paused, thinking of Michael.

The grief still lingered and would never truly leave, but it was no longer a cold, aching void. Instead, sorrow had shifted into hope, warm and alive in his heart. He would treasure the precious memories of those he had lost until the Rising came, when all would be restored and they would be reunited for evermore.

Tristan took his time joining Christiana in bed. He moved slowly, his eyes sweeping around the room, taking in every beloved detail. A candle flickered on the bedside table, and the crackling fire cast a gentle glow.

Tristan recalled Michael's words from many years ago when, as a child, he had ached for a place to belong, for a home. Michael had told him that being together is what made a home. Whether within the walls of a castle, a canvas tent in the mountains, or a beer-soaked tavern on the edge of battle—Tristan had always been happiest where his family gathered. He anticipated the remaining winter nights bundled up in the castle with everyone he loved in this world, safe and happy. Together.

Tristan was home at last.

And in the spring? Who knew what might come, everything was a possibility. He gazed down at Christiana, his eyes shining.

"What is it?" Christiana whispered, wondering at the joy on her darling's face.

Later he would whisper of his love for her, of his hopes and dreams for their future...but he couldn't speak in that moment. Tristan blew out the candle and gathered her into his arms for what he hoped would be a very long winter.

# Author's Note

The prayer Tristan recites twice in this book is slightly altered from the original, which appears in the 1928 Book of Common Prayer.

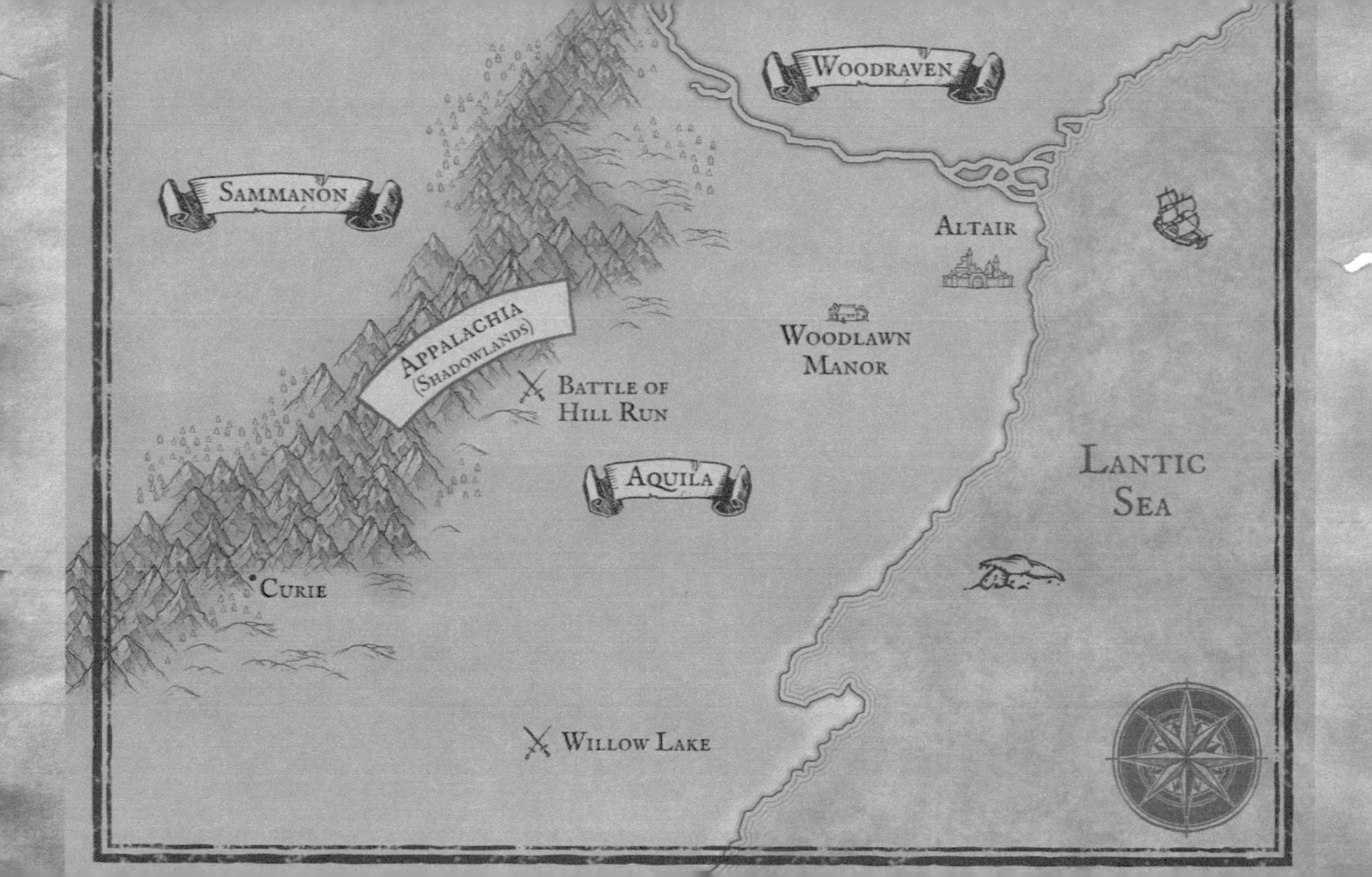

WOODRAVEN
SAMMANON
ALTAIR
APPALACHIA
(SHADOWLANDS)
WOODLAWN MANOR
BATTLE OF HILL RUN
AQUILA
LANTIC SEA
CURIE
WILLOW LAKE

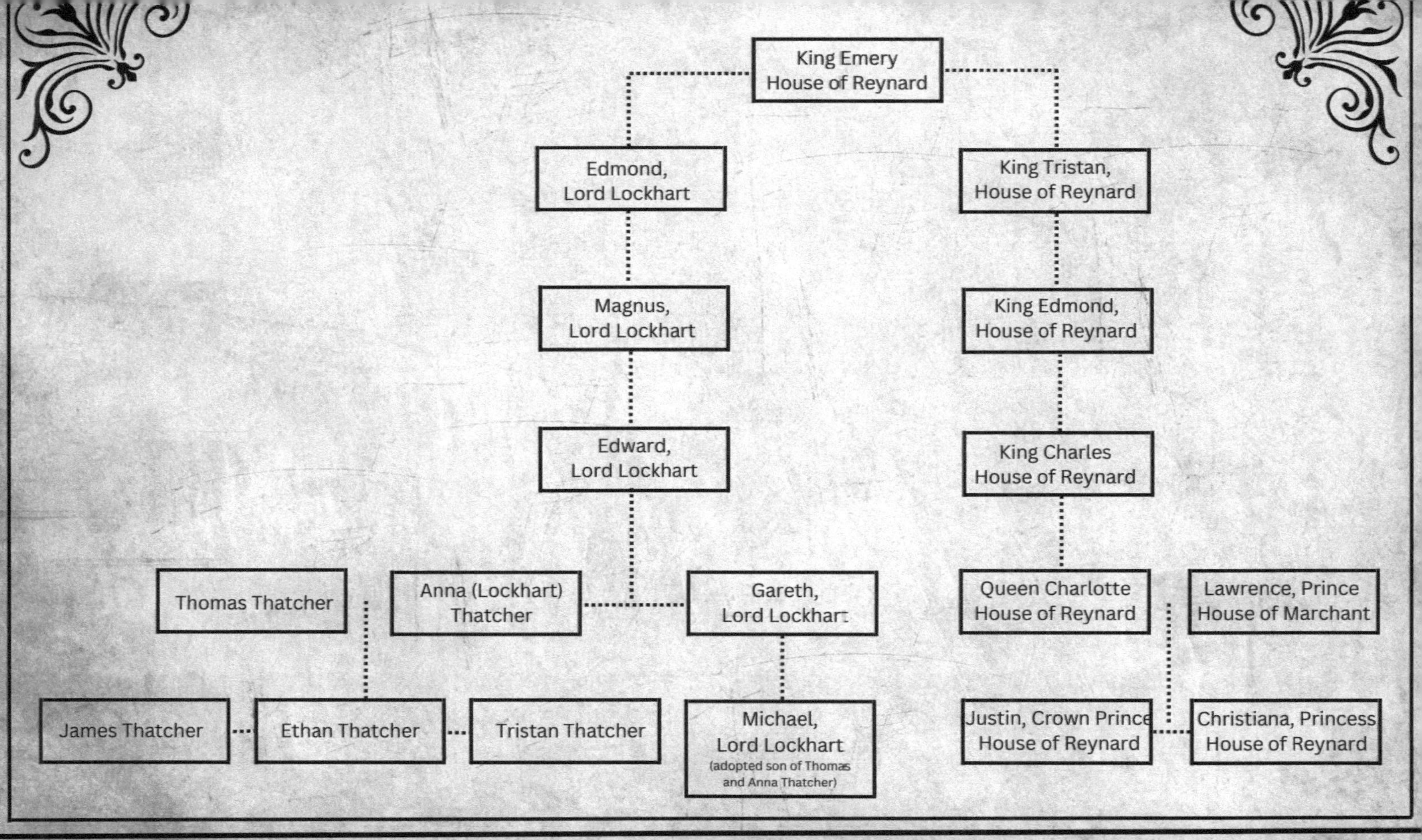

King Emery, House of Reynard
Edmond, Lord Lockhart
King Tristan, House of Reynard
Magnus, Lord Lockhart
King Edmond, House of Reynard
Edward, Lord Lockhart
King Charles, House of Reynard
Thomas Thatcher
Anna (Lockhart) Thatcher
Gareth, Lord Lockhart
Queen Charlotte, House of Reynard
Lawrence, Prince, House of Marchant
James Thatcher
Ethan Thatcher
Tristan Thatcher
Michael, Lord Lockhart (adopted son of Thomas and Anna Thatcher)
Justin, Crown Prince, House of Reynard
Christiana, Princess, House of Reynard

# Playlist

| | | |
|---|---|---|
| Prologue | Mrs Brown's Lullaby | Patrick Doyle |
| Chapter 1 | Mr. Knightley | Isobel Waller-Bridge, David Schweitzer |
| Chapter 2 | I Wish I Had A Hundred Years | Fernando Velázquez |
| Chapter 3 | River Flows In You | The Piano Guys, Eli Nelson |
| Chapter 4 | Father Comes Home | Alexandre Desplat |
| Chapter 5 | Persuasion | Regency Players |
| Chapter 6 | Walter's Burial | Marc Streitenfeld |
| Chapter 7 | Home Alone/Dad Arrives | Fernando Velázquez |
| Chapter 8 | Wayfaring Stranger | The Longest Johns |
| Chapter 9 | Goodbyes | James Horner |
| Chapter 10 | Secret Toast And Jam | Patrick Doyle |
| Chapter 11 | Harry In Winter | Patrick Doyle |
| Chapter 12 | Sweet Water | David Arnold |
| Chapter 13 | The Laurence Boy | Thomas Newman |
| Chapter 14 | Carriage Ride | Alexandre Desplat |
| Chapter 15 | Two Socks At Play | John Barry |
| Chapter 16 | Spring | Thomas Newman |
| Chapter 17 | Premonition | Tommee Profitt, Fleurie |
| Chapter 18 | Lord M | Martin Phipps |
| Chapter 19 | The Great Secret | Patrick Doyle |
| Chapter 20 | The Calm Before the Storm | David Arnold |
| Chapter 21 | Herald of the Change | Hans Zimmer |
| Chapter 22 | Hall of Prophecies | Nicholas Hooper |
| Chapter 23 | Moving On | Michael Giacchino |
| Chapter 24 | The Kiss | Nicholas Hooper |
| Chapter 25 | Campfire | William Ross |
| Chapter 26 | Off To War | James Horner |
| Chapter 27 | Another Year Ends | Patrick Doyle |
| Chapter 28 | The Courier | Randy Edelman |
| Chapter 29 | What It Means To Love | Evan Call |
| Chapter 30 | Planting The Fields | Marc Streitenfeld |
| Chapter 31 | Dual | David Arnold |
| Chapter 32 | Cholera | Alexandre Desplat |
| Chapter 33 | Rolfe Proposes | James Horner |
| Chapter 34 | Vesper | David Arnold |
| Chapter 35 | Stevens Solitude | Stephen J. Anderson |

# Acknowledgements

When I was about eleven or twelve, my overactive imagination conjured up a daydream about a boy. He had lost his family and was searching the world over for them. Every night once I was in bed and supposed to be asleep, I would meet up with this boy and we would go seeking his family together. Eventually we found them: a father and older brothers who loved him so very much and rejoiced at being reunited once again. The brothers went on to have many adventures. Since this was in essence a type of fairy tale, in their grand tradition the youngest son was the hero of the story and eventually won the heart of a princess.

The thing is, even as I grew older and life sped on past, I never abandoned the boy to the sad pile of other long-forgotten things from childhood. He stayed with me, and we grew up together. He was always within reach when I needed to escape the harsher realities of life. His story seeped into my very bones, becoming a part of me in a very real way.

As you have already guessed, this is how *Until the Rising* came to be. Deep down I always knew I wanted this story to be told, but writing a book is an act of pure courage or outrageous insanity (or more likely a combination of the two). It took a long time to arrive at a place where the story was bursting to break free, to have life breathed into it. But once I started, I never looked back.

And here we are.

I started this book entirely alone, but by the time it was released, I had developed such a vibrant community of fellow authors and readers, it's hard to pinpoint who to thank. If I missed someone, the fault is entirely my own.

Three cheers to my beta readers, there were so many at different stages of writing (some of you brave souls even read it more than once!). Thank you to Becca, Eddie, Journey, Ruth, Emily, Jamie, Brandi, Amy, Meredith, Meaghan, and Lauren.

Thank you Eddy Efaw for introducing me to the Rabbit Room, Hutchmoot, S.D. Smith, and Andrew Peterson (even if my friend Becca insists she had been trying to get me to listen to Peterson for years and I should know by now to always do what she says). Though they may never read this book, S.D. Smith and Andrew Peterson had an enormous impact on me at a crucial point in my life. It was while reading Smith's Green Ember series to my girls that it suddenly occurred to me, I can do this! I had already gone through four or five drafts of *Rising* by the time I was introduced to Peterson's music and books, but his emotional thumbprint is all over this little book of mine. I cannot overstate the incredible influence he has had on my writing.

Anne J. Hill was one of the first people I met when I started tiptoeing into the bookstagram world and she graciously took me under her wing. Thank you for the guidance and advice on all things book related, for introducing me to Riyria, and all the late night cozy chatter analyzing the best angle from which to shoot an arrow at some poor nameless soul from a tree.

To everyone with Flash Fiction Magic—I wish I could give every one of you platters of cheese toast. Thank you for all the crazy that has kept me sane.

While editing this book, I signed a contract with Quill & Flame Publishing House for my urban fantasy romance novel, *Unleashed*. They not only welcomed me with open arms, but took *Rising* on as their adopted child. The entire Q&F team threw their support behind me, and for that I am eternally grateful. Their encouragement and support was invaluable, especially in the last rush to get this baby out into the world. Thank you to AJ Skelly for the formatting and all the virtual coffee. So much love to Vanessa Burton for the laughs and gossip, Crystal Grant for your quiet yet sly wit, and Brittany Eden for being the very best at the business of writing. And dear Anna Augustine—every book should have a fan like you behind it. Thank you for the art and graphics, for the reels, and most especially your enthusiasm for the Thatcher boys.

I don't think this book would have seen the light of day without my cheer squad: Emily Barnett, Andrea Renae, Rachel Lawrence, and Katee Stein (all brilliant writers themselves). Emily was my last beta reader and gave me the courage to keep going when I was ready to chuck the whole thing. Thank you for encouraging me to make Ethan's role a bit larger, and of course for That-Which-Shall-Not-Be-Named. Andrea, thank you for the wonderful genealogy, and Rachel for all the precious fan fiction. Katee, I'm so happy I get to include you in this slightly revised edition. I hadn't met you when this was first published, but you've become invaluable to me as both a friend and an author. Few understand this world as well as you do, and I'm always thankful for your input.

I cannot say enough about my fantastic editors, Claire Tucker and Emma Flournoy. Claire especially—not only did you tame this wild beast of a book, but you did so with a kind and gentle spirit for this new author (along with an incredible array of Tolkien and *Star Wars* references). Words fail to express how thankful I am for you—not just your amazing skills as an editor but more importantly, for your friendship.

A huge thank you for Brigitte Cromey for helping me with this sneaky second edition and for loving Tristan as much as I do.

To my husband Mitch—it is no small thing for one's wife to suddenly begin writing a book. Sorry about the messy house. And the laundry. And the late dinners. And the occasional small fire from a long-forgotten stewpot.

Dearest Becca. You were here for the beginning of it all and this book would not exist if it were not for you. Thank you for everything.

For my girls—you have changed the trajectory of my life twice now. Once by being born, and now for being the reason why I wrote this book. Someday, when you are old enough to read it, I hope it brings you joy and courage.

Lastly, to the readers. Thank you for trusting your heart with this book. May it nourish you well.

*Soli Deo Gloria*

# ABOUT THE AUTHOR

Although born into a decidedly non-magical family, Amber fell through the wardrobe at a young age. Driven by a chronic case of lively curiosity, her many widespread interests and passions (including the baffling use of snails in medieval illustrations) have influenced her storytelling. Winner of the 2024 Eric Hoffer award, Amber has three books currently to her credit, including her debut coming-of-age fantasy, *Until the Rising,* as well as her urban fantasy duology, *Unleashed* and *Released.* Her stories are best known for their richly defined characters, emotional intensity, and courage shining brightly even amidst the darkest moments.

When not writing, Amber can be found wrangling her three slightly feral daughters in central Texas.

Other books by Amber Kirkpatrick

**The Aquila Chronicles**
Until the Rising
In These Night Seasons (2026)

**The Changed Duology**
Unleashed
Released

The Wizard of Wynedale Wood (2027)